Portia Da Costa is one of the most internationally renowned authors of erotic romance and erotica, and a *Sunday Times*, *New York Times* and *USA Today* bestseller.

She is the author of seventeen *Black Lace* novels, as well as numerous short stories and novellas.

Also by Portia Da Costa

How to Seduce a Billionaire

PORTIA DA COSTA

BLACK
LACE

7 9 10 8

Black Lace, an imprint of Ebury Publishing
20 Vauxhall Bridge Road,
London SW1V 2SA

Penguin
Random House
UK

Black Lace is part of the Penguin Random House group of companies
whose addresses can be found at global.penguinrandomhouse.com

First published in 2015 by Black Lace

www.eburypublishing.co.uk

A CIP catalogue record for this book is
available from the British Library

ISBN 9780352347909

Typeset in Janson Text LT Std by Palimpsest Book Production Limited,
Falkirk, Stirlingshire

Penguin Random House is committed to a sustainable future for
our business, our readers and our planet. This book is made from
Forest Stewardship Council® certified paper.

MIX
Paper from
responsible sources
FSC® C018179

Printed and bound in Great Britain by Clays Ltd, St Ives plc

Prologue

He was tall, dark and handsome. Always tall, dark and handsome. A romantic cliché, but who was she to argue with her subconscious?

Dream Lover didn't speak as he climbed into bed with her. He rarely did speak. Her fantasies were visual, not auditory and her own sighs and moans were all the soundtrack that she needed.

Falling back against the pillows, she let her imagined lover take the lead. His smile was enigmatic as he loomed over her, a subtle play of light and shade, but his eyes were vivid and dark with desire. Aquamarine and too brilliant to be natural, they almost dazzled her as he moved in close to kiss her. His lips were mobile and velvety, and the contact compelled her mouth to yield, his tongue demanding entrance, and thrusting fiercely.

Oh yeah!

Fantasy hands settled on her body, the contact firm but not rough as he explored her. He cupped her breast, squeezing lightly, thumb flicking back and forth, driving her crazy even though he'd barely begun his magic. She squirmed, every bit of her coming to life. Especially certain bits . . . The touch of his fingertips was smooth and warm, sliding easily against her skin. It felt lovely and made her wriggle even more . . . until an intrusive memory popped unwelcome into her mind.

A nearly-man, someone she'd once dated and hoped for great things with, he'd had callouses on his fingertips when he'd touched her. They'd felt horribly rough against her skin when he'd tried to sneak his hand up her blouse, and it'd destroyed every chance she might have had of getting turned on.

I'm my own worst enemy. Everything has to be perfect when in real life it probably never is.

As she banished the thought with a furious shake of her head, her hair lashed against the pillow as if she were already in the throes of orgasm. Still without speaking her phantasm-man soothed her, gentled her. His touch both calmed her down and shook her up at the same time, and he stroked her breasts, one then the other, alternating, knowing just when to switch. Then, kissing harder, he drifted that enchanted arousing hand further down, cupping her crotch in a light grip that employed a pinpoint degree of assertion and confidence. Her legs lolled apart of their own accord, making room for his exploration. Seducing him . . .

Of course, it went right. Why wouldn't it? It was all idealised. Questing, he parted the hair of her pussy with those perfect fingertips, dipping in to touch her clit. She gasped, always astonished to be so wet at these times. Lost in her fantasy though, it was easy to get slippery and silky, effortlessly easy.

She cried out, her own voice sounded shockingly loud. Usually she was able to keep the noise down in a shared house, barely articulating any more than wordless Dream Lover did. For a moment, she worried that her house-mate Cathy would hear her, but then told herself not to fret. She'd never heard any sounds of erotic partying from Cathy's room, and her house-mate led a happy, uninhibited sex life with a real, live lover. Cathy was normal, and shared good times with her steady man.

She's younger than me too.

No! Another intrusive thought . . . It was a weird night tonight. Somehow she was more turned on than usual, and yet at the same time less able to concentrate on making Dream Lover real.

What had got into her? Had she lost it completely, from all this incessant brooding on . . . her situation?

Closing her eyes tight, she focused on the dream man who was making love to her. He was passionate and beautiful, and though she still saw no exact likeness of him, he was somehow clearer. She didn't force the issue though. She had other priorities. Something else she needed to keep from slipping away . . . Sensations that could be as fugitive as they were precious and exquisite.

Stroking, stroking, stroking. The pressure, the pattern just right. No man would ever match her own fingers. No man would ever map her own body as she did.

No man had ever even had a chance to try, because no man was perfect.

Stop it! Don't go there. Focus, idiot!

Slipping, circling, swirling, Dream Lover banished her conundrum. His touch and the way it journeyed over the folds and dips and hotspots of her sex was matchless; dominant without being domineering, powerful without being rough. The gathering pleasure made her rock her hips, jerk and thrust against the contact. But Dream Lover was Dream Lover and he didn't miss a beat.

Gasping, she rose to him again, imagination finally taking over, the fantasy and the sensations becoming one. As if sure of her readiness, the man she'd conjured up moved over her, gracefully settling between her legs, his idealised cock pressing for admittance against the entrance of her sex.

The unknown country.

But it felt right. It felt wonderful. Hot. Solid. An iron-stiff rod pushing inside her, yet living and sensitive. Driving, thrusting, possessing, the rhythm divine and metronomic. The way he knocked against her clit with each plunge triggering pleasure that bloomed like fireworks, streaming up into the heavens and taking her with them.

Her teeth clamped hard together, keeping in her shouts, but inside she cried, *Oh thank you, thank you, thank you!*

Whoever you are . . .

Afterwards, she lay still and gasping. Wrung out like a dishrag, sweaty and dishevelled.

This was getting ridiculous.

You need to get a real man, you bloody fool. You need

to find out what it's really like. Nobody but a nun is still a virgin at twenty-nine nowadays, regardless of whatever life 'stuff' happens to them.

Holding out any longer for some crazy ideal of a perfect man was stupid. There *were* no perfect men, and if she kept holding out for one, she'd find herself holding out forever, and end up as a dried up spinster with only her sketching and good works or whatever to keep her occupied. She'd bet good money that any normal woman would be prepared to sleep with more than a frog or two in the hopes that one of them might turn out to be moderately princely.

Waiting for desire was daft. The years were flying by. She had to go half way, and take a risk; *work* to feel passion. Just sitting around expecting lust to suddenly arrive, kaboom, was pathetic.

Next time a nice man with potential crossed her path, she had to give him a chance, and not keep turning away because he wasn't Dream Lover.

As long as he's just a little bit tall and dark and hand-some . . .

Shaking her head, she sat up and smoothed down her nightgown.

Time to draw . . .

1

'Oh no! Why today? Why do you have to do this to me?'

Jess Lockhart stared up into the pouring rain and almost shook her fist. She would have done it if there hadn't been cars whizzing by, driven by people who'd think she was a loony; cars that flung up sheets of muddy spray that soaked her shoes and legs as they passed.

Why had this happened just when she wanted to look her best at work? She didn't normally dress up. Smart casual, in fact very casual, was her usual look. But today she wanted to appear a bit more polished, just in case, because of the mighty, exalted VIP who was visiting.

Not that the new owner of the insurance group she worked for was likely to descend from on high to tour the cubicle farm. Why would he? He was a businessman, a tycoon, a financier. He wasn't interested in what the lowly drones at the coalface were doing, just the monetary assets that Windsor Insurance, his new acquisition, represented.

'Why does nobody I know ever drive past?' Jess growled at no car in particular.

This was the busiest part of the city and not everybody was going in the same direction, but surely somebody else was heading for Windsor Insurance? But most likely they wouldn't even recognise such a rain-soaked and bedraggled mutt as their work colleague.

Now, if she'd got up in good time, she could've checked the weather forecast and known that sharp, heavy showers were on the way. But no, she'd been awake half the night, stupidly fantasising about Dream Lover, and then equally stupidly trying to capture his image on paper. Consequently, when it was time to get up, she'd slept in, woolly-headed and weary. If she'd woken up at her normal hour, she could have begged a lift from Cathy, but she'd left it too late. Cathy was an angel, and she'd offered to wait . . . but that would have made her late for work too.

Now you're paying the price for your midnight shenanigans, dimbo, and as you didn't even have the foresight to bring an umbrella, you're going to get soaked to the skin between the bus station and work. Brilliant!

Blinking water out of her eyes, Jess realised that the hair that had begun as a chic and elegant up-do was fast collapsing, its structure undermined by the teeming deluge. With a muttered oath, she pulled out the securing clip, and slung it aside in disgust, to run her fingers through the thick straggles of her sodden hair.

So much for 'maple syrup' low-lights and a twenty-quid conditioning mask.

Just about to retrieve the clip, she darted back from the kerb's edge. Despite the double yellow lines and 'No Stopping' signs, a vehicle actually was pulling up beside her now, its slowing speed only splattering her with a light swish of rainwater this time. Her hairclip was crushed to shards beneath the wheel of a distinctive, retro looking powder blue car. A long, low, classic Citroën. An uncle of hers had driven one once upon a time, and she'd always loved riding in it, because of the way its suspension made you feel as if you were floating on air. Happy, innocent days those had been, when she and her sister had accompanied her uncle's family on sketching holidays to Cornwall.

But what was a vintage 'blue whale' like Uncle Mark's doing here in this neck of the woods, jostling amongst the school run SUVs and the hot hatches and the occasional luxury saloon or hybrid?

Looks like I'm going to find out.

A figure within the blue car leant across the passenger seat and rolled down the window.

'Can I give you a lift somewhere?' said a deep, musical voice, easy on the ear, but very 'not from round here'. The accent was hard to pin down though – basically British, but with bits of other things – especially amongst the drumming rain and the honking car horns.

Jess blinked again. And not just from the water running into her eyes. It was like a double recognition. *Really* weird, making her feel weird too, as if she'd been whirled around several times, far too fast.

No, surely not . . . Surely it's not him . . . or him!

The man in the car was the spitting image of the pictures she'd seen of today's VIP visitor . . . and he could also have been Dream Lover at a pinch.

The familiar but unfamiliar man grinned, his face lighting up in a sunny, happy, amused expression, glowing somehow, almost dazzling. Eyes that were a bluish green – bluer than his car, but not as green as the actual green of leaves or grass – almost seemed to twinkle at her.

Dear God, it is him! It's the VIP! The new big boss of all bosses!

'Lift?' he prompted, making Jess realise that she must look a complete fool, standing there, wet and bedraggled, with her mouth hanging open, and was probably compounding that impression with every second that passed. Yet still she stood there, and time seemed frozen, apart from the ominous approach of an incoming traffic warden, heading along the street.

But what was this handsome devil, this mighty captain of business, doing cruising along, driving himself in an obviously ancient car when he should be riding in a limousine with a brace of PAs and a chauffeur to look after him? And the VIP's clothing didn't fit the surroundings either. He looked as if he was on his holidays. His suit was light-coloured, fawnish linen, stylish but slightly crumpled, and he wore his flower-patterned cheesecloth shirt with the tails out.

It's definitely him though. Handsome as the devil, but nothing like your everyday average billionaire tycoon. Definitely eccentric.

'Thanks, but it's all right. I'm nearly there. I

wouldn't want to trouble you, and I'll get rain on the upholstery of your car. Thanks . . .'

He laughed softly, cheerful and clearly entertained by her absurdity.

'Sod my upholstery, it'll survive.' He quirked his dark brows at her, and his smile was oddly entreating. 'Please won't you get in? You're getting drenched, and I'll never forgive myself if you end up catching a cold or flu when I could've prevented it. I'm not a pervert or a kidnapper, honestly.' He glanced quickly up the street at the approaching warden. 'I think I'm going to get a ticket any second if we don't move on.'

'Okay then. Thanks.'

Jess slithered into the passenger seat, embarrassingly aware of the slim skirt of her one good suit riding up her thighs. Her tights felt horribly slimy on her wet legs, but she'd wanted to look 'well put together' today and groomed, so she'd worn a pair. Normally she relied on a spot of fake tan.

'Where to?' The VIP arched his eyebrows at her again. And what eyebrows they were! Dark and very firmly marked, they were a perfect match for the near-black brown of his slightly tousled hair and the sexy roguish stubble of his semi-beard.

I don't think Dream Lover has ever had a beard.

'Um . . . Windsor Insurance. It's about two monoliths down, on the left. You can't miss it. There's this silly picture of a castle on the logo.'

And it's your latest acquisition, Mr Beach Bum Billionaire, I think you'll find.

'A silly castle, eh?' he observed, setting the car in gear, eyes on the traffic, yet still making her feel as if he was scrutinising her intensely. 'And what are you then, the lost princess?'

'Nope, just a serf. A minion. A lowly member of one of the claims teams.'

'Oh, not so lowly. Not from where I'm sitting.' Before Jess could even form a response to that, he gestured towards their destination, which now hove into view on the left. She hadn't noticed but he was driving quite fast in the wet and had navigated his way neatly through the hurly-burly of the morning rush hour. 'That it?'

Was he even going to mention who he was? Maybe not. Maybe he wasn't going to bother inspecting the troops, after all, and was just going to hang out with higher management echelons?

'Yes . . . Yes, thanks. You could drop me just here. That's the staff entrance.' She nodded to where some of her work colleagues, most of them considerably dryer than she was, were filing through the double doors.

As she put her hand on the car door handle, he stayed her, his fingers on her arm. It was the lightest contact, but she almost rocked in her seat, imagining the same lightness of touch in another context. A night-time context, slight and gentle, but the beginning of more, so much more.

Jess! What the hell . . . What . . .

Incredibly, her body roused. It was so sudden and so incongruous that she almost swayed in the seat.

Why now? In these circumstances? In the rain, with a man she'd met seconds ago, and would prob-ably never meet again, other than perhaps a nod of acknowledgement as he swept through the claims department on some kind of royal progress.

And yet, it'd happened, shaking her in a way that had always seemed like some magic unknown, a state fantasised about and achieved in solitude, but never experienced out here, in the real world. How could one fleeting touch from this displaced beach bum catch her unawares and take her effortlessly to the domain of Dream Lover?

Staring at him, she could almost see her every thought mirrored in those tropical ocean eyes. As if he knew her. Totally. Understood her lack of experience, and comprehended that she didn't *want* to lack experience, but simply didn't want to throw away something precious in a meaningless act with someone she didn't quite care enough about.

'Are you okay?' He frowned. Looked puzzled. Probably not as completely bedazzled and befuddled as she was, but somehow, amazingly, affected by the moment. 'Do you have towels in there?'

'What?'

'Towels. For drying yourself.'

'Er . . . No, not really, it's mostly hand-dryers.' Now there was a point.

He leant forward, popped open the glove compartment, and fished out a box of man-size tissues, as yet unopened. 'Take those. They'll be better than nothing. Your boss should provide better facilities for his staff than just hand-dryers. Especially in this soggy climate.'

'Oh, I couldn't . . .' Easy for him to be Lord Bountiful. Nobody would get soaked to the skin by dank northern weather on his tropical-somewhere hideaway or any other parts of a billionaire's exalted world.

'Oh, go on. It's just a box of tissues.' He reached over, unzipped the top of her tote bag and shoved in the box of tissues. 'Now, off you go. You'll be late, and we wouldn't want that, would we?'

'No, we wouldn't,' she shot back at him, glad to have retrieved her backbone from somewhere. He'd given her a very brief lift – and the weirdest jolt of pleasure – but he wasn't the boss of her . . . even if he was.

'Thanks again,' she cried, opening the passenger door and shooting out before things could get any weirder.

Soft laughter rang in her ears long after she'd entered the building, echoing as if imprinted on her brain.

2

Portrait of a young woman as drowned rat. I wouldn't want to draw that!

Jess could still see her face in the ladies' room mirror. Her makeup had mostly gone to hell, as had her hairstyle, leaving her looking generally gobsmacked and waterlogged.

And the man who'd given her an almighty shaking up for a variety of reasons had seen that impressive look, and obviously found her a rich source of amusement.

Arrogant bastard! In your world there'll always be a nice dry car to take you where you want to go! No slumming it in the rain like us plebs . . .

Now though, at her desk, an hour later, she felt warmer, better, and at least slightly dryer. His big box of tissues had helped with the blotting, and she'd set it beside her computer, like a talisman. She entertained silly, subversive thoughts about hanging on to it when it was empty, as a keepsake of their 'moment'.

Or at least your *moment, Jess. Ridiculously bad timing. Couldn't have been worse.*

Silly mare, she chided herself, yet, even as she went through routine tasks, she tried to reclaim the sensations.

Heat, even though she was shivering. Heart racing. The deep, slow, honeyed surge, low in her belly. Astounding . . . alarming . . . wonderful! Everything she could induce in her fantasies, yet never feel here in the real, living world!

Unfortunately, though, the man who'd induced those feelings would never know it. Hell, he'd probably completely forgotten her even before she'd reached the door to the building, even though the smell of his gorgeously spicy cologne was still powerful and exotic in her brain.

Those blue-green eyes. That sunny smile. They were still with her too. And she kept seeing his strong, lightly tanned hands, so relaxed yet sure on the steering wheel . . . and in everything they did, probably. Could this man be the full-on placeholder for Dream Lover? A face she could picture in her fantasies? An avatar to make do with until somebody real came along? If they ever did . . .

Banishing that grim thought, she felt her fingers itch to start doodling, and after a sly look around, she succumbed, pretending to jot notes on her pad, yet in reality pencilling the curve of that smiling mouth, that sexily stubbled jawline. Just elements. She daren't get absorbed in a full face sketch or she'd get no work done and somebody would notice. Not a good strategy at the best of times, but doubly unwise today. Everybody was supposed to look super-efficient, and wholeheartedly dedicated to insurance, for the 'royal' visit: the arrival of the group's new owner to inspect their very humble and fairly insignificant division. Which was weird, but apparently the VIP's eccentric habit.

And management doesn't know the half of it. She grinned to herself while she doodled the curve of his gorgeous lips on her pad. *That stuffy lot upstairs will have a fit when they see your flowered shirt with the tails hanging out.*

So, she'd actually met Ellis P. McKenna, international financier and general all-round filthy rich tycoon. One to one. He was the scion of a billion-dollar entrepreneurial family who'd bought out Windsor Insurance as part of a group along with a large number of other financial concerns, just like someone going out and buying three sweaters in different colours rather than only one. If actual whole companies were so easy to acquire and dispose of to him, it didn't bode well for the little people like her who worked in them.

We all might be just as disposable as cheap jumpers if you decide to keep this operation lean and mean, Mr McKenna.

Jess shuddered. She needed her job, because she didn't have any reserves. Ensuring that her gran had been comfortable at Baxendale Court in her final years had hoovered up every scrap of Jess's modest savings, and she was still gradually paying off the loan she'd taken out to make up the difference. She didn't regret a thing, and would do it again in a heartbeat, but it had left her finances since then a tad precarious, even long after Gran had passed on.

Impatient suddenly, she flung down her pencil, breaking the point and attracting curious looks from Jim and Michelle, who shared her 'pod' of desks.

Oh, come on, Mr McKenna, let's see you again. We'll all sit here tugging our forelocks for a bit, then we can get back to our normal drone activities . . . and I can be sure that Dream Lover is just Dream Lover, a man I once met for about thirty seconds.

Would he even acknowledge her? Or just swan past, barely noticing the faces behind the desks? She pushed his box of tissues to a more prominent place. Perhaps that might remind him?

Even as Jess was thinking that, there was a faint jumble of voices out in the corridor, a small commotion like a looming weather front. People around her sat up straight, fiddled with their ties or smoothed their hair. Michelle even pressed her lips together to refresh her lipstick. Ridiculous! The VIP would come blowing through the office, barely breaking stride, a self-identified deity amongst them, hardly bothering to acknowledge the individual insects he now employed.

The minor hubbub intensified, still approaching. Unconsciously, Jess did the smoothing of the hair thing too. She'd drawn it back now in the best 'do' she could manage at short notice and with her clip smashed and gone, a ponytail at the nape of her neck, secured by a covered elasticated band she'd discovered at the bottom of her bag. She patted at her blouse too, the only part of her ensemble that had more or less avoided getting soaked. Unlike her skirt, which was soggy round the hem, and her shoes, which audibly squelched when she walked. She could have changed into her comfy shoes, but they were far too casual. Ah, the irony, considering that Ellis McKenna was more casually dressed than anyone here.

Jess's heart thudded. Some of those voices were distinct now – those of her bosses – but another one also sounded vaguely familiar.

Oh holy shit, you are *tall, dark and handsome, Mr McKenna!*

The potential candidate for Dream Lover met the height credentials too.

Flanked by the Windsor Insurance bigwigs in their best dark suits, stringently ironed shirts and sober ties, the man with the vintage Citroën strolled into the room, looking like a shabby but dazzling peacock god surrounded by a scuttling murder of crows. Sharp aquamarine eyes scanned the desks and the people behind them, registering, summing up, and passing by with the efficiency of a Terminator. It took but a split second for him to find her . . . and smile.

Oh no!

Without any warning to his entourage, the newcomer abandoned them and strode towards her. Jess had the ridiculous urge to shoot to her feet.

God damn it, he's not a king or anything! I haven't even decided whether he's Dream Lover or not yet.

Sitting tight, she offered him a friendly smile. He had stopped and given her a lift, after all. 'Hello, Mr McKenna,' she said quickly, getting in there first, amazed that she suddenly felt both super-confident and quivery as a jelly inside. He was definitely having Dream Lover effects on her.

His gaze flicked to her nameplate. 'Hello, Ms J. Lockhart. Have you dried out yet?'

'Yes, thank you.'

His brow puckered as he took in her still damp hair, and then, as he peered around the edge of her desk, her wet-hemmed skirt and her sodden shoes.

'Fibber,' he said in a low voice, possibly audible only to her as he leant closer. Jess gripped the edge of her desk to steady herself, made woozy by a sudden waft of his intoxicating male fragrance. It seemed stronger now than it had been in the car.

Who the hell were you intending to impress that you needed to top up your cologne?

His Mediterranean eyes, and the way they flashed, supplied the answer.

I've told you before! Don't be idiotic, Jess, you're nothing to him.

But against all reason, that was wrong. The way he looked at her said she *was* something to him. Something she couldn't completely believe. She could almost imagine she was *his* Dream Lover.

He didn't say more, but his intent expression, and the little quirk of his firm, rosy, biteable lips said their conversation was merely postponed, not over. With a wink, he turned from her, his sharp eyes focusing elsewhere, this time on a step stool against the filing wall, close to her desk. Swooping down, he drew it out, and then leapt lightly up onto it, just a yard or so from where Jess was sitting.

'Right, everyone. I guess you know who I am, and if you don't, I'm Ellis P. McKenna and three weeks ago I took Windsor Insurance into the UK portfolio of the McKenna Group.' He beamed around at every-body. Jess didn't know what the men in the section were making of this, but she could feel a cresting wave of fluttering female excitement building in the room. *Stop showing off*, she wanted to say to him, even though every part of her subconscious and most of her conscious mind loved his display. His body was lithe, but strong-looking, and its proximity was like having some kind of sweet, heady alcoholic syrup bubbling inside her. He was inducing all the reactions that her fantasies managed to trigger, but which never occurred outside of them. Against her will, she found herself zeroing in on his waist . . . his linen clad thighs . . . his crotch . . . Wondering and wondering.

Desiring . . . At last. An actual living, breathing man. It was just like in the car. She was experiencing real female lust for a male who wasn't simply a figment of her imagination. All her adult life she'd wanted this to happen, and she'd believed she was weird and a freak because it hadn't. She'd never experienced the siren call. Never want to give . . .

Blinking, she realised he was speaking again. But there had been a pause. A pause where he'd looked back into her eyes, and, yes, watched the birth of her physical attraction to him. Had he sensed its unusualness?

'What I just wanted to assure you all was that there won't be any redundancies or any cuts in salaries. Well, not at this level.' He winked again, to all the desk-bound assembly in general. 'I haven't decided about this lot yet though.' He made an elegant sweeping gesture to the suits in his retinue, then beamed again, obviously highly amused by their discomfiture.

'Well, that's it really. I'm not one for speechifying. I just didn't want anyone to worry.' He leapt down from his vantage point. 'As they say in the movies, "Have a nice day."'

Yes, please go. I can't think. I need to settle down. Go away, Mr Dream Lover McKenna. Just walk out of my life so I can keep you in my fantasies.

A new emotion sluiced through her, as shocking and intense as the lust she'd felt. It was a black, aching sense of loss and despair. Why feel what she felt now, for a man she'd never see again? Why couldn't it have happened with someone attainable, with whom there might be a future? And more to the point, somebody that she liked, not this clearly supremely arrogant alpha male.

But Ellis McKenna didn't walk. He stayed where he was, scoping her, and frowning.

'You really are still a bit damp there, Ms J. Lockhart, aren't you?' The frown deepened, became layered somehow, as if his attention to her was operating on multiple levels at once. 'We can't have that. I'm not keen on the idea of an employee of mine coming down with pneumonia on the very first day I meet her. I think you'd better come with me.' Imperiously, he held out his hand, as if to draw her up from her seat. 'Please?'

And there it was again, that strange hint of entreaty in his eyes. That very human quality, a need for genuine interaction, however brief.

What the hell is going on? This is just barmy!

Still not sure whether she was succumbing to a consummate manipulator, or a man's real wish for her company, she took the offered hand, snatching up her bag from the side of her desk. His fingers closed around hers, firm and unyielding as if he thought she might flee if he let up on the hold. It was impossible not to follow him now as he led her the length of the desk farm, running the gauntlet of dozens of pairs of curious eyes tracking their every move.

'Where are we going? You can't just waltz me away somewhere,' she hissed, in the lowest voice she gauged he could hear without it carrying to the curious ears of her colleagues.

'I can. I'm the boss,' he said, twinkling at her over his shoulder.

'You're only the boss of me as an employee, not as a person. I ought to report you to my union rep for harassment.' And in any other circumstances, it might have been harassment, but this . . . this was something else entirely.

He stopped as they got to the lift, and released her hand.

'I'm sorry. I'm being a bit of an arse, aren't I? Do you want to go back to your desk?' His expression was still that curious blend of provocation and appeal. He was daring her to walk back between the rows of avidly gaping faces, yet hoping that she wouldn't call his bluff.

But what on earth is he planning?

Jess shot into the lift, and almost adhered herself to the far wall, about as far away from Ellis McKenna as she could get. After pressing the button for the top floor, he winked at her, and leant against the opposite wall. Why did she feel disappointed that he didn't lunge in her direction?

But, he didn't need to lunge. He just did it with his ocean-green eyes, scrutinising her from head to foot while a little smile played around his lips.

Jess wished, wished, wished she looked more impressive. She lifted her chin and eyeballed him back boldly, but she was all too aware of the soggy hem of her skirt, her squelchy shoes and the stringy wet strands of her hair. Still, pretending she looked fabulous, she stayed strong, trying not to be intimidated by his effortless, scruffy glamour and his sexual aura, an emanation so intense it was like a mist that filled the cabin of the lift.

Oh shit. Oh Lord. I want him. I've no practical idea how to do sex, but I want to do it with him, even if I will be the most hopeless lay.

Ellis tilted his head a little, his eyes narrowing almost as if he'd heard her. For about a fifth of a second, he caught his plush lower lip between his teeth, and looking at him, at that complex expression on his face, she could imagine that it wouldn't matter to him that she was inexperienced. Whatever happened, he would be good enough for both of them. He'd be sensational.

The 'ding' of the lift arriving at their destination made her jump, physically. They'd been in the lift less than thirty seconds but it felt like a lifetime.

'Where exactly are we going?' she asked, following him as he strode out of the lift, then paused to wait for her.

'I've commandeered old Jacobson's office for the day. He's slumming it, in with one of his henchmen.' Ellis winked at her again. 'He says he doesn't mind in the slightest but I can see he's really fuming inside.'

Jess had no idea what Mr Jacobson, the head honcho, looked like when he was fuming. He hadn't even been the one to interview her, and staff on her level never really interacted with senior management.

Looks like I'm interacting with a level of management way above 'old Jacobson' today. It isn't possible to reach a higher level than this.

'I hope he doesn't decide to take reprisals on people like me when you've flitted on to wherever you plan to flit to next,' she said crisply, as Ellis ushered her into the Executive Director's office suite. Jacobson's secretary gave her a curious glance, but only momentarily. The woman barely seemed to have eyes for anyone but Ellis McKenna.

'No interruptions please, Ms Brown,' he instructed, pausing at the older woman's desk to bestow a brain-melting smile.

'Of course, Mr McKenna,' she replied, sounding suspiciously breathy.

You make all women crazy, don't you? Jess accused him silently as he held open the door to the inner sanctum for her.

The way his beautiful mouth quirked seemed to suggest, once again, that he'd heard the thought.

It was a large office, with a very fine leather-topped desk, banked computer workstations to one side, and an 'informal' area over by the floor-to-ceiling windows that looked out over the busy street below. Across the rooftops, in the distance, there was a tantalising view, between two high rises, of the city park, a bit of breathing space amongst the built-up metropolis. There was even the faintest glint of the boating pond, the glitter of water.

Two long settees faced each other at right angles to the triple-glazed glass, with individual armchairs drawn up to the sides and a couple of small, low tables strategically placed.

But wasn't really the seating arrangement that caught Jess's eye. It was the collection of items assembled, some on one of the tables, some on one of the couches.

Ellis led her to the nearest couch.

'I think you should take your skirt and your shoes off.'

Jess gasped. What the hell?

The dazzling, roguish god laughed, his white teeth glinting.

'No, I'm not planning to ravish you . . .' He paused, and for a moment a more saturnine expression crossed his face. 'Well, not unless you absolutely insist. But really, your skirt is still wet at the hem, and I swear I can hear your shoes squishing as you walk.' He nodded at the offending footwear. 'It's bloody cold today, considering it's supposed to be summer round here at the moment, and like I said before, I'd never forgive myself if you ended up catching a chill.'

Thunderstruck, Jess said the first thing that came into her head. 'Why? It's not your fault.'

'Oh, I think it is, in a way. The big boss is visiting, so you chose to wear a smart but rather flimsy suit and insubstantial shoes. It *is* my fault.'

'That's nonsense. I always dress smartly for work.'

He narrowed his sea-blue eyes.

'All right . . . Yes, this isn't my usual work suit. It's my interview suit. And these are my best dressed up shoes.'

'Well, take them off for a while then. I've had the heating turned on, so we can slip your skirt over the radiator and your shoes beneath.' He leant over and patted one of the curious items on the nearest settee: a thick, fluffy bathrobe in navy blue. 'You can wear this while they dry off, and we can have a nice little chat and drink some hot chocolate. That'll warm you up.' He nodded towards a tall vacuum jug standing on one of the tables, with china cups and saucers, and a basket with what looked like home-made cookies nestling in a white table napkin. How had he assembled all this stuff in just an hour? Had he decided the moment he'd first seen her that he'd hijack her from her desk like this?

'I can't take my clothes off just like that. It's . . . um . . .' She clasped her bag, as if it were a weapon with which to defend herself from him. 'I mean . . . you're like the super duper boss of me. I only met you for a few minutes less than an hour ago, and this is an open office, for God's sake!'

'Who do you think is going to ogle you? It's just storage across there, as far as I can tell, and I don't think the birds are particularly interested in us.' He gestured towards the building across the road. He was right; the only living creatures that could overlook them were a few pigeons roosting on the windowsills across the way. 'I'll turn my back, of course.'

The situation was hurtling into the surreal. Jess

shook her head. It was as if she'd stepped through a magic portal at some time since the blue Citroën had drawn up beside her. Or maybe that was the event horizon, entering his car.

'Okay then, if you don't trust me not to look, Jacobson has a small executive bathroom.' He waved towards a door at the end of the computer bank. 'You can change in there instead.'

Stop acting like a ninny, Jess. Just treat this like a game, a hoot. Pretend it's all a big giggle and an adventure. He'll be gone in a few hours, and he'll most likely never come back. You'll laugh about this afterwards and he is fabulous fantasy material . . .

'I trust you not to look, but I think I'll still change in there.' Kicking off her wet shoes, she swept up the thick, luxurious robe and then hurried off towards the door to Jacobson's bathroom.

This was the weirdest situation she'd ever found herself in, and she needed a moment to regroup. To think and to look at her reflection in the mirror and convince herself she wasn't in an extended and augmented version of one of her own erotic fantasies. A freaky dream that she'd wake up from in a minute, and then have to drag her half-asleep body out of bed, to go to work.

And she needed a minute away from the challenging, macho aura of Ellis McKenna . . . The only man she'd ever met who actually honest to God turned her on.

3

Ellis pursed his lips as the door slammed.

What the hell are you doing, man? Being Mr Impulsive and playing up to your reputation for eccentricity is one thing . . . but this, this is different.

She's different.

Jessica Lockhart. What was it about her? Everything about her initial impression upon him had been unpromising, and yet, oh dear God, he'd been aroused the minute she'd slid into the Citroën in her soggy suit and her waterlogged shoes, and with her dark, saturated hair hanging in thick, wet rat's tails.

Frowning, he retrieved her shoes, imagining the shapely feet they'd protected. He wasn't a foot fetishist, but it was easy to imagine the lovely legs those feet were attached to. And the luscious thighs. And the lithe yet curvaceous hips.

His mind flashed a vision to him of those enticing legs and hips naked, and the mysterious grove of her sex, fully revealed to him. If she were a natural brunette – as he had every reason to believe – she'd be dark-haired down there too, the contrast against her creamy skin stark and stunning.

But great legs and an enticing little pussy were characteristics of a thousand girls. What was it about this particular girl . . . this woman . . . that had hooked him? Still musing, he placed the shoes close to the radiator, but not close enough to ruin them by cracking the leather.

Maybe it was the fact that he *did* perceive her as a girl?

But she isn't one. She's a woman. Later twenties. Not all that much younger than me, if truth be known.

But his journey through the valley of grief had aged him prematurely. Not physically, but emotionally. He felt as if he was a thousand years old in loss and regret, but in reality, thirty-six was no age at all. And he'd found a way to deal with his life as it was. A set of workable parameters . . .

But even so, that still didn't explain why Jessica Lockhart shook him up like this. She didn't remind him of Julie. Not in the slightest. They were entirely different types, except perhaps for that elusive quality; that of being untouched, yet curious. The way his wife had been at the dawn of their relationship.

A sudden image of Julie in her wedding gown pierced him like burning spear, hitting so hard he almost cried out, his excitement and arousal instantly forgotten.

No. No. No. That's the past, a paradise that can never be revisited. That state, that love that I once had . . . That's a closed book now, and never to be reopened.

He turned away from the window, and the vision

of the waterlogged metropolis and its unknown humanity, all hurrying about their business. Not that he'd even been seeing them.

The room, for all its sterile utilitarianism and lack of real character, was warm now, both physically and in an obscure, discreet sense that had everything to do with the woman he'd brought up here.

Perfection was a thing of the past for him now, but he could still have something different, something distracting. The pleasures of the flesh in all their delightful forms were still available to him, and some amenable company for a strictly limited while would be welcome.

Hmm . . . flesh. He was back to musing on her thighs again, and back to considering the mouth-watering curve of her bottom as she'd walked away in her trim but damp skirt. His fingers flexed, anticipating soft skin and firm musculature, as he imagined touching and squeezing, not to mention exploring and perhaps even a bit of judicious spanking, should things develop along those lines. She hadn't ever played any kinky games, he'd wager the entire income from this rather mundane company on that certitude.

What will your cries of surprise be like, Jessica? Will you moan with pleasure when I touch you? Will you whimper and cry out my name when I'm between those silky thighs of yours, thrusting?

Ellis McKenna smiled to himself. Life still had the potential to be good, even for him, and as he unscrewed the top of the vacuum flask, the hot, rich cocoa smell only added to his excitement and the gathering thrill.

His cock leapt, as he imagined those deeper pleasures, better even than the luscious taste of chocolate.

He always felt better when he was planning a seduction.

4

The robe was divine, if huge. Its quality was all that Jess would expect from a multi-millionaire, a man used to the finest of everything.

How wealthy was he? It sounded as if his entire family was wealthy, loaded with old money.

She ran her fingers over the deep pile of the towelling, loving its density. Was this one of his personal robes? He'd obviously driven himself to Windsor, but that wasn't to say he didn't have a cadre of minions who'd arrived here separately. PAs and concierge type people who could source anything he desired at the snap of his long, elegant fingers. It'd been around an hour since she'd got out of his car. Plenty of time for diligent gofers to convey this robe from his hotel, or somewhere, to here. She tweaked the lapel as she peered into the mirror.

Oh, hell, Jess! Just look at you! What a fright!

All semblance of style had fled from her hair, and even an attempt to dry it on one of Jacobson's towels hadn't done much to improve matters.

Was this what women looked like fresh from Ellis McKenna's bed? Hair all messy, recently ravished body swathed in his dressing gown? She breathed in deeply, but the garment mainly smelled of laundry. Mainly.

There was a hint of something, something spicy but very faint, an echo of the delicious aura of shaving lotion that hung around him.

Perhaps he *had* worn it before her? A heavy shudder rippled through her, dark and deep.

Damn! I can't lurk around in here, fiddling with his bathrobe. It might not even be his. What if old Jacobson has a dressing gown fetish and it's his, not Ellis McKenna's?

Again, the surreal nature of the day hit her. How had this happened? It was all completely crazy, like a badly scripted film.

And yet it was real, and there was a beautiful man who could have been the star of last night's fantasy waiting for her out in the office, a man who could do things to her without even touching her. Without her even knowing anything about him other than his public persona in the broadest of terms.

As she put her hand on the bathroom doorknob, she wished she knew more about him. The takeover of Windsor was a done deal, nothing any of the staff could do about it, so she'd not really taken much interest in Ellis McKenna. There'd been a rather small photo of him in the staff newsletter, and a lot of financial stuff, but she'd not really thought about the man himself. Now she wished she'd Googled him, found out more about him as a person rather than a business Leviathan. At least that way she'd have had a better arsenal at her disposal in order to deal with him. Facts. Mundane or otherwise, to ground her and stop her mind racing to those most dangerous places in his presence, the unknown country of bed and sex and pleasure.

He rose as she entered the room, unfurling himself from the furthest sofa, elegant and sleek, sophisticated despite his crumpled, lived-in clothing and the fact, she now noticed, that he wasn't even wearing any socks inside his casual canvas shoes.

'There, that's better,' he said, advancing on her, hand outstretched. For a moment Jess wondered what he was doing, but then he took her damp skirt from her, and darted across the room to arrange it carefully across the radiator. The room was nice and warm now. Had Ellis been feeling the cold? His holiday clothing seemed to suggest he'd recently arrived from hotter climes.

'Please, Jessica, sit down and relax,' he urged, returning to her and slipping a confident arm around her shoulders as if they were old friends, old lovers; almost as if he'd eavesdropped on her fantasies. He guided her to one of the sofas, and then set her pulse racing all over again by flopping down beside her, rather than on the one opposite. 'Hot chocolate?' he asked, nodding to the tray at his side on one of the small tables.

'Yes, please!' The lovely cocoa smell made her stomach rumble. There'd been neither time nor appetite for breakfast this morning.

'And cookies too, by the sound of that growling stomach?' His grin was so impish, so boyish. Somehow it was hard to take umbrage at his high-handedness, or be awed by his status. He was clearly enjoying himself. Why shouldn't she enjoy herself too?

'Absolutely. I didn't have time for breakfast this morning.'

'Tut, tut, Jessica! That's very unwise. Breakfast is important. Even if your hideous ogre of a new boss is visiting.' He put one of the large white china cups into her hands, tucking a couple of biscuits onto the saucer. For the first time, she registered the narrow golden band on his ring finger. She'd seen it before, she realised, when ogling his strong, elegant hands, yet somehow skipped over it. He'd been just an unattainable man giving her a lift, his marital status not an issue when barely moments of interaction were involved.

'In fact, especially when the big ogre boss is visiting,' he continued, 'you never know quite what you'll need all your strength for.' He gave her that wink again, so sly and naughty, a clear sexual challenge.

Stay calm . . . stay calm . . . Men as hot as he is are natural flirts, even when they're married. They just can't help themselves.

The hot chocolate was divine though, and just cool enough to allow a long, reviving sip. She took one, then another, and then met his sea-blue gaze.

'You're not an ogre, Mr McKenna, and nobody calls me Jessica as a rule, just "Jess".' Good God, she couldn't imagine ever saying that to old Jacobson in this room, but it seemed easy with Ellis McKenna.

'"Jess" . . . I like that.' He paused, and took a sip of his own chocolate, his tongue lingering suggestively over his lower lip. 'And I'm "Ellis" . . . and you don't know me well enough to know whether I'm an ogre yet. But I'm hoping we can rectify that soon.'

Jess nibbled a biscuit. Finished it. It was heavenly, soft and buttery and crammed with juicy sultanas, but she barely tasted it. What was he talking about? Was he really coming on to her? She sat up straighter on the deep sofa, trying to regain a semblance of control of her wits. Sitting here, with this beautiful man, and feeling his effect on her, was addling her brain.

'Look, Mr McKenna, what am I doing here? I'm just your employee. One of thousands I don't doubt. I . . . I shouldn't be sitting here with you, half dressed, scoffing biscuits and drinking hot chocolate. It's . . . um . . . well, it's not right.'

He laughed, a clear, light, joyous sound. Damn him, he was so relaxed. This was all so easy to him, while she had no clue how to act.

'I'm "Ellis". Call me "Ellis", I beg of you.' He set down his cup and swivelled to sit and face her. 'And you're not "just" an employee to me.' He fixed her with his penetrating gaze. 'Don't you realise that?' A slight, intent frown puckered his brow, almost as if he wanted to see her – read her – more accurately.

Jess put her cup aside, even though the chocolate was delicious, and reviving. She didn't want to spill it because her hands were shaking madly. 'No, I don't realise anything. This is all too weird. Fantastical . . . like something out of one of those novels with a pair of handcuffs or a lace blindfold on the cover, not real life.' She flashed a pointed look at his ring finger, then cursed herself for a prissy Victorian miss. But then, she was one, really, wasn't she? Apart from the era.

And it didn't sit right with her, him making a pass when he was married. It wasn't . . . heroic.

'I'm real,' said Ellis softly, reaching and enfolding her fingers in his. Raising their joined hands, he tilted his left one, making the narrow ring glint. 'And if that bothers you, Jess, I'm not married any more. I'm a widower.' For just an instant, the playful light went out of him, and his face was stark and sad. Then, just as quickly, his sunny charm was back again, on full beam, like something he could flip on and off at will.

Jess's mind prepared to run off down a path of speculation. Just how long ago had his wife died? Did he still love her? She opened her mouth, to say 'I'm sorry,' but then, almost as if to rein her back in from such thoughts, Ellis gave her what could only be described as a quelling look, and started to rub her palms and her fingers, massaging firmly but at the same time with great gentleness. No discussion of his marriage allowed then.

'You're cold. Why is that? The heating's almost tropical now, but you're still shivering,' he said. There was speculation in his eyes, and on his handsome face, almost puzzlement.

He doesn't get it because he's not used to women who don't have a clue. He's used to partners . . . and a wife . . . who know how to respond.

The realisation made her shake harder. Ellis's smooth brow puckered in a frown, and then his eyes widened, and brightened. He looked as if he were about to gasp. And perhaps to accuse her of her 'secret'.

'I'm sorry. I'm just nervous. You're my big boss and you could sack me, just like that.' Such nonsense. She

HOW TO SEDUCE A BILLIONAIRE   39

barely knew him but she knew instinctively that even
though he was a demigod of wealth and power he
would not go back on the word he'd just given to
everyone. He was a good and fair man and he wouldn't
just sack anyone out of hand.

Strong, smooth hands tightened around hers. He
tipped his head on one side. 'I told you all. I'm not
planning to sack anybody,' he confirmed, pausing to
flick his tongue out again, provocative and swift,
touching his lower lip 'although I would like to offer
you a new position, Jess.'

Oh God . . . Oh God . . . Oh God . . .

The devil-glint in his eyes was unmistakable, even
to her.

But why, why? She was just . . . just herself . . . and
he was the Master of the Universe.

But as fast as the demonic sparkle had appeared,
it was gone, replaced by what seemed awfully like
remorse.

'Ah, I know. Too much, too soon. Please forgive
me, Jess.' He sighed, a deep gusty sound. The quality
of his hold on her changed, and became even gentler,
less charged. He frowned again, and then ran his hand
up her arm, under the big, loose sleeve of the robe.
'Is the rest of you as cold as your hands?'

A rapier stab of pain hit her, almost palpable. She
was cold, in every sense. There was something wrong
with her. She'd never felt anything with a man. If it
hadn't been for her lurid fantasies and her episodes
of self-pleasure, she'd have been convinced she was
an ice-ball of frigidity.

Until today. Oh the bloody idiotic irony of it all.

She'd finally met a man she could fancy, even if she wasn't sure she actually liked him all that much. Dream Lover . . . but certainly not Mr Right.

'What's wrong, Jess?'

'I'm not cold. I'm not . . . It's just . . .'

He surged forward, and suddenly she was in his arms. 'I didn't mean it like that. No, never like that.' He kissed her hair, lightly and chastely. Too goddamn chastely. 'Your skin is cold. You *are* shivering.' He pulled away a little way, and gave her a smile, possibly the sweetest one she'd ever seen, yet she guessed he could wield it like a weapon when he needed to. 'I bet your feet are cold too. Let me give you a foot massage, Jess. I'm really good at it. Go on . . . give me a chance.'

He was right. Her feet were like blocks of ice. And his hands were warm, so warm . . .

'Yes, I think I'd like that.' She'd like it a lot. His hands on her. Feet were a safe location though, not dangerous. 'My feet are a bit chilly. It was the soggy shoes, I guess.'

Oh, what the hell am I babbling about? The most gorgeous man I've ever seen . . . He made a pass at me. I'm sure he did. And of course . . . I back off. I am frigid!

Ellis slid off the settee and settled on his knees in front of her. Grinning up at her, he shrugged out of his jacket and flung it haphazardly in the general direction of the seat. As it slid off onto the floor, he ignored it, and unbuttoned his cuffs, rolling up the sleeves of his pale patterned shirt.

Flowers. Delicate little flowers, in blue and green. How can he be wearing a poncy flowered shirt and still be the very essence of a man?

Then he laid his hands gently upon her.

The sensation of his touch was so intense that she gasped, and the gasp was reflected in his face in an expression of puzzled surprise, that morphed into triumph. Well, not exactly, more a strange satisfaction. 'Whoa, don't worry. I won't hurt you,' he said quietly, his thumbs starting to work, firm yet gentle, and somehow managing not to tickle, even though she was usually ticklish.

Instead, banners of heat unfurled inside her. They started in her chilly feet, but within heartbeats deployed in other areas too. Her throat, her back . . . deep in her belly.

Oh hell, I don't know whether I like this. Oh God, I do! Yes, I do!

How could he do that? How could he caress her feet, yet it feel like he had his hands all over her body, moving, moving and pleasuring? The urge to wriggle was excruciating, like an engine revving inside her. Equally intense was the desire to plunge her fingers into his thick dark hair and draw his face towards her. So he could give her another pleasure elsewhere that she'd only fantasised about . . .

She clenched her fists hard on the seat beside her.

'What's wrong? Don't you like it? Your feet really are chilled.'

'I'm fine. It's all right. But maybe I should be going. Everybody will wonder what the hell I'm doing up here. Especially old Jacobson and his cohorts.'

Ellis's fingers stilled, but he didn't let go. In fact, for a moment he looked down at her foot, in his hands, and Jess almost imagined he was going to dip forward and kiss it. Good God, she was going mad!

'Why would you care what he thinks? What anyone thinks?' His eyes were harder suddenly, but still beautiful.

'Of course I care.' She tried to pull away her foot, but his hold was implacable. Both feather-light and unyielding at the same time. 'Mr Jacobson is my boss. He'll still be here when you're long gone, and things might be weird for me if I hang around much longer with you.'

He gave her a long look, a strange complex scrutiny. Was he weighing up what to say next? And what the hell might that be in this bizarre, peculiar situation. The weirdest she'd experienced in her life.

'Nothing will happen to you, Jess. Nothing that you don't want to happen.' His thumb moved slowly over her skin, and then, just as if she'd been prescient, he did swoop forward and press a kiss against her toes. 'And if anything I've done today makes life awkward for you, Jess, you have my word that I'll do everything in my power to set things right. That's a promise.'

His voice was vehement, almost wild, and his eyes harder than ever. But Jess hardly noticed it. All she could register was that kiss, that fleeting kiss, his mouth against the tender skin of her foot.

'That's stupid. Why would you do that? I'm nothing to you. Just one of thousands of drones you employ.' Her voice sounded strange to her own ears, reedy, almost feverish.

He released her foot, but before she could spring away, he captured the other and kissed that too.

'I'd do it because I want you, and I think you want me.'

Jess's mouth opened, but she couldn't frame words. She blinked, only just resisting the urge to shake her head and clear it. So she could wake up from this weird extension to one of her own night-time fantasies and find herself back at her desk, doodling a sketch on her notepad, trying to capture the essence of the eyes, the lips, the hands of a man she'd never see again.

'Ah . . . I see I've gone too far again,' murmured Ellis, releasing her foot and pushing himself upwards, sitting beside her. 'I'm sorry, I do that . . . I do it a lot . . .' He snagged his plush lower lip between his teeth. His eyes glittered. 'But mostly, the women I do it with are right on the same page with me. Often several pages ahead.' Was that a world-weary note? As an ultra-wealthy, no longer married man he was a prime catch.

Jess was still numbed. Every nerve in her body was in a firing tumult, yet incapable of making her move. Overload. That was what it was. Overload.

He took her hands and kissed them too, one after the other.

'What's different about you, Jess?' His scrutiny bored into her, blue-green fire, setting her alight, freeing her from her paralysed state, sending new patterns of instructions to her nerves and sinews, the blind, carnal command to surge forward, throw her arms around him. Kiss him . . . touch him . . . know him. Know him and compel him to know her.

Don't be bloody ridiculous!

She tried to struggle. To rise. He still held her in that tender, implacable way.

'What is it? What is it?' he continued softly, as if musing to himself as he raised her hand to his lips again and kissed her palm this time, gentle yet provocative. She felt the brush of his soft stubble against her skin. 'There's something about you, some mystery, and it's driving me crazy. Making me act like a barbarian.' He kissed the other palm this time. 'It's exhilarating though. Exciting . . . Are you excited?'

'No, not in the slightest!' Finding strength at last from somewhere, Jess snatched her hands away, and sprang to her feet. She was such a liar. She'd never been more excited in her life. In every sense of the word. 'And there's nothing in the slightest bit special or different about me, Mr McKenna, as you'd quickly discover. Now, may I go? I've a lot of work to do.'

Not waiting for his answer, she marched across to the radiator and her skirt. For an instant, she considered retreating to Jacobson's bathroom again, but it would only waste time. Instead, she quickly shrugged out of the robe, tossed it over the radiator and reached for her skirt. Trying not to imagine what Ellis McKenna was seeing, she stepped into the skirt and zipped it up smartly. The hem was almost completely dry now, but it wouldn't have mattered if the entire garment was dripping wet. She had to get out of there.

Her shoes were almost dry too, when she stepped into them.

Damn, her bag was on the settee, close to where he was sitting, and watching her. His eyes were bright, yet his expression was slightly perplexed; he was still puzzling over her. Probably quite a new experience for someone so confident in himself and his ability to weigh people up.

You've probably never met a virgin over twenty-five before, so you don't recognise one when you see her.

'You *are* special, Jess, and I'd love to know your secret . . .' He rose to his feet, but didn't approach her. It felt like a standoff, the *O.K. Corral*, or a *Fistful of Dollars*. 'You're bright and intelligent. You're smart and brave. And you're beautiful. But there's something else. Will you tell me?' His gorgeous eyes narrowed, and he drew out the moment. Then he deployed a weapon the Man with No Name had never possessed, his beautiful, quizzical, complicated, almost entreating smile. 'Please?'

'Alright already, if you insist.' Her heart revved up. What the hell was she doing? 'That secret you're so desperate to know is . . . I'm a virgin!'

5

'Wow!'

Apart from Ellis's exclamation, the proverbial pin could have dropped.

What the hell is wrong with me? Why did I say that? Why did I tell him, of all people?

Hearing the 'V' word from her own lips like that was a shock. It did not compute. How could she possibly have revealed her most intimate secret, the one that not even her closest friends were privy to?

How? How? How? To this man . . .

'Well, I'm not sure quite what I was expecting, Jess.' Ellis McKenna looked almost as shell-shocked as she was, but he smiled too. A small, subtle, almost wondering smile. There was no mockery in it, but perhaps just the beginning of challenge. 'But somehow, now you tell me . . . I can see it. A purity . . . No sexual calculation . . . You're just a beautiful, honest woman. Thank you for telling me. I feel honoured.'

Jess affected a shrug, trying not to show how flustered she was. 'I probably shouldn't have told you, Mr

McKenna. It's not really a big deal, or an issue.' She strode forward. Action seemed to be the only possible way to control her shaking. Steeling herself she moved closer to him, snatched up her shoulder bag, and then, in a supreme effort of control, she stopped herself shooting away from him, and held out her hand. 'I think it's better if I just go now, and get back to work. It's been . . . interesting . . . and it's broken up what would otherwise have been a humdrum morning. Thank you for the chocolate and cookies.'

He regarded her steadily, then accepted her hand, and shook it, no nonsense, releasing her again immediately. He made no attempt to stop her when she walked away.

Planning to open the door, walk out and not look back, Jess cursed inwardly when she found herself turning. The part of her he'd rocked to her very foundations just couldn't resist one last glance. She had to print him in her memory. Despite everything, she'd still draw him . . . and finally give Dream Lover a face.

He didn't look smug and macho. He was barely even smiling. He still looked a bit puzzled, at a loss. Had he expected things to go differently? It seemed as if he had.

Yet his voice was confident and even. 'My name is still "Ellis", Jess, and thank you . . . thank you again for telling me your secret. You're very brave.'

Oh damn him, the devil. He was getting to her with niceness now, as well. Not that it mattered. She'd never see him again.

'Goodbye, Ellis.'

Before she could balk again, she opened the door and walked out, keeping her face as straight and composed as she could, and just nodding fleetingly to Jacobson's secretary as she passed.

'So, what's he like? What did he want? Did he make a pass at you?'

The questions came thick and fast over tuna salad in the canteen. Jess would have gone out and found somewhere to eat alone, away from her well-meaning but nosy work-mates, but she knew it was better to brave their curiosity sooner rather than later. And besides the rain was still pouring down outside.

'No! Don't be ridiculous,' she said quickly, smiling in a way she hoped looked nonchalant when she was as far from nonchalant as it was possible to be. 'He just wanted to make sure I didn't catch a cold. I think he's a bit eccentric, to be honest, a bit weird. Maybe not quite right in the head.'

I couldn't fake it with you, Ellis McKenna. You saw through me. You knew there was something. I'm going to have to try and pull the wool over everybody else's eyes though.

'Well, that's a damned shame,' said Pamela, who was in Jess's section, 'He's the fittest thing I've seen in here for a long time. In fact *ever*. It's disappointing that he didn't make a move. Still, I suppose if he's married and all that . . .' Clearly every female in the place had immediately checked out his ring finger.

Emma, the third girl at their table, piped up, 'Well, I'd have made a pass at *him*. Even if he is married. He's freaking gorgeous!'

Jess stabbed at a cold green bean. Her appetite was non-existent. The only thing she fancied was hot chocolate and cookies, and she'd walked away from those, along with a certain other temptation. The one she didn't want to get into with the women around this table. They were all buddies, like Cathy at home, and some of them told very wild stories about their sex lives, but Jess had always managed to dance around the subject of *her* sex life. Or total lack of it. It would've been far too embarrassing to reveal that she was still a virgin. She always talked vaguely of boyfriends that she'd had before she'd taken this job. It'd been all too easy to let her lunch buddies assume she'd done the deed with at least one or two of these mythical men.

'He's a widower, apparently,' Jess pointed out, pushing her plate away.

'Wahey, so he's available! God, I hope he comes here again. Some of the rest of us might get a crack at him next time.' Emma's appetite appeared to be improved by the news of their visitor's marital status, and she reached out to stab a choice bit of tuna from Jess's plate. 'Imagine it . . . He looks like a film star and he's a billionaire. What's not to like, eh, Jess? You missed your chance. You should have jumped all over him. He must have fancied you or he wouldn't have invited you up to the inner sanctum.'

'He *is* very handsome,' Jess admitted cautiously. It was a lie, really. Ellis McKenna was far beyond simply handsome. 'But it wasn't anything like that. Honestly. He just singled me out because he'd given me a lift in the rain. I think he just wanted to quiz a typical employee about day-to-day life at the Windsor coalface. Nothing more than that.'

Two sets of wide eyes said 'yeah right', but neither girl pressed. She wondered if they really *did* know or suspect her secret, but they were too nice to ask the awkward questions.

'Anyway, it's certainly brightened up a crappy day for us all, hasn't it?' observed Pam, with a dreamy expression on her face. 'I thought this place was the dump of all dumps, and the last chance saloon job-wise, but just thinking about working "under" Ellis McKenna makes it worth staying put.'

'He's only visiting for the day, love,' countered Jess. 'A royal visit to inspect the drones and all that. We'll probably never see him again.'

Again, came that stab of pain. But why? Realistically, Ellis McKenna could never be more than a fantasy object, the future face of Dream Lover. He'd given her a foot massage and made a pass of sorts, but he'd probably already forgotten her. Any ideas that he might be the one to help her get rid of something she was getting mighty fed up of saving . . . well, they were patently ridiculous.

'Ooh, I don't know,' said Emma. 'I was talking to someone from personnel who knows a bit more. Apparently, he actually has a house in this area. Some stately pile or other that belonged to a Brit branch of the McKenna family.' She paused and took a long slurp from her juice carton. 'With any luck he'll decide to settle down there and he'll be popping in to see us every day!'

'Ah, but doesn't the McKenna empire have holdings

all over the world? They must have posh pads every-where,' Pam said thoughtfully, 'America and Australia, at least. He's probably lived all over the place, and if he's got the pick of them, why on earth would he decide to take up residence here in the arse end of the universe?'

America? Australia? Well, perhaps that explained the hard-to-pinpoint accent. Like everything about him, his voice had intrigued her. He'd sounded, well, basically English, but with other notes too, a bit American but not quite wholly so.

You speak like velvet, every syllable a seduction.

'Well, he obviously likes the arse end of the universe,' said Emma, her eyes widening. She was staring over Jess's shoulder towards the serving counter at the other end of the canteen. 'At least this particular cheek of it . . . I do believe our glorious leader is down here to dine amongst us plebs! He's just walked in.'

Don't look round. Don't look round.

Jess had to grit her teeth to stop herself rubber-necking. The volume of chatter in the room had quadrupled in the last few seconds, and everybody she could see was staring towards the counter. The men all looked surprised and curious, and the ones who were chatting up a female lunch companion looked downright annoyed! Every woman in the room was clearly bedazzled, just as they'd been during Ellis's royal progress through the work-floor.

'Aren't you going to look?' demanded Pam. 'I'd give even money he's looking for you.'

'Don't be daft. He's not interested in me. All this

"getting down with the employees" and chatting to random people . . . it's just an act,' Jess said, stabbing at the remnants of her salad again, 'a ploy to seem like the big nice guy super boss. There'll probably be redundancies next week, when he's gone, regardless of his bullshit for the troops.'

'Why so bitter? You said he was nice,' Pam said, her eyes still scoping the far end of the room.

He is nice. He's more than nice. But I . . . I . . . I can't forgive him. He's started something, and he'll be gone in an hour and I'll never see him again.

She'd feel differently tomorrow. Probably mightily amused by it all. Perhaps grateful, and changed too, and ready to be bolder and, well, live a little.

But today, now, it was all too confusing. 'He was perfectly fine,' Jess said, 'but let's face it, he's an obscenely wealthy man who employs us, amongst many, many thousands of others. He hasn't got where he is today by really being "nice", has he? It's all an act.'

'Well, we'll soon see . . . Incoming!' Emma's eyes were bright and her face pink . . . and suddenly wreathed in her best 'pulling' smile.

Oh no!

But, it was *oh yes*. Ellis McKenna slid into the spare seat at their table of four with a belated, 'May I join you?' Setting his cup in front of him, he grinned as if he completed their chatty foursome every day.

Jess couldn't speak, but at least she wasn't the only one. The others were gaping at their new companion, as subject to the 'dazzle' effect as she was. Although perhaps for not quite the same reasons.

Ellis took a sip of what looked like jet black coffee and said, 'Not bad . . . not bad at all.' He took another sip, and then lounged back in his chair, beaming at them. 'Seems a decent canteen. The only shortcoming I can see is that there's no hot chocolate on the menu, but that can be rectified.'

Did you just wink at me? Oh you, devil, how could you? Stop it!

'So, ladies, what do you think of the food? How's that tuna thing?' He nodded to the food still on Jess's plate. 'Nothing wrong with it, I hope? Nothing I need to look into?'

'It's excellent, actually.' It was normally one of her favourites, but a certain person had put the kybosh on her appetite. 'I'm just not particularly hungry today.'

'And why is that? Nerves about meeting the big horrible ogre who's just bought the company?'

Pam and Emma giggled. How the hell could she give them a 'cool it and behave look' without him noticing? They were exchanging looks and Jess had seen that secret code, and been part of it herself, when one or other of them had fancied a new male employee, and set their sights on the guy, here in the canteen. The look meant it was time to scuttle off and leave the field clear to the one who hoped to 'click'.

'No, not that at all.' Jess paused to deliberately stab up a tuna chunk, convey it to her lips, and then chew. It tasted of nothing. 'I think you've proved to us all that you're not an ogre, so there's nothing to be nervous about.'

It was Ellis's turn to laugh. 'Now that's a shame. Obviously rumours of my power and awesomeness have been grossly exaggerated. I'm crushed.'

'Look, it's been lovely meeting you, Mr McKenna,' said Pam, already on her feet, 'but I'm a dutiful employee and I have some stuff to catch up on . . .' She grabbed Emma's elbow. 'And so has Emma. Please excuse us.'

Emma clearly didn't really want to be excused, especially as she was sitting right next to Ellis, their bodies almost touching, but she complied with a smile, and 'Catch you later', then followed the other girl away from the table.

'Nice girls,' observed Ellis, leaning forward again, eyes alight. 'Very tactful . . . very perceptive.'

'Yes, they are nice. They're my friends. And we were enjoying our lunch together.'

'I'm sorry . . .' Oh, what an obvious, big fat lie. 'But I wanted to continue our conversation and I thought this would be less conspicuous than summoning you upstairs again.' His long, slightly tanned hands were on the table now, just inches from hers. Oh God, he wasn't going to try and grab her, was he?

'What do you mean, less conspicuous? Everybody's looking at us, Mr McKenna, in case you hadn't noticed?'

It was true. Everyone in the immediate vicinity appeared to be hanging on their every word, some blatantly, and some trying for at least a semblance of stealth.

'I tend to have that effect,' he said with a lift of his

dark eyebrows, 'but you're right. This is quite a public place for the kind of questions I'd like to ask you. What say we go out for lunch? You're not really eating that, and I know several places not too far away where the cuisine might be a bit more tempting. How about it?' He looked as if he might reach out and take her hand, but Jess hid both quickly, in her lap.

You're the temptation . . .

It was true, but to succumb was pointless. It would only make things worse. He was muddying the water. She only wanted a face and a body to star in her fantasies. There was no possibility of more, and she didn't want to spill all the details of her non-existent sex life to a man she'd never see again. Especially one who was starting to make her cross as well as turned on, what with his arrogance and his alpha male games.

'That's very kind of you, Mr McKenna, but I'm afraid I've already got my lunch here, and to be honest, I don't want to answer any questions. Not unless they're to do with my performance as an employee here.' She gave him a very firm look. 'I really think that's all you're entitled to, don't you?'

He shrugged; a beautiful, loose, mammalian movement, accompanied by a boyish, rueful smile. 'You're right, of course. But I just wanted to get to know you better, Jess. No pressure. No questions if you don't want any. Just a bit of time spent in each other's company.'

What was he playing at? Why was he playing with *her*? She was an ordinary woman, a middling happy insurance clerk heading for thirty. Her life wasn't perfect – whose was – but mostly she liked it the way it was.

Ellis McKenna was as alien as a man from another planet. In every way that mattered, their worlds could never really intersect. Stop the madness now.

Coward, Jess. Coward . . .

'I don't think that's really a good idea, Mr McKenna. I'm me and you're you.' She looked around. 'I . . . I feel uncomfortable with you here. It's making people stare at me. I like fitting in here. I like my job. But it's going to get weird if people keep seeing me with you.' She drew in a deep breath, preparing herself. 'I really do wish you would go . . . Please.'

He frowned. Was he cross? Annoyed at not getting his way, as usual? Then he smiled again, shrugging that fabulous shrug. 'All right. I see that. I'm being a bit of an oaf, aren't I?' His fingers flexed, as if he really was fighting the urge to reach out and grab her hand. 'I'll leave right now, if you'll promise me one thing. No . . . two things.'

'What things?' *Just go . . . go . . . you're driving me crazy and making me want what I can't have. Well, not with you . . .*

'One, you call me "Ellis".' He reached into his inner pocket and drew out a couple of business cards. 'And two, you'll at least consider having dinner with me some time. Away from here. Nobody need know.' Reaching in his pocket again, he brought out a pen. 'This is my private number . . .' He scribbled it on the back of one of the cards, and then pushed both cards and the pen towards her. 'Can I have yours?' He waited, in one of his cleverly executed micro-pauses. 'Please?'

She hesitated. People were watching, but she no

longer cared. Exchanging numbers was like . . . serious . . . like a man properly interested in a woman, wanting a real date.

'I could get your number from your personnel file, but that seems underhand. I'd rather you give it to me willingly, Jess.'

Give it to you willingly . . .

For a flash moment, a hot, vivid image rocketed into her brain. Herself, with Ellis, giving something willingly. Something she wanted to give. Oh God, how she wanted to give it. And, if she was going to, why not with him? A fabulous, beautiful, once in a lifetime man.

Snatching up the pen, she scribbled her mobile number and her home number on the back.

He beamed. 'Anything to get rid of me, eh?' Pocketing the card and the pen, he stood up.

'Yes . . . anything to get rid of you . . . Ellis.'

Laughing softly, he waggled his fingers at her in a mock wave, then, just before he turned and walked away, he murmured, 'I'll be in touch, Jess. I mean it. Enjoy your lunch.'

And then he was gone, leaving a hum of conversation lingering behind him . . . and Jess wondering what the hell she'd just done.

I'll be in touch, Jess. I mean it.

Yeah, right. And pigs might fly.

Back home that evening, Jess twirled Ellis McKenna's card between her fingers. She wasn't going to call his number because she didn't think he'd intended her to, and he most certainly wouldn't call her. It'd just been him going through the motions. Kindly perhaps, to make her feel special for a moment, but probably hoping she knew the score, really.

What a day. Probably one of the strangest of her life, and although Jess would have liked to discuss it with Cathy, in one way she was glad her friend was out with her boyfriend, and possibly not back for the night.

It was an ideal opportunity to review her encounter with a billionaire, and try and make sense of it. Especially as Cathy had left a note telling Jess there was half a bottle of white Zinfandel in the fridge that needed drinking up.

Why did you come to Windsor Insurance today, Mr McKenna? Because you were bored? Because you really are an eccentric weirdo, and you enjoy doing unexpected things and wrong-footing people, women and employees in general alike?

It had been a whim, really, she supposed. Windsor wasn't the biggest insurer in the country, but its share in the market was growing. A nice profitable plum to be harvested by the McKenna group. And Ellis McKenna had probably thought it was a bit of a wheeze to drop in on the staff of its main northern HQ, simply because of the coincidence of him having a house in the area . . . which he probably didn't visit much anyway.

You are *weird, Mr McKenna.*

Ellis, he'd insisted.

You're weird, Ellis. Gorgeous but decidedly strange.

Maybe it was the loss of his wife that had affected him? It must have been devastating, enough to throw the hardest head off kilter. Or maybe he'd always been capricious, and into playing mind-games?

She could clearly picture him nodding in agreement, imagining him right here in her bedroom with her, in a way that was far clearer than her hazy erotic fantasies about Dream Lover.

Even though the wine had been open a day, it was still cool and delicious from the fridge. Jess set her glass aside, not wanting to swig it down all at once. She'd bathed and changed into her pyjamas early, and was in bed, with the sound turned off on the telly, and all her 'stuff' spread around her on the bed.

A pristine new drawing pad. Freshly sharpened pencils and a proper putty eraser. Some snacks, although she'd have to be careful not to get crisp grease on the paper. Her old laptop, with Firefox open at Google search.

She'd told herself not to get involved in finding out about Ellis McKenna, and that it was better just to remember today as unusual, interesting and, yes, sexy. The day a billionaire had kissed her feet, and got her in such a kerfuffle she'd told him she was a virgin. But she couldn't help but be curious about him. The bloody man had had an unprecedented effect on her and she just couldn't sweep that aside. It had to be acknowledged. *He* had to be acknowledged. And known, if only a little.

The next half an hour was both fascinating and frustrating. How could there possibly be so little information about Ellis McKenna in this no-secrets digital age? Oh, she found business statistics about the McKenna group, some background about his extended family, who seemed to be spread all over the world, but mainly in the States, Australia and also in the UK

. . . She also found pictures of what must have been the 'old' Ellis, clad in razor sharp suits and with a razor sharp haircut. One full length shot even showed 'proper' shoes, hand-made no doubt, in gleaming leather, rather than the footwear he wore now, that looked as if he'd walked right off the beach.

Yet apart from his age – thirty-six – and some academic stuff and more notable business achievements, there was tantalisingly little personal information to be found on Ellis himself. Just snippets in news archives.

Clearly, even in these times of celebrity exposés and phone-tapping, if you were rich enough, you could still fly pretty much beneath the radar. She couldn't even discover what the name of this supposedly local house of his was, or the specifics of its location.

But there were one or two brief news pieces on the death of his wife. A horrible tragedy that the press had found so juicy they just had to pursue the details.

Billionaire's Bride gunned down in Mall . . . McKenna's little angels slain.

It'd happened five years ago, in a popular, newly opened shopping mall. Ellis's wife Julie had been out for the day, with their two daughters, Annie and Lily, when a gunman, believed to be high on drugs, had run amok, mowing down a dozen or more shoppers in a rain of bullets, including the McKennas. The two little girls had been just five and seven at the time.

Icy horror gripped Jess, just from reading the piece. It must have been devastating beyond belief. With a history like that it was no wonder Ellis was a bit strange. And no wonder he hadn't offered any detail beyond the fact he was a widower.

I should have been nicer to him. Poor man.

Jess picked up the card. Should she call him? No, it was silly. If he could make a pass at a random virgin like her, he probably had a whole little black book full of much more experienced girlfriends who could offer him the solace of physical pleasure. The brief oblivion of the flesh that would momentarily dull the pain of his loss.

Hmm . . . the glass she'd been randomly sipping from was empty. As was the bottle.

Thinking about the loss of loved ones would make her maudlin, and that wouldn't do anybody any good. Not her. Not this strange, beautiful, arousing man she'd never meet again. Time to put a positive spin on her peculiar day.

Time to draw. And perhaps do other things.

She flipped open the drawing pad, and shuffled to sit up against the pillows with it resting on her knees. Reaching for one of her good graphite pencils, she set to work.

Sometimes, Jess had a knack of being able to draw from memory, or from a combination of memory and pure imagination. Tonight those skills seemed a bit addled, surprise, surprise.

She worked on an eye, crinkled at the corner, as if he was grinning or laughing. She laboured over a mouth, curved, playful and sensual.

She made a mess of his nose, making it too straight and sharp, rubbing out several times.

But damn it, she couldn't seem to put the whole face together.

Maybe I should call you after all, and ask you to pose for me, you aggravating man!

Shaking her head, she tossed the card away across the bed. That way madness lay.

Her drawing wasn't working for her tonight. Time to try something else. Rising from the bed, she went and turned the light off, relying only on the silent flickering from the television for illumination.

Then she returned to the bed, shoved her stuff aside and smiled to herself. Dream Lover had a face now, at least, so why not enjoy him? Use her strange day and her encounter with a billionaire, rather than let it go to waste, and just fade away?

Shooting a quick glance at the drawer in her bedroom cabinet, she wondered about the cheap and cheerful vibrator and a small tube of lubricant she kept in there. Why not, she had the house to herself and no worries about being overheard?

But even so, she didn't fancy the noise the rather basic toy made. The sound was like another presence in the room, and she only wanted it to be her and Dream Lover.

Her and Ellis.

What would it be like? Being with him? Because of who and what he was, a deluxe experience, no doubt. No coupling in an ordinary suburban bedroom like this one, no way.

Unfastening her pyjama top, she formed a picture of a gorgeous hotel room, acres of space and a huge, white bed made up with immaculate, luxurious linen. She switched perspective, seeing the room from the aspect of the sumptuous bed itself, with herself at its centre, clad in equally sumptuous lingerie: an ivory silk camisole, fastened up the front with delicate pearl buttons, worn with the tiniest matching thong, and white hold-up stockings with a thick welt of intricate lace.

Bloody hell, I look fab!

She'd never fantasised in quite this detail before, but somehow it was easy. But what about her lover, her dream . . . Ellis McKenna?

Both in the fantasy and in reality, she looked up at the ceiling and closed her eyes. Would he come to her naked, or clothed in something? Well, initially . . . She imagined him bare-chested but wearing silk pyjama bottoms. Never having seen his unclothed chest, she imagined it smooth. Or maybe just a little bit of dark fuzz, to match the hair on his head, and that sexy designer stubble he wore.

He didn't speak, but he advanced towards her and lay down gracefully on the wide, white bed at her side. Astonishingly, she almost experienced the dip created by his body for real.

Cupping her breast, she replaced her own fingers with his. She knew his touch already. He had beautiful hands and he used them well. He was as much an artist as she was, in this at least. His thumb glided over her nipple, masked by the silk, strumming it in a way that was both arousing and frustrating. It made her want more. Silently directing the action, she willed him to undo the phantom silk ribbons and bare her.

'Delightful.'

The sound of his voice was so real that it shook her from the fantasy for a moment. This was a first. Dream Lover had a voice now too, why hadn't she expected that, knowing the real man who was the template had such an intriguing layering of accents within his basically English tones? A British education, enriched with time spent in other lands; Australia, America.

'You're beautiful, Jess.' The words were like caresses in themselves, exciting her even more, as if the syllables played over her nipples . . . and her clit. She moved uneasily, plucking lightly at the former; wanting to rub the latter, but holding off. To make things last.

I'm not beautiful. Not really . . .

But in the fantasy it was easy to believe it. To feel powerful and seductive, and regard him with sultry amusement as he undressed her. Those eyes of his, so gorgeously coloured and mutable, they flared with heat as he teased open the notional ribbons and bared her breasts. She arched upwards as he swooped down, kissing her nipples, licking and sucking them. Dimly at the back of her mind she knew the pleasure came from her own hand, but what her imagination was creating for her was more real than ever before, painted in a thousand colours, informed by the actual experience of Ellis McKenna and his dazzling good looks.

Dream Jess dug her fingers into Dream Lover's thick silky hair, compelling him to lavish her bosom with kisses.

But she wanted more, and because he was idealised, he knew what that was. Still plaguing her nipple with his tongue, he reached down, pushing his fingers beneath the tiny silk thong to find her centre. She imagined that she might be shaved down there, trimmed and groomed, and he zeroed in on her clitoris with no pause or hesitation.

'Do you like that?' he whispered. Jess didn't hear her own voice, as she mouthed the words, just his.

'Yes . . . yes I do. Give me more!'

The stroking, the circling, the rocking and rubbing, it became more. She made it so, but it felt like him. Strong fingers, deft fingers, perfectly precise.

'Yes, that's good,' she cried, squirming about. There was nobody else in the house, so she could be loud. Nobody else in the vast, soundproofed hotel room, so she could even scream if she wanted to. 'But I want you. I want you to fuck me. Now!'

So demanding. But this was her show. She was in charge.

'Your wish is my command,' Dream Ellis said, with that low devilish laugh, from the real world. Twisting his hand in the dream, he tore away her G-string, ooh wild! Then he reached down, unfastening his pyjama bottoms and moving forward, ready to cover her body with his own.

'No! Let me see it first!'

If wasn't as if Jess had never seen a cock before, even if this crazy scenario had been actually happening. Despite her lack of sexual experience, she was no prude, and she'd enjoyed images of naked men online and in magazines. And at her life drawing class, she'd seen her share of 'equipment', though never been especially impressed.

Now, she could be impressed. She could extrapolate. Make Ellis huge!

Dropping out of the dream for just a second, she thought, *Maybe his is huge!*

What a whopper . . . towering, reddish, proud. Pointing at her.

I bet he really is big. He's got that swagger. Primal. Potent.

She imagined how it might feel to her touch, and how warm and hard it would be. She squeezed, not sure whether he'd like that, but Dream Ellis groaned, pleasure not pain.

'Okay then . . . I want it in me. Get to work, Mr McKenna.'

Not Dream Lover. No more kidding herself.

'With pleasure.' Dark-eyed, he resumed his approach, moving between her thighs, positioning himself. And this was fantasy again, no consequences, so no condom.

Again, she was in the realm of conjecture, with nothing but tampon use and unsatisfactory and abortive exploration with her vibrator as a guide. And the latter hadn't worked out well, had it? Doubts threatened to pull her out of the dream, but she shook her head against the pillows, as if to banish them. The real first time would, no doubt, be uncomfortable; this fantasy was idealised, so all possible pain was banished.

Surrendering again, she soared, the pleasure from her own fingertip ministrations transmuted by the power of imagination. Becoming more and different sensations.

Her dream lover billionaire entered her, and she welcomed him, in both worlds drawing up her knees to cradle his body, his lean, powerful, pumping hips.

The rhythmic impact of him knocking against her, again and again, juddering her clit in sweet, percussive jolts of pure sensation.

And the kisses. The wicked words. Rude, delicious things he said about her body, her heat, her tightness. Somewhere at the back of her mind, Jess knew she'd laugh her head off afterwards about the absurdity of her own inner dialogue, but right now, when it mattered, it excited her more.

Just as her inner voice had become his, the relentless massage of her fingers became his thrusting, and the combination, persistently applied, could have just one outcome. Her back arched, her legs waved, and her pussy flexed and clenched as she hit her climax.

It was deep and shattering, a harder coming than she'd ever reached before, and she wailed out, coherent yet incoherent, 'Ellis! Ellis! Ellis!'

Afterwards, she wasn't sure whether she'd passed out or not. She probably hadn't, but it almost felt that way. It was as if the spirit of Ellis McKenna had not only fucked her senseless, but turned into a tornado that had swept her up and dashed her against the wall, again and again.

'Bloody hell,' Jess whispered as she sat up again, aware that she'd been shouting and yelling, perhaps even screaming, during her orgasm. Her whole body still seemed to be thrumming, especially her sex, the sensation far finer and more affecting than anything either of the cheap vibrators she'd tried could ever have produced.

'Bloody hell . . .' She righted her pyjamas, still panting for breath, still tornadoed-out.

Would the real thing be like that? Would it be like that with *him*?

But with a man there would be so many other variables. What *he* wanted. His staying power. His preferences. His physicality.

She'd no doubt that in purely physical terms bedroom-Ellis was as gorgeous and as aesthetically pleasing as boardroom-Ellis. But realistically, he was only ever going to be her fantasy, wasn't he? And other men would as surely have their foibles and quirks and imperfections, just as she had hers.

But why can't *he be more than fantasy*, a sly, subversive voice whispered. The card was there on her bedside table. She could ring him.

Don't be daft. He didn't mean it. He was just amusing himself, and ringing him would only lead to total embarrassment. He certainly wouldn't ring *her*, and that was for sure.

Yes, better this way. It'd just been a crazy thing that had happened, and she had to look on it with a laugh, rather than a what-might-have been.

But she would do something about it. Make it work for her. All this sitting around waiting for a man to desire was pointless and cowardly. She had to give men a chance. More of a chance. Billionaires that looked like beach-bum angels were a rare and special case. With everyday men, you probably had to give yourself more of a chance to know them before lightning struck and you realised you *wanted* them.

Finally, she'd got her breath back. And now she needed a drink, perhaps a midnight snack, and a wash, to clear the sweaty, sexy grunginess from her body.

Thank you, Ellis McKenna. You're a beautiful fantasy object, and you've made me get my act together. We'll never meet again, but our 'moment' was well worthwhile.

Rising from her bed, she headed for the bathroom door, full of resolution. And confidence.

And a little touch of wistfulness as the sight of the card caught her eye . . .

6

In his apartment overlooking the Thames, Ellis
McKenna twirled the business card between his fingers
and stared out across the river. He saw no lights from
late night river-craft. He saw no familiar night-time
skyline. He saw no 24/7 bustle of the busy sprawling
metropolis.

'Jess,' he said to himself, enjoying the name on his
lips, short and sweet.

Well, it hadn't been the usual way he met women
for brief, sexual friendships, had it? With hindsight,
he realised he'd never actually seduced an employee
of any of the many McKenna-owned companies. And
he probably shouldn't start doing it now. It was bad
form. Exploitative . . .

*And I'm not even sure you're the sort of woman who'll
be satisfied with my 'parameters', Jess, and one of my three
or four week only relationships? You deserve something real,
not a shallow fling.*

Even so, her image tormented him. He'd have
to get her out of his system, because never again

could he allow a woman to be *in* his system. That was the domain of Julie, whom he'd loved, and always would do.

Sex was okay. Sex was often glorious. Sex was a panacea. Sex purely for physical exhilaration and release wasn't betraying what he and Julie had shared, because that had been more, so much more.

So it was probably best to purge himself now of any disquieting and obsessive thoughts about Jess Lockhart. They could enjoy one of his four-weekers together, and have a high old time of fucking and mutually satisfying sex play, and afterwards they'd move on, refreshed and sated and with stronger hearts, to face *both* their sets of demons.

Jess's demon was that she was a virgin, and even though she'd not expressed it in words, she very patently and obviously didn't want to be one. She wanted sex. He just knew she did.

But do I have the right to be the first?

Now there was a thing. Yes, Jess almost certainly did want to be rid of her virginity, but he sensed she was an old-fashioned girl, well, woman, and didn't just want to throw it away with just any old man.

You'll be all right with me, Jessica Lockhart. I'll make it good for you. Good, with no regrets.

He could imagine her now, in his bedroom here perhaps, her lovely body relaxed and spread before him on his wide, comfortable bed. Her creamy limbs glowing against the immaculate sheets. She had gorgeous legs, he'd seen them, and he'd wager a chunk of his very considerable fortune that the rest of her was just as delicious.

'Jess,' he groaned, slipping the card that bore her number into his pocket. His cock was aching furiously, and unfastening his robe, he revealed it as he leant his head against the tempered and one-way glass of his magnificent-viewed window. Clasping his length in his fist, he began to work himself slowly, picturing Jess moving uneasily in his bed, plagued by the same fires of lust that tormented him now.

Had she fancied him? Yes, he was sure she had. He could tell the signs. Bright eyes, flushed face, the pert, spiky way she'd responded to him. She might be a virgin, but she was a sensualist too. He'd no way of knowing *why* she was still virgin well into her twenties, but a gut instinct told him it wasn't because she was cold. Quite the reverse. When she did have sex, when she was relaxed, she would enjoy it. She'd *love* it! And God, did he want to be the first one to light the blue touch paper on an inferno of passion and response.

Working his hand and his hips, he thrust his cock to and fro in the glove of his curled fingers. His pre-come flowed from his tip, the silkiness of it lubricating the slide of his flesh, mimicking the silk that would flow from Jess's sweet puss when he prepared her long and slowly with pleasure and orgasms.

I'll introduce you to sex with every power at my command, beautiful girl. That'll be my project, and my pledge to you. I won't let some clod who doesn't appreciate you be the first.

Clamping his fingers tighter around himself, he imagined the sweet, tight grip of her sex, rippling and pulsating around him as she came, for the first time, around a man.

'Oh dear God,' he chanted as the white heat of

pleasure barrelled down his spine, and through his loins, jetting out as semen that spattered in sticky bursts against the window.

Oh Jess, he thought again, smiling as he slumped against the strong glass, anticipating the delicious times that lay ahead with a bright, delicious woman.

But first, he had a cleaning up job to do. Laughing softly to himself, he fastened his robe, and headed for the utility room, his heart feeling lighter than it had done in a long time.

7

I'll be in touch, Jess. I mean it.

Four days had passed. Four crazy days. Four days of people at work asking stupid questions about whether she was going to see 'the big boss' again, and her saying 'No, of course not, don't be ridiculous.' Pam and Emma were particularly disappointed.

But Jess *had* considered calling or texting Ellis McKenna, because it had been four days of thinking about him, non-stop. She'd put his number in her phone's address book and once or twice, she'd been right on the point of calling it, and some dumb thing or other had happened, and the opportune moment had been gone. After about the fourth time, she'd decided it was fate and a message from the gods that it wasn't supposed to be.

So when her phone made its text noise while she was on the bus home, and there was the name, 'Ellis', she cried 'Fucking hell!' and dropped the thing on the floor.

'I beg your pardon?' remarked a cheeky lad in the seat opposite, retrieving the phone for her.

'Thanks! Phone spam! I hate it!' replied Jess, almost shaking too much to tap the icon to read the message.

Hi Jess, how are you? Would love to take you to dinner. How does La Girandole at eight tonight sound? Let me know. I promise not to behave like an oaf this time. E

In her mind's eye, she saw that devilish smile. His confident swagger.

Yeah, right, and you'd be heartbroken if I turned you down. Some girl you picked up on the off chance. Not.

That was harsh, she knew, but still, she started to compose as polite and friendly a refusal as she could manage in a text. Then deleted it. Then took another shot at it. Then deleted that and typed:

I'd love to. Shall I meet you there? J

Within moments his reply came.

Wonderful! I'll pick you up about seven thirty. Address?

He probably knew her address, from her personnel file, but she suspected he was trying not to seem too controlling, too stalker-like. She tapped in her address and added *Looking forward to it!*

She imagined him sitting there reading it, somewhere, in car, at his home perhaps? Maybe in a lull in a high powered meeting?

Me too! See you soon. E

What the hell had she done? This was crazy. Anything might happen. But she *wanted* it to happen.

I might end up having sex with you, Ellis.

The final frontier.

I want sex.

True.

But not meaningless sex.

He knew she was a virgin. Could he possibly

understand what a huge great big enormous deal it would be to her, *not* to be one any more? Some women, younger women, slipped off their virgin status with barely a second thought, but for her it'd be tantamount to metamorphosis.

Ellis McKenna was a beautiful man, and the odds were that he was an experienced and skilful lover. But he'd probably lost his virginity in his teens. Twenty years ago? And it wasn't the watershed for boys that it was for girls, surely?

But I could wait for Mr Right another ten years or so, and then I might have a horrible time of it, even if I love the man. Why not take a gamble on a gorgeous billionaire? You've fantasised enough about it, you silly mare.

Yes, she saw his face every time she touched herself now. And his body. Stifling her cries in her pillow, she'd pleasured herself every night since she'd met him, picturing him naked again and again, or maybe partially dressed, his flowery shirt unfastened. His lightweight linen trousers open . . . Clothed or stripped it was so easy to imagine a sleek and lean, magnificent physique.

Take a chance, Jess. Stop dithering. Stop debating. Stop just dreaming and start doing! You've got a date with a real life sex god, so just go for it!

Even if she did meet her one true love one of these days, he'd expect her to have some experience at her age, surely? Nobody seemed to care about virginity any more, except her, so the man she eventually married or lived with would probably actually be pleased that she knew how to 'do sex'.

When she reached home though, she ran upstairs

and flung open her wardrobe. Where was Cathy when she needed her? But her friend was out again, with her own bloke, off to a concert straight from work, and probably not experiencing the slightest qualm whatsoever about the possibility of sleeping with him. In fact, eagerly looking forward to it!

Primping and preening probably more than she'd ever done for any date before in her entire life, Jess tried to keep her mind in neutral, focusing on the tasks in hand.

The trouble was, now the decision was made, the fantasies flooded in, distracting her.

It always came back to Ellis McKenna's body again. Muscular or sleek? Smooth or hairy? Big or average? Not small . . . no, not small.

Images from life drawing class jostled in her head, phasing into her own imaginings of what lay beneath the linen suit and the flowered shirt. She saw Ellis reposing on the sheet-covered couch, or standing on the plinth, unashamed, a man she actually desired rather than a convenient human shape that happened to be male.

Stop it, Jess. Get on with what you're supposed to be doing. You don't even know if you're going to see anything tonight! It might be just a nice dinner and chat!

Easier said than done. In case of 'the eventuality' she had to look good from the skin out, and none of her lingerie was really of the seductive category, just pretty and not especially provocative. All her clothes were like that, she realised. Smart and well chosen, elegant and flattering, but nothing to knock a man dead. No wonder she'd had no enthusiasm for getting out and meeting someone; she hadn't even provided herself with the right tools for the hunt.

Finally, it came down to a dark rose pink silk top and matching skirt. A wedding outfit that had drawn some compliments. It *had* even led to a date, but just one of those very occasional and awkward encounters that she specialised in. He'd been nice enough, but there'd been no second outing.

And there probably won't be one after tonight, either. Even if we do *sleep together.*

While she was grappling with her slippery, freshly washed hair, and trying to get it to stay up when it when it wanted to stay down, her mobile beeped.

A text. Swinging between relief and despair, she hardly dare look.

If he'd changed his mind, she'd be free of all this stress and internal debate, what a relief!

If he'd changed his mind and she'd never see him again, oh no!

Change of plan, Jess. I'm running late. Sending car to collect you. See you at restaurant. Hope to be there to meet you, but if not, table booked in my name. I've ordered champagne for you while you wait. E

Now! Now was the chance to back out. Say thanks, but perhaps not a good idea after all.

You birdbrained wimp, Jess! Don't be stupid.

Shoving her phone right to the bottom of her bag, out of reach, she returned her attention to her hair. Best to leave it down really. Wasn't that how virgins always wore it?

*

La Girandole was a glorious place: glamorous, but quietly discreet, and surprisingly welcoming to those of a nervous disposition. Jess had never dined there – it was well out of her normal price range – and on arrival, she was treated like a princess. Ellis's instructions, no doubt, as just the same thing had happened with the luxury hire car that had collected her, and then glided through the night like her very own personal fairy-tale carriage.

The *maître d'hôtel* guided her to a table by the window, overlooking a pretty ornamental garden, complete with pond. Billionaire businessmen could obviously score the best spot in the room at next to no notice, and Jess was glad of the table's combination of secluded intimacy and a prime view of the rest of the room and the other diners.

After the ritual of tasting and approving, she took a long, grateful sip of her champagne. As glorious as the venue, it was spectacularly delicious. Crisp and buttery and complex. It danced on the tongue, heady and potent, yet slipping down with dangerous ease.

Don't get legless. Just let it take the edge off the jitters.

To keep from devoting herself to nervous drinking, Jess people watched. The diners were almost exclusively couples. Some of them were upscale, wearing clothes that were obviously expensive, but others were surprisingly informally dressed. Jess relaxed a bit. Her pink silk, medium heels and casual hairstyle fitted nicely somewhere in the middle.

A lot of the couples were gazing into each other's eyes and smiling 'those' smiles at each other. If she hadn't been so distracted by the way her own evening might go, Jess would have played a game of 'who's going to end up in bed together tonight and how soon', to pass the time.

Her attention was drawn to a sophisticated young woman, seated at another premier table. She had startling black hair and wore a beautiful vintage dress. Her companion at the table was an older man, and they were totally into each other, it was clear from across the room. He put his hand over hers, the touch light yet meaningful, and they laughed together, blissfully easy and comfortable in each other's company.

I wish I was at that stage with Ellis McKenna.

But that was pie in the sky, she reminded herself. Odds were that they'd never get there and it was madness to think beyond tonight or, at best, a couple of discreet assignations in luxurious hotel rooms.

Nothing wrong with that. Accept things for what they are . . . and make the most of it!

She had a shrewd idea that she was the only virgin in the room though.

Five minutes passed. Then ten. It wasn't easy to pace herself with the sublime champagne, but she tried. What if he didn't come? What if she'd been stood up, and the *maître d'* came gliding up to the table any minute now, with whispered apologies?

Well, sod it. I'll have a meal here anyway. Even if I have to pay for myself!

Just as she thought that, a rustle of interested voices shattered her fears. Her attention shot to the doorway.

Oh Lord . . . Oh Lord . . .

Gone was the beach bum, and in his place a god of sophistication and sex approached. Ellis, in a glorious dark grey-blue three-piece suit, still light-weight, but cut slightly more sharply. No tie. A white shirt with narrow, impressionistic stripes in two toning shades of blue. And unless she was very much mistaken, he was wearing socks this time, a couple of shades lighter than his suit.

His dark hair was combed back more smoothly tonight too, emphasising his broad, imperious brow.

Jess logged all this in a split second, for future reference, despite being half-stunned by his glamour.

'Jess . . . I'm so very sorry for keeping you waiting. Please forgive me.' As he reached the table, he moved right beside her and lightly kissed her cheek before taking his seat.

Jess touched her cheek. It felt like he'd done something to her skin there, changed it forever. He'd taken her 'cheek' virginity . . . no, that was a stupid notion! Was she squiffy already?

But he'd bestowed the kiss completely naturally, as if they were established lovers, just like so many others in this beautiful, luxurious room.

'No problem . . . It's very nice here, and the champagne is gorgeous. Thank you . . .'

Laughing inside at herself for some kind of star-struck fool, but also strangely unashamed of it, she gazed at him. Met his smile. He seemed pleased with the way she'd revealed herself, touching her cheek like that, but, hey, he was a man and that was the way they were. Why take offence when he was making no attempt to hide how happy he was to see her?

'Good! I'm parched. I'm looking forward to a glass

of that myself.' He filled a flute, and topped hers up. 'What shall we drink to?' He lifted his glass to hers.

'I don't know . . . Just a pleasant evening, I guess?'

'Indeed. And more than pleasant, I hope.' His sea-blue eyes glittered, making her far dizzier than the champagne ever could.

They clinked their glasses. Jess managed not to shake and to drink her gorgeous wine like a normal person. Well, almost normal . . .

'I . . . I don't know why I'm here,' she blurted out. 'Why did you ask me? You don't know me, and I'm sure I'm not your usual type.'

As she put down her glass, Ellis reached out and laid his hand over hers. 'I don't have a type, Jess,' he said, his voice soft, and strangely kind. 'You're here because you're a beautiful, interesting woman and I'd like to spend time with you. Time when we can just be two people enjoying each other's company, rather than boss and employee. Although, technically, I'm not your boss. I own the company, but Jacobson and his team still run Windsor.'

'So, do you make a habit of floating in from your exalted realm now and again to select interesting women?'

He laughed again, that sweet, young sound. Women at adjacent tables looked around, and Jess's spirits soared. These glamorous sophisticates who dined at high end restaurants all the time, they were jealous of her!

'You make it sound like a bad thing.' He beamed at her. 'I want you to have a lovely evening, Jess, and I'll do everything I can to ensure that.' He was still holding her hand, and his thumb moved evocatively against her palm, caressing her. The back of her neck prickled as if the little hairs there might be standing up, and she almost laughed. Apparently that wasn't just a cliché in books after all. It actually happened.

'I believe you . . . I think.' She tried to do a smile, like the sophisticated women did, hoping it didn't turn out goofy.

'Don't you trust me?' Ellis's smile *was* sophisticated. But then, he had a lot of practice at it, presumably.

Jess opened her mouth to answer, but when Ellis's attention flicked away from her, she realised the *maître d'* had arrived. Saved by the menus! She wasn't sure she did trust Ellis, but telling him that without sounding like a ninny would have been difficult.

The menus were huge, but the selection of dishes was relatively small. All good stuff though, mostly classic French, but some tempting traditional English fare too, yum yum. Choosing would've have been a nice diversion from awkward questions, but one dish leapt out at her.

'Mmm . . . chicken pie. Would you think I was awfully unsophisticated if I opted for that?'

Jess just stopped her jaw from dropping. Was Ellis reading her mind? Listening to her idiotic musings on sophistication or lack of it? 'No, actually, I was just going to choose that myself. Sounds divine . . . Well, it all looks fab, but that's what I really fancy.'

'Brilliant! We're already on the same wavelength,' he said, his eyes challenging her again. They were back to trust country again. 'How about a starter?'

Her appetite was alive and kicking, surprisingly,

but it probably wasn't a good idea to eat too much
. . . be too stuffed . . . if there were to be 'afters' after
the afters. 'Well, they all look good, but I think I'd
just like the pie, please.'

'Good idea.' He quirked his eyebrows at her, as if
he'd heard this inner debate too. He lifted a finger,
and the *maître d'* came gliding back to them. 'Chicken
pie for two, please.' His eyes were still on Jess.
'Selection of vegetables? And chips?' She nodded.
'More wine?'

'I think I'm okay with what we've got, thanks.'

'Smart woman.'

Then they were alone again. What now?

'So, why Windsor? What drew you to insurance?'

Yuck, work talk. Hadn't he said they were getting
away from that? Or, bizarrely, was he actually a bit
nervous himself? Not as much as she was, but still, it
almost seemed that way.

'I needed a job. There were vacancies. I could do
the work. It's not too far from where I live. I just
happened into it, as simple as that.'

Which was true. She'd been lucky in these times.
With her employment history, a lot of other people
would still be searching.

'No burning need to ensure the Great British
Public get the policies they need then?' He took a sip
of his wine, everything about him teasing.

'Don't make fun. You've bought the company. You
must think it has some value.'

'I'm sorry. It seems a well-run operation. A good
acquisition.' For a moment, he looked serious, like Mr
Business, then his beautiful mouth curved. 'It's just

you. You seem as if you ought to be doing something different. Something a bit more "out there", you know? Something more imaginative.'

I would. But I had commitments. I owed someone big time. Someone I loved.

'Well, I did have plans once, but life, you know . . . sometimes it has plans for you that you didn't foresee.' She reached for her wine, took a fortifying sip. 'I'm not complaining. Far from it. But I had to do something, and it put me on a different track.'

Ellis reached for her hand again, squeezed it gently. 'You don't want to talk about it, do you? That's okay. There'll be another time. Let's just stay on the light stuff, shall we? Where do you live? What do you do for fun? What about friends?'

God, that was almost as problematical. He'd probably think she was a sad little thing, with her quiet life, and rarely a boyfriend. And never really a sniff of sex, even though that was entirely her own choice. Her being particular and holding out for an ideal that probably didn't exist.

But . . . Ellis had said *another* time. Which suggested there might be another date after this one?

'Well, I just live a quiet life, you know? I share a house with another girl, and we're good friends. Sometimes we go out to the pictures, or for pizza, or just for a drink. Although not lately, because she's got a steady bloke. I see a couple of girls from work for girly nights out occasionally, but it's not really a regular thing.' *I'm babbling again, yattering on like a fool.* 'I love to read. I love television . . . good stuff . . . not rubbish. Documentaries etc. I go to an evening class too.'

'What are you studying?' His voice was intent, as if he really cared. Either that or he was a supreme social animal, able to feign a believable simulation of interest where none existed.

'It's an art class.' She didn't really want to tell him it was life drawing. Not yet, at least.

'I knew it! That's your thing, isn't it? What you should really *be*, rather than working in insurance. There's this certain quality about you, as if you're looking at things in a way most normal people wouldn't.'

That was true too. But who else would have noticed that?

'I just draw a bit. I'm not that good.'

'Oh, I bet you are. Did you go to art college? Were those the plans you had to abandon?'

Jess never really talked about the twists and turns of her life much, but suddenly, she wanted to. Even with this man, in this situation.

'Yes, they were actually . . . but like I said, life happened.'

'Tell me. I want to know . . .' Something of a shadow passed over him, and he started twisting his wedding ring around. Jess had a shrewd idea that he didn't even realise he was doing it. 'I'm interested in how people deal with life . . . and its happenings.'

Jess faltered at first, but gradually, inexorably, it became easier to talk. Ellis seemed to have slipped into a quiet, receptive mode, passively encouraging now, rather than jabbing in with questions. She found herself telling him about the death of her parents when she was a child. How her granny had taken her and her sister in, caring for them with a deep and generous love, and then, when the tables had tilted, and dementia had struck, how Jess had taken time out of *her* life to pay back the love she'd been given, nursing Gran until she'd just been too ill to care for adequately at home, and she'd had to spend her last years in the best private care establishment Jess could afford.

'You put your life on hold,' said Ellis quietly, after their food had been served. 'That's a beautiful thing, Jess. A lot of people wouldn't have done it.'

'I couldn't have done anything else,' she replied. It was a fact. She'd never even considered any other path. 'Of course, I stormed about it inside quite a bit. I'm only human. But she was so wonderful to me and Mel. She deserved to be cared for in return.'

'And so you never got to go to art school, yet your sister got a shot at university? That's hardly fair.'

'I don't begrudge her it. She's smart. Much cleverer than me. And art is something I can still do without formal training. I don't need it to be my job or anything, does that make sense? In fact it's *better* if it isn't my job. It's fun. It's a bit of a laugh sometimes.' She paused, and chewed a fork full of pie. Damn, it was good! 'And you'd probably laugh too if you saw some of my efforts.'

'That, I would really like.' He paused to top up her glass, although she'd noticed that after one small glass himself, he'd switched to water. 'I'm not an art expert or anything, but I would like to build a bit of a collection of things that I like. No particular style . . . just what appeals to me. Do you show your work?'

Jess giggled. Uh oh, had she already had too much fizz? 'I told you, it's really not that good. Like I said, it's just a fun thing. A hobby.'

'Seriously though, I would like to see your work.' His sea-blue eyes narrowed. 'And before you say anything, I'm not patronising you. I really am interested.'

'Okay . . . perhaps I could send you something?'

'Why send? Why not just show?'

'I . . . well . . . I suppose I wasn't expecting to see you again after tonight.'

Ellis picked up his knife and fork, and stabbed determinedly at his food. 'Well, at the risk of sounding like a domineering martinet, you *will* be seeing me again, Miss Lockhart. I insist on it!' He softened the decree with a grin.

Jess's innards trembled a bit. Her appetite wavered. She focused in on her plate, the food, the moment.

Don't look ahead . . . not even further than this . . . and especially not . . . later . . .

'So, what's your speciality?' asked Ellis, his voice crisp, as if he was changing the subject without changing it. 'Still life, landscapes, figure drawing?' His long lashes swept down. 'Life drawing?'

Oh, those penises . . .

'Yes, I do life drawing. And before you ask, I draw naked men. In fact that's the class I'm taking at the moment and, at least fifty per cent of the time, the models are male.' She kept her chin up, challenging him to challenge her. 'I've dabbled a bit in various forms and styles, but I like life drawing best of all, if you must know.'

'Really.' His eyes flashed, and he pushed away his plate, nearly empty. Jess looked down at her own, mainly because she could feel a wild blush warming her cheeks, and discovered she'd eaten all her own dinner too. 'Dessert?' he asked, but she had a feeling he was asking something else entirely.

'Thanks, but I think I'd just like coffee instead, if you don't mind? But you have some. I'll bet the puds here are something else.'

He blotted his lips with his table napkin, then dropped it beside his plate. 'Coffee sounds good. Shall we take it in the bar? We could find a nice secluded corner. I'd really like to hear more about this life drawing.'

I'll bet you would.

A few minutes later, they'd found that corner. La Girandole was part of Green's, the best hotel in the city centre, and the bar was on the rooftop, commanding a dazzling view of the lights, the traffic and the ebb and flow of the nightlife below.

Jess got in first. 'Look, just because I'm a virgin, it doesn't mean I faint at the sight of the male body. I can look at a . . . a cock without having a fit of the vapours.'

'I hope you won't faint at the sight of mine.' Ellis reached for his demitasse.

Ah, here we go . . .

'It depends on how big it is.' She'd been doubtful when Ellis had suggested she have a brandy, but she reached for her glass now, and sipped carefully. Aromatic fire bloomed inside her, meeting and matching a different fire, a different bloom. 'Most of

the guys at life class are about average.' The temptation to glance away, blushing harder, was almost a
compulsion, but she resisted. Ellis's eyes were dancing.

'I guess I'm average.' He shrugged, then grinned
like a schoolboy. 'On the bigger side of average.'

'Well, you would say that. All men like to think
they're big.'

'Is that a fact?' Ellis drank some coffee, then licked
the trace of it from his lower lip. The fire flared,
almost roared. 'And if you are what you say you are,
who are all these men you've discussed cock dimensions with? Surely the issue doesn't "arise"' – he rolled
his eyes, having the grace to look shame-faced – 'if
you never go to bed with them?'

'I was speaking generally.' General nonsense. Due
to too much champagne and brandy. Too much Ellis
McKenna.

Setting his cup aside, he reached for her hand.
'Why are you a virgin, Jess? You're intelligent and
beautiful. Compassionate. And certainly sensual . . .
Is this something else you put on hold? It's unusual
for a woman, well, in her twenties.'

'I'm thirty in two months.'

Ellis frowned. What, disappointed because she
wasn't young and fresh, even though she was a virgin?

'Look, forgive me. If it's some religious or ethical
choice, forget I ever said anything. I'll shut up and
never mention it again. I'm just a clod of a man,
thinking with his dick, like we all do.'

Part of her wanted to pull her hand away from his
grip; part of her loved it. The warmth, the promise;
the strange sense of safety. She looked around the

softly lit room. Were any of the other patrons aware of the tumult inside her? It seemed not. Nobody was even looking their way.

'Nope, not ethical. Not religious. Just life.' How to explain it? 'There wasn't much time for dating when I was living with Gran, and afterwards I just kept waiting for a man to come along. One I knew I *wanted* to do it with. But he never did. They always seemed nice, but nothing more.' She shrugged. 'I'm too choosy, I guess.'

'No, just discerning,' said Ellis quietly. He looked away, almost as if he were embarrassed. 'But how about now? Are you prepared to give me a chance?' The grin came back. His thumb moved slowly against her palm. 'I'm not particularly nice, but I do have other qualities to recommend me.'

'Oh, really?' It was all she could manage, thinking about those qualities. He was, to put not too fine a point on it, drop dead gorgeous. There was no better candidate for making Dream Lover real, because he was handsome in a characterful way, not a pretty boy. And the more she saw of him, the more she was certain that he had a lean fit body beneath his clothes, one that moved well, with effortless grace and power. He was elegant, refined and, despite his somewhat eccentric choice of daywear, and his fondness for facial stubble, obviously deeply fastidious.

That was the problem. Ellis McKenna was probably *too* perfect. She might actually have been better off with a man with one or two faults, because even though she could readily admit she wasn't bad looking, she didn't class herself as fantasy woman material.

'I'd say I'm a good choice as your first man,' said Ellis breezily. Maybe that was the fault? He had no shortage of self-confidence . . . of arrogance. 'I like to think I'm considerate. I want a woman to enjoy the experience at least as much as I do. And I do know quite a few tricks.'

I bet you do, you devil.

'I'll take that under advisement. Although I'm probably better off starting with the basics, rather than tricks.' He was stroking her hand now, soft and slight, driving her crazy. 'And I can't see why you'd want me. Don't you prefer a woman who knows her way around a mattress?'

'I do as a rule, but who's to say you're not a natural? I sense an ocean of erotic potential, just waiting to be awakened. Someone waiting for all that as yet untapped carnal enthusiasm to be . . . well . . . tapped?' He raised her hand, dusted a kiss on her knuckles, and then freed her. Before she could react, he reached for her glass of brandy and put it into her hand. For shock? What on earth was he going to say next? She took a brief swig, welcoming the fuzz of heat.

His eyes narrowed. He looked calculating. 'You have touched yourself, surely? You know what pleasure feels like?'

Jess hit the brandy again, too much, and started coughing. Ellis tapped her on the back with a firm thump, then rubbed the spot he'd slapped, gently massaging.

Summoned by a gesture Jess had been spluttering too hard to see, a waiter arrived, and Ellis requested water. The man was back in a flash, with a crystal glass filled with iced mineral water, and Jess sipped from it gratefully.

'Better now?' Ellis said after a few moments.

'A bit . . . yes . . .' She glanced around. Surely they were being watched now, but it seemed not. Maybe people were all too wrapped up in each other to notice. It was all couples again. Probably couples who'd soon be going to bed together, with no hang-ups and no stupid virginity to contend with.

'Was I too personal?' Had he moved away from her on the banquette? Pulling back because she was acting like a nervous nelly? It was hard not to sigh and want to kick herself. Why couldn't she just be a bit more sophisticated about this? Surely it was possible to be sophisticated *and* a virgin . . . although in her case, it seemed not.

'No . . . well . . . yes . . . I'm a grown up. I should be able to answer these questions without having some kind of choking fit. Like I said, I'm nearly thirty, not a silly teenager.' She sipped some more water, just for something to do.

This was all crazy and stupid. She wanted Ellis McKenna. He was the first man she'd ever really wanted. But she was screwing everything up. Big time self-sabotage.

'You're not silly. It's a big thing, talking to a man about intimate issues when you're not used to it.' He paused, and gave her a quirky little smile. 'And I should have more sensitivity . . . more *savoir faire*. But . . . well . . . I want you, Jess. And I think you want me. But maybe you're not ready?'

I am! I am! I am!

But maybe she wasn't. She'd lay good odds that he had a room reserved, somewhere in the hotel below them. A room that any woman in her right mind would be rushing to with him, right about now.

'I don't think I am,' she admitted glumly. 'Sorry.'

'No need to be. We don't have to rush.' He lounged back against the banquette. 'Let's just enjoy ourselves here for now. Get to know each other first, eh?'

'Okay.'

Sod it! Sod it! Sod it! she screamed inside, livid with herself. Then, she was even crosser when a couple at a nearby table rose as one, their faces wreathed in mysterious smiles. The woman turned and headed for the door, her walk elegant, sensual, confident. The man followed close, his hand brushing the small of her back in an intimate gesture, and his companion reached behind, to confirm his touch.

They're going to bed. I wish it could be that easy.

8

Too fast, you fucking idiot. Too fast.

Ellis cursed himself inside, even as he made small talk. Why had he pushed? Jess wasn't like his normal dates, so why had he tried to treat her like one?

He felt like a fool. Where was his sophistication? His experience? Instead he'd lumbered like a bull at a gate because he wanted this unusual woman so very badly. It was important to be circumspect, and take his time with her, but inside, the spoilt greedy boy in him was furious. Furious with himself for cocking it all up. Metaphorically grabbing for the goodies far too soon.

And yet, it was a good thing just to talk. In fact it was a very good thing, and often missing from his brief liaisons. There was a sweet relief in conversation, without pressure. At least now he didn't have to worry about failing her in bed, and not being the perfect lover she deserved for her first time. Oh, he had the technique and all . . . but his raw hunger for her might make him rush too fast there too.

But she was so haunting, so different . . . so goddamn beautiful. That pink outfit, it made her look like an elegant angel. The skirt was just the right length to show off her astonishing, shapely legs. And her hair was like silk. Her lips, blush rose, almost made him insane.

Damn, he was hard. Hadn't she noticed? Maybe it was her innocence. She didn't look blatantly like an experienced woman. He suddenly wished he could pose for her . . . then she'd *have* to check out his body!

A germ of an idea formed. A tactic. Not so much for him, as for her. Maybe another night though. He'd messed things up enough already with his crass question, fucking idiot that he was. He needed to dial things back a notch. She'd be worth the wait, he'd stake his fortune on it . . . and he was a billionaire, last time he'd seen the figures.

'Maybe we should check out some galleries? Is there anything notable in the area?' he asked on the spur. 'I must admit that when I come up here at weekends, I mainly doss around the house, watching the telly in between dips in the pool. Maybe we could go for a drive or something? Lunch somewhere first, if you'd like that?'

She gave him an odd look, a little crooked smile as if she'd seen right through him. *Please believe in me*, he wanted to say. *I might be making small talk, but I mean it. I can't bear not to see you again.*

'Sounds good. I'd love to. Thank you, lunch would be great . . . if you're sure?' She toyed with her coffee cup. 'I thought you'd have moved on by then. I mean, don't you have business interests all over the world?'

'I do, but I like to come up here when I can. Windermere Hall is a family place. I've been spending quite a bit of time here, in between London business and fly-aways.' That impulsive urge swept through him again. 'In fact, I've decided that I'd like to spend even *more* time here. I like the countryside and I like the vibe, and virtual offices make it possible to work anywhere nowadays.'

'Oh . . . right . . . That's great.' She sounded so unsure. Not quite trusting. Oh why wouldn't she trust him? How could he get her to let her guard down?

For God's sake, you stupid bastard, I wouldn't trust you if the positions were reversed!

He had to slow it down, way down. But maybe not *too* far. After all, this thing would only be lasting a few weeks at most.

'I'll take you home now.'

Wait? What? Oh no . . . She'd been right. It wasn't easy.

If only I'd loosened up. Acted less uptight.

'But . . . I thought . . .'

'Let's take it slowly, Jess. It'll be better that way. We only met today, and you are . . . what you are.' He rose to his feet, and reached out for her hand, drawing her up too. 'We need to get to know each other. Be friends first, then lovers, eh?'

It made such sense. What was it, barely more than twelve hours, thirteen, fourteen, since that old blue car had pulled up beside her? And now here she was, disappointed because he'd not rushed her headlong into bed, and ushered her skilfully into the world of not being a virgin.

But I want him! I barely know anything about wanting, not really . . . but I want him!

Smiling and chatting as normally as she could with Ellis, Jess allowed him to escort her down to the lobby and out of the hotel. Was he aware of how glum she was inside? How angry with herself? He probably was, but was too much of a gentleman to act in any other way than as if the evening, and she, were both perfect. The Citroën was waiting for them when they stepped outside, driven round for him from the parking area by a porter. Did everybody get that service at Green's, or was it just billionaires?

The powder blue car glided through the town like an air-sprung ghost. With every yard it covered, Jess cursed herself more and more.

Blithering idiot, you should have gone for it! Just look at him . . . he is Dream Lover. He's glorious. And no matter what he says, you might never see him again.

She'd kick herself, she knew, if that happened. This might be it. All there ever was of her 'relationship' with the mysterious, glamorous, handsome man beside her.

He was quiet, almost as if his thoughts were as troubled as hers. Watching the road and the traffic, he turned and stole a quick glance at her occasionally and smiled, but said nothing.

In what seemed like no time, they were drawing up outside her house.

This is stupid. You're a coward.

'Ellis?'

He turned to her, and it was the unmistakable rush of hope in his eyes that did for her.

'Will you take me back to the hotel? Now?' Aiming for his forearm, at the last minute, she swerved and laid her hand on his thigh. So muscular. So hard. Solid against her fingers beneath the fine cloth of his suit trousers.

The rush of hope flared to something else. In the darkness, he focused on her. His beautiful oceanic eyes widened. 'Are you sure?'

'Yes, I am. I'll probably be rubbish in bed and a complete nervous nelly, but I'll try and do my best.'

Ellis's bark of laughter made her flinch, but before she could even start feeling terrible, he swept his arms around her, and pulled her against him. It wasn't a voracious kiss, raunchy passion and all that, just a hug. A happy, enveloping hug, his face pressed against the side of hers, lips in her hair.

'You won't be rubbish, you crazy woman! You'll be wonderful!' He nuzzled his face against her, rubbing like a cat somehow, affectionate yet primal. 'It's me who should be worried about being rubbish . . . not being able to contain myself enough to make your first time great.'

'I'll take my chances.' She reached up and cupped his jaw. Oh, how silky his demi-beard felt. Not scratchy or stubbly at all. It was soft against the skin of her palm as she angled his face to hers. *Now, fool, go for it!*

She compelled him to kiss her.

His lips were soft too, pliant yet with strength beneath. They lay against hers, latent and promising, then began to move a little, but subtly. As he buried his fingers in her hair, steadying her, she wound her arms around him, sliding them beneath his jacket.

He was so warm. Warm lips. Warm body. Heat flowed into her, bringing confidence, reassurance, and simple pleasure at the contact. A wave of his deliciously spiced cologne billowed up where she'd pushed aside his jacket. It hit her senses with all the power of the luscious champagne she'd drunk earlier.

Kissing him was easy, and lovely. His tongue didn't push, but she felt it, brushing like a feather against the seam of her lips, speaking to her silently and promising. Everything.

He kisses like Dream Lover only a hundred times better!

Drawing away from her, he looked into her eyes, his own as brilliant as aquamarine suns. He didn't say anything, but she was glad of that. It was as if he knew precisely how delicate the moment was. She saw him swallow, his strong throat undulating, then he pressed forward again, bestowing another measured kiss.

When they broke apart again, he said, 'Good God, woman, we're making out in a parked car! I haven't done that in ages.' He grinned. 'I'm so excited I nearly forgot where we are.'

You are! You are excited! Jess glanced downwards. *In every way . . .*

There it was, the tell-tale bump in his perfectly tailored trousers. Had it been there before? Probably not. It hadn't taken but a few seconds for him to get rampant.

With a struggle, she tore her attention away from Ellis's crotch, and looked again to find him watching her, mischief dancing on his face because he'd caught her checking out his equipment. As if of its own accord, her hand snaked out, and cupped him.

'Oh! Oh, yes!' he gasped. The words were barely audible, little more than an exhalation, yet they echoed in Jess's brain, a clarion of triumph, his, not hers. His hips bumped, pushing his body against the contact. His long lashes fluttered and he looked angelic, divinely suffering.

Was she hurting him? No, not that. But how could such a simple touch pleasure him so, a man as experienced as he was? Tentatively, she moved her palm against the hard knot, and he jerked again, rocking in synchrony. The beast itself twitched. It was so hot through his clothing, and seemed to have a life of its own, distinct from its owner.

'Mm . . . that's lovely, Jess. Lovely. You have a wonderful touch.'

Still she erred on the side of caution. She knew anatomy. She'd read erotic books. If she went in too heavily, she could hurt him. But still, she pressed lightly with her thumb, exploring the shape.

'If we weren't parked on a public thoroughfare, I'd ask you to unzip me, love.' Ellis's voice was husky, sultry. 'But I think I'll have to wait for that pleasure. I know it'll be worth it.'

'I hope so,' Jess said, laughing nervously. This was crazy; any passing neighbour might look in, attention caught by the beautiful vintage car, and see what its occupants were doing. But she couldn't take her hand away. It was as if the living bulge in Ellis's trousers was magnetic and her fingers were metal.

'I know so!'

When she withdrew her hand – reluctantly – Ellis drew it to his lips and kissed her palm, slowly and with intent.

'Do we really have to drive all the way back to the hotel? What about your place?' He nodded to the house, currently in darkness, save for one small lamp lit in the sitting room. They always left that one on when they were out. Cathy was clearly not yet home.

'I suppose so.' She hesitated. It seemed weird. She'd always imagined some hotel or other as the location where she'd eventually lose her virginity. Somewhere a bit nice, but unspecific. Just the act itself was the important thing. Her body, and the man's.

'Sorry, I'm getting ahead of myself again,' said Ellis, kissing her hand again. 'Forget it. I don't want you to feel uncomfortable. You've got me so crazy that I want you anywhere, but if you prefer neutral ground, I think I can keep myself in check long enough to drive to the hotel, or even to my place. It's your choice, Jess. I just want you to feel at ease.'

It could all go pear shaped now. Hesitation could lead to postponement. Postponement could lead to, well, him changing his mind in the cooler light of day, and thinking, *What the hell was I doing? A nearly thirty year old virgin? Not really . . .*

'No, it's okay. Cathy's not home. My room might be a little bit untidy if you don't mind slumming it . . . and I think I might actually feel more relaxed, in my own space. Do you know what I mean?'

'Oh, you angel!' Grabbing her by the shoulders, he kissed her hard and quickly. Then in a flash –

perhaps before she could change her mind – he was out of the car, round to the passenger side, and handing her out into the night air. Within moments they were on the pavement, and hurrying inside.

Jess was self-conscious, aware that her cheeks were pink and blushing, and that any passer-by could read from that exactly what she'd been doing with Ellis and to Ellis in the car. He, on the other hand, appeared sublimely unconcerned, as cool and suave as ever. Jess daren't look at his groin to see if he was still sporting his erection, but she didn't doubt that he wouldn't be embarrassed if he was.

But there was only one other person in the street. A middle-aged woman in a fleece and jeans, with her dog on a leash. The bumptious canine was bounding around, and his owner's full attention was on him, rather than a pair of potential lovers thirty yards away on the other pavement.

Never before had her own front door seemed so daunting. She could still change her mind once she was inside, but somehow, it didn't seem that way. The threshold to the house was like jumping off a cliff, like skydiving. Once she was in there was no return. Her fingers fumbled with the key, clattering against the lock. Ellis took it from her and manipulated it easily.

Key into lock. A simple act. But suddenly a metaphor.

Hearing her gasp, Ellis glanced at Jess, and saw that she was on the same page. Good grief, she was blushing like a schoolgirl. Exactly like the virgin she was.

'You're adorable.' Ellis touched her cheek, pressing his palm against the heat. 'You're beautiful. Don't be anxious, Jess. I desire you . . . you desire me . . . We'll have a wonderful time together.'

As she turned her face to kiss his hand, he tried the door, ready to push it open. Jess leapt away from him, as if there were a throng of people waiting inside, but he corralled her, his arm sliding around her waist.

'Don't worry,' he reiterated, 'it'll be fine. Now, is there an alarm code we need to deal with?'

'Yes, it's 1812.' She grinned, as if finding the nerve she'd momentarily lost. 'And yes, I know, it's pretty obvious.'

'Only to a music lover or a history nut.' Ellis winked at her. He needed her to relax, but he felt more apprehensive himself than he had done for a long time with a woman. Why did this feel like as big a step somehow as his first ever fuck after Julie?

Once inside, he silenced the beeping alarm, and returned Jess's key to her, watching her lock up again and slip her key in her bag.

'Cathy can get in with her own key. Wouldn't want some slimy burglar to come in and nick things while we're . . . um . . . While we're busy.'

'While we're making love,' Ellis corrected her. Again, he felt different. Normally he would have said *fucking*, but that was too crude and blatant a term to use at this critical moment. Not because she was a virgin, but because, well, she was Jess, and not like his usual women in almost every other way too. 'Now, lead the way to paradise.' He gave her a gentle little push on the rump, and suppressed a gasp. Just the

lightest contact with her beautiful, rounded bottom
made his aching cock jump hard.

Christ, it's as if I'm the virgin here, not her.

He hoped to God he could stay in control of
himself. What good to her would he be if he lost it
and came before she was ready? This was all about
her. Her pleasure. Her experience. It had to be
wonderful, and the start of something even better.

But not in the long term. Not with me.

That shouldn't have bothered him as much as it
did.

9

Jess's whole body sizzled as she climbed the stairs, with Ellis just behind her. At least it felt that way.

He's looking at my bottom. He must be. That's why he's here. For the sex. It's not like he's doing it for charity or therapy. He's a man and he wants action.

Yet that was harsh. Ellis McKenna was arrogant and controlling, but he also seemed to have a gentler side. He could have been taking any one of dozens of sophisticated, cosmopolitan women to bed tonight, but he was here in a modest house, in a quiet road, on the outskirts of a small northern city, about to initiate a virgin.

'This way,' she said, opening the door to her room, her sanctum.

It wasn't exactly a self-contained flat, but it'd formerly been occupied by an older relative of Cathy's family who'd liked her own space and privacy. So the room was large, with a queen-sized bed at one end, and a sofa and low table at the other, facing her television. Some of the furniture was quite old, one or two pieces genuine Victorian, and the décor was warm oranges, reds and ochres, in soft prints, almost womb-like. But, in contrast, her little en suite was all modern, white and chrome.

On the walls she'd hung some prints, a bit crowded together in an eclectic mix: Pre-Raphaelite *Beata Beatrix*, Manet's *A Bar at the Folies-Bergère* and Renoir's *La Loge*. Impressionism was her favourite 'ism', she supposed, but she loved other kinds of works too. She had one of Klimt's gilded ladies, *Adele Bloch-Bauer 1*, because she loved the unabashed opulence of it and the exquisite but strangely static expression. All her choices were the biggest hits of art, really, but she wasn't ashamed of liking the popular, because things were usually popular for a damn good reason. Because they were great; because they were sublime. But, descending to what some might have classed as ridiculous, she'd hung some of her own work too, in a statement of self-belief. Not her life drawings though, just a couple of her golden oldies, a seascape painted on a rare and treasured art holiday, and a watercolour of a pretty local view.

Ellis studied her selection of greats with a thoughtful expression, and a nod here and there, as if their taste in art was aligned. Glancing from the Manet to the Renoir, he said, 'These are in the Courtauld Gallery, aren't they? Have you ever seen them in the flesh, so to speak?'

A regret nothing to do with her lack of a sex life swept through her. 'No . . . no I haven't. I suppose I should have, but somehow I never got around to it.

Maybe one day though. How about you, have you seen them?'

A stricken look descended upon his handsome face. 'No, me neither. I've never been to the Courtauld. It was on our family to do list, next time we visited London.'

'Oh . . .' What to say? There must be a million wonderful things he'd planned to share with his wife and girls.

Ellis's jaw tensed, then it was as if he mentally shook himself, pushing that ever present grief to the back of his thoughts. As if to distract both her and himself, he zeroed straight in on the sore thumbs in her little gallery.

'Your work?'

'Yes, they're nothing special. But I do love doing larger works. Sometimes. Haven't really had the opportunity lately. I should make the effort though.'

'You must,' he said firmly, turning from the art, and coming to her. 'You're very good. And I'm not just saying that. I'm not a major connoisseur but I know what I like and what I believe is worthwhile.'

Am I going to be worthwhile?

He stood, looking down into her eyes, and there was a glow in his that gave her hope. They'd moved on from art now . . . or perhaps to another kind of art. Plucking her bag from her shoulder, he tossed it lightly onto the settee behind them, then slid her pashmina off her shoulders, dispensing with that too.

'Don't be anxious, Jess. You'll enjoy yourself. You're a beautiful woman, and a sensual one, I can tell. It'll be like falling off a log, believe me.'

'Last time I fell off a log I grazed my elbow, banged my hip, and got a mild concussion.'

Ellis laughed softly. 'I always was one for pathetic figures of speech.'

He took her mouth then, in another of his long, sweet, probing kisses. She tensed at first, but the stroke and rhythm of his tongue, moving in her mouth, and the way his hands swept over her back and buttocks in a smooth possessive glide was almost hypnotic. Within moments, her tongue pushed back, twirling with his, and her hands went on a journey of their own.

His body was hard-muscled, electric with energy beneath his clothes. He rocked against her touch, making rough little sounds of appreciation against her lips. What she was doing must be right. Either that, or he was a very good actor. Maybe a bit of both?

But not even the best actors could get erections to order. Unless he'd taken a little blue pill when he'd excused himself briefly back at the hotel. He was rampant against her, rocking his hard shape against her belly, circling and circling.

'Mm, you feel good, Jess Lockhart, really good,' he growled, tracking his kiss across her cheek and hair-line, 'So inviting . . .' He cupped her bottom to hold her tighter against him, belly to belly, pelvis to pelvis.

You're the one that's inviting. You're bloody well irresistible.

It was true, so true. She'd travelled further and faster with him, and in less time, than she'd achieved with any of her very few attempted boyfriends. This handling, this fondling and exploring; it'd made her freeze before. Not quite to the stage of flesh-crawling, but definitely a shudder or two, not of the good sort.

Now she wanted more, more, more, and deeper, more daring.

Ellis's fingers were on the little covered buttons at the back of her top now, popping them with the consummate ease of the frequent seducer. He eased back from her, and before she could stop him – not that she wanted to – he'd grasped the hem of her silky top and was easing it up. As if she'd undressed for men since she was a teenager, she lifted her arms and let him slide it off over her head, ruffling her hair as he went. When he'd tossed away the garment, he smoothed the dark strands out of her eyes, running his fingers over her brow, almost reverently.

The urge to cross her arms across her chest was hard to quell, but she resisted. She didn't know what to do with her hands though.

'Lovely,' he whispered, then quickly shrugged out of his jacket, flinging it away after her top. After unbuttoning his waistcoat, he took both her hands in both of his, and placed them flat on his chest. 'I'm just a man. I won't bite. Well, not unless you want a little love-nibble here and there.'

'I . . . I know. But I can't help being nervous.' His heart was thudding beneath her fingertips, its beat scarily steady. But then he was used to all this. 'Would you mind if I took a moment? Powder my nose and all that.' She needed the bathroom, but she needed a moment away from the intensity of him more.

'No worries. Take all the time you need.' He gave

a funny little shrug. 'Just don't jump out of the window and flee from me, eh?'

She let out an edgy little laugh. 'There is no window. It's a new bathroom. Sort of squeezed in. I'm trapped with you, whether I like it or not.' He took his hands from hers, releasing her, and she almost darted away.

'I'll make sure you like it.'

When she was gone, Ellis shed his waistcoat, unbuttoned his shirt, and then kicked off his shoes and peeled off his socks. He'd seduced a fair few women in his time, most of them lately, to fuck himself into forgetful oblivion, but it was a known fact that even the most practised lovers looked dorky when taking off their socks.

Barefoot, he padded around the room, looking at her things, and her prints and paintings again. Despite her modesty, her watercolours impressed him. There was a solid, vigorous quality to them, not usually seen in the gauzy medium. And odd little touches. A circling seagull in the beach scene appeared to have a contrail as if he'd been doing aerobatics, and in the countryside view, there were three rabbits sitting in a row on a knoll, in hear no evil, see no evil, speak no evil style.

Ellis smiled, turning to an investigation of the few clothes on view, tidy on their hangers on the front of the wardrobe door. Simple garments, but elegant. Understated. She obviously didn't have a lot of money to spend on clothes, but she looked after what she had.

You're a bit of a neat freak, aren't you?

It was true. The room was homely, but extremely tidy despite her claims to the contrary. Most women he'd spent time with lately tended to fling things about because they had people to clean up after them, but not Jess. Was her whole life just as tidy? Or was there a tumbling disorder of passion, just beneath the surface. He sincerely hoped so, and that he was the one to unleash her wild side.

Jess! Jess! Hurry!

He was eager to touch her again. Hungry to get started. It was hard not to want to rush, but he was going to have to try. Moving to the bed, he lay down upon it, staring up at the ceiling, trying to calm down. He let his hand drop to his groin, rubbing himself lightly and rewinding his fantasy. The caress felt good, but he wished the hand was hers.

Staring at the ceiling, he drew a lungful of her scent, lingering on the bed linen. Nice, but light; floral, almost sugary. Not the heady sophisticated fragrances he was used to, but pleasant enough. And it was the smell of the woman herself that mattered.

The bathroom door opened, and she appeared, wearing a short, turquoise, kimono type wrap. And looking uptight.

He sat up and held out a hand to her. 'Come here.'

She approached warily, like a fawn to his wolf.

'I told you. It'll be okay.' Clasping her hand, he pulled her down onto the bed at his side, setting her against the pillows. Her hair fanned out, thick and dark. For a moment he remembered Julie's hair, also lush and dark, then he shut the memory firmly away and half rolled over Jess, finding her lips, her sweet lips, kissing her hungrily. He smiled against her mouth, tasting mint. Sampling the bright clean taste, he slid his hand down her body, flipping open the robe's sash, then the light garment itself.

She was naked beneath. A moment of disappointment. He loved peeling filmy undergarments off his lovers. But the qualm was forgotten again just as quickly. Her skin was divine. Fine and smooth and warm, quivering beneath his touch. Was it in fear or anticipation? He suspected both.

But when he cupped her breast in his hand it fitted perfectly.

Excitement beat its mighty wings inside her. It was happening. She was naked with a man, and he was touching her. Exploring her. His thumb moved against her nipple, flick, flick, flick. Every stroke wound up something tighter inside her, filling her with energy, compelling her to move, making her want to suck on the tongue that possessed her mouth. As if some mighty puppeteer controlled them with strings, her thighs lolled apart, making space for Ellis's still clothed body to possess.

'Mm . . . yes,' he murmured, mixing his breath with hers, and taking command of the valley she'd opened for him. The knot of his sex was huge and hard, so close to her own centre that she felt it twitch and leap, even through his clothing. 'Good girl.' He rocked his body, pressing himself right against her clitoris, caressing her with his weight, his strength. He kept moving, kept kissing, kept gently squeezing her breast. The sense of winding, and of gathering intensified.

She churned against him, wilder and hungrier than ever.

Her heart swelled. It was all so easy. Why had she never anticipated this? There was no urge to shudder and flinch away as before. No sense of struggle. Quite the opposite. It was as if her body knew exactly what it was doing, and wanted to fuse with his, and climb right inside it.

And she was wet, too, probably making a mark on his trousers as she rubbed against him.

I don't care! I don't care!

She rubbed harder.

His kiss roved over her face, along the line of her jaw, and down her neck. Would he bite her? She almost wanted him to, but he just kissed. Probably a man as well versed in seduction as he was would avoid giving juvenile love-bites to his equally sophisticated lady friends. Not a good look if they were in the social eye.

'What are you thinking?' He reared up over her, his sea-green eyes tinted dark with lust. God, they were astounding. Even she would have got aroused, just looking into that stunning gaze.

'Nothing. Stupid stuff. Don't stop.'

He laughed low and wickedly. 'I don't intend to. Unless you say so.' He looked a bit more serious. 'But if you do want to stop, at any time. Just say the word.'

'I don't want to stop!'

'Good . . . you gorgeous woman!' He plunged down again, and before she could draw breath, his mouth was at her breast, kissing, nibbling, and ooh dear Lord, sucking!

If she'd been wriggling before, she was crazy now. The sensations were unbelievable. She grabbed at him, pulling at his body, digging her hand into his dark hair, tousling it and clasping him to her. His wicked tongue was even better at flicking and teasing than his clever fingers were.

As he switched to her other breast, she felt his hand settle on her bare belly. Then pause. He popped up again, and gave her a questioning look.

'Yes . . . oh, yes.' The words were so small that they hardly came out of her mouth, but he heard them, and acted.

His hand slid between her thighs, then his long fingertips dove into her pubic hair, seeking the unexplored land. Well, unexplored by anybody other than herself.

'Mm . . . wet. That's good, sweetheart. Very good.'

And yes indeed, she was. She'd checked in the bathroom, still surprised that it could happen to her. A primal fastidiousness had almost made her wash herself furiously, but she'd refrained. How stupid! He *wanted* her to be wet, and she wanted herself to be wet. It was a sign of success, or at least of a promise of it.

Oh! Oh my! Oh my God!

Not sure what she was expecting, she almost levitated. His touch was so light, like a dance on her clitoris, swooping and floating, so delightful that she let out a gasp, a laugh of happy surprise. Without thinking, she pressed her hand over his, laughing again.

'Ticklish?'

'No . . . yes . . . I'm not sure.' Rocking her hips, she somehow managed to match her greater actions to his precise ones. How could she do that? It was almost a miracle.

'But good?' He leaned against her, pressing his face into her hair, against her ear.

'Oh God, hell, yes!'

The wonderful waltz of his fingertips circled on, becoming more complex, more exploratory, more energetic but still sweet and airy. She shuddered wildly when he pressed the tip of a finger inside her. Automatically, she stiffened.

'Easy . . . easy . . . It's all right . . . it's all all right.' He let the finger rest there a moment, as if steadying her, letting her get a feel of something there. Smaller than what lay ahead, but something. 'Okay?' he asked, wiggling the finger just a little. 'Have you ever . . . how can I put this delicately? Have you ever used a sex toy?'

The memory ran through her like a shiver. She did shiver. But with a beautiful man's hand between her thighs at last, this was no time for being coy and prudish and shy. 'I've tried a vibrator. I've got a couple actually. I tried to . . . I tried to put it in, but I think it was too big.' Suddenly her ears seemed to sizzle, along with the rest of her. She was one big blush from the roots of her hair, to the tips of her especially-for-him pedicure.

'Was it bigger than a man?' He kissed her again, and his finger moved on, sleekly slithering around her folds and back to her clitoris.

'How am I to know? The guys at life class never

get erections. Well, there's the occasional semi, but nothing very impressive.'

It was Ellis's turn to laugh, soft and low as he cupped his whole hand against her pussy in a caress that felt almost as if he was cuddling her down there. She liked that.

'If I was posing for you, I'd be rampant as a tree all the time, knowing you were looking at me. I wouldn't be able to help myself.'

Pressing herself against his hand, Jess reached down, cupping his trouser-clad crotch in return. 'You feel pretty tree-like to me now. I . . . well . . . I think you're probably as big as the vibrator.'

Disturbingly, that was true. He felt huger than ever, so much bigger than where he was supposed to enter. And yet, even though there was apprehension too, a greater curiosity, and boiling desire, still over-powered it.

Her vagina, pussy, sex, call it whatever she would . . . well, it was meant to accommodate a man, wasn't it? Hymens were meant to be breached, and girls not much more than half her age were losing their virgin-ities every day, and were probably very glad to be rid of them.

'Well, thank you for that. A man likes to hear that he's impressive . . . even if he isn't.' Beneath her hand, his cock seemed to nod as if affirming that.

'Oh, but you are impressive.'

'Sweetheart, I think you'd probably be quite easily impressed at this stage of your sexual education. Certainly if you've never seen or touched a man with a full hard-on before.'

'True,' she said, feeling her state of excitement wandering away from her.

But, as if he'd sensed the little dip, Ellis began to kiss her again, light and feathery, exploring and teasing. Gentle, but also assured and competent. Jess smiled beneath his lips, welcoming back her arousal. God, he was clever. He knew just what to do and he could read her like a book. Which was scary, but also reassuring.

At least one of us knows exactly what to do.

10

'Do you fantasise, Jess? Do you imagine what sex is like? Most women do . . . even virgins, I'm told.'

It was her deepest, darkest secret, apart from actually being a virgin, but to her surprise, she wanted to tell him. She wanted to clear away the baggage of keeping things to herself, and keeping *herself* to herself. He wasn't Mr Right. She might not see him again after tonight, but there was some kind of bond between them, and there'd be an even stronger one, if not long-lasting, when she'd given him her virginity.

'Yes, I *do* have fantasies,' she said, surprising herself with the firmness of her voice. A miracle when he was inveigling his clever fingertips back between her sex lips. 'I . . . I was a late-starter, what with one thing . . . ooh . . . and another . . .' Stroking, stroking, stroking, he kept on stroking. 'But lately, I've been fantasising a lot . . . and . . . masturbating quite a bit too. More and more as time's been passing.' She bit her lip. Oh God, it felt so good, so amazing. Different to when she touched herself, but crazy-crazy-good. 'I . . . I thought I'd better make some pleasure for myself because it was beginning to look as if I might have missed the boat, Mr Right-wise.'

'Well, clearly all the men you've met so far must be idiots, or blind or something. How could they not want to seduce a goddess like you?' His fingertip pushed against her entrance again for a moment, but this time she pushed back against it, lifting her hips. 'Steady, gorgeous . . . steady . . . I'm going to make you come first. At least once. It'll relax you.'

'Is that a fact?' Christ Almighty, she was almost there, especially when he returned his devilish fingers to her clit, resting two against it, then stroking in long, firm, toe-curl-inducing glides.

'Well, that's the theory.' Was there a slight waver in his all-conquering, all-confident façade there? Perhaps not.

'Actually . . .' She gasped, her breath taken by the tingling, singing precursor to pleasure. 'There have been men who probably wanted to seduce me. But I didn't want to be seduced.'

'Until now.'

'Until now,' she affirmed, grabbing at him, at his shirt, his arms, fingernails digging in, 'so consider yourself honoured to be chosen.' Her hips jerked, jamming her sex against his hand.

'I do . . . I do, Jess . . .' He looked down on her, his eyes glinting, his lush mouth curved in an arch smile. 'Now . . . come for me, gorgeous. Come for me. Give it up for Mr Wrong. For Mr Sex . . .'

That did it. The laughter, again, tipped her over. Crying out, she soared, her centre rippling and pulsing, her heart on fire. The pleasure seemed to go on and on, buffeting her on a high, ever-peaking wave, before finally casting her ashore . . . in Ellis's arms.

Oh my God! She's amazing!

Cradling Jess in his arms, he hoped that she didn't notice the fact that he was probably shaking as much as she was.

It was a long time since he'd been with a woman who responded like that. Perhaps even ever. Her body was a natural for pleasure. Her reactions unscripted, and unmodified. She was a seductress without trying or even knowing that working hard at it was a thing.

You're a lucky man, McKenna. Happening on a peach like this when you were least looking for one. What a special and erotic woman you are, Jess Lockhart.

He stroked her brow, smoothing back her hair. Her forehead was broad, the skin there like cream. Long black lashes kissed her cheeks, veiling her eyes and her emotions, and frustrating his need to know how she felt.

'You okay, Jess?' He kissed each cheek, then her brow, running his fingertip along her jawline.

Her eyes snapped open, huge and shimmering, the brown irises like chocolate in crystal.

'Yes . . . very okay . . . thank you.' Her voice was almost transparent. She was still half out of it, not yet back on earth.

'Do you want to take a break? Chill a while?'

Please say no! he commanded silently, though he'd known he had to ask. *I can't wait. I want you now. I'm going mad.*

It was true. He was. Though he loved sex, and liked it often, he was aware of the superficiality of his relationship with fucking. It was an escape. A release. A pleasure shared with a willing woman, an equal exchange between two consenting partners.

But this . . . this was different. It was as if he was in an alien land, and though he liked it, that sensation of being a little out of his comfort zone unnerved him.

'Hell no!' Jess sat up, shaking him off. 'I want it all. I'm not a fainting virgin even if I am a virgin and I feel as if I just fainted.' She gave him piercing look, her beautiful eyes narrowed. 'I'm not turning back now, and I don't want to wait. I want to see what it's all about, and I want to know if you're as good as you seem to be . . . Mr Sex.' Her face crinkled in a grin. 'I love that. Mr Sex . . . it's perfect for you.' Grabbing at the front of his shirt, she pushed it off his shoulders.

'All off, eh?' He affected a stripper's shimmy. 'Your wish is my command, beautiful. There's nothing I'd like more than to get naked with you.'

Divested of his shirt, he slipped to his feet beside the bed and unfastened his trousers. Letting them drop, he stepped out of the pool of dark tailoring, then rested his fingertips at the hem of his jersey trunks. He tried not to grin too much. Jess herself was doing a valiant job of trying not to stare exclusively at his crotch and the way his bulging cock was tenting out his underwear. Her gaze skittered from his chest, to his shoulders, then hurtled down his body at top speed, skating over the critical area.

Then she frowned. 'What's wrong with your foot? What are those scars?'

The question surprised him. Even though his left foot occasionally bugged him, he never thought about the scars themselves, and his other lovers had never seemed to mention them.

'I was born with a club foot. I had to have an operation and it went a bit wrong, so I had to have another and another . . .' The pain was a dim memory now, but sometimes there was still a dull ache, and a peculiar sensitivity in the skin of his left foot that felt oh so much better when he went without socks. 'That's why I often go sockless when I can . . . That foot's a bit sensitive to pressure.'

'Does it hurt now?' In spite of everything, there was a sweet and genuine concern in her eyes. For a moment he entertained a mad fantasy of her falling to her knees before him, and smothering the foot in question with kisses, but he pushed it aside. It wasn't his foot that wanted attention now, it was the area she was still studiously avoiding looking at.

'Shall I take these off?' he said, flicking the waistband of his underwear and flashing her his most wolfish grin. 'There's nothing in them that should shock you if you've done life drawing.'

'In case it's slipped your mind, I did say that none of the models I've drawn have ever been in quite the state you are!' Doing a shoulder roll of her own, she slithered completely out of the short kimono. Ellis had to make a fist of his hands, and dig his nails into his palms. It was either that or come in his trunks at the way her lovely breasts moved with the action. Her nipples were dark, and delicately pointed.

'Well then!' she said, nodding towards his cock.

He hesitated.

What the fuck is wrong with me? Am I shy all of a sudden?

Ellis was proud of his body. He swam and cycled, and even ran regularly. The issue with his foot actually seemed to benefit from running rather than the opposite. He was in the best shape of his life at the moment, and he knew he wasn't lacking in the cock department either. So why was he shilly-shallying about with his shorts still on, acting as if he were the virgin, not Jess?

In a swift, rough, less than graceful move, he tugged down his underwear, stepped out of it, and kicked it away.

'Yikes,' was all she said, her eyes wide.

'I hope that's a good "yikes",' he said, settling on the bed beside her, his cock almost touching her thigh.

'Sort of . . . but it . . . you . . . well, you're bigger than I was anticipating.' She was looking at his nether regions now, her eyes wide with an amalgam of curious fascination, and yes, a bit of alarm. 'You're definitely bigger than my vibrator and . . .' A divinely cute blush was forming over her chest and in her cheeks. 'Well, that won't fit . . .' She glanced away for a moment. 'I suppose I should have persevered . . . but I didn't.'

A qualm of doubt gripped him. He was going to hurt her, there was no way around that. But he wanted her to feel good. Mostly for her, but a little bit for his own male ego too. He didn't like to fail.

But you failed Julie. You weren't there. Maybe you could have saved her and the girls.

The spear of pain shot through him, and for a dark

moment, he imagined his cock softening. It didn't, but he imagined it. Metaphorically, he gave himself a sharp slap across the face. All the more reason to get on with the job in hand; initiating Jess happily into the pleasures of fucking, while drowning himself in sensation at the same time.

'There's a difference between a man and an inanimate object. Well, sometimes not a lot, but in this instance some.' He slid onto the bed beside her, and taking her hand, placed it upon him. 'The cock is a greedy organ, but if its owner can stay in charge, it can be a well-mannered one too.'

Jess blinked, staring intently at her hand, and at him. She nibbled her lower lip. Ellis nearly howled with desire, her touch was so heavenly. Especially when she very lightly ran her fingertips up and down him.

'Mm . . . oh, that's good, Jess. Just right. Not too strong, not too half-hearted. Are you sure you've not handled one of these before?'

'No. Never.' Her thumb glided around him, slipping neatly into the groove beneath his glans. Good holy God, oh God, how did she know to do that?

'Oh yes, you gorgeous girl, yes . . .'

Girl? No, she wasn't one really. Just young in delicacy and innocence and sweet instinct.

For a few moments, he let her explore, and try different strokes. It was sublime, but he had to fight an inner battle with himself not to demand more, to thrust through her grip, command her to bring him off and watch the pearls of his semen jet onto her belly. Eventually, he took her hand from him, bringing it to his lips, saluting it with a kiss as he tasted his own flavour on her fingers.

'I wasn't too rough, was I?' She was frowning.

Ellis leant forward and kissed her brow, smoothing the lines. 'No. It was just right. Perfect. Just how I like it.' He gently stroked her fingers. 'And I'm not bullshitting you. I'm not just saying that. I love the way you touch me.'

Was that a line? Maybe just the tiniest. But she was good. She was damned good.

And now he wanted more . . .

Jess had a feeling that Ellis actually was bullshitting her. But she didn't mind. She'd choose to believe she'd got it right. It had certainly seemed the way to touch him. She hadn't had to think about it. Her fingers had just moved almost without conscious direction.

Maybe I am *a natural?*

Or maybe it was because she had such fabulous material to work with! Such fabulous *big* material. She couldn't suppress a shiver.

Ellis cupped her jaw and kissed her again, feathering his tongue against her lips and then pushing it in when she parted them. Him . . . in her. Just like down below, soon. He kissed her long and deep, thrusting with his tongue, almost as if he was acclimatising her to the idea of penetration.

'Do you want to try it now?' he whispered, the breath from the words soughing against her jaw. 'If you've changed your mind, that's okay. I'll bring you off again, and then you can do me. That'd be good too.'

'No! I've told you. I want it. I don't want to wait any more. Now's the time.' She laughed, to quell her nervousness. 'Then when I'm an old lady I'll be able to scandalise my grandchildren by telling them I had my first ever fuck with a billionaire!'

'Well, that'll make for one helluva "you kids today" story,' he said, looking down on her with a grin, 'although I must tell you . . . My family has billions but I'm not sure I'm worth that much as an individual. Well, not all the time . . .'

'In that case, you'd better leave. I'm only giving it up for a billionaire!'

Ellis rolled on top of her, kissing her ferociously. 'Wicked minx . . . I thought you were after me for my pretty face and my gorgeous body.'

What am I after him for? Am I even after him at all? I just want him . . .

'Who says I'm after you specifically? I just want to lose my virginity and you happen to be handy.' She settled her hand on his cock again, and gasped. Bloody hell, the thing was hotter and harder than ever!

'Let's get to it then,' he growled, lunging at her for another long kiss, and running his hands up and down her body. 'Do you have any lube? I'm guessing you might, if you've been experimenting with your vibrator . . .'

Yes, she did. 'There's some in the drawer, to your right.'

When she'd returned from the bathroom, she'd noticed he'd put condoms on the bedside table, and wondered about the lubricant. It made sense to be as super-slippery as possible.

'Good girl. That'll make things so much easier.' He paused, and to her astonishment, Jess saw that he was blushing ever so slightly. 'Do you . . . have you used tampons?'

'Yes. For years.'

'Good. That might make things easier too.'

Jess had never expected a cross-questioning, but it was actually reassuring, very reassuring, to be with a man who didn't seem to want to charge in blindly at her and leave everything to luck. A man who actually seemed far more concerned about her experience than his own.

'So . . . you don't subscribe to the wham, bam, thank you ma'am approach then?' she asked as he rolled back and pulled open the drawer, twisting to look inside it.

'That's for cavemen,' he pronounced, fishing out the tube in question. 'I pride myself on being a modern, reconstructed man. Now, open your legs, woman, and let me grease you up!'

Jess giggled. And then gasped and then sighed as he applied the silky goo with delicious, teasing strokes, making the readying into a gorgeous pleasure-feast in itself.

Within a few seconds she was rippling; a mini orgasm, her trembling flesh awash with gel.

'Good, that's good,' he crooned as she wriggled against the mattress, loving the sensations. 'Now, hold that thought.' He reached for a condom packet and tore it open.

'Shall I do that?' she asked, but he was already rolling the rubber down his length, fitting it carefully.

'No, baby . . . Just touch yourself, keep stirring the good feelings.'

In a moment, he was sheathed, and lying against her, the silky-fine rubber of the contraceptive brushing her leg. Sliding his hand down her inner thigh, he parted her legs wide, then, in a graceful move, got between them. His cock lay against her sex, pointing and high, as he kissed her again, and reached down to stroke her pussy.

'It might hurt,' he whispered, 'but not too much I hope. It'll be better if you can relax, not tense up, not fight me.' His fingers were right at the heart of her, at her entrance . . . adjusting himself. 'Just one good thrust. That'll be easier than a whole lot of anxious pushing and prodding about.'

'You say the most romantic things, Mr Sex.' In spite of the critical moment, she found herself grinning again, and it seemed to take hold of her. She was giggling at life's absurdity when Ellis jerked his hips and shoved imperiously, entering her body in that one good thrust, swift and confident.

'Yowch! Ouch!' It hurt, a keen, sharp and spiky sensation, and yet somehow she was still laughing as he slid in deeply.

'Sorry . . . sorry . . . sorry . . .' He was gasping. Panting. Good grief, *he* was the tense one, not her.

'No . . . it's okay . . . It hurts a little bit, but it's okay.'

Ellis held still, inside her, his entire body as rigid as his sex. He was taking his weight on his elbows, so as not to squish her.

'You're wonderful,' he said, the words low and

raw against her neck. His face was buried there, his lips against her hair. 'You feel wonderful. So tight and warm . . . Oh thank you, Jess, thank you, thank you, thank you.'

Thank you too. Thank you for this. I'm glad it's you.

It was all strange though. Being part of one joined-together person almost. Minds completely separate, yet bodies as close as two ever were. Suddenly she realised she was shaking, unable to get over the idea that a part of Ellis was inside her. People did this every day, but it was astounding to her, like something she'd just imagined happening that could never be real.

Tears trickled down her cheeks. Not from sadness. She couldn't even describe what the emotion was, but it overwhelmed her.

'Oh Jess . . . hush . . . hush . . . It's all right. I'm here.'

Nonsense words, but immediately she found her calm place again. He was there. Right there. The feeling new and piquant, not yet arousing, but huge with the promise of it. The solid presence of his cock inside her was a grounding somehow, stopping her from flying away in all sorts of mad panic and specu-lation about what might have been, how things could have been different.

Running her hands down his back and over his buttocks, she embraced him. His body felt strong and fine and warm. She didn't love him, and he didn't love her, but he'd been right. He *was* a good choice for her first man.

As her hands strayed to his bottom again, he made a rough, low sound and pressed his face against her shoulder. God, he was so excited, but he was clearly holding back for her, keeping still, letting her know him rather than rushing ahead.

'You should probably move,' she whispered. 'I . . . I'm not sure I'll be able to come. Not this first time . . . it's a bit too new for me. But you should.' She cupped the cheeks of his behind, urging him. 'You should come. You should enjoy it. I'll just enjoy the fact that you're enjoying it.'

Ellis lifted himself up a little, then looked down into her face. He looked thunderstruck almost, and his ocean-dark eyes were suspiciously shiny. 'You really are the most astonishing woman, Jess. You're completely amazing, you know that.' His jaw worked for a moment, as if he were containing great emotion, then he plunged forward, kissing her again, and starting to work his hips.

It still felt odd, a bit uncomfortable, but the real pain had gone, or at least backed down a notch or two, buried in the sensation of him sliding to and fro, filling her, then retreating, filling her, then retreating. Jess tightened her hold on him; he was her rock in a wild new physical world. It was impossible to quantify how she was feeling, but in and amongst the strangeness there was a quality of nurturing. There was something about him that wasn't quite the all-conquering hero, and she sensed that it confused him, and that it wasn't his usual experience . . . and she wanted to make him feel better, just as he was trying to make things as good as he could for her.

'Don't hold back,' she urged again, rising to his thrusts as a little thread of pleasure made its presence known amongst the twinges of soreness. Could she get there? Probably not. It was all too momentous. But she saw in that moment how the next time could be. And the next . . .

Not speaking, Ellis moved more urgently, sliding a hand beneath her, cupping her buttocks, tilting her so he could get in deep. His breathing quickened to ragged gasps, and the way he plunged gathered momentum, his hips bucking hard.

Buffeted, she clung on tight. He was fierce, but she sensed he didn't want to be, that he was still trying for self-control. In a moment of instinct she gripped his bottom harder, her fingertips exerting pressure on the slopes of his cleft.

'Oh God . . . Oh God.'

That was it. The tipping point. Almost growling, Ellis went rigid in her arms, then powered into her in one, two, three . . . a succession of primal shoves. When he stilled again, in far deeper than she'd thought would be possible, she imagined she felt a ripple deep inside her. Not her own body, but his, semen pulsing in the condom.

Again the ghost of pleasure stirred, perhaps from that more profound intimacy, but it just wasn't close enough, not without grinding herself against him, and she didn't want to do that. She didn't want to change anything about the moment.

And despite the intimacy, she had an uncanny sense that somehow, he wasn't quite with her.

The return to rational thought was almost painful, full of confusion.

What's the matter with me? I've just fucked the most lovely woman. A beautiful, wonderful generous woman who's given me something rare and precious as well as the most astounding pleasure. Why do I feel as if I want to sob like a baby?

It was because of Julie, the presence that never went away. The wife he still loved. She'd been a virgin on their first night together, and Ellis had been with no other virgin before or since . . . until now.

I've betrayed her.

The thought didn't make sense, and he could almost hear his late wife laughing fondly at him, and telling him not to be idiotic because she wanted him to be happy again and take pleasure in sex, because it was natural and good.

But still he felt the guilt. Not just over Julie, but over Jess too, because he was also betraying *her*, by thinking of another woman even while he was still inside her.

No more though. He'd taken what she'd freely given him, and now it behoved him to give to her in return. Even in the madness of his own orgasm, he'd been well aware that she hadn't shared it with him.

Not to mention the fact that he was still sprawled on top of her, flaked out, and he was probably crushing her.

'Are you all right, Jess?' he asked, levering himself off her. God, his voice sounded weird, as if he'd just been turned and tumbled inside an industrial rockbreaker.

'Yes . . . I'm okay. I'm fine.' Her voice sounded

feathery though, as if indeed she'd been struggling to breathe while he'd lain on her.

'But you didn't come, sweetheart.' Hauling in a breath himself, to clear his head, he came up on his elbow and looked down upon her. She was lying with her eyes closed, her limbs spread akimbo on the bed, her lips parted, chest lifting.

Oh God, she looked divine. A primal rogue male urge powered through him. His post-coital *tristesse* was speeding away now, and hell, he was Mr Sex again. If he hadn't just come a few moments ago . . . The spirit was already aroused, even if the flesh needed a minute or two to recover.

You're disgusting, McKenna.

And yet the natural urge soothed him. It *was* healthy. It was good. And ignoring it and wracking himself with guilt certainly wasn't. No amount of breast-beating, hair-tearing and sackcloth wearing would bring Julie and Annie and Lily back, and they'd have been the first ones to remind him of that fact.

Jess was the one who mattered here and now. He laid his fingers lightly over her lips, blocking in the words, *It's all right. I don't need to come.*

'Before you say it . . . I think you do need to come, darling.' He leant forward and kissed her lips. 'You *were* getting there, weren't you? Despite having your virginity stolen from you by a ravaging horny beast.' He kissed her again, feeling himself on surer ground, sexual playfulness. 'You're a natural sensualist, Jess. I can tell. And if you'll let me, I'll give you another orgasm to prove it.'

Her eyes snapped open, and what he saw in them

made him want to cheer. She was right there with him. Her expression became sultry and she licked her lower lip.

'If you must,' she said . . . in the arch and husky tones of a practised seductress.

'I must!' he countered, sliding his fingers into the heat and silky wetness of her sex.

Jess knew she was right. He had gone away from her somehow in the moments after his climax. But in the moment after *that*, he'd come right back, and focused solely on her well-being. Slowly and sweetly, he'd coaxed her into another orgasm . . . and another. Even when she'd wanted to stop him because she'd caught sight of a little blood smeared on his fingertips.

Now, in the aftermath, while she waited for Ellis to emerge from the bathroom, she could only think of the leaving. She didn't want him to leave, but she knew he would. This was no tender dawn of a new relationship between two fated lovers. Nothing with a future. He'd had that before with the wife he'd adored and lost.

When he reappeared, he'd climb into his clothes and he'd be gone. In all likelihood she'd never see him again. Unable to watch him go, she rolled over in bed, facing the wall, and pretended to sleep. He could let himself out, slip the key through the letterbox and hi ho Silver, away!

The door opened quietly, and she tensed so hard that every muscle ached, including the ones that had seemed to receive their first ever workout tonight. Her body felt odd, bits of her vaguely displaced, as if when Ellis had withdrawn he'd somehow left a ghost behind.

Don't be daft. Now just stay still. Let him go graciously. Don't be whiny and clingy.

Footsteps padded across the room, and then, to her astonishment, she felt colder air on her back as Ellis lifted the covers and climbed into bed beside her, moving up against her. He was wearing his jersey boxer briefs, and he wasn't erect, but he was in bed with her.

'Um . . . what are you doing?' she asked in a small voice, irrationally feeling that if she spoke too loud she might spook him and he'd jump out of bed again.

'I thought I'd stay for a while,' he said, draping an arm companionably along her flank. 'It seems a bit callous to shag and run. Especially when you're new to all this. I thought you might like a bit of company until you go to sleep . . . unless you'd prefer me to clear off, that is?'

No!

'No, it's all right. Do stay. I'd like that.'

'Good. I feel a bit sleepy. I always do after good sex.' He adjusted his position in the bed, giving the pillow at his side a bit of a punch. 'I'll slip away before dawn though. Don't want to embarrass you with your house-mate.'

'She'll see the strange car. She'll know there's someone here.'

'You don't think she'll mind, do you?' His body was so warm against her, and glorious. Not in a sexual way now, although she knew it wouldn't take much to stir that. Just companionable. Something she realised she'd yearned for, and hoped for, just as much she'd anticipated losing her virginity.

'No. Not at all. She'll probably be thrilled that I've finally brought a man home.'

'Does she know you were a virgin?' Jess could sense curiosity in him, and she wasn't surprised. She had been a phenomenon, a rarity, hanging on to her hymen quite so long.

'We've never discussed it, but I'm sure she's suspected it.' A blush rose in her cheeks, just at the thought.

'Will you tell her?'

'I really don't know. I'll see. I'll see if she asks about the car tomorrow.'

There was something about Ellis's strangely non-threatening presence that soothed her though. She'd face Cathy when she had to face her. Now, Jess realised that she was tired, dog tired, despite everything. She wanted to sleep, and maybe just pretend for a while that Ellis was Mr Right, here with her. It was nonsense of course, and she knew she must be ultra-careful not to let her mind and her heart go that way. He might be staying for a little while, but he would go soon. And go for good.

Glad of her weariness, and surrendering to it, and to the heat of Ellis's body against her, she pushed away the bitter pang that thought provoked.

11

Rising out of sleep, Jess suddenly jolted awake, dislocated somewhere between fantasy and reality.

Oh my God. Ellis. Oh my God. I . . . we . . . had sex. I'm not a virgin any more.

He wasn't lying beside her any more either. He was sitting on the edge of the bed, fastening his shirt. Even though she'd barely moved, he turned to her, as if aware that she was fully awake now.

'I think it's time for me to go now. It's half past five. I heard your friend come home a little while ago, but she's retired to her room. Best that I go now and avoid making any awkwardness for you.'

Did he have to? Good grief, Jess *wanted* the awkwardness. Suddenly she was wide awake and she wanted to show this gorgeous man off. She wanted Cathy to know that the days of her house-mate being a virgin who couldn't find a man to fuck her were now officially over. She'd found a prime specimen, even if that man was just a one night stand and not Mr Right.

'Would you like a cup of tea or coffee before you go? It won't take a moment to make some and I could do with a cuppa myself.'

Ellis frowned. Oh hell, he must be used to needy women trying to cling to him. She'd probably just committed a cardinal sin, but perhaps it was just as well. There'd have to be a clean break and he was all the more likely to speed away now, to get out of her pathetic coffee-offering clutches.

So, don't clutch, Jess. Coffee is just coffee. Say goodbye, no fuss, no drama. Accept you had a beautiful initiation, and always remember Ellis as a glorious one-off, never to be repeated.

'Sure, coffee would be good. I'd love some.' He gave her a crooked little grin. 'We'll have to be quiet as mice though, so as not to wake your friend up.'

'Don't worry, she's a very sound sleeper.' Jess fished around for her robe. She couldn't see it, but an instant later, Ellis had retrieved it and was draping it around her shoulders. Close, he seemed about to kiss her, but Jess knew that would be fatal to her peace of mind, so she shot out of bed and out of his reach, provoking another of his frowns.

'I'll let you finish getting dressed, while I make the coffee.' Not trusting herself to look at him, even though there was nothing she wanted more in the world – almost – than to feast her eyes on him, she beat a stealthy retreat and headed downstairs to the kitchen.

It took her just a few moments to make coffee, the best instant. Cradling hers, she sat down at the kitchen table, staring around at the room that looked so normal, even at dawn, so completely the same as ever, when she'd changed so much.

All the years of waiting, wondering, saving herself, wondering whether she was an idiot for saving herself . . . all over now. And with a man she might never see again. What to do now, that was the question?

Actual sex hadn't been stupendous, but it hadn't been awful, and the other bits had been so out of this world that she was sure that actual sex would be equally as gorgeous when she got the hang of it. Frowning, Jess took a sip of her strong coffee, relishing its power.

But what if the out of this world bits – the foreplay – are only out of this world with Ellis?

Now there was a question. One she hardly dare contemplate. What if Mr Right and Mr Sex could never actually be combined into one man? Maybe it didn't matter if you loved Mr Right enough?

'Why such a stony frown?' Ellis's voice was low, out of respect for Cathy, as he sidled into the room and slipped into the seat opposite Jess. He sipped his coffee immediately, letting out a soft sigh of satisfaction. Obviously he wasn't a purist and liked instant as well as freshly ground.

'Just mulling over some issues.' No use getting into it with him now, or revealing anything that could be construed as trying to cling on to him.

'Issues concerning me, and what we did last night?'

Bugger!

She hardly dare look at him, yet at the same time, she couldn't stop. He was dressed now, apart from his jacket that he'd slung over the back of the chair, but his dark hair was still a bit wild. It was easy to imagine the naked form she'd seen last night, and which she'd slept snuggled up against. How was it possible that she'd been to bed with such an unimaginably fabulous man?

Oh God, I want him again. Am I a sex maniac, who just didn't realise it?

This was crazy. She needed to stop ogling him, and just send him away. But all she could think about was going back to bed with him again, which she knew in her heart and her gut would be better than ever this time, even the actual fucking.

'Yes, a bit. It was a big thing . . . It is for any woman.' The moment after she'd said it, she realised . . . and started giggling. Apparently she'd got a juvenile dirty mind too.

Ellis smirked. 'Why, thank you, I'm flattered.' His handsome face straightened, became more serious. 'But I know what you really meant. And you're right.' Cradling his mug, he stared into it for a moment. 'I know the actual act wasn't quite perfect . . . but you enjoyed the other stuff, I can tell.' His eyes flashed. 'And we can work on the main event next time, eh?'

Oh . . . Oh God, the temptation.

'I did enjoy the other stuff. And the act itself . . . in a way.' No use denying it. 'But I don't really think there should be a next time. I mean . . . You're you, and I'm me. You won't be around here much longer, and as you're so utterly irresistible it's not a good idea for me to get addicted to you, is it?'

Ellis laughed softly. 'You won't get addicted. You're

far too sensible. But I do think you ought to take advantage of me.'

'How do you mean?'

He took her mug from her hand and set it aside, then clasped both her hands in his.

'I've got a proposition for you, Jess. What I think is a sensible, logical arrangement for both of us. It's temporary, but we both get benefits.' His eyes were bright, full of that peculiar blend of mischief and faint melancholy she was beginning to become familiar with.

'Go on.' No harm in hearing him out, even if she was pretty sure it wasn't anything she could accept.

'I don't do commitment, and "long term", as you'll have gathered. I had the perfect committed relationship once, but I lost it. I'll never have that again, and I accept that.' For a moment, his whole face went hard, and Jess wanted to fling herself around to his side of the table and hug him, in an attempt to soften the obvious pain he felt. 'But I do like sex, and . . . well, seductions, "liaisons", call them what you will. I like those a lot.'

His eyes narrowed, and Jess realised she must have betrayed something in her face. Puzzlement, perhaps disapproval? Although she wasn't sure quite what it was that she felt. If she'd had, and lost, what he'd had, she wasn't sure how she'd conduct herself afterwards, so she couldn't judge him.

'Sex isn't a betrayal of her memory,' he said, his voice low. 'It's not the deepest core of what we had . . .' He hesitated again, pursing his lips, his fight against revealing himself too much very obvious. 'Julie and I had fabulous sex, but it wasn't everything. Love was everything . . . is everything.'

'And that *would* be a betrayal.' It had to be said, and though Ellis didn't visibly flinch, Jess felt it.

'Yes.'

'I see.'

Did she? Did she really? Jess clamped down on something inside her that was trying to protest.

'So . . . that's it for me. I don't do anything longer than a few weeks. Four or five, tops,' he said more briskly, smiling a tricky, charlatan smile that Jess knew was another mask. 'How would that be for you, Jess? If it's no good, just say so, and we'll part as friends.' His expression became more seductive, even trickier, but in a different way. 'But we could be good for each other during our "liaison", Jess. You're a smart, beautiful and intelligent woman. One of the most interesting and intriguing I've ever met.'

Oh, you sweet-talking bastard, you!

'Thank you . . . I think.' The warmth from his fingers was doing dangerous things to her. That, and the nurturing feeling he evoked too. It was a fatal combination. 'But why would I want to have a liaison or whatever with you? I know you're handsome and rich, and you're good at . . . *very* good at sex.' She looked away. Those sea-blue eyes of his were hypnotic, and added to the touch of his fingers, and what she could only describe as his aura. She'd thought such a thing was the province of fiction, but it was real and it was turning her head. 'But I'm not sure I'm a liaison type girl. Now I've . . . well . . . Now that I'm not a virgin any more, and I know I can enjoy sex, I think

I probably want to look for a proper relationship now, not a temporary "thing", you know?'

'You are a sensual woman, Jess. But you barely know anything yet . . . I could help you change that.' His voice was low and velvety, subtly cajoling. 'Spend a few weeks with me, and I could teach you everything you need to know . . . So that when your proper relationship with Mr Right comes along, you'll be able to blow his mind and have the best time in bed together right out of the gate, without a lot of fumbling and shyness and false starts.'

Oh, he was such an infuriating man. One minute beguiling her with his charm and his genuine kindness; the next arrogantly assuming all men wanted what he wanted, as if he were the last word on the preferences of his gender.

'If a man really cared for me, he'd accept a bit of fumbling and shyness at first. He might like it, because it takes the pressure off him to be a superstar in bed,' she countered.

'A woman who's a good lover helps a man to be a better lover. The days of men prizing virginity and scoring maidenheads like trophies are long past, Jess.' He was sticking to his theme, which spoke to his desire for a nice little interlude of sex with her. But one with a solid get-out clause when he'd had enough.

'So you didn't really enjoy what we just did at all, very much, then? You'd have preferred it if I'd had certificates in the *Kama Sutra*. With honours.'

'No! I didn't say that! You were gorgeous . . . Very little fumbling at all, and not too much shyness.' He winked at her outrageously and she suddenly wanted to punch him. 'But with a sensual nature like yours, and the looks and body . . . and brain . . . to match, you could be out of this world, Jess, really.'

Jess glared at him. Or tried to. He was somehow sexier than ever when he was being obnoxious. 'I don't know whether to tell you to sod off, or take you up on your offer. Just to take advantage of you.'

'I wish you would.'

'No . . . I don't think so. I think I'd prefer to muddle through in my own way.' He was too confusing. She just wanted him out of the way. Nobody had ever made her feel so jumbled up. In any way, never mind sexually. She was safer with him far, far away from her.

Ellis shrugged. Even that slight movement was so erotic she almost gasped. 'Very well,' he said, rising to his feet, 'I accept that. Not everyone's way is my way.' The devil, he was backing down now. She watched, expecting him to slip on his jacket and head for the door, but instead, he came around to her side of the table, and crouched down beside her, taking her hands in his again. 'Just tell me you don't regret what we did? At least not too much?'

'No, I don't.' It was the truth. And now, with him so close, more than ever. He *was* beautiful.

'One last kiss?' With utter grace, he was suddenly on his knees.

Oh Ellis, you beast. You're irresistible. A kiss, but don't ask for more.

She nodded and leant forward. He cradled her head in the very lightest of holds and dusted a kiss like thistledown on her lips. It was so delicate it barely happened; so seductive it sent molten fire rampaging through her. Deep in her belly, desire gouged at her, effortlessly reignited. Not stopping to think, she dug her fingers into his thick, silky hair, and drew his mouth to hers again. This time, his tongue quested, asking for entrance; which she granted.

Without her knowing quite how he'd achieved it, he drew her down, out of the chair, and onto the kitchen rug, still kissing her. She wound her arms around him, her tongue jabbing at his, fighting back. The line of his back was strong and lithe beneath her hands as she ran her them up and down, caressing him through his waistcoat and trousers.

He broke the kiss, heaving for breath. 'Jess, I know you don't want much of anything more to do with me, but please, let me love you one more time. Let me show you how it can be. Just the once. I won't bother you again. I *owe* you this!'

His mouth came down hard on hers again, the kiss devouring. Even if she'd been able to speak, Jess knew that she wouldn't have had to tell him the answer was yes.

She knew that he knew. How could she say no? His mouth, his body, his hands, they were like forces of nature that swept her onwards, brushing aside all qualms. A born again wanton, she swirled her hips against him as he kissed her, loving the jut of his erection and the way her shimmy-dance made him moan like a wild thing.

It was only when his hand slid inside her robe, pushing it open, that she snapped open her eyes and saw the weird stain on the kitchen ceiling that looked like Australia, that she remembered exactly where they were.

'For God's sake, Ellis,' she hissed, pushing him off her and clutching at her robe, 'we're in the kitchen. We can't do it here. Cathy might hear us and come down any minute.'

Ellis sprang to his feet, reaching down to draw her up too. Plucking at the revers of her robe, he set it aright and tugged her sash back into place. 'Come on then,' he said, taking her hand, 'we'll have to go back to your room.'

'I don't know . . .'

'Oh yes, you do. You're right on the same page as me, Jess.' She was already moving, compelled by his eyes as much as the way he urged her forward. 'Give me one chance to show you a better time.'

'Okay.'

She followed him up the stairs, grimacing at how loud their footsteps sounded. They'd crept down, but they were thundering up, and predictably, a voice rang out.

'Jess! Is everything all right?'

Ah, Cathy!

'Yes, everything's fine. Go back to sleep. Sorry about the noise.'

'Don't worry about it, kid. It's about bloody time. Have fun!'

'Oh bollocks,' whispered Jess.

'Don't worry,' said Ellis, low and almost laughing. 'Sounds like she's on our side.' He pushed open the bedroom door and drew Jess inside.

'But she might hear us!'

'We'll have to try and be quiet. You'll have to contain your screams of ecstasy.' Ellis's hands slid under her robe, cupping her buttocks as his mouth came down on hers again.

'What about *your* screams of ecstasy?' Jess countered, in between kisses.

'I'll just have to bite my lip, won't I?' His hands tightened on her bottom, squeezing and manipulating her cheeks. The sensation made her blush. It was so exciting, so naughty, especially when he rubbed his crotch against her belly at the same time.

They kissed for a few moments, rocking against each other until Jess was gasping. It was like a spring winding inside her again, sensation gathering and gathering. Her pussy ached. The desire to be touched was like a madness in her blood and she grabbed at Ellis's hand and drew it between her legs, hitching her thighs apart a little at the same time so she could jam his fingers against her.

'Oh yes . . . oh yes . . .' he crooned, 'that's right, beautiful Jess. Take what you want. Demand it. It's your right.' Nimble fingertips worked their way through her pubic hair and found her centre, making her squeak at the contact, she was so primed for it. Ellis's other hand shot to her lips, silencing her with a touch of his forefinger. 'Hush . . . keep it inside. It'll feel better . . . I promise you.'

His fingertips rocked and circled, just as her hips rocked and circled. She was wet already, in the zone, so quickly her mind couldn't keep up.

'Good . . . oh sweetheart. Are you there yet? I bet

you are. Just relax and let it happen. It's so easy, so easy.'

His voice and hand *made* it easy. It'd never been this way before. Even in her fantasies with Dream Lover she'd had to work for it.

You are *Dream Lover, you bastard!*

Burying her face in his shoulder, clamping her teeth together, she came hard, her pussy pulsing and fluttering against his touch. Her knees lost all strength but he flung his free hand around her waist and kept her upright.

'Right . . . let's get down on the rug. Less noisy than bedsprings.'

While she was still reeling from the sensations, he manhandled her to the bedside rug, settling her down with beautiful gentleness, and then dragging the pillows off the bed so she could rest her head on them.

'Have you got a thing about doing it on the floor?'

'I've got a thing about doing it.' Ellis grinned, settling himself beside her. 'Anywhere would be paradise with you, gorgeous.' He reached down and quickly cupped her sex, the gesture tender, almost companionable. 'But I want to take you to paradise too . . . while I'm in you.'

Kicking off his shoes, he unzipped his trousers and shimmied out of them, then dragged his underwear off over his feet too. Jess's eyes widened when he shoved his shirttails out of the way and his cock bounced up, looking bigger and harder than ever, if that were possible.

'I hope you've got another condom for that thing,'

Jess said, watching the rigid flesh sway, primitive yet elegant.

'Don't worry, I'm always ready.' From the pocket of his waistcoat, he flipped out a familiar package.

I'll bet you are. Always prepared for the next panting woman who falls at your feet.

But why be irked by that? She knew the score. He wasn't making any promises, just offering her no-strings 'educational' sex.

Ellis tossed the condom to her, but flustered, she dropped it on her belly.

'You should put it on me this time. That's another thing you need to be able to do for Mr Right when he appears.' He lounged back on the rug, a male odalisque.

'All right, but you'll have to keep it still.'

'Haven't you practised on a banana?'

She spluttered with laughter. 'No! Of course I haven't! I've got better things to do with bananas.'

'Of course you have.' He grasped his cock, as if offering it to her. 'And it's much better to practise on the real thing anyway . . . But be gentle with me, eh?'

She had a good mind to grab him and give him a good shake, but even she knew that that mighty male staff needed very mindful handling.

Gingerly, she tore open the packet. The thing would be useless if she ripped it, and it felt very slithery in her fingers. Odd, but not unpleasant to the touch, very slick. Instinctively, she pinched the teat, then set the contraceptive over the broad tip of Ellis's cock.

'Good, now roll it down. That's right. I won't break, actually . . . you're doing great.'

The fine latex rolled down his length with ease. A piece of cake! Admiring her handiwork, she started to lie down on the rug, in readiness.

'No, I think you should be on top this time, Jess. You should ride me.'

12

Uh oh . . . Dream Lover had always seemed to be on top. Always the one to take charge. Getting astride your lover was probably second nature to most women, but she wasn't most women. Not by a long chalk.

'What's wrong, Jess? Don't you fancy taking the upper hand?' His eyes sparkled. 'You'll enjoy it. You'll be a goddess looking down upon your humble minion, whose flesh exists only to service you.'

Oh, men did talk nonsense sometimes, and obviously they talked the most nonsense of all when they wanted sex.

'If you say so.'

'Don't worry, it'll be good for you. You can control things better this way . . . ensure you get the pleasure you deserve.' He took her by the wrist, urging her towards him, towards the mighty structure towering up from his groin.

Still in two minds, Jess got astride his thighs, loving his hot skin against hers. She tugged at the sash of her robe, but somehow it'd got tangled. With a growl, she wrenched it aside, the thin strip of satin still around her waist.

'Divine.' He half sat up, reaching for a breast and cradling it. Jess arched her back, loving that too. How was it that the way she curved fitted exactly into his palm? As if they'd been constructed to fit each other. Perhaps it was the same down below? She glanced again at his erection, jutting up so close to her, sturdy and ruddy through the thin latex.

'I still don't know how that goes in me. It's such a monster.'

'Why thank you, ma'am, every man likes to hear words like those.' He squeezed her nipple, a little harder than he'd done thus far, and a bolt of fierce sensation assailed her clitoris. 'Do you like that? A little spice with the sugar?'

'I don't know . . . I don't *not* like it.' She gasped when he did it again.

His grin was wicked. 'Ooh, we're going to have so much fun when we know each other a little better.'

But they probably weren't ever going to do that. This was supposed to be one last shag. And if that was the case, what the hell was she waiting for?

Jess came up a bit on her knees, hovering over him, putting her hands on his chest to steady herself. As she did so, Ellis slid his hands beneath her thighs, in a cupping hold, fingers in, thumbs out. 'Don't worry about me getting in too deep. I'll support you. Just take as much as you want. As much as you feel comfortable with.' His hold on her was firm. He was supporting her. She'd no doubt that if her thighs began to ache with the effort of keeping her aloft, she could relax and he'd take her weight in his strong, sure grip. 'Now guide me into you, and relax, baby, relax, relax, relax.'

Leaning forward, resting on one hand, Jess reached down. Ellis's glans was hot and hard to the touch. The surface of the condom was pleasantly silky. Manipulating him carefully, she guided his tip to her entrance, trying not to tense up, trying to forget the discomfort of his first thrust.

'That's it, Jess. I've got you. Sink down a little.'

Gulping in a great breath, she did just that.

Ooh, there was a little twinge. But somehow being above, and in control after a fashion, made it feel entirely different. It was still a stretch to get him in, but easier, so much easier than before. The twinge faded, enveloped in a greater and much more delicious feeling. Gorgeous fullness.

'More?'

'Oh yes . . . more . . .'

She pressed down as he let her descend. Inch by inch, inch by inch.

'Oh my God . . .'

'Oh my God . . .'

They spoke as one, then laughed together, the sensations of *that* making Jess gasp.

'I can hardly breathe. This feels amazing. You feel huge.'

Ellis groaned, shifting his hips. Jess's eyes nearly crossed and she felt as if the top of her head might lift off, but the gentle hold of his cupped hands under her haunches kept her grounded. 'I'm not hurting you, am I?' His voice was tight, and she could see the cords of his neck taut with the effort of self-control. He was fighting not to thrust up, and jam in deeper.

She wanted him to. She wanted all of him. She wanted more . . . and perhaps not simply his body.

No, don't go there. Just enjoy the moment. How many women in this world get one quite like this? There can't be all that many godlike hunks as handsome as him around. And if they are, they're still not him. Not my Dream Lover.

Pitching forward, she attacked the buttons of his waistcoat, then his shirt, parting them. The skin of his chest was super-smooth. Did he wax, or was he just naturally sleek that way? His body was tanned, but lightly so, creamy-golden. On a whim, she plucked at his nipple the way he'd tweaked hers, and inside her, his cock jumped and twitched.

'You like that?' She leant close, aware of his cock moving within her as she echoed his words.

'Mm . . . yes. Strong sensations. I'm not a masochist though. I'm not a sub. Quite the reverse.'

More unknown territory here. She knew the words. She'd read stories. But the reality of that subject matter was a new world beyond the one she was already exploring. Curiosity stirred.

'Oh,' she said, wondering . . . wondering . . .

It was better that they part after this, but what would it be like to take up his offer, and explore those worlds with him? Could she keep her emotions safe, and still be educated? Was it worth the risk?

'What are you thinking about, beautiful Jess? You're frowning? Are you sure you're okay?'

'I'm fine . . . I'm more than fine . . . Just mad thoughts.'

'I'll bet they're no madder than mine.' He winked at her, and lifted his hips, pushing in deeper. It was hard to think at all now . . . but one tiny, detached little bit of her wondered if he'd sensed the direction of her thoughts. She closed her eyes, just in case, concentrating on the gathering knot of pleasure that circled around the juncture of their bodies. 'Feeling good?' Ellis asked, the words husky.

'Yes . . . oh yes . . .'

'Why don't you touch yourself? Stroke your clit. I'd love to see you do that.'

New heat sluiced through Jess again, but almost immediately she laughed at herself, inwardly, for being an idiot. How could she be embarrassed about pleasuring herself when here she was sitting astride a man's loins with his cock high inside her? She snapped her eyes open, to find Ellis studying her face, rather than her body, his own expression a beautiful amalgam of sultry and intense, wound up.

'Men like that, don't they? To see women touching themselves.'

'Well, I don't know about other men, but I do. I can't imagine anything more provocative right at this moment. Do it, Jess, put on a show for me. If you give yourself pleasure it'll be easier to come with me inside you.'

With no further ado, and no more words, Jess slid her hand over her belly and down to her sex. When she touched her clit, and began to circle and stroke it, she let her fingers stray a little in the action, to touch Ellis's shaft where they were joined.

'Oh, you're a seductress, aren't you?' His fingers

curved in, cradling her bottom and squeezing her in time to her own strokes. The two caresses seemed to meld into one compounded pleasuring, so intense it made her sway, and the sway made Ellis groan in turn.

Oh God, I'm so near ... so close ... I can't look at him. It's all too much.

And yet she had to look. He was too beautiful not to look at, this rogue angel of a man with his fabulous eyes, his devastating smile, and his roguish piratical stubble-beard. Moving beneath her, he bucked upwards, while holding her, pushing in yet deeper. Was he close too? Or did he have reserves of control from years of fucking?

The agonised set of his jaw, and the way his shining white teeth were clamped together suggested that the reserves were flagging. That she, the virgin with no experience, and even fewer sex skills, was getting to him somehow. She *did* have power, and shimmying down onto him, she rode a surge of sensation that arose both from his solid flesh inside her and the reaction on his face.

Try this, Mr Sex!

She flexed her inner muscles, clamping on him tightly, embracing him within her.

'Oh God, Jess!' he shouted, despite all his promises to be quiet, and the power surged again, like a force of nature, like a silent rising roar of complete triumph.

Moaning herself, watching the ecstasy in his face, she tried to clench again, but couldn't. Her control was gone, her body was pulsing and gripping on to him all of its own accord, while wave after wave of bliss washed through her loins, and deep inside her, she registered an answering pulse. Ellis was coming too, his semen spurting out into the condom.

This time when he put all his clothes on again, they stayed on.

'I'd love to stay and spend the day in bed with you, Jess, but I need to be in London in – ' he checked his slim watch ' – in about three hours. I've got people flying in from Europe to meet with me, and it'd be bad manners to just brush them off, even for a woman as gorgeous as you.' He leant forward and kissed her.

Jess lifted her hand to cup his face as he drew away, loving the soft silkiness of his beard. She lingered. This would probably be the last time she ever touched his face.

In three hours . . . When was that? She glanced at her alarm clock and got a shock.

'Oh, fucking hell! I have to be at work in less than an hour.' She leapt up off the bed – where Ellis had picked her up and gently laid her down after they'd finished – and almost knocked Ellis over.

He grabbed her by the shoulders. 'Hey, don't panic. I'll ring your boss and say you won't be in today. Heck, you might as well have the rest of the week off.'

'I can't do that! You can't do that! What will people think?' She scowled at him. 'You just drop in from on high at Windsor for a day, but I have to work there, and I'll be the subject of constant speculation . . . It'll just be . . . It'll just be weird.'

Ellis's expression grew more solemn. 'Of course you're right. I've no desire to make things awkward for you, Jess.' He paused, rubbing his chin where she'd touched him. 'Could you ring in sick? Take a day that way? After all, you have lost quite a bit of sleep.' The wicked man winked at her.

'I could, but it doesn't seem right. I hate doing things like that.'

He reached for her again. 'That doesn't surprise me. You're a very decent and right-thinking woman, Jess.' His lips settled on hers again, sweetly and lightly. 'Why don't you get dressed and I'll give you a lift to Windsor? I could make you some coffee while you're showering.'

No! It was too intimate. Too nice. The longer she hung onto him, the longer she'd want to. She had to get back to normal. Ellis was a beautiful, time-out-of-time experience, never to be repeated.

'That's kind of you, but I'll get a lift with Cathy. You need to be on your way, Ellis. It's . . . it's been lovely, but we both know that's it. You'd better go now.'

Ellis rocked back as if she'd hit him. 'Well, that puts me in my place, doesn't it?'

'But you said you don't do relationships and all that, and I'm not looking for a relationship with you anyway . . . So it's better not to drag things out.'

She felt terrible now. There was a stricken look on his face. More than she'd expected. After all, not seeing her again would be a very small disappointment with another liaison just around the corner. Nothing really . . . Not to a man who'd lost the love of his life in such hideous circumstances.

'Look, I had a lovely time. I can't imagine a better

first time, because you're a lovely man, Ellis, and you've made me feel wonderful.' Out of his line of sight, she clenched her fists, horrified by the inadequacy of her own words. 'But we're just ships that pass in the night, aren't we? Admit it.'

He looked at her very steadily. 'We could circle each other for a while. We could have a good time. There's much more to sex than what we shared last night . . . much more . . . It would be a joy and a pleasure to teach you a few more tricks.'

'I'm not a performing sex poodle, Ellis!'

'I didn't mean it like that, Jess . . . I'm not putting this very well.' He reached for her hands, holding them quite tight. 'But we could be good to each other for a little while, and then part as friends.'

It was tempting, so tempting. It twisted her heart.

If I get more of him, I'll want more of him. I already know that. I'll want more than he can give and I'll spoil it.

'Let's part as friends now, Ellis. Please.'

The line of his jaw was taut. Was it genuine disappointment? Or simply annoyance at not getting all his own way, which was what he was probably used to. Perhaps a little of both, she suspected.

'Are you sure? Is that what you want?'

'I think it's for the best, Ellis,' she said, compelling her voice to remain steady and composed and not emotional. 'Don't you?'

'There are different kinds of best, but I accept your decision, Jess.' He gave a resigned little shrug. 'We part as friends. No hard feelings.' He leant forward and dropped a kiss on her brow. 'I had a great time, and I thank you for that. And if there's ever anything I can do for you . . . Anything at all . . . Don't hesitate to contact me. I'll be glad to help, and I really mean that.'

It was a lovely offer. A gracious, non-macho response. But it also seemed so formal, and so sterile, after the sweaty, threshing intimacy they'd shared.

'Sure I can't give you a lift to work?' He released her hands.

'No, it's fine. But thank you.'

You're an idiot, Jess Lockhart. A total idiot, she told herself a few moments later, as she stood in the doorway, in her robe, watching him climb inside his blue whale of a Citroën, and drive away.

13

'You're an idiot, Jess Lockhart. A total idiot,' said Cathy as they sat at traffic lights on the way into town. 'Even if there was no future with him in a proper relationship, you could at least have had a nice little fling with him. I would have . . . in your situation.'

Unsurprisingly, Jess's friend had tackled her almost as soon as she'd closed the front door, demanding to know who the drop-dead gorgeous man with the old blue Citroën was. Cathy had admitted to watching from the upstairs window as Ellis was leaving, and didn't hide the fact that she found his good looks stunning.

Thankfully, the bigger issue, the fact that Jess had finally 'done it', was taken as read.

'I know . . . I know . . . but it just didn't seem right. I can't explain it.' Jess yawned, lack of sleep suddenly catching up with her when there'd been no sign of it earlier. 'But I can't just go from being a non-fling type person to being a . . . well, being a fling type person. Not overnight.'

'Well, you obviously went from something over-night to something else, didn't you?' Cathy put the car in gear and they sped off. 'And don't try to deny it.'

Jess didn't say anything. There was no point in trying to deny anything, but somehow explaining why she'd decided to lose her virginity to Ellis McKenna was beyond her at the moment. She still didn't under-stand it herself.

'And with a billionaire too! Which makes it all the more barmy that you won't see him again, doesn't it?'

Jess nodded, even though Cathy's attention was on the road. Any woman in her right mind would have at least agreed to see him again once.

'Can't you contact him and say you've changed your mind? Even if you just keep it casual. You really need to get into the swing of full-on dating now you've finally taken the plunge, Jess, and you'll probably get some gorgeous presents out of it, at least.'

'I'm not interested in his money, or anybody's really. I only want to find the right man . . . and Ellis just isn't that. Not really.'

It was true about the money. Yes, it would be nice to have a bit more, and to know she had something in reserve to cover some unforeseen disaster, but Jess was old fashioned and for her money had to be earned via a proper job, all above board.

'You could have given him a chance to be Mr Right, you know. Clicking with a guy at first sight is very rare, and you usually don't realise you really like them until after a few dates, perhaps even longer.' Cathy started to slow the car. They were approaching

Windsor Insurance. 'And that's pretty much the same with sex. For it to be really good, you have to get to know each other's likes and dislikes, and work at it a bit.'

Ah, but it was toes-up fabulous right from the start with Ellis. Even when it hurt a bit.

But she didn't tell Cathy that as they said cheerio, and she got out of Cathy's car.

Even though she'd changed irrevocably overnight, as the morning wore on, Jess realised that Windsor Insurance was just the same as ever. Not out and out horrible, but not exciting. Excruciatingly boring. With her eyes half-closing every other moment or two from fatigue, and her concentration shot to hell, Jess decided to ask her supervisor if she could take the afternoon off from her hours of accrued flexi-time, and luckily, it was okay.

Not only was she bone-tired, and incapable of concentrating on anything other than thoughts of Ellis, and her own ensuing decision never to see him again, she was drawing a lot of curious looks and comments from Pam and Emma, and others. Two and two were being put together, connecting her obvious weariness and the sensational VIP who'd paid so much attention to her only the other day.

'Meeting someone this afternoon, Jess?'

'Seen the big and gorgeous cheese lately, Jess?'

'Something keep you awake all night, Jess?'

With laughter and evasion, she fielded the friendly probes, but she was glad to get out of the building at last, and in a very rare indulgence, she took a taxi home because she was convinced she'd fall asleep on the bus and miss her stop.

Letting herself into the house only made her think of letting herself and Ellis in last night, and on reaching her room, she could have sworn that she could still smell his cologne. And though that was probably her imagination, she was quickly convinced she could smell another odour.

Sex. The act of sex.

She'd done it now, and she was different, a new kind of woman. All morning she'd been acutely aware of every part of her body, especially the intimate zones. All of them. Her mouth, where Ellis had kissed. Her breasts and thighs and buttocks where Ellis had stroked and touched her.

Her pussy, where he'd possessed and pleasured her, the awareness there most intense of all, in a bizarre kind of sensory high definition.

Did the scents of their joining still linger in the room? Perhaps that was just an olfactory illusion, but if she was going to catch up on sleep, she'd probably better change the sheets.

Drawing in deep breaths, she seemed to see things, too, as well as smell them.

Ellis's beautiful naked body as he walked towards her. Ellis on the rug, half dressed, his erection high and proud. Ellis's sea-blue eyes, puzzled and perhaps annoyed when she'd resisted his blandishments and the temptation of a sweet sexual fling.

Sod the sheets. The effort of re-making the bed was too great, and yet exhausted as she was, she knew sleep wouldn't come, so she made some tea and brought it upstairs to drink. In an effort to stop herself thinking too much, she settled down to draw a little, but there were no prizes for guessing the subject of her sketches.

The soft graphite pencil skimmed over the page at lightning speed, sometimes recording in sharp, crisp detail, sometimes capturing a dreamy, impressionistic essence. Either way, she'd never been able to record images quite this fast before. Never been quite this good?

Ellis in his clothes. Ellis out of his clothes. Ellis's face. Ellis's hands. The curve of his shoulder. The sharp line of his hipbone.

The proud elegant jut of Ellis's cock . . .

She hid the latter at the bottom of the pile as soon as it was done.

Well, looks like you're my muse now, Mr McKenna, for the time being at least, even if you'll never be more than that.

And inevitably the muse of her fantasies too; Dream Lover for the foreseeable future. He was her blessing, and the beautiful scourge of her peace of mind, all in one glorious package.

Her eyelids drooping at last, she lay down on the bed, aware even as she drifted off that she was lying where Ellis McKenna had lain last night.

Ellis's main meeting during the day had remained inconclusive, and unresolved. He'd had to apologise to the attendees and arrange to reconvene. It'd been either that or be preoccupied and inattentive throughout the entire proceedings, and it was something he'd never once done before, even after intercontinental travel or the most athletic all-nighter with a woman. He despised bad-mannered business behaviour, and the only time he'd ever come close to it was 'before' . . . when there had been sleepless nights comforting his daughters when they were ill or teething, and even then, cherishing his family life, he'd mostly stayed home the next day with them too.

Pushing memories away, he sighed and finished his tea, then stretched out on the leather-covered couch in his London sitting room, wondering what the hell was wrong with him. No, scrub that, he knew exactly what was wrong with him. A case of totally unforeseen confusion and frustration over a certain Jess Lockhart. It had to be that, because normally he could function on a ludicrously tiny amount of sleep. Today he'd been all over the place, musing on the woman who'd turned him down.

Intellectually and even emotionally, he understood her choice. Even admired it. Women he'd known who were infinitely better off than Jess had attempted to cling on to him, as much for his wealth as for his qualities as a man and a lover, and yet she'd shown virtually no interest in his money at all.

Yes, he could see and respect why she'd told him to go, but the primal caveman beneath was roaring almost constantly at being denied the beautiful prize.

And beautiful she was. Far more than she obviously realised. A characterful beauty, lovely in depth rather than just gloss. Innocent, yet profoundly sensual. Another quality of which she was barely aware. She was a goddess of untapped erotic potential, and what a thrill and a feast of pleasure it would be to help her comprehend and enjoy her own powers as a seductress.

I can't just give up on you, Jess Lockhart. I'll persuade you to give me another chance. I must.

It would be intriguing to see more of her drawing and painting too. She had definite talent and she ought to be living creatively rather than doing drone work in one of his companies. Perhaps he could do something about that.

He started to wake up, the fatigue fading as purpose revivified him. He reached for his phone and opened his organiser. Meetings were stacked for the next few days, and he squashed the urge to cancel the whole lot. Other people's lives and jobs depended on his decisions, and he couldn't just chuck everything aside to satisfy his libido, not even for Jess. He'd have to stay in town this weekend, alas, but next weekend was all his, to be spent at Windermere Hall, his bolt-hole.

It was a long time to wait in order to be with her, but perhaps that was a good thing in a way. Nothing would be worse than making her feel crowded and harried. This way she'd have time to rethink her choice, look back on their night together, and perhaps come around to the idea of giving him another chance. And in the meantime, perhaps flowers? They were a cliché, but still. Perhaps a basket of something too. Gourmet goodies, hot chocolate, those cookies she'd liked, similar indulgences. That way he could give her a luxurious treat without overpowering her. It felt crass to send more intimate gifts, like exotic lingerie and sex toys, to a near-virgin. He could lavish such items on her later.

Smiling, he tapped the shortcut for his concierge service. His heart lifted. He hadn't felt this optimistic and excited in a long, long time.

14

It'd been a weird week. The weirdest. But then again, most of her time seemed weird now, since the visit to Windsor Insurance of a certain VIP.

She'd done nothing but think and fantasise about Ellis McKenna, the man she'd told herself sternly to forget.

Fat chance of that!

For one thing, there were the flowers. A gorgeous sheaf of white and orange roses, exquisitely velvety and fragrant. They'd provoked a raised eyebrow from Cathy, and more scorn when Jess had insisted she wouldn't be seeing him again.

'You idiot. It's obvious he likes you. Couldn't you just give him a chance? Use him for sex? God knows you deserve to let your hair down.'

Jess had umm-ed and ah-ed. Cathy was right. It didn't make sense to turn her back on him, even if there was only a fling on offer.

But you know what'll happen. You'll get addicted.

And when the end came, she'd probably wish that there'd never been a beginning.

The ominous thing though, was that it might already be too late to avoid that.

Then, the basket came. An overflowing hamper of edible goodies from a local luxury food store. Hot chocolate, probably the same brand she'd drunk that first morning, along with cookies and cakes and unctuous confectionery, along with speciality teas and coffees.

'I guess you'll have to send it back,' Cathy had said, almost visibly drooling over the abundance, and already pulling open a package of triple choc cookies.

'I think that would be ungracious, don't you?' Jess had grabbed a cookie and taken a heavenly bite.

Both women had laughed. And it was right. Ellis had been kind and it would be rude to reject that kindness. But the thank you note would have to be very carefully worded. Perhaps a proper old-fashioned card, sent to the address on the business card he'd given her?

Life seemed to go on as normal, when in fact, it was totally different.

Jess was different. Ellis McKenna had changed her. Physically, almost infinitesimally, but in every other way the transformation was massive.

She felt different. And her mirror told her she looked different; a vague, discreet change, but there all the same. Something in the way she held herself was new.

I'm not a virgin any more. A beautiful and sophisticated man desired me, and gave me pleasure, and I gave him pleasure.

It was like that 'aura' phenomenon she'd once

mocked, an inner glamour. At first when men had looked at her with curiosity, appreciation and interest, she'd thought it was due to Ellis's performance at Windsor that first morning, dragging her upstairs. But the changes were apparent in locations other than her workplace. Men giving up seats for her in cafés and on the bus, suddenly restored to old-fashioned chivalry. At art class, several male classmates who'd previously kept themselves to themselves began to chat, comparing notes and techniques, and to compliment her fulsomely. One newcomer, Josh, had suggested 'coffee' some time, no pressure.

He was actually quite nice, and not bad looking too, and if Jess's metamorphosis had come about in any other way, she might even have capitalised on her new poise and self-confidence, and made a tentative move herself. Who knew where and when Mr Right might appear?

But unfortunately, the quest for Mr Right had been completely derailed by the arrival of Mr Sex in her life!

Despite the strangeness of her week, she still felt good about it. Sort of. Every unoccupied moment, she thought about Ellis.

She was thinking about him when her sister Mel rang one evening.

'You sound a bit distracted, sis, are you okay?' her sibling said after they'd done a bit of catching up, mainly Mel's news about her life as a young professional, and her relationship with Simon, the man she lived with and adored. Mel was bubbly, and their chats always made Jess smile, even though there was often probing about her life, and the third degree about any potential men in it.

Well, there's one now, sister dear, after a fashion.

'I'm fine. Everything's fine. Just same old, same old, you know?'

She could almost see Mel narrowing her eyes. The younger Lockhart was perceptive.

'It's a man, isn't it? You've met someone . . . What's he like? Do I know him?'

'No, it isn't . . . well, yes, sort of. Just someone I met through work. It's nothing serious. Just casual. I probably won't see him again.'

There was a pause. Mel was probably shaking her head now. 'You don't do casual. You're not a casual person.'

'Well this is very much a ships that pass in the night situation, Mel. Nothing more than that.'

'Give him a chance, Jess. Please . . . I know you're choosy. But give him a chance. Is he nice? Good looking?'

Like a god . . .

'I don't know . . . It's tricky. He is very good looking indeed. And nice . . . in a way. But he's not a prospect, if that's what you want to know. There's no future with him, and that's a fact.'

'If you say so . . . but still, maybe you should give him a chance? Have a good time, if only on a temporary basis? You know I don't pry . . . but I worry. But . . . well . . . I know you've missed out on a lot, Jess, and for my sake too. I want you to have fun. Stretch your wings. Have a life.'

'But I've got a life!'

'You know what I mean.' The sisters didn't discuss intimate matters, but Jess had a shrewd idea that Mel knew how things were with her . . . on that score.

'I've got a life, believe me.'

Mel laughed, and said warmly, 'Well, I'm glad to hear it! Good for you. Now get out there and live it, making a start with this good-looking and nice in a way guy, whoever he is.'

To Jess's relief, Mel didn't push things further, and turned the conversation to questions about Cathy, whom she also knew, and other mutual friends.

But her sister's words stuck in Jess's mind, long after Mel had rung off, a counterpoint to the vivid presence of Ellis there.

So, now I've finally got this 'life' I was so desperate to have, what do I do? she asked herself when riding home on the bus on Friday. *Only live half of it? I've held back from relationships, chasing some impossible ideal, and now that I've been gifted a chance for something really exciting, thrilling, and insanely mad and wonderful, what do I do? I dither and consider turning away from it . . .*

Reaching into the pocket of her bag, she fingered Ellis McKenna's card. And her phone. But just as she drew it out, ready to call, a rather disapproving looking woman with blue-rinsed hair, and a meticulously co-ordinated beige casual outfit took a seat beside her . . . and frowned pointedly at Jess's phone.

Okay, I'll call him when I get home.

She didn't need to. When she turned the corner into her road, the Blue Whale was parked outside their house.

Oh hell! Oh hell . . .

There was a big difference between resolving to do something, and having it forced upon her, but there was no way around confronting him now, because he'd clearly spotted her. He was out of the car, and strolling towards her already. A beach bum sex god in his pale linen suit and another of those questionable flower-patterned shirts.

'What are you doing here? I thought we agreed . . . not a good idea and all that.'

So gracious, Jess, especially when you were on the point of changing your mind.

Ellis gave her a sunny grin, and before she could elude him, he leant forward and gave her a kiss on the cheek, before tucking her arm in his. Jess almost tripped. Inside she was whirling, and all the hormone reactions she'd convinced herself were wildly exaggerated by recollection were now firing on a thousand pumping cylinders.

He felt so good. He smelt so good. Dear God Almighty, he looked utterly divine!

'I thought I'd try again to win you over. I know you like me a little bit, and we're great together in bed . . .' He waggled his dark eyebrows at her like an inveterate Lothario. 'I didn't think there was any harm in trying to persuade you to change your mind.' He paused as they reached the gate, and he opened it for her. 'And . . . well . . . it's the weekend, I'm up here on my own, and I'm lonely.'

Jess looked at him sharply. There was such a keen note in those last words. They were stripped of all the rakish joviality that he was so prone to. She could almost imagine him in agony, remembering family weekends, joy, companionship, now all lost.

The losses from her own life rose up and stabbed at her. She knew some of his pain, even if the particular quality of it was different, and company at least helped a little bit. Whatever he was going to suggest, she decided that she'd probably go along with it, even if she had to nominally drag her toes a bit, for form's sake. He mustn't be allowed to think she was easy. She *wasn't* easy. Well, not with anyone else but him.

'You assume a lot,' she said, opening the door and letting them in. The thirty-second warning on the alarm beeped out, and she cancelled it. Cathy was out this evening, and possibly for the rest of the weekend, and had clearly already left. 'What if I had plans?'

Ellis followed her into the living room, and when she turned to him, he gave her a long, old-fashioned look. Okay, so he knew without having to be told that she didn't have any plans.

She flung down her bag. 'So, what are you proposing? Let's hear it.' Holding his gaze was difficult, as wicked lights danced in his eyes now, the moment of sadness gone.

'I thought we might spend the weekend together. Fling a few things in a bag and I'll whisk you away to Bluebeard's Castle with me, well, until Sunday evening at least. We'll have the place to ourselves. My housekeeper has left me an abundance of food and wine, and I'm very good at reheating her delicious concoctions.' He moved close to her, and laid his hand on her waist as he looked down at her. 'And in between all the indulgent eating and drinking, we can satisfy our other appetites in privacy and comfort. What do you think?'

'So it's a sex weekend.'

'Not necessarily *all* sex, although as far as I'm concerned, that's not a bad thing.' He kissed her for the first time. A quick, teasing peck, but it almost made her sway with desire. 'You could bring your art materials. Windermere Hall has some beautiful gardens – not that I know anything about horticulture – and if you get tired of sketching flowers and stuff, you can always use me as a model for a bit of life drawing.'

I've been using you as a model all week.

Which was true. At life drawing class, the tutor had remarked on the fact that what she'd produced was some of her very best work, even though it didn't look a bit like the model they were working with.

'But what about Cathy? I can't just swan off . . .'

'Can't you? Where is she now?'

'With her boyfriend.'

'And where will she be most of the weekend?'

'With her boyfriend. But you're not *my* boyfriend. You don't do relationships.'

'Very true.' His long, elegant hand curved around her cheek. 'But I do excel at nice sexy weekends. Especially with a woman I both admire as a person as well as have the horn for. Will that suffice?'

Yes. No. Stay. Go. Exist . . . or live a little!

'Yes, it will. But I'll need a quarter of an hour or so to get my things together and quickly check if there's anything needs doing that I should have done.'

'Anything I can do to help?'

'Not really.' Any help with packing would involve him going up to her bedroom with her, and that might mean starting the sex weekend straight away. She wanted him, boy how she wanted him, but she was curious to see Bluebeard's Castle aka Windermere Hall.

'Okay, I'll watch TV.' Without further ado, he flung himself down in an armchair, and in time-honoured man style grabbed the remote and started flicking through channels. 'Glad you liked the flowers and the other stuff,' he added over his shoulder, nodding to the roses, in pride of place in a vase on the sideboard.

'They're gorgeous. It was all gorgeous . . . *is* all gorgeous,' Jess answered, flustered. 'You're very kind.'

'And you deserve gorgeous things.' With a wink, he returned his attention to the television and, half apprehensive, half elated, Jess raced up the stairs, wondering what the hell one generally packed for a two-day erotic marathon.

'How come you have a house up here? I'd have thought you'd have lived in a luxurious pad in London or some honking great mansion in Gloucestershire or some posh county like that.' They were gliding along a country road, out in the green belt, but only about ten minutes from where Jess lived. 'This seems the last part of the world where a globe-trotting billion-aire might live.'

'You'd be surprised, Jess. This part of the world is actually billionaire corner. I know of two others who live not ten miles away from here. I'm not sure they're both billionaires in their own right, but probably not too far off.' Ellis took a remote out of his pocket, as the car slowed before a set of imposing wrought-iron gates with a coat of arms in the centre of each one. The McKenna crest? When he pressed the button, the gates swung open.

'You're kidding!'

'No . . . God's honest.'

They cruised up a short drive, flanked on either side with well-manicured turf. Jess managed to tear her attention away from Ellis, whom she'd been discreetly ogling throughout the whole journey, and focus on the smallish but nigh-on perfect Queen Anne house that stood at the end of it. It was a poem in creamy stone, red roof tile and narrow, immaculate, white painted window frames.

'It doesn't look a bit like Bluebeard's Castle,' she said, already loving the symmetry and harmony of Windermere Hall. It looked so calm, yet so elegant. 'It's far too refined and genteel for a den of iniquity.'

'Oh dear . . .' Ellis stopped the car on the gravel out front. 'I hope the refined ambience won't put you off rampant sex.' He winked, then leapt out, shooting around to open the car door. 'There's a rackety old stable that hasn't been renovated though . . . We can indulge our animal passions there, if you prefer?'

'Don't be silly.'

Ellis laughed as he took her bag from the boot, then escorted her indoors.

The entrance hall boasted a mosaic floor and a wide sweeping staircase, and there were a number of doors leading off in all directions.

'Not all the rooms are decorated,' said Ellis, dropping

her bag for a moment. 'The place has been in the family for a long, long while, but nobody did anything with it. The branch of the McKennas that lived here fizzled out, and it just got left.' A shadow crossed his face. 'After my wife died, I didn't want to live in America or Australia, in the homes we'd shared. I wanted a bolt-hole that was really out of the way, and when I found out about Windermere Hall, it seemed liked the perfect spot. So I had it fixed up, but just enough for a sort of country bachelor pad.'

To bring your women here, I guess. The ones you fuck for a few weeks, trying to forget the life you once had.

It was sad, but not pathetic. He'd found a way to endure, to go on with his life in the face of deep loss. If sexual pleasure helped him deal with emotional agony, who was she to criticise his choice of therapy?

'It's beautiful . . . really beautiful . . .' she said as he led her into an airy, comfortably furnished sitting room. It was an elegant space, just like the hall, but not intimidating. The deeply upholstered sofas, covered in gold and umber brocade, were inviting, and unbidden, Jess imagined making love there, in front of the fire, when darkness fell.

If we wait that long!

Turning to Ellis, Jess knew she couldn't. Wait, that was. Pent up yearning almost made her sway. Throughout the week, she'd done so much fantasising about him, and replayed what they'd done together that first night so often, that she thought she might explode if something, anything, didn't happen between them almost immediately.

From virgin to sex fiend, do not pass go.

Had he read her eyes? He gave her a long, considering look. 'Would you like something to eat? A drink maybe? Perhaps a nice, long, relaxing bath?' He was going through the motions, trying to be a gentleman, bless him. But something about the way he stood, a coiled, alert quality, told her he didn't want to wait too long either.

'No . . . no, thanks. I . . .' She swallowed, then dropped her shoulder bag on one of the chairs, and walked over to him. 'I want something else.'

'Oh Jess, my lovely Jess. I was so right about you.' He cupped her cheek in that delicate yet strangely predatory way he was so good at. 'You're a quiet storm, woman. A hurricane of hidden sensuality, just waiting to let rip.'

His outlandish words nearly made her giggle, but almost immediately he took her lips in a deep, ravishing kiss, consuming the laughter from her mouth before she could utter it. Mastering her with his tongue, he slid his strong fingers around her head, digging into her hair, holding her at the base of her skull, while his other hand travelled the length of her back and settled on her bottom, gripping there too.

When he pushed her pelvis against his, he was as hard as a rock.

She ground herself against him, body on autopilot, knowing exactly what to do. Her own hands journeyed beneath the jacket of his lightweight suit, clutching at his gorgeous, muscular bottom through the thin layers of linen and underwear.

He was everything wonderful. Dream Lover made flesh, and given a face. A handsome, angelic yet powerful face that looked down on her with unfettered hunger when he broke the kiss.

'What do you want, Jess?' His fierce expression gentled into a grin. 'What do you want to try first, beautiful sex pupil?'

'I don't know. You're the expert.' It was hard to think straight when his crotch was still pressed against her and his cock seemed to be getting harder and hotter by the second.

'Well, what do you fantasise about?' He slid his fingers around to her face, tracing her jaw, playfully outlining her mouth, thumb on her lower lip. 'Vanilla or kink?'

'Both . . . a bit . . . but vanilla stuff mostly. Not being very "advanced" and all.' He was squeezing her bottom, fingertips pressing the crease through her light, silky skirt, and it was hard to concentrate. She'd swiftly washed and changed into something a bit more alluring while he'd been waiting for her: the short, flirty skirt and a fine knit cotton cardigan, in a matching turquoise.

'Do you read erotica?' His hand settled on her throat, then travelled down her chest, fingers spread warm and deft in the V of her cardigan.

'Yes . . . sometimes . . . I mostly read crime or horror, or biographies, but I have read some erotic novels.'

'So . . . what do you like? *The Story of O*? Henry Miller? Anäis Nin?'

She laughed, even though he was tackling the buttons of her cardigan, using one hand with amazing dexterity. 'No, they're mostly stories about handsome and domineering billionaire sex maniacs if you must know!'

It was Ellis's turn to laugh, as he prised open her cardigan, and revealed her bra. Jess was acutely aware that the bra was rather thin and her nipples stood out like little corks, clearly visible through it.

Dumbo, they're supposed to do that. That's why you chose this bra? Why be so bashful?

'You mean, like me?' He started stroking her nipples through the sheer fabric.

No, not like him. Not like him at all. There was no man like him. Ellis was tricky and clearly liked his own way, but there was something almost sweet at the heart of his considerable charm and powerful charisma.

'No, the guys in the books are a bit on the arrogant side for my taste.' She caught her breath as he delicately closed his finger and thumb on her nipple for an instant, making her hips jerk. 'You're arrogant, Ellis McKenna. Arrogant as hell . . . but you're, well . . . you're more human somehow.'

'I'm glad you think so.' He gave her a sultry, heavy-lidded look. 'Shall we sit down? I think this will all be so much more pleasant if we're comfortable.' He guided her towards one of the lush, cushion strewn sofas. When she sat, he took her by the shoulders and urged her to lie back against the deep upholstery. She tried to reach for him, but he took her hands, one by one, and set them on the seat at her sides. 'Let me do the work,' he said softly, leaning in, his breath warm against the side of her face.

'Are you trying to take charge of me, like the men

in the books?' She wanted to embrace him, but her hands were tied by invisible bands, as if he'd shackled her. Energy gathered in her loins, and she wanted to touch herself, but she couldn't. She wanted to rock about, to give herself some ease, but he hadn't given her permission to.

'Might be,' he said, nipping at her ear, then tugging with his teeth. How the hell could that have an effect between her legs? And yet it seemed to, stoking the need. 'So, these book guys . . . did the fact that they were dominant excite you? Did you play the same scenarios in your own fantasies?'

'No . . .' Liar! 'Well, maybe a little bit. But it's hard to imagine the complex stuff when you haven't even passed the first, simple test.'

He plucked at her nipples again, first one, then the other, more assertively this time. 'Well, you've passed that with flying colours now, Jess. You're already a star pupil. Do you want to progress?'

Her mouth was dry, and her heart was thudding. Below, desire gouged at her, yet still she was unsure. She wanted something, but didn't want to run before she could walk.

'I don't know . . . maybe. On some level. But I think I'm a feminist really, well, a bit of a one. Generally, I don't much like the idea of men having the upper hand.' She clenched her fists beside her, and immediately, he reached out and unclenched them for her, spreading her fingers flat on the cushions, the action firm yet caressing.

'How about if it was just for a strictly specified period, and the moment you stopped enjoying it, you could just say "cut"?' His eyes were so brilliant, she hardly dare look at them, yet she couldn't turn away. He wasn't smiling, but there was the ghost of it around his beautiful lips.

'That might be all right,' she whispered. It was hard to breathe. The weight of anticipation and wanting seemed to press all over her body. 'But wouldn't that mean I was really the one in charge of the game?'

Suddenly, she found herself smiling back at him. They were already playing some sort of game, and it dawned on her that she liked it. She liked it a lot.

'The game? Oh, Jess, you get it don't you? Yes, you'd be in charge, even though it'd seem as if the poor stupid man, namely me, was the one calling the shots.' He lifted one of her inert hands to his lips and kissed it passionately, covering its entire surface, finger after finger, with the touch, touch, touch of his soft, velvety mouth.

'Okay then, let's do it.'

'Very well.' He paused, and it was long one, ramping up the tension. She almost thought he'd changed his mind, and she couldn't see his eyes because he was still studying her hand.

But just when she was about to break the silence, he said, 'Close your eyes.'

15

She was divine. Perfection. Her lush dark eyelashes floated down, right on cue. Ellis loved Jess's glossy brown hair and the way it hung gracefully on her shoulders. Her face was an artist's, fey, but also strong. Her special imagination was writ large in her clear, elegant features; she was both dreamy and determined. He nearly moaned aloud when she licked her lips, his cock lurching heavily.

Turning her hand, he kissed her palm again, opening his mouth and caressing it with his tongue.

'Oh,' she said, gasping, getting his drift. Her erotic imagination was precocious too, for a near virgin. Perhaps it was those books? He suspected that they had only piqued a sensuality that already ran deep.

'Hush . . . Don't speak. Keep it all in. Focus in on what I do to you. Don't waste energy.'

She pursed her lips, swallowing. It was an effort for her to keep still, he could tell. She was bursting with erotic spirit, with desire.

Whipping off his jacket, he flung it away, then slid

down to kneel on the carpet. With his hands on the insides of her knees, he parted her thighs to the limit that her slim-fitting skirt would allow. Her pussy, still hidden, seemed to call to him, inviting him to admire and touch and taste, but she was all delights to him, and the sight of her lovely breasts made him suppress the sort of gasp a randy schoolboy would have let out at the sight of them.

Jess wasn't heavy-breasted, but she had sweet curves. A beautiful pair of handfuls, he thought with a smile. The smile broadened when he noted that the simple but pretty bra she was wearing fastened at the front.

Well done, beautiful girl. Smart thinking.

He popped the clasp, baring her. Her mouth worked, as if she was still fighting not to gasp or moan. He wanted to moan, himself. Her nipples were ador-able, fiercely erect, dark, reddish brown and puckered. When he laid a fingertip against the left one, she did let out a gasp, and her whole body seemed to shudder finely.

'Naughty, naughty . . . what did I tell you? Behave yourself, Jess.'

He touched her other nipple, flicking it lightly, and she moved slightly against the cushions, as if unable to keep still.

Good God, she was so exciting! Especially when her eyes suddenly snapped open and she gave him a slight, but deeply feminine smile. Despite her lack of experience, in every way that mattered she knew every-thing. She was a woman of power, indulging his foibles . . . because it pleased her to.

Her eyes closed again, but a ghost of the smile still lingered.

He stroked her nipples, toying with her, one moment gentle as a feather, the next, tweaking, almost pinching. She licked her lips again, and he almost leapt to his feet, tore open his trousers and crammed his cock into her mouth, the temptress! But he'd sworn to himself that before the hour was out, he'd introduce her to the flip side of the coin, before he asked for that bounty for himself.

Leaning in, he drew a nipple between his lips, and started to play that way too, sucking lightly, then fluttering with his tongue. She gasped and in his peripheral vision he could see her fingers twisting and clenching, clearly fighting the compulsion to grab him by the hair so she could control what he was doing.

But with more self-control than he might have exerted, she remained still. Even when he created a deep, drawing suction on the beautiful tip of her breast, almost moaning in his throat as her whole body shuddered.

Driven almost mad by her reaction, he maintained the intensity, reaching up to fondle the other nipple at the same time. She was rocking in her seat now, and despite his instructions, she reached for him, digging her long, flexible fingers into his hair, and putting pressure on his scalp. It hurt a bit, it actually hurt, but as he mouthed her, he couldn't think of anywhere he'd rather be at that moment. The little pain almost made him harder, even though he'd never really had masochistic tendencies.

Switching to her other breast, he plagued her, exerting tiny retribution for what her fingertips were doing. She moaned, then with a sudden sharp cry, she curved forward, over him, burying her face in his hair, and kissing it.

'You want to come, don't you?' he demanded against the feverish skin of her breast, blowing on it. 'Admit it, Jess, admit it!'

'Yes, I do, you monster! You know that!' She was panting, gasping for breath. 'Bloody hell, Mr Sex, I'm almost there already! I didn't think it could happen this way.'

'It doesn't often,' he said, lifting his face and looking up at her, awe-struck, 'but you're a miracle, gorgeous girl, a miracle of sexiness . . . One in a million.'

Her face flushed with desire, she smiled at him, half out of it with excitement, half supremely in control and triumphant. 'If you say so.'

'I do say it. But now I'm going to do something that just can't fail to get you off.' With one last kiss to her blushing bosom, he reached for the hem of her skirt, pushing it upwards.

16

Oh my, oh God, he was going to do *that*. He was going to put his glorious face between her legs and kiss her pussy.

Dream Lover had done it, of course, but there was a considerable difference between imagining what something was like and actually experiencing it. And somehow, being gone down on seemed more intimate even than fucking.

Sprawled on the deep upholstery, she was exposed to him, and soon she'd be more so. The ordinary but luxurious surroundings only ramped up the intensity. It seemed as if anyone could walk in any moment and see her exposed breasts, and now, her bare thighs.

'Don't worry, there's nobody here but us, nor is there likely to be for the whole weekend.' His fingertips glided up her legs. Her skirt was at her crotch now, and a second later, up around her waist. The light from the standard lamp just behind the couch created a golden pool around them, and made Ellis's dark hair gleam when he dipped forward and kissed the base of her belly, his lips hot through her knickers.

'Divine,' he murmured, but Jess didn't know whether he was praising her posh new underwear – that she'd fooled herself she wasn't buying just in case she ever saw him again – or the slight curve of her belly or her eau de toilette . . . or even the faint odour of her excited sex.

She didn't care. Whatever it was, the heat in his voice filled her with a potent cocktail of power and anticipation.

'Now let's get these off.' Retreating a little way, he reached out to pluck at the elastic of her knickers, then pulled them down. The action was quick, almost ruthless, the product of his own obvious eagerness. When he'd bared her, he tossed away the flimsy garment and shuffled forward again, between her thighs, pressing them more open with his palms on their inner slopes.

Trembling again, Jess couldn't look. She wanted to, but the sight was too decadent. Her inner vision defied her though, and showed her his intent expression as he admired her pubic curls, and the hungry fire in his eyes and the way he licked his lips. She clicked the shutter in her mind, imagining a sketch. One she might do for her own delectation, or for his. Maybe hers, on reflection, to remember this moment, when he was long gone.

No! Don't think of that now.

'Don't worry,' he repeated and she could feel his breath on her thighs and her belly, he was so close. 'You'll like this, Jess. I promise you . . .' With his thumbs, he combed through the soft hair, making a parting, the ultimate exposure. Still, she saw it in her mind. Like any woman, she'd been curious, and looked, with a hand mirror.

Waiting, waiting, waiting for contact, she felt his breath again. He was blowing on her, making a tropic wind flutter across her clitoris. It was unbearably gorgeous, tantalising, plaguing. It made her want more. Much more. Devouring pleasure.

He moved in, but to the side, rubbing his soft stubble over the insides of her thighs, all the time inhaling, then exhaling, creating the zephyr. At the end of her tether, she grabbed him by his thick dark hair and imperiously conducted his mouth to her pussy.

Moisture met moisture. His tongue was bold and muscular, immediately licking her in long, comprehensive strokes, passing over her clit, but also exploring her folds and diving like a tease into the snug entrance to her vagina. As he probed there, his tongue a point now, he settled his thumb squarely on her clitoris and rocked it in a circle.

'Oh God! Oh God!' she wailed as he manipulated and probed, teased and rubbed, triggering a climax that howled through her like a hurricane, hard and intense, as if she'd been waiting for it for years. Maybe she had? Soaring, she couldn't think, but she could feel and sense that she'd never had an orgasm quite like this . . . at her own hand or with this man who had his face between her legs.

Her eyes snapped open and she could see concentration on his face, through the haze of bliss. And a frown too, of pain. She was pulling his hair.

'Sorry!' she gasped, still riding the wave. It was difficult to force her fingers to release him, messages getting mixed and muddled along her nerves.

But she managed to.

'Thank God for that,' he gasped against her tender membranes, laughing as he still lashed her with his tongue. For a moment, he pulled back, shaking his head, maybe to ease the pain at the roots of his hair, then he dived in again, licking, licking, licking.

'Ellis . . . please . . . I want you in me now. Fuck me, please!'

Lifting his face again, he grinned, his sea-coloured eyes flashing as if lit by lightning. 'As you command, Mistress Jess.' Taking her by the hips, he shuffled her down onto the thick rug set before her sofa. It should have been awkward and laughable, but somehow she descended with a modicum of grace, settling on her bottom.

Ellis moved like a god, even when he was crawling about on the floor, working to unfasten his trousers and shimmy out of them, and his underwear.

'Have you got a condom?' He wasn't the type, she sensed, to ever forget such things, but the whole having sex thing was all so new to her that she couldn't help but ask.

'Of course,' he answered with a gentle grin. He was ragingly aroused, his cock like a thick ruddy bar, hungry to possess her, but he was a kind man too. A man she could always trust that he'd take care of her. 'Trouser pocket.' He nodded, indicating she should get out the contraceptive, while he pulled cushions from the settee down onto the floor with them.

Strangely, it didn't seem odd to be sitting on a rug with her breasts and pussy on show, searching for contraceptives, while an equally half-naked man lounged back and watched her. She fumbled, though, when Ellis idly took himself in hand and started stroking his length. He clearly didn't need any extra stiffening, so he was just doing it for himself and because she aroused him.

Good heavens, I'm a goddess!

She prised the sheer but strong rubber tube out of its wrapper.

'Want to put it on for me again? You have a lovely touch.' With his cock in his fist, he seemed to be offering the star prize to her.

'Okay. I do need the practice.'

Pinching the rubber tip, she positioned the contraceptive and rolled it down. It went on like a dream, no hesitation.

'Next time you should try rolling it on with your mouth.'

Yikes.

'I think that's just a bit advanced for me as yet. Let's put it on the task list for later, eh?'

Ellis smiled, then his long eyelashes fluttered. Jess realised he'd gone back to idly stroking his now-rubbered cock.

'Mm . . . that's nice,' he said with a sigh. 'But I think I need to be inside you pretty soon. I just can't wait any longer to be up to my balls in your divine little puss.'

Jess shuffled around, preparing to lie back and open her thighs wide for him, but he halted her, taking her hand and conducting it to his cock.

'Squeeze me. Just there.' He folded her fingers around him, just beneath the glans and positioned her thumb just beneath the groove. 'I've gotten myself a bit too excited, love. I need to slow down so I can last longer, and this'll help.' He exerted a light pressure, his thumb on hers.

Jess pressed lightly where he'd indicated, careful not to go at it too hard. Clumsy handling could hurt him and put him off altogether, and she was always mindful of her paucity of experience.

Ellis's long lashes fluttered. 'Mm . . . yes . . . that's good. Just a little more, and I think we've got the beast tamed.' His eyes flashed open again and he gave her a silky grin. 'I want to last . . . to give you pleasure . . . not just go bang, bang, bang, oops, that's the end of it.'

Still holding his cock, Jess looked at Ellis in wonder. She had no other men to compare him with, but received wisdom told her that most men would never be so honest about their sexual capabilities and performance. The proud alpha males in the books she'd read certainly never admitted that there was a possibility of premature ejaculation.

'Am I being a bit too "human" for you? Admitting that I might not be a super-stud?'

Was it so obvious on her face? At his urging, she released his shaft, and relaxed back onto the thick rug. Ellis moved forward and placed a cushion beneath her head.

'No . . . I like "human".' She paused, reaching for his shoulder, to pull him towards her. 'I haven't any experience, but I don't expect you to be like the men in the books who go all night without a break and can get it up again within ten seconds of coming . . .' But she grinned up at him as he reared over her, settling between her thighs, his heavy cock resting on her belly for a moment. 'Although I have to say, you don't do so badly. I think you're probably about as near to the fantasy as a girl's likely to get.'

'Why thank you, Jess. You're always very good for my ego.' Resting his weight on one elbow, he reached down, took hold of his cock, and pressed it against her pussy. Jess gasped, when, instead of pushing into her, he started to rub the hard, latex-clad head of his penis round and round, using it as a sex toy almost, to pleasure her.

Jess fell back, closing her eyes, sighing. The way he played her was astounding. Inventive. He didn't throb like a vibrator, but the heat of him was almost as stirring as the thrumming might have been, and the pattern he created was hypnotic and complex.

'Mm . . . that's nice,' she whispered, instinctively swirling in a counterpoint, lifting to him as sensation built and gathered.

'Good.' His voice was taut, and when she glanced down, she saw he was controlling himself again, even as he used his own flesh to caress her.

'Please, Ellis, I want you inside me. I don't want you to have to wait. I've come already and you haven't . . . it's . . . it's not fair.'

'I live to serve you, beautiful princess,' he murmured, moving into position, settling his shaft at her entrance. Again, she felt a qualm of fear. He was a big man, and she was only a step or two away from her virginity. 'I wish I'd thought to provide some lube again.' He'd read her moment of pause.

'I don't need it! I'm wet as wet can be . . . thanks to you. Now get on with it!'

Ellis laughed. 'You're a miracle, woman. Truly you are.' Pushing with his hips, he started to enter her.

There was pressure, but her body yielded instantly, easily this time. Maybe she *was* a miracle, or maybe all women were in this respect, taking the solid club of flesh into themselves, the tribute of a randy man.

She hitched her hips, pressing close to him. He hitched his hips too, working himself in more deeply. Already, his body was familiar to her, and she bent her knees, bringing them up to let him in as far as he could get.

Marvellous. You're marvellous to me, Ellis McKenna. I never expected it to feel this good . . . and you're not even Mr Right, just the man who crossed my path at the moment when I got fed up of waiting.

A shudder swept through her, but not from sex. The concept of 'Mr Right', it troubled her suddenly. Did he even exist for her? What if . . .

'Hey, where are you?' Ellis backed up a little, weight on his elbow so he could trace her cheek with his fingertips. 'You've gone somewhere, Jess. Come back to me.'

She blinked. How bizarre. In this moment of ultimate intimacy, she'd been thinking. Thinking far too much. Dangerous thoughts too.

'I'm here now,' she whispered in reply, winding her arms around his back, pulling him hard against her, 'I'm here and there's nowhere else I'd rather be.'

'Damn straight. Me too,' growled Ellis, swinging his hips, getting his rhythm, banishing all qualms with his beautiful physical presence and his power.

It was as if she'd never had that wobble, never paused for thought in her relentless rise to pleasure. Ellis's every thrust was like the priming of a mechanism, the tensioned ratcheting of some infernal fabulous engine, taking her higher and higher. Sublime sensations flared every time his pelvis knocked against hers.

'Oh Jess, Jess, Jess . . . I wanted to hold on, to last, to introduce you to the concept of having your brains fucked out.' He laughed, and the rumble of it, passing through his body to hers, almost made her eyes cross. 'But I'm so excited I want to grab at pleasure, take it now, like some hideous chauvinistic bastard.'

'Then take your pleasure. Take it. I've come already.' Holding him tighter, she flexed her fingers, as if the pressure might compel him to break loose and come. The fact he was so concerned with her pleasure over his almost made her feel guilty.

'Not yet, Jess, not yet.' He looked down into her face, frowning. 'It's a point of honour . . . I don't leave my lovers high and dry if I can help it. Not ever.'

She didn't want to think about his other lovers, nor even the wife whom he'd adored.

'Touch yourself,' he commanded, then kissed her neck, drawing his tongue over a sensitive point before pulling back again. 'Touch yourself, and let me watch your face while you come.'

'I don't know if I can . . .'

'Try it.' His words were soft, but there was a deeper thrill in them too. A thrill like a silver cord that twined around her clit. He was in charge. It was how he lived. And right here, right now, beneath him, she loved it. Sliding her hand between their bodies, between her skin and his, she found her centre and started to rub. As the pleasure surged, and Ellis redoubled his efforts with thrust after thrust, she closed her eyes again, half expecting him to tell her to open them again.

But he didn't. And it was easier. Even though she was denied the sight of his passion-wracked face, and everything that was handsome about it. His brilliant eyes, his strong mouth and white teeth, the roguish beard . . . his wild hair. She saw those in her mind, almost mutated into a work of art, as if she'd painted him, the greatest she'd ever create because he was the ultimate model.

'You're so beautiful,' he said, his breath coming in gasps, the raw sound of it ramping up her sensations. He was so close. She wanted to tell him he was the beautiful one, not she. 'You look like a Madonna . . . not rock star Madonna . . . a painting . . .' He paused to kiss her again, almost savaging her throat. She could feel his teeth against her skin. 'You're like this image of an exquisitely divine woman yet with an erotic secret, like the *Mona Lisa* . . . a mystery. An eternal mystery.'

Her fingers stilling on her clit, Jess laughed, 'I thought men turned into animals when they were . . . were fucking. But you, you're some kind of crazy poet, Mr McKenna. I never imagined it would be like this.'

'Oh, I'm an animal all right.' He laughed too,

through gritted teeth. 'Now come on, play with yourself for me. I want to feel you orgasm around me, so
I can come too.'

He fucked harder. She rubbed harder, locking her
ankles around his hips in an instinctive action as if
she'd been making love with men for a decade, not
just for little more than a week. The way their bodies
realigned knocked her fingertips harder against her
sensitive flesh, and within a few more strokes, the
crescendo peaked and she orgasmed hard, shouting
out 'Ellis! Ellis!'

With her last speck of presence of mind, she gritted
her teeth then. It was either that or cry out something
else too. Something very, very silly, which beyond the
heat of the moment wasn't even true. Probably . . .

17

'I thought that lovemaking might have given you an appetite?'

Kitchen time again, although this gleamingly well-appointed and tastefully renovated haven was a world away from the slightly ramshackle space Jess shared at home. She and Ellis were sitting at the scrubbed oak table eating a scratch supper of cheese and cold cuts and fresh bread. Ellis had offered Jess wine, but she'd asked for water instead, and they were both drinking Evian.

It seemed important to be sharp and clear for every moment of their time together. There was no knowing whether this 'friends with sexual benefits' experience would even last beyond this weekend, and Jess wanted to be in full command of her senses for every single second of it. She didn't want to miss a thing.

He was right though. She wasn't particularly hungry, although she'd been well impressed with Ellis's domestication when he'd offered to prepare a proper meal, or at least do fresh vegetables to accompany one of his housekeeper's dishes from the freezer.

'Ah, but the lovemaking was so good that the satisfaction has spread over into my other appetites.' She grinned at him. For all his own sexual appetite and confidence, she was well aware that he was concerned lest he short-change her, and not give her the very maximum degree of pleasure.

You're a very strange alpha male indeed sometimes, Ellis McKenna. Very real and humane, even if in most ways, you're straight out of fantasy.

'That's great to know.' He smiled. 'I want you to have a good time with me. I want sex to be all wonderful things for you, Jess.'

'Well, I think it's fab so far!'

Yes, it was fabulous. But that wasn't the only fabulous thing. Miraculously, despite every extreme difference between his life and hers, she felt comfortable with Ellis McKenna. As if he was becoming a friend as much as her sex tutor. Just look at them now, sitting so companionably together like this, both in dressing gowns like the one she'd worn back in old man Jacobson's office, sharing the most casual of meals. Ellis's mobile phone sat beside his plate, and from time to time, he checked it and answered messages and emails.

Just like a real boyfriend. As if we've been together for years rather than barely a week.

How good would that be? To be at that stage?

The thought made Jess shiver, but she controlled the reaction. Even so, Ellis looked sharply at her, as if he'd picked up her tension subliminally. He reached across and touched her hand.

'Are you really okay? I mean it. You're not just saying you're all right, when really you've got doubts.' His sea-blue eyes were probing.

She did have doubts. But probably not quite the ones he suspected. She needed a diversion, and focusing on his hand over hers, she found it.

His fingers were long and elegant, but capable. A work of art.

'I'm fine, Ellis. I'm having a good time.' She reached into the pocket of her dressing gown, where she'd stowed a couple of pre-sharpened pencils and a small Moleskine drawing book, one of her few extravagant indulgences. Such high-end papercraft cost more than she could really afford, the amount of them she got through, but they were worth it. A kind of pledge to herself that her art was worthwhile.

'Could I draw your hand? I love drawing hands and you've got really nice ones.'

He looked a little surprised, but then smiled, flexing his fingers before draping his tanned hand over the cheerful, striped tablecloth.

'Like that?'

'Yes, that's great. It won't take long. I'm no Leonardo. I just do simple sketches.'

They both fell silent as she went to work, beginning by measuring by sight, against the edge of her pencil, then setting down a few key reference points and lines. It was his right hand and, as she sketched, she couldn't help but imagine that beautiful hand doing other things.

Holding hers, as a lover would. Touching her hair, and her face. Travelling over her body. Finding intimate trigger points and creating sublime pleasure. Astonishingly, even though she'd thought herself totally focused on the work, her body roused again, right in the places where those fingers had wrought their magic.

Focus, woman, focus. It's the anatomy of his hand you're supposed to be concentrating on . . . not where it's been!

And yet, as her pencil seemed to glide and work of its own volition, she found herself thinking of Ellis's hands elsewhere, perhaps touching other women. Women with whom he'd shared his non-relationships, and before that his adored and beautiful wife, Julie. Was that why he'd offered his right hand? So she didn't have to draw the ring, the symbol of what he'd lost and what kept his heart closed off?

A shaft of jealousy pierced her, and the pencil jagged. She reversed it, and used the eraser-cap attached to the non-business end, a feature she'd found useful for very quick sketching.

Jealousy was a stupid emotion, both in general, and most definitely in respect of Ellis. He'd stated the ground rules, and they were what they were. Theirs was a very temporary coming together for a specific purpose. Which made jealousy irrelevant. She'd never possess him sufficiently to even merit jealousy.

And yet still you feel it, you silly mare. He's not yours. He'll never be yours. Get real!

'I wish I could draw,' said Ellis suddenly, almost causing Jess to make another boo-boo. 'I could do with more hobbies. Something more creative to do with my time.' He'd been studying his own hand almost as intensely as Jess had, and now he looked up. 'Maybe you could teach me to draw while I'm teaching you how to make love?'

'I'm no teacher, Ellis,' she said, making the final touches, defining the way a vein ran along the side of his thumb, using a very fine shadow. 'I've got far too much to learn myself, without trying to instruct someone else.' In a fit of *joie de vivre*, she signed the work. She often didn't but somehow it seemed important now. 'I would have thought a man like you would have loads of exciting stuff in his life . . .' She looked up at him, and gave him an interrogative glance. 'Social events . . . sports . . . stuff like polo and yachting and other rich men's pastimes. What is your "thing", Ellis? It's not fast cars, unless you've got something far more souped-up than the Blue Whale in one of your garages somewhere.' On the question, she turned the notepad towards him, so he could see the result.

Ellis stared at his imagined hand for a few moments, but Jess had a feeling he wasn't seeing it, even when he said, 'That's amazing.'

Something about his voice and his demeanour froze her, and when she said, 'Thanks,' the word was barely audible.

'My thing?' he went on, his voice musing, and what Jess saw in his face almost made her flinch. 'I don't have a "thing" like that. I don't think I ever did. It was all business and working with my father and my uncles until I met Julie . . .' The words somehow faded, volume leached out of them by emotion. 'Then she was my "thing" and our little family was our "thing" . . . I mean, we had lovely homes in a variety of places, but we always lived quietly, happy and self-sufficient unto ourselves, without need for any glitz or glam. Just hanging out, having fun, a bit like this really. Me and Julie sitting at the kitchen table . . . Annie and Lily drawing . . .' He pursed his lips, as if fighting for control. 'Though with crayons, mostly, and pictures of Daddy with bright blue hair and feet like a Sasquatch.'

Oh God, what had she started? Why had she asked? His eyes shiny with unshed moisture, Ellis looked older than his years suddenly, his glorious features rendered haggard by a deep and manifest suffering. He was a man who had everything, but who also had nothing. He'd lost the best part of his life, and it was clear that it could never be replaced.

That was why he lived this strange existence, not like a man of his status. Nothing mattered any more, not really. His world was only half a world with no Julie and their beloved daughters in it.

'Oh Ellis, I'm so sorry. I shouldn't be so nosy. It's none of my business.' She reached out and touched his hand as he'd touched hers. 'I've hurt you now. Made you remember unhappy things.'

Ellis shrugged, and gave her the sort of smile that was a hard fight.

'You haven't hurt me, Jess. Not at all. What happened to me happened . . . I can't change that. And I don't mind talking about it, not really. It's a fact of my life and I deal with it. I should talk about Julie and the girls more. It'd probably be cathartic.'

Did he mean that?

'Well, I've more to do on this . . .' Jess nodded at the sketch, which did need more modelling. 'You can always talk to me, while I work. If you think it'd help?'

The air seemed to still. Why had she said that? Hadn't she prompted enough anguish already?

'You're a kind woman, Jess,' said Ellis quietly, settling his right hand back onto the table, and letting it go loose when Jess reached out to adjust the position. It was a yielding somehow, and more than physical. 'In that sense, you remind me of Julie. She was sensible, compassionate, understanding . . .'

'I'm not perfect. I think bad thoughts about people, and I get cross sometimes. Lash out a bit, you know?' She remembered raging sometimes to her sister, about how things had turned out, then afterwards feeling the deepest remorse, and trying to make amends in any way she could.

'Julie was cross with me. That last day, five years ago.' Ellis's voice was so low, Jess hardly dare breathe, or look at him. She focused hard on the image on the paper.

'She was right to be,' he went on. 'I'd promised a family day. Made quite a big thing of it, and the girls were excited . . . and then I'd had to back out at the last minute, and deal with a sudden crisis at work. When we parted, there was a chilly edge between us . . . which was quite rare, because we were usually the best at ironing out our snags.' Jess was studying his right hand, but peripherally, she was aware of his left hand too, and the way he was running his thumb to and fro across the inner face of his wedding ring. A compulsive action of which he probably wasn't even aware.

'But she knew you loved her. It was just a hiccup,' she pointed out gently.

'Yes, but the last time I ever saw her, she was frowning at me. And I could tell that Annie and Lily were picking up on it.' The thumb rubbed and rubbed. 'She texted me later from the shopping mall where she'd taken the girls. A few sweet words. It was just like her . . . I was going to reply, but I never got the chance. By then she was gone, and they were gone. Shot by some lunatic on a rampage. And I should have been there to protect her. To protect them all.'

Jess shot him a look. He was staring at his hand on the table, his face strangely composed. No hint of tears now. Numb, really.

That's it. The core of the loss and guilt. The reason you have to shut down and not allow yourself to feel.

She wanted to say he shouldn't blame himself. But she knew she'd have blamed herself in his place. It *wasn't* his fault, but he still felt responsible. A bit like her own feelings when she'd eventually given in, and had to seek a place in professional care for her gran. It wasn't her fault things had turned out that way, but still she felt guilty. Even now.

Ellis looked up at her, then down at his left hand, shaking his head, then relaxing fingers and thumb. 'Actually, I think I do feel a bit better for that. Thank you, Jess.' He gave her a small, wry smile, and a sort of ripple seemed to pass through him, a bracing up. 'Now, let's have another look at this.' He reached out and took her small drawing pad in his hand and studied it more closely. 'You know, you shouldn't be working in an insurance office – even one of *my* insurance offices – if you can do *this*! You should be making art all the time. Really you should.'

Confession time was over, precious as it had been. Scary as it had been. With an effort, Jess filed the moment away, turning a key on it as she sensed he wanted her to. She too focused on the drawing.

Did he really mean what he'd just said? Did he really think art was a viable future for her? Most people who knew about her drawing admired her work, and a couple of people had even bought sketches, but at an art group she'd once joined, then left again shortly after, there'd been some cuttingly patronising observations.

'I think I'm too naively representational to be a real artist. Too figurative. I just draw what I see, or see in my imagination, and sometimes I just copy from photographs.'

Ellis gave her a level glance. Thank God, he seemed to be shaking off the pain she'd almost forced on him. 'I like representational. I like things to look like what they are. And all these pseuds who pay thousands for square blobs of grey paint and the like . . . well, they want their heads testing!' He gave her a more playful smile. 'And that includes my mother. She has a Rothko, a Pollock and at least one de Kooning, and she thinks they're the bee's knees. But me, I'd far rather have *this* on my wall than splodges and splatters worth millions.' He pointed to her sketch.

'You're proving to be very good for my creativity, Ellis. I got extra special praise at life class this week, because of you.' She blushed, remembering how every study of the male model had turned out as Ellis himself.

'How so?' He gave her a wicked smirk, as if he already knew what she'd been up to.

'Well, even though we had a perfectly good male model, every drawing I did seemed to end up looking a bit like you.'

'Really?' The grin broadened. 'So you've compromised my reputation, have you? Naughty girl.'

'It's all right. Nobody will recognise you with your clothes on.'

'Even so, it's still taking a bit of a liberty, isn't it?' He winked at her. 'I think you owe me for using me as a muse without my permission.'

He was working around to something. Something risqué and sexual. She was glad of it. And not just because she was rapidly becoming addicted to the risqué and the sexual with him, but because it would distract his attention away from the sad thoughts that had descended upon him a few moments ago; the ever-present grief over the death of his family. At least in this, the physical, she could help him.

Bring it on, Mr Sex. I'm ready, willing and able to oblige you.

'What were you thinking of in terms of a recompense? You know I'm not exactly an accomplished sensualist yet. You're going to have to give me a nudge in the right direction.'

'Bullshit, Miss Lockhart, you're a sensualist to your very fingertips. It's all there. I think the fact that you're an artist proves it. All you needed was the slightest bit of encouragement.' He beamed at her, his eyes dancing. He'd obviously already decided what he wanted, and mentally sifting through the activity cards of what they'd done and what was yet to be attempted, Jess had a pretty good idea what it might be. Reaching for her water bottle, she took a sip to freshen her mouth, then ran her tongue around her lips in a way she hoped was sufficiently provocative.

'God, you're a hot piece! I don't think I've ever known a woman as quick on the uptake.'

Jess suspected that his wife might have been such a woman – Ellis and Julie must have been totally attuned to each other – but it was best not to mention that right now.

'Do you want what I think you want?' She pushed her chair away from the table. Making ready . . .

'Of course I do.' Ellis did the same too, swinging out to sit at right angles to the table, and setting his feet wide apart on the tiled kitchen floor. He was barefoot, and she got the urge again to kiss the source of his childhood pain, but she suspected that he'd prefer her not to dally. With a slow nod, he indicated that she get down on the floor, between his thighs. In the lap of his robe there was significant tenting.

Jess slipped into place, opening her own robe as she went. Ellis's eyes flared with heat, his glance darting from her breasts to her pubis as if the sight were entirely new and delectable to him. Her body warmed, blushed. Part excitement, part pride in herself and her own desirability that Ellis had revealed to her.

Tugging on his sash, she parted the wings of his robe and his erection sprang up at her, rosy and fierce.

'How long has it been like that?' she asked, eyeing the magnificent totem.

'Pretty much since I picked up a certain pretty but

slightly waterlogged woman and gave her a lift to her workplace.'

'Don't talk daft.'

'It's not daft,' said Ellis, gently mocking her northern phraseology. 'You excite me, Jess. You set the blood flowing to the critical zones every time I see you, every time I think about you.' He took himself in hand, lightly drawing his fingertips up and down his length. 'Would you believe that when I've been in London, there have been nights that I've had to masturbate like a teenager to get to sleep because I couldn't stop thinking about fucking you?'

Jess's blush deepened. God, he was a thrill! 'Was that before or after you'd actually had me?'

'Both.' He leant back in his chair, pushing his robe well out of the way. 'Kiss me, Jess. Lick me. Caress me with your sweet lips and your nimble wicked tongue.'

'It might not be all that nimble,' she pointed out, almost cross-eyed in her intimate proximity to Ellis's erect cock. This was the closest look at it she'd got so far, seeing detail she'd never observed in the at-rest specimens at life class. For a moment, the artist in her battled with her lust. What a challenge it would be to draw this thing before she fellated it!

'Your tongue is very clever when we kiss . . . just do the same.' Ellis adjusted his position in the chair, making himself even more inviting. Jess hid a grin. He'd slightly misconstrued her hesitation there. 'Kiss whichever bit of it you fancy, as a start.'

She licked her lips, and leant forward.

The head of Ellis's cock was very shiny, the taut

rosy skin coated in a veil of slippy-silky pre-come that was flowing from the tiny love-eye. With closed lips at first, she pressed her mouth against the tempting plum-shape. One kiss. Then another, moving around the head, exploring. The pre-cursive fluid was slick against her lips, and when she parted them, and sampled it, the taste was bland. A little musky, a little salty, but not in a strong way.

'Yes, that's nice. Do more of that. You're a natural, my darling. You're amazing.'

Not sure that such praise was merited – quite yet – Jess found that what was natural was the desire and urge to lick. Her tongue seemed to know what it was doing, at first cautiously, and then more boldly sweeping over his contours. She swept around the groove that demarked his glans, first from one side then the other, then returned to the very particular little indentation, a kind of notch, on the underside. When she furled her tongue to a point and jabbed there, Ellis moaned like a soul in torment and clasped his hands around her head.

'Oh yes . . . oh hell yes . . . that's the sweet spot, Jess. Oh, that's so good, you clever little goddess. Do more of that.'

Your wish is my command, she would have said, as he'd done, but her lips and tongue were otherwise fully occupied.

She swirled and slithered and flickered at him, but always came back to that sensitive notch, and the finely raised filament that pointed down the underside of his cock from it. He shouted out her name again when she dashed her tongue rapidly back and forth right there.

While he was still shaking his head from side to side and praising her to high heaven, Jess decided to try something a little different. Grasping Ellis's length in her hand, she lightly ran her fingertips up and down the upper side, while caressing the ridge below with the flat of her thumb.

If she hadn't been using her mouth on Ellis, Jess would have smiled again. Grinned. Laughed out loud. Shouted out herself, in triumph. The sense of power was intoxicating. The control she had over him. She might be the one on her knees, in the supposedly subservient pose, but she'd never felt more in command of a situation before in her life. Ellis was a slave to sensation, a slave to the pleasure she was giving him. A pleasure she could increase or deny as the whim took her. A pleasure that seemed to flow through her and transmute into gold within her own body.

Using her mouth on Ellis was making her own sex rouse and grow hot. Desire ground low in her loins, and she knew that even if her lover-man was going to be pretty much incapable for a short while when she'd finished with him, she would take her own pleasure, her own release, at her own hand.

'Oh Jess, Jess . . . suck me. Suck me now.' His voice was a ragged edge, yet warm. He wanted her to do him, but there was still a respect for her there, despite his near delirium. He honoured her, and was grateful for her gift to him.

Very well then . . . seeing as it's you.

Smiling inwardly, she parted her lips, let him in, and began to suck.

*

Oh, holy hell, she was amazing!

Ellis dug his fingers into Jess's thick dark hair, trying not to be rough, but not quite in control of himself. The way her tongue danced, the deep, sweet suction she was orchestrating. The way she handled him as she used her mouth; the sight of her perfect, lithe body crouched at his feet. That was, when he was able to see straight in the midst of the sublime pleasure she was creating.

How can you do this? Your first time sucking a man . . . You're a prodigy, a divine genius, beautiful Jess Lockhart.

If it had been any other woman since Julie, he would have now have been questioning her claims of inexperience. Such mouth skills as these were exceptional even in women who'd been pleasuring men for years.

He believed Jess utterly though. She was all truth and honesty, and she'd been a physical virgin, there'd been patent proof of that. In another woman, he might have suspected one that 'did everything but fuck', but not Jess.

She'd been a consummate fantasist, that was for certain, her erotic daydreams no doubt rich and vivid, fuelled by art and sensual reading and perhaps other sources of erotica.

But in every way that mattered, she'd come to him in innocence. He *knew* that. He'd been her first fuck . . . and now he was the first man to whom she'd ever given head.

Oh, you lucky, lucky bugger, McKenna. You're arrogant, capricious and contrary, and you still get rewarded with this!

This . . . an increase in delectable, devilish suction. This . . . virtuoso fondling with the tips of her fingers and thumbs, travelling up and down his shaft, and also experimentally and with sublime delicacy, straying over his tensing balls and the excruciatingly sensitive plain of his perineum.

Her fingertips danced like fairy feet over his genitals, while her lips and tongue were those of an angel divine. White, boiling sensation surged down his spine like a wave, and his hips started to buck.

No! He couldn't just do that!

How the fuck could he stop himself?

'Jess . . . Jess . . . let me slip out. You don't have to let me come in your mouth.' His voice sounded like an alien's, not his, torn to shreds by the fight not to ejaculate.

His closed eyes snapped open. She wasn't letting go. When he looked down at her, there was a supreme smile of triumph in her eyes.

Beautiful, despite having her lips stretched around him, her face blazed with power, and as her tongue jabbed hard at his tender spot, he growled out her name and shot his seed into the warm haven of her mouth.

18

Afterwards, he swept her up to bed and made love to her slowly and thoroughly, mapping her body for all the places where she best liked to be touched. And the ways she liked to be touched and kissed there.

Fierce kisses on the side of the neck while he was fucking her sent her into orbit!

'I must be into vampires.' Jess touched her fingertips to a spot close to where her neck met her shoulder. It was tender. 'Have you marked me?'

Ellis sat up and leant in close. 'A little bit. You might have to put a bit of makeup on that at work.' He kissed it again, exquisitely gently this time, stroking the little reddened place with his tongue. 'Or you could take a few days off on the sick. Nobody's going to dare sack you or discipline you now, you know.'

'I do know. I get some very funny looks around the place at Windsor now. Both from bosses and other employees. I'm sure they're all dying with curiosity, desperate to know whether anything happened as a result of that performance of yours in the office.'

'I'm sorry,' said Ellis with a shamefaced grin, 'I was terrible, wasn't I?'

'Not terrible,' countered Jess, sitting up, and automatically tweaking the sheet over her breasts. It still seemed weird to be in a bed with a man. 'But certainly noteworthy. Things like that don't normally happen at Windsor. In fact I think they probably don't happen in most insurance company buildings. Except in films . . .'

Ellis was looking at the sheet. Jess shrugged and let it drop. His smile widened, yet somehow, it wasn't a desiring leer, more a satisfaction that she was relaxing her inhibitions when they weren't making love, as well as when they were.

'Believe me, it *is* the first time I've done something like that in a business or workplace environment. I like to drop in on acquisitions, and surprise the management teams. But I've never hijacked a woman before . . .' His eyes lowered a moment, as if veiling a thought from far away, another life, perhaps. 'Although I once swept Julie out of a very, very posh party so I could make love to her. Not long after we first went to bed.' Ah, she'd been right . . . the ghost of Julie was always with him. The woman he'd loved so deeply. The wife he probably still loved as much as when she'd been alive.

'I hope she told you off for being imperious.' Jess was surprised at her own words. She hoped she'd not spoken out of turn, but somehow she was almost coming to know Julie, through Ellis, and to feel a kinship with her. She was relieved though, when he smiled broadly.

'She did. In that respect she was much like you. She didn't take any shit from me, I can tell you.'

Jess didn't know what to say at that, but suddenly, with a flourish, Ellis threw the sheet aside. 'We left your drawing book down in the kitchen. I'd like to see some of the other work in it. I think I'll go and fetch it. Can I get you anything while I'm down there? Something to eat? Or drink? A glass of wine?'

She'd not wanted alcohol earlier, but now, a glass of something not too strong would go down nicely. 'Mm . . . yes. I wouldn't mind some wine.'

'White? Red? Rosé? Champagne?'

'What? You've got rosé? I didn't think wealthy sophisticates approved of pink plonk for the masses.'

Ellis laughed, reaching for his robe and shrugging into it. What a shame to cover such a body up, but hey. 'I might have plenty of money, but I'm no sophisticate, Jess my sweet. I'm a total philistine, really. Much to my mother's chagrin.' He strode to the door. 'Rosé it is . . . and some nibbles. Making love to you makes me really hungry.' He winked at her. 'Back in a trice, baby!'

Jess took the opportunity of Ellis's kitchen raid to dash to the bathroom and freshen up. Like the kitchen, the master bathroom was modern and beautifully appointed. The major rooms that had been restored so far were more in keeping with the house's Queen Anne history, but clearly some rooms were entirely new in the renovation. In front of the big mirror, she studied her reflection, looking for more differences, more signs of her new eroticised state.

You just look the same . . . only a bit more so.

She was still herself, but somehow ever so slightly larger than life, as if some of Ellis's special charisma had flowed into her via osmosis when they'd been joined. Or maybe it was her own specialness? And sex had made it flower?

On the shelf in front of her, she studied Ellis's toiletries. Cologne, shaving lotion, something called 'skin and stubble balm'; all with a white label as if they'd been specially blended and formulated for him. Only the best for Mr McKenna.

At the end of the shelf, in a space he'd obviously cleared for her, bless him, she'd placed her own bits and pieces. Because to her great surprise, he'd invited her to share his bedroom. To sleep with him. All night.

'Um . . . are you sure?' she'd asked. 'I was assuming you didn't actually sleep with your conquests. I thought that was something you . . . well . . . would only have done with your wife?'

He blinked, looking at her, clearly surprised. 'To be honest, I've never actually brought a woman here before. I've invited lovers to my London pad, and to various hotels, but never here.' He gave her a wide grin. 'You're the first.'

But not the last . . . probably.

That thought, now, cast her down a bit. But she gave herself a stern inner shaking. The rules of this arrangement must never be forgotten. She could allow herself to be fond of him – hell, she couldn't stop herself, she was already infatuated at least – but possessive thoughts, and 'forever' thoughts were forbidden.

He isn't Mr Right. He's Mr Handsome, Mr Rich, Mr

Generous and Mr Sex, but that's it. And that's good. That's the deal.

Shaking her head, she fluffed up her hair, attempting to dispel her disquieting detour and focus on the now.

Yet she couldn't. Not entirely. It was too late. She wouldn't allow herself to say the words. Or even think them.

But picturing Ellis in her mind – his eyes and his smile, and every wonderful thing about him – the twist in her heart said everything the forbidden word couldn't.

He was waiting for her when she emerged, flipping through her Moleskine. A bottle of wine stood in a cooler on the bedside table at his side, and he'd already poured two glasses.

'Are all these hands and eyes and ears and mouths mine then?' he enquired, passing her wine to her.

'Yes, I must admit they are. You're pretty much my muse at the moment. Hence your unexpected appearance at my life class.' She took a sip of the rosé. Ooh, it was nice. A girly wine, but Ellis seemed to be enjoying it too. She didn't have many other men of her acquaintance, but the few she did have would have pulled a face at pink wine.

He grinned, almost radiantly. 'I've never been a muse. I rather like the idea. It makes me feel really valued.'

Jess frowned. 'Don't you feel valued because of the work you do?'

'Pah! Just pushing money around . . . anybody can do that. But being a "muse", now that must be rare.'

'I guess it is. I've never really had a regular one before. Apart from an actor in a vampire show once.

I drew him a lot at the time. He was a blond though. Not a bit like you, but hot all the same.'

'Do you have any pictures of him?'

'Oh no . . . well, yes, I do. But a lot of my framed stuff and my art materials are in storage, with my gran's old belongings.' She frowned again, realising how she'd let her art aspirations lapse in recent years. Circumstances and all that, but still. 'I've not done as much as I should recently. It was difficult to work on anything big when I was looking after Gran, and afterwards it just seemed like too much of an effort to start with paints or pastels and the easel and the whole shebang. I just drew in notebooks to keep my hand in, and signed up for the occasional class, now and again.'

'You shouldn't let it lapse, but I can understand why. I used to do all sorts of things before Julie's death, family activities mostly . . . but since then, it's mainly been work, a bit of exercising, and reading and watching television. Pathetic, really.'

'And the occasional woman,' Jess pointed out.

'Yes, the occasional woman.' He grinned.

So, I'm just a part of one of his 'hobbies'.

'A self-indulgence?'

He had the grace to look shamefaced. 'Yes, you could say that. Sounds a bit despicable, doesn't it? As if I treat women as a disposable commodity.'

It did. A bit. Yet there were extenuating circumstances.

'We all have to do what we have to do to get by.'

He gave her a long, considering look. 'We do. I'll drink to that.' He leant across and clinked his glass to hers.

The rosé was delectable, fresh and sweet and fruity. Very, very cool. It wasn't strong, but suddenly she wished it was, a bit.

'And you, how do you get by? I . . . I feel that's what you're doing, Jess, getting by. Instead of living life to the full.'

He was right, so right, but the truth hit hard. She'd been marking time so long she'd almost come to accept that as the norm. Waiting for Mr Right. Waiting and hoping that her gran would get better, even long after she'd known that was impossible. And afterwards left with a void where all that waiting and hoping had been. To her horror, tears threatened, but she fought them, taking a deep swig of her wine. No way did she want Ellis to feel sorry for her. It was demeaning, and she wanted to keep things light, and fun for both of them. Focus on the sex weekend.

Her glass was empty and, wordlessly, Ellis reached out with the bottle and topped her up. There was sympathy on his face, but more than that, almost as if he understood the complexity of her feelings, the mirror of his own.

Gah, no getting away from it.

'Yeah, yeah, yeah . . . okay, so I am marking time. I have been for months . . . years . . . I suppose I've just got into the habit of hiding from life.' The tears welled up again, and this time she couldn't quell them. 'How pathetic is that?'

Blinking, she sipped more wine, staring at the shimmering pink. But after a moment, Ellis reached out and took the glass from her, and a moment later, he put a box of tissues within hand's reach, the same kind he'd given her when they'd first met. Then, he shuffled across and put his arm around her, easing them together back against the pillows.

Oh hell, don't blubber, you silly sod!

Jess crammed half a box of Kleenex against her face. She tried to sit up. She wanted to create distance between the beautiful, glamorous man at her side, and herself, the snivelling, spluttering, unattractive wreck. But Ellis wouldn't allow it. He increased his cradling hold on her, wrapping both arms around her, and raising one hand to stroke her hair and encourage her to bury her face in his towelling-clad shoulder.

Oh God, it felt so good. She needed this! She had Cathy and other friends that she talked to. She spoke on the phone with Mel, her sister, often. Mel visited whenever she could, so it wasn't as if she was without people in her life.

But none of that was the same as the simple comfort of arms around her, the hugs she'd lost when the woman who'd brought her up had died.

Alas, though, the relief of being held only freed the floodgates of long held-in weeping. Grabbing on to Ellis with one arm, and blotting her face continually with her free hand, Jess surrendered herself to it. If being a weeping ninny temporarily dissolved whatever attractiveness she'd had for him, so be it. Ellis wasn't shallow, and he knew pain himself. She'd never imagined she'd release emotion like this with any man, not even the eventual Mr Right, but with Ellis McKenna, it seemed okay.

After a moment, as the storm began to abate, it dawned on her that Ellis was talking quietly to her, his voice gentle and soothing. Most of his discourse seemed to consist of 'hush' and 'it'll be all right' and 'let it all out', and other variations on that theme, but even though it made her feel slightly like a hysterical child or a panicking pet or something, she relished the warm, nurtured feeling it gave her. An educational sex weekend was all well and good, but there was a lot to be said for a bit of good, old-fashioned TLC too.

'I'm sorry,' she said at last, when her voice came out normally instead of accompanied by hiccups. 'You must think I'm a total idiot and about as sexy and seductive as a floor mop.'

'You're a strong, compassionate woman with real feelings. I'm honoured that you'd open up to me. I prefer that. I prefer honesty and a real person rather than someone who brushes the deep stuff aside and just acts like a sex kitten all the time.' He reached out and smoothed her hair out of her eyes. 'You're beautiful on every level, Jess Lockhart, believe me.'

'What, even with red eyes and a red nose?' She managed a smile. She couldn't help it. The sheer glow of him would lift the lowest of spirits, even if she thought he was probably bullshitting her a bit.

'Even then.' He gathered up some of the tissues and tossed them in the general direction of the waste bin by the bedside table. Most of them went on the floor, but he seemed not to notice. 'And believe me, Jess, I do know how you feel and I respect those feelings. You lost someone you love, just as much as I've lost Julie and Annie and Lily.' He pursed his lips, as if fighting emotions of his own.

Wondering if the two losses were comparable, Jess still nodded.

'Thank you, Ellis. Thank you for being a very decent man.' She paused, aware that she'd stirred up his own grief for him. 'I didn't mean to come here and remind you of . . . of what you've lost too. Some kind of fun sexy companion to distract you from all that, aren't I? This is supposed to be an erotic education weekend, not my misery-fest.'

'There's plenty of time yet. And we've got to pace ourselves, haven't we?' His beautiful eyes twinkled. 'It's *quality* not quantity that's preferable, I think . . . Don't you?'

But it's all quality with you.

She didn't say it, but nodded in agreement. 'Quite right, Mr Sex. Especially for a novice like me. In the novels they go at it hammer and tongs for hours on end. It's a wonder the heroines can walk sometimes, the amount of action they've had.'

Ellis laughed softly. 'I'd rather have you in a fit state to appreciate my mad sex skills, Ms Lockhart, than gratuitously over-fucked, just to slake my appetites. And right now, I think it would be nice to get some sleep, and refresh our batteries for a deliciously sensual and educational day tomorrow, eh?'

Surprisingly, she did feel sleepy all of a sudden. 'Good idea. But are you sure you want me here? I don't mind sleeping in a guest room or whatever, if you need your space.'

'I'm quite sure. Do you want a spot more wine, to help you sleep?'

'No. Thanks. I'm good.'

But was she 'good'? she wondered as they made their preparations for sleep. She'd shared a bed with him before, but somehow now, it seemed so much more intimate here. Back at home it'd been casual, almost accidental, but this was a conscious act of closeness.

And as strange as it was wonderful to a person who'd never shared her bed with anyone ever in her life . . . except this man.

Yet when she tried to sleep, frustratingly, it wouldn't come.

Perhaps it was the strangeness of another body in the bed, even though Ellis was not a duvet hog, an over-hugger or a spreader-outer. In fact he slept still and neatly, on his back, with one arm draped backwards over the pillow, like a male model posing for an Old Master. The curtains were open, and moonlight sliced across the room, illuminating him and adding to the sense of a work of art. Moving as covertly as she could, Jess eased up into a sitting position, so she could admire him, feast on his beauty.

Ellis's handsome face was serene in sleep, and she experienced an almost overpowering urge to reach out and trace its contours with her fingertips. Even in the intense milky moonlight, there wasn't quite enough light to set about drawing him, but she would have loved to attempt to capture him right at that moment.

He was the perfect subject. His tousled hair, his straight nose and full, sensual mouth framed in that demi-beard that always felt so strangely soft . . . even when it had brushed her inner thighs when he'd given her head. She'd always believed that kissing and making love with a bearded man would be less than ideal. All that scritchy-scratchiness and stubble. But somehow, with Ellis, the sensation of whiskers only added to the deliciousness of every kiss.

A great sigh gusted through her. It wasn't just his cute little beard, or his gorgeous eyes, or his superb body. It was far more than that which had dazzled and ensorcelled her in such a very short space of time. It was the man himself, his kindness, his strength and also his vulnerability.

She was obsessed now, she knew it, and more.

Oh, bloody hell. I love you, Ellis McKenna. It's ridiculous, and I don't know how it's happened so fast. I knew I shouldn't have let you get close. I should probably never have succumbed to you. Never have agreed to the sex education thing . . .

But inside, it had always been impossible to say no, and now she was in far too deep, hooked too firmly. And possibly forever.

Even if he asked to see her again – to extend their relationship to his customary three or four weeks – it would probably be a good idea to gently part from him after this weekend. It would only hurt more if she didn't make the break as soon as possible. Right now, he was still mourning his wife, and might always mourn her. And even if, eventually, he got past the most painful stage of his grief, it might not be for a long, long time. It might be years before he was ready to even get close to love again . . . Years after his interlude with her was long over, long forgotten.

I know I'm not unworthy because I'm not rich or famous.

I know I've got desirable qualities . . . and a lot to offer you . . . but you're just not ready for me, Ellis, are you? Not yet.

Even though she was trying to keep still and not disturb him, she couldn't contain another deep sigh.

I've arrived too soon in your life to be your second wife.

There. Now she'd said it, if only to herself. She'd barely known Ellis McKenna two weeks, and the parameters of their brief relationship had been clearly laid out from the very beginning . . .

Just as she'd always known would happen, she'd subconsciously recognised Mr Right the instant she'd first seen him. Fallen head over heels in love in the rain.

Slowly, carefully, she lay down again, closing her eyes but still seeing Ellis.

Mr Right, but Mr Emotionally Unattainable. The man I love who can never love me back.

Ellis sat up in the moonlight and looked down at the woman lying beside him. She was still as a mouse, a vision of breathtaking beauty in the silvery glow flooding in through the gauze curtains at the window. That image of a pure Madonna-like figure came to him again, but still, the tiny, barely discernible frown on her forehead told him she was probably actually awake, or only dozing in the same troubled, shallow sleep from which he'd just surfaced.

What's wrong, Jess?

He almost said the words, then stalled. What if she said the words he subconsciously feared? The words he didn't want to hear because he could never,

ever reciprocate. Even the idea of reciprocating filled him with guilt. It would be a betrayal. Not Jess's fault, just his.

You can't give her anything meaningful, man. You're empty of all that now. You gave it all to Julie. There's nothing left for another woman on that score, even if she's adorable. And you'll only hurt her if you don't disabuse her of any false hopes you've already given her.

And yet . . . and yet . . . he must have her for a little while longer. He was too greedy for her loveliness. A good man would sit Jess down for a firm but gentle chat tomorrow, and suggest that they part as lovers but remain solely friends from now on. He could still help. Still support her in her future goals. She had to stop working at his stupid insurance company because she was totally wasted in that world.

His spirits lifted. Yes, they could be friends. He could be her sponsor. Her own high principles meant she'd cruelly missed out on a formal art education, but he could give her that now. He could open doors for her. Make it possible for her to make a living using her God-given talents in a creative future that fulfilled her.

Oh, really, Mr Philanthropy? While your body is still howling for her other God-given talents?

Even now, with such 'noble' thoughts in his mind, he was getting a hard-on. Even knowing it was madness to continue this, his lizard-brain was chanting fuck, fuck, fuck.

As if she'd sensed his inner turmoil, she started to stir, and he almost smiled. She was trying to feign a natural rousing, when they both knew she'd been lying awake, turning things over in her mind, just as he'd been turning them over in his mind too.

'Can't you sleep, Jess?'

She blinked, and her eyes snapped open, brilliant with full awareness and no hint of sleepiness. In the moonlight, she gave him a nervous little grin that only increased her irresistibility. It was all unaffected, sweetly natural, but it only made him want her more, even though her delicious body was completely covered, right up to her chin.

'I did sleep a bit . . . but I guess I'm just not used to being in bed with another person.' The little frown pleated more deeply. 'I like it, really I do, but it's just different, you know?'

'True. Very different.' In an attempt to be altruistic, and do what was best for her, he said, 'Would you prefer a bed of your own, Jess? You might be able to sleep then. I'll go to one of the guest rooms, and leave you in peace.'

'No!' She reached out for him, her hand warm on his forearm as he sat up. 'Don't go. I'm sure I'll be able to sleep.' The act of reaching for him had caused the sheet to slip, revealing her breasts. Ellis's cock lurched to hard, heavy stiffness just at the sight.

Good God, man, you're an animal.

But he couldn't help himself. He wanted her so much, and when she moved uneasily, she brushed against him and that made her smile.

'That might help me sleep.' Her grin was so sultry, so beguiling. Everything about her dazzled him, especially her deep, innate sensuality. Again, he exulted in being the first man to tap that vein of fundamental sexy womanliness, even though he was far from worthy of the gift.

'It'd certainly help *me* sleep.' He moved in again, pressing himself against her. Her body was warm, fragrant and cuddly. Cuddly but so desirable he could barely see straight. He wanted to enfold her in his arms, rock himself against her, touch her and pleasure her. 'We should make love like spoons . . . that's a nice, drowsy, easy way to do it in the middle of the night. Snuggly . . . not too athletic. Much more fun than hot chocolate for getting off to sleep.'

'But I like hot chocolate.'

'So do I, but I like shagging more.' There were practicalities though. Momentarily he turned away, and plucked a condom from the nightstand. He'd tossed a few there earlier on, and there were still a couple left. 'Hold that thought while I rubber up.'

He enrobed himself by touch, his lower body still beneath the bedclothes. It was easy. He was so massively stiff. 'There, that's better!' He rolled in close again, throwing an arm around her hips, turning and drawing her to him, her sweet rounded bottom against his aching groin.

If you were a decent man, McKenna, this would be the last fuck. After tonight, you should back away from sex with her. Not let things get too complex. For her sake as much as yours.

He wasn't sure he could do that. He *had* to have this weekend. The prospect of it was too exquisite to cut short . . . but when it was over he would attempt to make a clean, kind break with her, because it was the best thing *for* her. Now was now though and he had the most divinely seductive woman against him, her body warm and willing. He'd make it sweet and good for her tonight – even if that wicked lizard-brain was suddenly entertaining lurid notions about the firm lobes of her bottom, stroking it and maybe a little light spanking. More education to be imparted there, but probably not by him. Not if he were to do the right thing.

'Now, let's arrange ourselves, gorgeous. Tilt your hips and lift your thigh a bit . . . that's it. That's the right angle.' Guiding her limbs into position, he poised himself at her entrance, and reached around and down to test her readiness. She was a slender woman, and she seemed to fit him perfectly. There was no awkwardness, no arm going to sleep; she seemed to know exactly how to conform herself to him.

And she was wet! Deliciously slippery. He'd been wondering about lube, because this was still all so new to her. But her body was totally prepared to receive him, silky and welcoming. With a further little tilt of her hips, she silently invited him to proceed. So, gripping her by the waist, he did just that.

Oh heaven . . . oh heaven . . . Jess's sex was tight, but sublimely accommodating, letting him in but also gripping him at the same time, an inner caress.

'Mm . . . that's so good. You feel so good, Jess. So perfect.' The words were banal, but the glorious sensations dissolved his vocabulary, almost stripped him of his mind, leaving only pure feeling and happiness, without the complications of emotional analysis and the inner whirl of right-wrong-right-wrong. Right here, right now was where they both should be, bodies joined, and to hell with tomorrow.

Sliding his hand around and between her thighs, he dived in with his fingers to stroke her folds and her clit. His touch made her moan and wriggle and contract herself around him and the way that felt on his cock made him clench his teeth, fighting for control. Hell, this was supposed to be gentle and lazy and easy and he was a wild man already. He blinked hard and grimaced, glad she couldn't see him fighting not to thrust like a raving maniac and come straight away.

Focusing, he stroked her, loving the delicacy and responsiveness of the hot flesh beneath his fingers. There was a piquant pleasure in playing his fingers against her entrance too, where their bodies were joined, and his latex clad cock was buried in her. He dabbled there, and she reciprocated by massaging him. He could feel the tense and relax, tense and relax from both within and without.

Concentrate, you bastard, he told himself sternly. *Concentrate on Jess and on giving her pleasure*.

He returned his attention to her clitoris, rolling it and playing with it, swirling his fingertip around it as if it were a smooth, living jewel.

'Oh yes, oh yes,' she chanted, squirrelling her divine bottom against him, her nether cheeks against his belly, their shape inducing those tricky thoughts of putting her across his knee and playing other such tantalising games.

Cool it, idiot. Think of Jess, not your fucking self.

With his free arm tight around her, and his fingers moving rhythmically between her thighs, he jerked his hips in short, shallow thrusts. He didn't need to be deep. The sensations were miraculous, and even more of a miracle was her high, sweet cry and the way her body began to clench and clench and clench around him as she came.

Knowing he could relax now, he released his guard . . . and thrust deep, coming gratefully with a long, heartfelt groan.

Here comes the rain again . . .

The next morning, it was teeming down, a heavier downfall than the one that had first brought them together, almost as if the heavens were conspiring to keep them sequestered in the house. In intimate proximity. With no semi-awkward thoughts about 'going for walks' and getting out and taking some other exercise, they had the perfect excuse for staying in and making love.

The perfect excuse for making the best of our limited time before we part.

But it wasn't all sex and, despite her concerns, Jess was astonished again and again to discover how easy and companionable it was to be around Ellis out of bed. He didn't make her feel as if she had to be 'on' all the time, or make constant conversation. Over breakfast they read the papers together, making only occasional commentary, as if they'd been sharing their coffee and croissants all their lives.

'You don't really live very much like a billionaire at all, do you?' She looked around the kitchen. It was beautifully restored and had every modern appliance tastefully integrated, but the fact that they were in it, alone, having prepared their own breakfast, only attested to his modest way of living. 'I mean, Windermere Hall is lovely, but it's not huge and dripping with gold fittings and wall to wall bling, is it? And you've no vast armies of lackeys at your beck and call either.' She appraised him, too, currently dressed in his robe. 'And most of the time, you don't really dress like a high-flying businessman either, do you?'

Sitting opposite her, Ellis poured two large breakfast cups of coffee. He might not ever really look or act the billionaire part, but he still took her breath away. Just the triangle of lightly tanned flesh in the neckline of his dressing gown was getting her going.

'Oh, I've got those battalions of PAs and lackeys a plenty on the business side, and staff who come in to muck out after me both here and at my London place, but I haven't really led the wealthy life all that much since I was a child, in my parents' world. After university, I pretty much grew out of that madness, and Julie preferred the simple life too, even though her family are almost as rich as mine.' He frowned as he set aside the cafetière. Was the brew too weak or too strong, or was it painful memories that made his smooth brow crumple? 'We had homes in both Australia and America, in fact several . . . but they were . . . are . . . quite modest places compared to the sorts of pads our families have in those countries.'

He edged her cup towards her, and when she added milk, it was the perfect colour. 'So, where do your parents live at the moment?' While talking about his wife wasn't entirely a no-go area, it did seem to make him melancholy, so a change or slight shift of subject was in order.

'My father mainly lives in the States, where the primary power base of McKenna International is, and my mother lives in Australia. They're divorced, but thankfully, everything's very amicable between them. In fact they're still good friends. My mum has always had her own money too, so there was never any fighting over the settlement and she still retains some McKenna shares.' He sipped his own coffee and shrugged, then added a dash more milk.

'But you don't live in either country. So do you ever see them? Surely you must if you're running parts of the business empire or whatever.'

'They both have houses in London and in Scotland and elsewhere . . . I've lost track. I'm mainly based in London because I oversee European operations, so I visit them and we spend time together when they're in this country. Oh, and a great-aunt of mine owns a medium-sized Caribbean island, so sometimes various bits and pieces of the family go there for holidays.'

'Neutral ground for you?'

He nodded. Then heaved a sigh.

'Maybe I should take you there for one of your educational weekends?' Somehow, the enthusiasm had gone out of his voice.

'Ah, I see . . .' Jess didn't quite, but she could guess.

'I can't hide anything from you, can I? And yes, you're right, that was where Julie and I spent our honeymoon.'

'I'm sorry, I shouldn't have reminded you.'

He reached for her hand. 'Don't be sorry. The hang-ups are mine. You don't have to dance around anything to do with what's happened to me.' He took the hand he held, and conveyed it to his lips for a quick kiss. 'In fact, I probably should start revisiting places. I mean it . . . about the educational weekend on Augusta's island.'

'Oh, I don't know . . . What would your family think? How would you explain me?'

He squeezed her hand and released it, then pushed the plate of croissants to her. Carbs to calm the nerves. 'Don't worry, I've never considered that I have to explain myself or my friends or my life to any of them . . . And Aunt Augusta is a decent old bird. She doesn't really leave her bedroom all that much anyway because of her health issues. I have a shack of my own and my own beach there too, so we'd have total privacy, or we could mingle if you prefer, if anyone else is visiting.'

He was obviously just talking for the sake of talking. He'd never want to take another woman to his honeymoon hideaway.

Jess nibbled a piece of her croissant. 'You mean a shack like this shack?' She gestured around her at the fine kitchen, and the lovely Queen Anne house beyond.

'Well Blue Breezes is actually quite shack-like. In fact it's very small and rustic . . . But it does have all the amenities, water and electricity and so on.'

'It sounds idyllic.'

It did. She could imagine spending a weekend like this, just the two of them, enjoying each other's company, and each other's bodies, but under blue skies and alongside a long white beach, lapped by a warm sea. Perfect romance.

'It is,' said Ellis, 'you'd love it. I'll fix something

up for us if I can get away soon . . . and you can tear yourself away from the joys of insurance for a few days.'

'Deal,' said Jess, as they returned to their companionable perusal of the newspapers.

It won't happen. By the time you can get away, we'll probably no longer be together.

With an inner shrug, she pushed away that sobering thought.

Later, they lazed beside the indoor pool together, Ellis either reading reports of some business thing or other that Jess didn't enquire about, or working on his laptop, while she sketched and sketched and sketched in a free and inspired way that she hadn't achieved in a long time. For a while she'd been aware that her art was sometimes tighter and more constrained than it should be, but now that sense of constriction was totally gone.

It's you. You've set me free, she silently told the subject of most of these liberated new efforts. *Not just in sex, but everything else. I can't believe it.*

Most of the drawings she did were of Ellis, but she also tried a few little 'impressions' of the beautiful, airy, conservatory-like room and one or two small still lives. The tray with the jolly red teapot and their teacups; a potted palm, its fronds leaning gracefully over the tiles; Ellis's robe thrown over the back of his lounger-chair while he swam. She wished she'd brought her pastels and had had time to dig her easel and her watercolour paraphernalia out of storage, but that was probably straying a bit too far from the main purpose of the weekend.

Later in the morning, towards lunchtime, Ellis suggested that Jess have a swim too.

'But I haven't brought a costume.' It wasn't really a protest. There was no need to worry about stripping off now, not for the man who'd already seen her body, and deemed it beautiful. She wanted to get naked with Ellis at every opportunity. He'd made her love her own skin, and that was amazing.

'And your problem is?' Grinning, he stood up, shucked off his trunks, and kicked them aside.

'Nothing.' Jess answered his smile as she unfastened her cotton blouse. In a couple of moments, it and her jeans and her underwear had joined Ellis's swimming trunks, abandoned.

They swam for a while, lapping together. Jess had a shrewd idea that he was probably halving his pace so she could keep up with him though, and eventually, he paused in the deep end, drew her to him, and kissed her hard. He was fully erect and, embracing, they slipped and slid against each other, the water like warm silk around them.

Eventually, when Ellis drew away from her, he said, 'So, are you ready for lunch . . . or something else?' His eyes were like dark stars, and the expression in them made as clear as his rampant flesh did what appetite he planned on satisfying first.

The pool-side tiles were hard but Ellis made a bed for them of towels and lounger cushions and robes, then drew her down upon it. The pocket of one of those robes yielded a most convenient condom.

'Have you ever done a self-portrait?' he asked as she settled down upon him, her sex yielding to his cock as if that too was something that had been occurring easily and naturally for months and months.

'Not really . . . I've thought about it . . . Oh God,' she gasped as he reached forward and spread his hand across the dip of her groin, slipping his thumb into her cleft and settling on her clit.

'You should. I'd love a portrait of you.'

'But I'd have to use a mirror. It'd be reversed . . .' His caress made her shudder with exquisite sensation, even as the seed of interest, in a work of self-portraiture, took root.

'You'll look just as beautiful. You can try it in the big mirror, up in the bedroom . . . Later.' His thumb circled, circled and pressed. 'Now, come for me, Jess. Come for me now. I want to hear you moan.'

It was so easy to comply. It was happening almost before he said it. Her happy cry rang out, resounding and echoing off the surface of the water.

Later, Jess emerged from the bathroom, drying her hair, to find Ellis sitting in his bathrobe, on the ottoman at the foot of the bed, with her big sketch-book on his lap. He had a pencil in his hand, and was glancing intently from the surface of the paper, to the free-standing pier glass, which he'd moved from its place in the corner of the room right into the centre, a few feet from where he sat.

'What's this? Decided to have a crack at sketching?' Jess crossed the room to him, only to discover the paper was blank.

'I would like to learn, one day, but I was hoping you'd do that self-portrait for me.' Setting aside the sketch pad, he rose from his place, and made a sweeping, mock-courtly gesture, inviting her to sit down.

'I'm not sure I can . . .' How could she explain to him that it was probably one of the greatest challenges? Unless you were a total artistic genius, that was, and though she knew her own talent, she wasn't quite that amazing.

'Oh, you can. You can do anything, Jess.' He gave her a sultry smile, quirking his wicked eyebrows at her. 'Just look at all the other things you've learnt to do in the last week or so. You've discovered mad skills you never knew you had . . . from a standing start.'

'Well, that's easy . . . Like falling off a log.' She grinned at the echo of their exchange, that first night.

'Especially when you fall divinely off that log and onto my cock.'

'So refined, Mr McKenna.'

'But you have a rare natural talent for both drawing and sex, Ms Lockhart. It would be a shame not to leverage both those gifts to the full.' He glanced at the pristine, and yes, very tempting sheet of paper. 'Just give the self-portrait a try . . . Just for me.'

Why not? It would be an intriguing challenge. And somehow, she wasn't afraid to fail in front of Ellis. She'd always been very conscious of the times she didn't get something quite right before, especially at art class, but this strange yet wonderful man simply wasn't judgemental. She could trust him.

Really?

Really.

'Okay, I'll give it a shot, but I'm not promising any masterpieces, and I'll probably have to do a few preparatory sketches and finish the whole thing at some later time . . . when there's not quite as much distraction.' She winked at him, and prepared to sit down.

'Uh oh . . . that's not quite what I wanted.' Ellis nodded towards her, and it dawned on her that he was indicating the thick fluffy robe.

'I can't sit here starkers and draw myself!'

'Of course you can. What difference does it make? It's a warm room . . .' He moved closer to her, and reached to cup her face, dipping in for a quick but fierce kiss. 'And I know how much you like taking your clothes off for me, don't deny it.'

True. She'd stripped off and swum naked. Why not draw naked too? The heat in Ellis's eyes only stoked that new-found urge of hers to show off for him.

'Well, this'll be a first. Life drawing myself.' She tugged open the cord of her robe and then eased the loose garment off, first one arm then the other, leaving it pooled around her.

'I should hope it's a first!' Ellis exclaimed, laughing. 'Unless it's half and half posing and sketching at this class of yours.'

'No, I just draw. That hall is cold. I don't know how the models put up with it.' It was true, and goosebumps were very tricky to capture with charcoal.

The drawing pad felt very odd against her naked thighs, and the sight of herself in the mirror made her want to giggle as much as anything, even though the way Ellis was devouring her with his eyes was provoking other sensations too.

'Don't watch me! This is tricky enough as it is. Can't you read the paper or something?'

'You're a cruel woman, Jess Lockhart. You sit there looking like temptation incarnate and you want me to read the paper?' He was grinning though.

'Well, the self-portrait is your idea, mister.'

'Fair enough . . . I'll try not to make you nervous.' Reaching for his tablet from the bedside table, Ellis threw himself on the bed very theatrically and began to flick through pages. 'See, not looking!'

How long would that last? Not very, Jess suspected, but she set to work.

The task wasn't quite as difficult as she'd antici-pated. It was just a case of laying down the basic forms, like any other life drawing. Ovals, rounded corner rectangles, circles. Lines measured by sight, using her pencil. The figure would not recognisably be her for quite some time, and she suspected that to get it something like, she'd have to spend several sessions on it. Especially as she couldn't quite concentrate on it in the way she usually did.

Despite his protestations to the contrary, she knew Ellis was watching her. She could feel his scrutiny flowing over her like a heated wave. If she'd been using coloured pencils, there would have been a lot of pink involved for the flush on her cheeks and her throat and shoulders. And tints of rose and brown on her fiercely puckered nipples. Weirdly enough, as she began to fill in more detail of the curves of her breasts, and their dark, sensitive tips, the more and more puckered and more sensitive they became.

And as her nipples ached to be touched, so did her

sex. Who would have thought life drawing could be so erotic? Usually, despite the nakedness of the subject, it was an ironically chaste and sexless activity.

'Can I look?' said Ellis after a while.

'You're looking already, Mr McKenna. Don't think I don't know that.'

'Busted. But you didn't really think I could keep my eyes off you, did you?' Rising from the bed, he came to sit beside her on the ottoman, looking over her shoulder at the sketch pad on her lap.

'It's *very* good.'

'It's only rudimentary . . . It needs a lot more work.'

'Still, it looks like you.'

'But the face is a just an oval blob!'

Ellis leant forward, looking closer, and she could feel his hot breath on her arm, and her breast. 'But it's a very lovely blob, and besides that, you've captured your gorgeous breasts perfectly.' He reached out, and she thought he was going to touch the paper, but instead, he changed direction at the last instant, and cupped her breast, his thumb lying against her nipple.

Jess's lashes fluttered down, and she leant into the contact, shimmying, the pad on her knee and the pencil clasped in her fingers forgotten. There was only the reality of Ellis and his touch.

'No, you should look,' he said in her ear, breaking away to take the drawing materials from her and setting them aside on the bed. 'Look at your subject. Really look.'

'You sound like my art tutor.' Her eyes snapped open, and she looked at the reflection in the mirror. Ellis certainly didn't look the least bit like Mrs

Mulgrew, the patient, long-suffering teacher of the Intermediate Life Class.

'Do I look like him?'

'Not in the slightest. She's a woman in her sixties who wears kaftans and has a crew-cut.'

'So no one I need to be jealous over, then?'

Are you jealous? I thought you wanted me to be ready for lovers . . . after you?

She pushed the thought away. It was easily done, feeling the firm stroke of Ellis's thumb against her aching nipple, and *seeing* it, in the mirror.

'No,' she said, feeling awareness of anything but Ellis, in this room, go floating away. He was sitting up close now and he slid his free arm right around her, to cup her other breast.

'Lift your arms, clasp your hands at the back of your head and bring your elbows in tight.' Now there was a similarity to her art tutor. He was specifying the pose. She obeyed him and he cupped one breast hard, and played with the nipple of the other, rolling it and pinching it. 'Keep looking. Keep looking.'

The most exciting view. A beautiful man, toying with the breasts of a beautiful woman. A wanton woman, who rocked where she sat, excitement gathering in her belly and her cleft. A woman whose face and neck and chest were rosy with arousal.

Her attention skittered sideways, to the huge bulge in Ellis's dressing gown. He leant in and pressed his face against the side of hers, then mouthed her ear, nipping it. 'Naughty, naughty . . .'

Her, or him? It didn't matter. He nibbled and kissed,

and pinched and rolled, and then, without warning, released her.

Only to shimmy his way out of his robe, so they were both revealed.

Jess didn't know where to look now: at the reflection of Ellis's cock, or at the beast itself, almost touching her hip. Catching his eye in the mirror, she shuffled closer so it was pressing against her. When it twitched, she licked her lips, and he growled.

'You're a she-devil, Ms Lockhart. The sexiest, most seductive piece of work I've had the pleasure of in a long time.'

Was that true? He must have his choice of women, even given the fact he only did short-term 'arrangements'. But he made her feel seductive. Provocative. He made her feel she could do anything and say anything.

'Touch me, Ellis. Touch my pussy.'

His ocean-green eyes flashed, and against her, his flesh surged.

'Gladly.' Still cradling a breast, he slid his hand down her flank and across her belly, diving in to obey her. His hand was nimble and tanned, and the tendons tightened and relaxed, tightened and relaxed as he began to work her.

Oh, that was so delicious. Jess arched her back, and tilted her hips, to give him better access, and ride his fingers.

'More. Harder,' she commanded, her voice taut. He obeyed, fulfilling the urge for the vigorous handling that filled her.

Sensation gathered, and she swayed, digging her

fingers into her own tousled hair, and rolling her shoulders. The pleasure gathered and wound around the spot where Ellis was rubbing her, but still she wanted more.

'Put your fingers inside me. Put two inside.'

'Hell yes,' he said, his voice ragged in her ear. In the mirror she watched the way he crooked his wrist to obey her. His fingers were narrow and elegant, but they felt huge as he pushed them into her slippery channel. She dropped a hand herself, to slide in beneath his so she could massage her clit while he flexed the fingers inside her, stretching her opening, and stimulated the sensitive nerve endings there.

'Yes. Yes. That's good.' She sat down, pushing his intrusion deeper.

'Fucking hell. It's amazing!' he agreed, laughter in the way he said it, and pride too. Awe, even, she realised vaguely.

She rubbed herself harder, gripping his fingertips, squeezing them. Then she didn't have to work to do it, as the sharp, grabbing rhythm of her body took over as she climaxed. The expression on her own face was too raw to look at, so she clamped her eyes shut as she panted and gasped her way through the fierce, sudden orgasm.

After a few moments, she slumped against him, his fingers still inside her, slippery with her silky arousal.

'You're wonderful, Jess,' he told her softly. 'I liked that . . . You taking charge. I like to be the boss as much in the bedroom as in the boardroom, but sometimes, there's something thrilling about being told what to do by the right woman.'

'I like telling you . . . I wouldn't want to do it all the time. It's hard work being in charge. But for a change, yes . . . it's exciting.'

And it was! Ellis was a fantasy figure of power and alpha manhood. Having him at her disposal was like an aphrodisiac spirit flooding through her veins, making her voracious for him. She'd come, but she wanted more, more, more.

When she snapped open her eyes again, she saw she wasn't the only one. In the mirror, Ellis's handsome face was an icon of desire, his eyes black with lust, and lower down, his cock stood out like a club, thick and rosy and shiny at the tip with pre-come fluid.

'That's what you do to me.' Dipping in, he kissed her neck, and she caressed his thick, dark hair. She slid her hand across and enclosed his shaft, almost stunned by the heat and the rock-like hardness.

'I want this now.' She gave him a squeeze. 'I want it in me . . . as far as it'll go.'

How long was it since she'd been a virgin? It seemed like a century of ravishing passion since then. She looked the same, but in every way that counted, she knew she was unrecognisable.

Ellis's smile was sultry, saturnine. She squeezed him again and he gritted his teeth, laughing.

'And you shall have it, madam.' He was looking at her in the mirror, at her eyes, then, his gazed dropped to her hand around him. 'Can you draw that?'

It was Jess's turn to laugh. 'Not right now. I think my concentration is shot. It'd be a scribble.' She waggled her eyebrows at him. 'A very *big* scribble, but a scribble all the same.'

'But what about some other time? Later? From memory . . . like the way you're going to finish that portrait off for me?'

She drew from memory. Could she? Of course she could. But that would be one she'd never be able to take to life class to show her fellow artists.

'No, not for public consumption. Just for ourselves. A memento.'

For just an instant, a dark cloud scudded across the day. Yes, soon this would all be past, and drawn mementoes, and memories, would be all she still had of him.

Jess shook her head, making her hair fly in both their faces. None of that now. No negativity. Enjoy the moment. There was plenty *to* enjoy!

'I could try,' she said, 'but it'd be very distracting. I might have to keep handling the real thing to refresh my memory!'

'I'm sure that could be arranged.' Ellis reached to brush her hair from across his face, kissing a hank of it as he did so. 'Now, do you think we could fuck? I'd really like to watch that too, but we might have to move the mirror around.'

New heat flooded through Jess's body. She wanted him. She wanted to see him in her. Something else to draw later, perhaps? An action study . . .

When she released him, Ellis rose to his feet, and walked to the mirror. 'Tell me when you think it's in the right place.' He pushed it on its castors until it was at right angles to the ottoman they'd been sitting on.

Somehow he'd managed to get the positioning and

the angle perfect. When she glanced to the side, there she was, centre stage, sitting on the ottoman, a study. Woman waiting to be fucked. As Ellis crossed to the bedside drawer and retrieved some condoms, she printed the arrangement of flesh and the setting in her mind. Then she became part of a different composition as he moved into the frame to join her, elegant and sleek as a classical statue, yet also raw and lewd with his rampant erection rearing up, pointing high from his body.

Tossing the condoms onto the seat beside her, Ellis moved in front of her, as if to display his cock to her. His mouth curved in a devilish smile as he took himself in hand and rubbed his flesh against her bosom, anointing her with his silvery pre-come. Without having to think, Jess cupped her breasts, making an inviting channel around him. She looked down at his marvellous shaft nestled there, but in her mind she could see the outrageously erotic reflection in the mirror. Him looming over her, his heavy reddened erection against her paler skin.

'God, that's wonderful!' Resting his hand on her shoulder, he rocked back and forth, thrusting between the pressed together curves, his cock slippery and hot, rubbing against her. The sensation in this was mostly for him, but still it excited her madly. Her loins ached, her nipples so tightly erect they were almost stinging.

'I'm selfish, aren't I?' he said, still moving. Jess glanced to the side, but not at her body. It was Ellis's thrown back head that caught her gaze. The taut look of pleasure on his face, his gritted teeth, his wild dark hair.

He was gorgeous, and she wanted him. Wanted him in her. When he turned to the mirror, and their eyes met, a message seemed to pass between them and he said, 'Yes . . . yes . . . let's fuck.'

Withdrawing from the niche she'd made for him, he slid his hands beneath her armpits and drew her up, giving her a long kiss on the mouth that also managed to be a full body kiss too, when he pressed the full length of his chest and torso against her. His cock was like a brand of iron against her thigh, his tongue just as hot in her mouth.

'Kneel on the ottoman,' he commanded when they broke apart. 'Hold onto the bedrail . . . so I can handle you. Part your legs.'

Shudders of anticipation coursed through Jess's body. They seemed to begin at the very crown of her head and raced right down to her toes, in waves of heat. But she assumed the position in the most graceful way she could, still not watching the mirror, but disposing the arrangement of her limbs in her mind, framing the image again . . . for later.

'Dear God, Jess, you're incredible.' Ellis's hand settled on her back, flat and with his fingers spread, and he stood there for a moment as if he were sampling her somehow, tasting some discreet essence with his fingertips. Then, setting a knee between hers and one hand on the rail, he reached to slide his other hand around and underneath her ribcage, to cup her breast, squeezing it as he pressed his cock against the curve of her bottom.

Jess stole a look at their reflection, at the shapes they made, the colours. Ellis's tan was light, but gilded, and her own body was creamier. His hair was like dark silk, and hers perhaps a shade or two lighter. Her nipple was dark brown against the side of his thumb. His wedding ring glinted, reminding her, reminding her . . .

What would it be like if there was no wedding ring, no lost and beloved wife and children? If Ellis were truly free, truly available to her.

You probably wouldn't be here, fool. He wouldn't be diverting himself with brief and temporary sexual flings, and he wouldn't have looked twice at you.

Ellis thrust himself closer against her, and in the mirror, his eyes blazed, compelling her attention. 'Jess, don't go away from me like that. You're beautiful and I want you, believe that.' His left hand moved tantalisingly on her breast, and then, after one last possessive squeeze, he slid it down over her midriff and then her belly, to cup her crotch.

Tightening her grip on the rail, she closed her eyes, giving herself up to his divine touch, and letting it expel all angst and maverick thoughts from her mind. Now was all that existed. All that mattered. She might never have had this beauty . . . it should be celebrated, only celebrated.

Pushing back against him, she used her entire body to caress him as he caressed her. She let her head fall back against his neck and her hair trail over his shoulder, moaning as the pads of his fingertips played magic games against her clit. Opening her eyes, she cast a sideways glance back at the mirror, desire surging as she did so, fired by the sight of themselves, rubbing and rocking against each other, impressions in cream and gold skin, and hair richly dark. Excitement, and gathering orgasm placed a hazy filter across their adjacent forms. They were shapes, patterns of lust and need, almost abstract now as her lashes fluttered, and her sex fluttered, and her thoughts fluttered too, losing coherence as she soared into climax.

She stiffened against him, arching; her long lashes flickering as her eyes almost rolled up. Against his fingers, he felt the beat, beat, beat of her flesh, pulsing in orgasm, and in his ear, her wild, repeating, heavy gasps, marking each beat. The sounds were music to him, though he doubted she was even aware that she was uttering them.

God, I was so lucky to find you, virgin-goddess. You're perfect, Jess, a wonderful woman and made for love and sex.

And for true companionship.

As her crisis subsided, he slid his arms around her to support her, shocked by the thought that was occurring to him again and again. Jess was sharply intelligent, and funny, and great to be with, as well as a supreme natural lover. He caressed her more gently, cradled her more closely, as if that might in some small way compensate her for what he couldn't give her. What, in another world, he would have happily wanted to give her, but in this one, he couldn't.

He could only enjoy this jewel for a limited time, before he had to set her free to find some man who *could* give her everything and who was worthy of her. It wouldn't be long, now that she herself was empowered and ready to look for that man, and at least he himself could take some small solace in the fact that his selfish lust had enabled her to find her shine as a fully sexual being.

In the mirror, her body was a gorgeous sight, sleek and flawless. In his hold, the heat and vibrancy of her was a jolt to his senses, tasking his ability to keep his cock in check. He had to have her. She had to have him. Fucking was simple, pleasure unalloyed, closeness without the moral and philosophical complications of his life, filled with the emotions of fondness and respect that could be enjoyed, even by him.

'You're not looking in the mirror,' he said, rubbing his face against her hair. 'You look divine. You should see yourself.'

'I look like a shaking wreck with a red face and my hair all over the place,' she said huskily, but when he flicked her hair out of her face, and she twisted round to look at him, she was smiling.

'That's a great look on you.'

'Idiot,' she said, adjusting her position.

'Idiot with a massive erection,' he countered. 'I really need to do something about this thing.' He rubbed himself against her again, and she reciprocated, swirling her hips and making him groan.

'Yes, it is rather monumental, isn't it? I guess I need to oblige you then.' Her voice was pert, and when she craned around again, her eyes were sultry. She even winked at him. God, she was ready to go again, sublimely voracious.

'I'd be grateful.' He kissed the back of her neck again, and reached over for a condom, ripping open the package. He was conscious of her watching the procedure as he rolled it onto himself, then adjusted their positions. Grabbing her by the hips, he helped her to kneel right up so he could gain access to her, then he stood against the edge of the ottoman, between her thighs.

Yes. Exactly right now. Her cleft was so hot against the tip of his cock, through the latex. The moment of anticipation was heart-stopping. He almost wanted to freeze time and stay there, even though he knew that the entry into her, and the glorious thrust and pull, thrust and pull of sex would be even more sublime.

'Please . . . don't tease me. I want you,' she whispered, more command than plea. She was so in charge, and he loved that. Complying, he pushed right in, the sensations almost lifting the top of his head off.

Heat. Enclosure, tight yet also yielding. Perfection. His inner greedy sex pig yowled at him to just go for it and fuck, fuck, fuck, and come, come, come in seconds. But the sophisticated man who took pride in pleasing a woman slowed him down. He pushed in a little deeper, and settled there, still, enjoying another miraculous frozen moment.

Turning to the mirror, he admired their conjunction, and the way his body was pressed against hers, both of them finely trembling. Jess had both her arms braced as she held onto the bedrail, and he was taking his weight on just one hand now, bending right over her.

Watching the progress of the other hand over her hip and around, and feeling the shape of her, and the slide of her perspiring skin beneath his touch, he sought out her centre once again.

He heard her gasp, and saw her rosy mouth open as he found her clit. Her teeth were clenched, in agonised ecstasy, as he rubbed her. As if knowing he was watching so closely, her eyes snapped open then, meeting his gaze in the mirror. Her pupils were black with lust, and she rocked and circled her hips as he pleasured her, causing delicious havoc where he was lodged, his cock deep inside her.

'Yes, yes, yes,' he chanted as her reflection licked her lips like a wanton. She was gripping him with her sex, matching each word with a clench of her inner muscles. He rubbed her more firmly, trying to make a pattern of it, swirling and slipping around in her delicious silkiness. She was so wet, so miraculously wet, so hot and welcoming that in his eyes tears almost formed.

He was conscious that even as he was trying to hold back, amazingly, she was too. 'Sweetheart . . . you don't have to wait,' he purred in her ear, tearing his attention from the mirror-glass and inclining over her. 'Take your pleasure now, Jess. Take it. You can never have it too much, or too often for me. It's a woman's prize to come again and again. Claim it. Claim it now. It's your right!'

'All right! I will!' She was laughing again, half out of it, then moaning and gasping. Her body stiffened, and stiffened again, and she cursed a blue stream as she climaxed around him, clenching and gripping hard, while her hold on the bedrail rapidly destabilised.

Ellis braced for them both, using his greater strength. The way her orgasming channel embraced him sent heat howling through his body, circling around him like an unstoppable wind, then barrelling back towards his balls and his cock. He wanted to hold on, to take her higher, and do it again, but his control was wavering, dissolving.

'Your turn. You now,' she hissed out, through her tightly clamped teeth, 'come now, you devil!'

Still so strong! So sure of what she wanted. Her body was barely beyond its virgin state, but she was a confident lover and seductress, bred in the bone.

'Yes . . . Oh God . . .' They were going to collapse in a heap though, when he lost control. So he summoned his last ounce of self-possession, and somehow, he knew not quite how, he took a quick tight grip on Jess, swung their bodies around together . . . and ended up sitting down on the ottoman, with her on his lap, and his cock deep inside her.

'I feel as if I should give you marks for that move . . . Nine point five at least,' said Jess, laughing, her flushed chest heaving.

'Cheeky witch! Just touch yourself!' he commanded, watching her in the mirror as she obeyed, while he grabbed her hips for purchase and thrust up, up, up inside her, deeper than before.

The sight was orgiastic, dazzling, animal yet beautiful as she caressed herself to pleasure again around his jerking, spurting cock.

Then all went white, and they both slumped back. Their blended voices laughed and sobbed in sweet release.

19

Sunday followed much the same hedonistic pattern as Saturday.

Chilling out. Drawing. Fucking. In approximately equal proportions.

Jess could not believe what a patient model Ellis could be, when she captured him again and again with her pencil. Somehow his beauty was infinitely mutable, and his body was always graceful, no matter how he stood or sat or lay. Of course, sometimes, Jess would be intent on a capturing a feature of his wonderful physique, correcting and reworking, correcting and reworking, again and again . . . and suddenly she'd look up and realise that a certain part of that physique was in a rather different state to the one it'd been in when she'd started the sketch. And with nobody but them in the house, it was the simplest thing in the world to move from life drawing into life fucking. Ellis had ensured that wherever they were in the house – and they *were* in the house, because the rain teemed down incessantly – there was handily somewhere to make love. The bed in the bedroom; the thick rug in the sitting room; another thick heap of rugs and pillows adjacent to where they sat and lounged in the pool room.

Sometimes Jess rode him; sometimes he fucked her masterfully in the superior position, and she folded her knees, to tilt up her body, letting him in deep. And sometimes they gave each other pleasure with mouths and fingers, eschewing penetration for the moment. Kneeling, lying, even standing in the shower, they tried it.

But they didn't do anything too kinky or experimental, the sort of stuff Jess fell into giggles over when Ellis teased her about her reading of erotic novels, and the contrast between those and her growing practical knowledge of the subject material.

'I think I'd prefer to perfect the basics for the moment,' she'd told him firmly when they were making love. Basically. 'It seems just like art. You have to get a solid grounding in the fundamentals before you start to get ambitious and move on to the more advanced stuff.'

'Very wise,' replied Ellis, his voice amused and conversational as he thrust smoothly into her. 'There's a lot to be said for good, no nonsense vanilla sex. Sometimes it's all you need.' Sliding a hand down her flank, he gripped her hip for purchase.

'You mean like now?'

'Yes. Like now. I couldn't think of anything, or anybody, I'd rather be doing.'

'Well, that's good to know . . .' Jess gasped as Ellis did a hip-swirl thing that felt quite advanced to her. 'But I would . . . um . . . like to experiment sometime.'

'And *that*'s good to know,' purred Ellis in her ear. 'But don't feel you have to do things, just to please me. You're wonderful in bed, Jess, just as you are. Some people end up being poor lovers because they're scared they're not acting kinky all the time. They think they're not sexy unless they're doing something extreme.' He kissed her cheek. 'Something other than perfectly delightful standard sex.'

Not that anything's standard about fucking you, thought Jess later, watching Ellis as he lay flaked out on his lounger, his body quiescent as he dozed and covered only partially by his unfastened robe and nothing else. *Everything about you is so much better than wonderful, sex or otherwise.*

And that was the problem. The other side to their weekend. She couldn't stop herself from wanting more of him. Just as she'd feared, Ellis McKenna was addictive, and it was far from just the sex. He was a kind and thoughtful man. Intelligent and funny. Cultured and yet with a keen sense of the absurd.

She couldn't imagine another man of his wealth and status being so domesticated either. If she wanted tea, Ellis made it. When she was hungry, he prepared a meal, either hot or cold, letting her help with simple tasks in kitchen companionability.

It's probably happened far too fast but I have fallen completely in love with you, Ellis McKenna. I shouldn't have let it happen, but it has. I want it all with you, and I've a feeling you're picking up on that, and it's a problem for you. Because you don't want it all with me, do you?

He was lovely, but to coin a cliché, they were ships passing in the night, and they should be heading for separate ports by now, not footling about together in the bay of completely impossible.

Watching him stir, and wrinkle his nose in his sleep, then shimmy slightly against the lounger mattress, Jess made a resolution. When the weekend was over she'd find a way to suggest, in the most tactful and hopefully not ungrateful-seeming way that they should call it a draw. She tried to formulate a script . . . she'd had a breathtaking time, blah, blah, blah, and that she'd always be fond of him and think of him as a friend etc., etc., but she accepted the major fact that he'd been at pains to point out. That he didn't do relationships.

Knowing that she didn't like deception and evasion, she knew she'd have to tell him that she *did* want a relationship, and that was why a clean break was better.

He'd appreciate that. He was a pragmatist. A realist who knew it was much better not to let things get out of hand.

But first, now, she'd draw him again. Make the most of her perfect muse, something he always would be, she suspected.

And when she'd drawn him, she'd suggest that they make love. If there was just this weekend, she'd better make the most of him.

So why was it, that when the time came to part, all her sensible, realistic intentions counted for nought?

As they sat in the Blue Whale, outside her house on Sunday evening, the words she had practised were impossible to utter. She'd replayed them again and again in her head, and they were balanced on the tip of her tongue, but she simply couldn't get them as far as her lips!

Instead of coming out with her 'it's better this way' spiel, she leant over and kissed him. And it was a decidedly 'can't wait until we're together again' kiss. She just couldn't help herself.

Ellis's fingers sank into her hair, holding her and taking control of the embrace, his tongue delicately toying with hers. It wasn't a kiss of out and out voracious passion, but there was an edge to it. It certainly didn't say 'just friends', and when he drew away from her, there was a slight frown on his forehead.

Now. Say it now.

'I had a wonderful weekend, Ellis. Just wonderful. Thank you for . . . for looking after me and everything.'

His expression was still quizzical, as if he was wondering whether she had the guts to say the words. The words he was perhaps hoping for?

'It was wonderful, wasn't it? I had a great time, Jess. A really great time.'

This time, he plunged forward for the kiss, holding her again.

'I'll be travelling all this week, and I don't know what my movements will be next weekend, but I'll call you. I'll call you as soon as I know what's what, and we'll fix something up.' His face was an odd mix of emotions. Warmth, genuine and unfeigned, but also a hint of confusion, as if he too was having trouble with his script.

'I'd like that,' was all she could say, even though inside her wiser self was still screaming at her to say what had to be said.

'And maybe we could try a bit of that experimentation?' He quirked his beautiful eyebrows at her. 'Only if you want to though. You know I'm perfectly happy with "fundamental principles".' The way he rolled his eyes and pretended to twirl a dastardly moustache made her laugh though. And made her want him again too, even after an entire weekend of satiation.

But after he'd brought her bags to the step for her, kissed her again, with an almost desperate intensity, and then sped away without looking back, Jess came tumbling back to earth and cold reality again.

I'll call you. It was the classic brush off line of all brush off lines, wasn't it? Especially when the couple involved had barely got to know each other in the first place. It was what the man – or woman – always said, in melodramas and romantic comedies, and while she believed that Ellis had far more class than to just disappear from her life with never another word, it somehow still felt like the end. He *would* most likely call her, and in the cooler light of day, very quietly and kindly he'd say exactly what she'd been unable to. That it was probably best they part now, and that he'd always think of her as a friend . . .

So much more sensible. So much for the better. For both of them.

In which case, why were tears pouring down her cheeks and causing her to scrabble in her pockets for tissues before she went inside to face the third degree from Cathy?

Ellis wasn't much of a drinker, but arriving home he went straight to the whisky bottle. A small measure of single malt would warm his belly. Help him think.

Why the hell hadn't he done what he'd told himself he'd do? Spoken quietly and gently and matter-of-factly to Jess, suggesting that they should not see each other again? He couldn't give enough of himself to her, and she deserved far more than just the torn and tattered scraps of his emotions.

You mustn't lead her on, you sod. You can't give her what she needs. You can't give any woman that, ever again. You lost Julie, through your own fault. You weren't there when the woman you loved needed you. You weren't there to save her. You can't just go on your merry way as if nothing happened after that. You don't deserve to. Ever.

He knew his reasoning was illogical, not rational. It was purely a gut and heart thing. But he couldn't forgive himself.

That day, five years ago, he should have taken Julie and the girls to the beach, maybe out on their boat, but oh no, instead, he'd put business first. God damn it, he couldn't even remember what the stupid emergency meeting had been about now. And his wife and daughters had gone for an indulgent day out at that new mall instead . . . and fallen into the random path of a crazed gunman. An unhinged weapons nut who'd shot up the pizza place where Julie and Annie and Lily had chosen to go for lunch.

If they'd been out on the ocean, they wouldn't have been there. Even if he'd gone to the mall with them, he might have been able to keep them safe, certainly put himself between them and the bullets.

But oh no, some pathetic business hiccup had to

come first. And the bitterest irony was, that had never usually been his style. Normally, Julie and the girls had always been his top priority . . .

Ellis poured another whisky, barely having tasted the first as it had gone down, still feeling icy cold despite its warming peat-scented glow. He didn't have to drive. A chauffeured car would be collecting him shortly.

He'd allowed his family to die, and he could never forget that. Never allow himself to, or allow himself to find a replacement, or a substitute for them. Sex, he could have. The pleasures of the flesh. But not that greater, more sacred union that he'd once cherished.

He had to keep the wound open by remaining alone. And he hadn't wanted it any other way. Not until he'd picked up a feisty, cross-looking but breathtakingly beautiful woman in the middle of a sudden torrential downpour of rain . . . and set himself on the tortuous path to a new kind of guilt.

20

'Good grief woman . . . what a body! How do you ever keep your hands off him long enough to draw him?'

Cathy had insisted on seeing the portfolio, and while Jess had managed to sneak a few of her drawings out of it and stash them away, there hadn't been a way around showing her friend some of her work, despite the fact that the vast majority of the drawings were nude studies of Ellis.

'It's a tough job, but somebody's got to do it. But he insisted on modelling for me. It was a case of "draw me like one of your French boys" and he just stripped off.'

Her friend's eyes narrowed. 'Are you sure he wasn't stripped off already? He has the look of a well-satisfied man about him in this one.' Cathy lifted one of the larger drawings Jess had done on the big pad. 'And if this is what he's like when he'd deflated, he must be pretty eye-watering when he's got a stiffy.'

'Cathy!'

'I'm only stating the patently obvious,' Cathy said. 'You're a very lucky girl. And to think you nearly gave him the elbow. You must have been mad to even think about letting him go.'

Despite her blushes, Jess shivered, as if temperature in the kitchen had just dropped dramatically. She *was* going to have to let Ellis go; if he didn't let her go first.

'What's up?' Her friend was nothing if not perceptive.

'It's not a proper relationship, you know. It's just a quick "thing". We've slept together a bit, but that's about the size of it, Cath. Nothing more. He doesn't want anything more than that. He's a loner, really.' Reaching for the drawings, she swept them up and put them into her portfolio, putting ultimate temptation out of sight. 'Shall we have a cup of tea? I'm dying for one.'

'Well, you can change the subject now, buddy, but I'm not letting you off the hook that easily. I think you need to talk about this. He might be a loner, but I know you . . . and I don't think *you* are a loner any more. Not now.'

'Don't be daft.'

'Make the tea, woman. And break out some more of those triple choc crumble crunch cookies he sent you. I think we're going to need them.'

Cathy was three biscuits in when she accused Jess. 'You're in love with him, aren't you?'

'No way! I hardly know him.'

'Yes way, kiddo. You've fallen hard. It's obvious in your face when you talk about him, and as for the drawings . . . well, I've never seen you do better. They're drawn with love, Jess, which is what makes them so alive, so luminous.'

Setting out to catch up with her friend's cookie consumption, Jess chewed mutinously before answering, 'It's not love, Cath. I like him. I really do. He's so gorgeous he's like a fantasy made real, and, let's face it, any woman's bound to have a special feeling for the first man she slept with.'

'I don't. It was a quickie behind the changing rooms at the sports centre, and it was horrible. Luckily, I can barely remember what he looked like.' Cathy dunked expertly.

'Well, a woman who had a nice first time. And I did. To the best of my limited knowledge, he's a pretty spectacular lover, and I'll always remember him fondly for that.' Jess dunked with less finesse and nearly lost her biscuit.

'"Remember him fondly" . . . you're talking like you'll never see him again. The man you love.'

'I don't love him and I might never see him again. We've not made any specific plans. It was just an "I'll call you . . ." and I've heard that line often enough, even if he's the only one I've ever slept with.' Jess took another cookie, but when she bit into it, it almost tasted like ashes.

'Oh, for heaven's sake, "I'll call you" isn't always the brush off, Jess. Sometimes it just means what it says. That he'll call you. He hasn't behaved like a git thus far. Why should he start now?'

Cathy was so sensible, so down to earth. She made it sound as if there was hope, when there really shouldn't be any. Jess started blinking as she stared fiercely at her teacup, furious with herself for feeling and behaving like a ninny. She just couldn't let Ellis McKenna get to her. She couldn't let her feelings for him take away her sense of her own agency and make her dependent on the very first man who'd crossed her bedpost. All these years, she'd managed alone, making her own way, not defining herself by any relationship with a man. Now was no time to change and become a whinging, whiney wimp, pining and wailing for someone she could never have.

A box of tissues slid across the table towards her. Damn, she was snivelling!

'He wouldn't be behaving like a git. It's just me behaving like an idiot, and getting all infatuated with the first man who ever fancied me.'

'You're not. And he isn't.'

'What do you mean?'

Cathy shoved the cookies her way now, and realising she'd eaten the other one on auto pilot, Jess took another. It tasted better this time. Fabulous in fact. Nothing but the best for Ellis.

'One, you're not behaving like an idiot. You've just fallen for an amazing, but probably emotionally difficult man. And two, plenty of men have fancied you.'

'Like who?'

'Men we've met when we've been out. You always pull admiring looks. And the guys you've been out with, they must have fancied you, even if you didn't let them get to first base.' Cathy frowned. 'And what about that nice bloke at art class you mentioned? Josh Somebody? Sounds like he fancies you.'

'Okay, so a few guys have been interested, and I *have* fallen for Ellis. What the hell do I do about it? There's no future with him. I think he intends always to be emotionally bonded to his wife, even if he sleeps with other women.'

'If he calls, you should keep on seeing him for as long as it lasts. Have fun. Have great sex. Get a few good presents out of him. He is a billionaire, after all.' Cathy's look was no nonsense, even if Jess was shaking her head. 'And if there is no future with him, at least you'll have something wonderful to look back on, and you'll probably get him out of your system better that way, rather than if you do a runner now and then spend the rest of your days wondering about the one that got away.'

Jess took a deep breath and drank some of her tea. Yes, she had to shape up. Ellis wouldn't call, but in the remote eventuality that he did, she decided that she would see him again. She'd be in control of her destiny, and pragmatic. He was just too wonderful to say no to, even if it would probably hurt more in the long run.

'You're right, Cath. He probably won't call, but if he does, I'll give him a chance.'

'Good girl. And he *will* call.'

'Ever the optimist. He won't.'

'Will.'

'Won't.'

Beside her plate, on the table, her phone vibrated and trilled. The display, whilst not exhibiting ten-foot-high letters of fire, might as well have done.

Ellis.

'What did I tell you?' said eagle-eyed Cathy, leaping up. 'I'll be taking a bath. You need your privacy, kiddo. And remember what I said. *Carpe diem* and all that.'

As she disappeared out of the kitchen, Jess tapped 'accept'.

'Er . . . hello?' *Great start. Sound like an idiot, why don't you?*

'Hi Jess, are you okay?' Ellis didn't sound like an idiot, just a man with a low, thrilling voice and an interesting all over the world accent. Just those few words made the tiny hairs on her skin stand up as if his breath had just drifted across them.

'I'm fine, thanks. I just didn't expect to hear from you so soon. I'm not complaining though. You just surprised me. Where are you?'

'I'm in the back of a limousine, going about as fast as we legally can down the motorway.' There was a smile in his voice, and Jess could see it in her mind's eye. Almost unconsciously, she drew her sketching pad towards her and fished around for her ever-present pencil. 'Where are you?' His oceanic eyes would be twinkling now, and she started to rough out the shape of one. She always started with the eyes.

'Sitting at the kitchen table, drinking tea and eating those fabulous biscuits you sent.'

'Are you alone?'

Jess's heart thudded. God, how she wished she was alone in her room, with the door firmly shut. Cathy had swept out, to give her privacy to talk to Ellis, but it wasn't the sort of privacy she suddenly needed.

'Cathy's around. She just went into the other room for a moment. I think she's planning on taking a bath.'

Ellis laughed softly. 'Mm . . . a bit too risky for anything risky then?'

It was, really. 'What on earth do you mean?' she said, knowing exactly what he meant.

'Don't worry, I won't embarrass you, sweetheart. I'll wait until I'm tucked up in bed in my wicked London sex lair before I do something about the way your gorgeous voice makes me feel.'

'Ellis!'

'Sorry . . . I'm a pig, aren't I?'

'No, not a pig. Just a bit . . . a lot more than I'm used to.' She paused, then hurried on. 'But I'll get there.'

Why the hell had she said that? It suggested that she was assuming there was more ahead between them.

'You will indeed, Ms Lockhart, if I have anything to do with it.' The smile in his voice was a seductive grin now. Jess focused on the sketch that was forming on the paper, to stop herself doing something very silly. 'But seriously, I phoned about next weekend. I've been looking at my schedule. I've a got a couple of crucial things with people who are only in town then, but my evenings should be free. Why don't you come down here and visit Bluebeard in his London lair? Maybe you could take in some galleries during the day, and we could meet up in the evenings . . . Have dinner . . . maybe have dinner brought in . . . so we've more time to spend experimentally in bed.'

It was all so matter of fact, but still the way he spoke made her want to be there. Right now. Tucked up in that bed, in Bluebeard's lair as he called it, doing, well, doing whatever. Jess imagined some sleek, white, penthouse space, with a bed a mile wide and multi-million dollar views over London. She'd no idea exactly where Ellis's apartment was, but she pictured a vista of the river, and a jewel-box of night-time lights. A beautiful sight, but no match for the man in that notional white bed with his epic body and his erotic imagination.

'Don't fancy it?' His voice sounded slightly less assertive in the tiny speaker, as if he was nervous about her response. He was a man of limitless wealth and power but these little instances when he didn't quite act like the all-conquering hero were strangely bewitching. His humanity and reality somehow managed to make him even more of a fantasy figure than ever.

'Oh yes I do. It's just that I'm not used to making travel plans on the hop. I'm not a particularly spontaneous person, you know?'

'You're spontaneous with me. You've taken chances with a very strange and arrogant man, Jess. You surrendered your virginity to me when we barely knew each other, when we'd only met a day or two before.'

He was right, but it just didn't seem like that. When she thought about it now, it was almost as if he'd been destined to be the one. That they'd been fated to meet and make love, even if there'd been no hint of it almost until the moment it had actually occurred.

'Yes . . . yes I did. You really must be Bluebeard, seducing me in a whirlwind like that. Who knows what you might do if I agree to come to London.' Her heart trembled, and so did much of the rest of her, especially the intimate zones. The vision of that vast acreage of white bed appeared again, with herself at the centre of it, her hands bound, secured to the brass bed-head with electric blue ropes. Wow.

'But you'll come?'

'I should hope so,' she shot back. *No doubt about that, with you.*

'Oh, I can guarantee it. As often as I can make it possible, gorgeous one.'

She was drawing his mouth now, that plush, beautiful shape. It could be so velvet-soft, yet so muscular and ruthless. Her sex fluttered, and in that other image, the London one, she saw him crouched between her thighs, kissing her core.

'Are you in the Mafia, Mr McKenna, because you've just made an offer I don't think I can refuse?' She was talking nonsense, he'd shaken her up so, with just a few casual words.

'Don't refuse it. Come to London. I don't want to wait any longer than that to see you.'

But it's only temporary. In a few weeks you'll move on. You'll be nice about it, but we'll be over.

It would be so much less painful to quit now, but still she said, 'Okay . . . I'll get on the internet and book a train ticket.'

'Don't be absurd, Jess. I'll arrange for one of the company jets to pick you up at the local airport, and a car to get you there. You're a very special woman and you deserve nothing but the best.'

It was an exciting thought, but crazy, really.

'Don't be daft. I can easily get the train. It doesn't take long these days.' She started to fill in a little of his dark, designer stubble as a frame for his divine mouth. Hair was something she'd always found tricky to interpret, but somehow it seemed easier when she was drawing Ellis. 'Just think of the rainforests, sending a jet just for one person. It's a kind thought, but it's not exactly environmentally sound, is it?'

'You're wonderful, Jess,' he said softly, 'but how about a compromise? I book your train tickets, first class of course, and the car to pick you up. Would that be agreeable to your eco sensibilities?'

Jess laughed. It would be lovely, actually. She'd only travelled first class a couple of times in her life, but the sense of specialness appealed to her romantic nature. So this would be a treat that she didn't have to feel too guilty about, something within the realm of the achievable for someone like her.

Unlike Ellis, who was still a creature of pure fantasy, even though their bodies had joined, and the sweat of their couplings had blended.

'Very agreeable,' she said, shaking her head to bring her back to some semblance of normality. Sometimes where Ellis was concerned, she just lost it. 'Shall I be ready at Friday teatime, after work?'

'Take Friday off.'

'I can't. I can't just keep taking time off at short notice.'

Ellis chuckled again. 'Oh, I think you'll find that you can. You can do anything you want, Jess. You're golden. You could not turn up for work for a year, and you'd still be able to go on drawing your full salary and benefits.'

'Oh, Ellis! What must the bosses think? They'll know that we're . . . um . . . having a thing.' Her pencil scratched off to one side, making a very weird shape. She quickly flipped to the eraser end and started correcting. 'It's very embarrassing.'

'You shouldn't care, Jess. You . . . you're a superior being. You shouldn't worry what a bunch of tin-pot managers think about you.' He paused, and she could almost see him frowning. 'I've told you before . . . You shouldn't be working in an office anyway. You should be pursuing an artistic career. You should take a degree course, the one you missed out on, at the very least. I could . . .'

'No! Let's not talk about this. I've told you. I'm happy with drawing and sketching as a hobby. I enjoy it better that way.'

'I'm sorry, sweetheart. I'm pushing and being controlling, aren't I? Hazards of the job, I guess. I'm used to making things happen.'

It was Jess's turn to laugh. 'You can say that again . . . and in some ways . . . most ways, I like it. Believe me. But I'm used to doing my own thing too, my own way. And it's probably not a good idea to get out of that habit. You know what I mean?'

She had to keep things real. Somehow. Because they'd go back to being real again, soon enough.

'I understand. I admire you for it.' He sounded sincere, but that didn't mean he still didn't want his own way, she guessed. 'But if you ever want any kind of assistance, in changing careers, I'm here for you Jess. I stand by my friends.'

Friend, and currently friend with benefits. That was all she would ever be. Why, oh why was she wanting more when she knew the score with him?

'Thank you, Ellis. That's a wonderful offer, and I'll keep it in mind. But I don't want to change the status quo at the moment.' Oh yeah, all that talk about letting life pass her by, and now she was dismissing a brilliant opportunity out of hand. But she knew the real reason . . . the ephemeral nature of this relationship. She always had to be mindful of that. 'I'll take a day off on Friday. But a proper day off, from my allocation. No funny business.'

Ellis laughed. 'Oh, don't you worry, there'll be plenty of "funny business" but I understand what you mean. I'll set up your travel arrangements and text you the details.' He paused, and she could almost feel him switching gear, and imagine the wicked twinkle in his eyes. 'Now, seeing as I have you on the phone, what are you wearing? Underneath, I mean . . .'

He couldn't resist it. He'd been feeling so horny since he'd left her at the door, and in such a mixed up, contemplative mood. Guilt. Desire. Hope. Hopelessness. Julie. Jess. All had circled in his mind, over and over, while at the same time, the caveman part of him had focused again and again on the sublime pleasures he'd shared, and planned to share again, with Jess Lockhart.

'Ellis . . .' Her voice was husky. She was trying to be reproving, but not really succeeding. He recognised that note in her voice, a certain timbre, the hint of a laugh. Even though she knew she ought to tell him she wanted nothing to do with his nonsense right now, he knew she was on the same page, sexy and willing.

'Oh, indulge me, woman. It's over two hours since I touched you and I'm going crazy here.' It was true. He was rock hard. Aching. There wasn't much he could do about it right now. Even he couldn't bring himself to masturbate in the back of the Bentley, speeding down the motorway, despite the fact that the windows were dark tinted and there was a privacy barrier between him and the chauffeur. It just seemed a bit tacky, a bit out of control.

But at least he could imagine Jess in a more private scenario. Properly alone, so he could direct her in a little movie that he could replay later to himself as he lay in his bed, in his apartment, high over London.

'But I told you . . . I'm in the kitchen. Cathy is around.' The words were a protest, but her voice was more velvet and full of excitement than ever.

'Then go to your room, you wicked girl. Do as you're told.'

'Are you trying to order me about, Mr McKenna?'

'Yes, that's exactly what I'm doing.' His heart thudded. God, his sex thudded too. This was going to be so tough, but so worth it.

'Very well,' she said, 'I'm on my way up.'

There were a few moments of semi-silence, with just the impression of motion, faint footsteps, a soft thud, thud, thud, then the opening and closing of a door. Bless the woman, she'd done just as he'd said. She was only playing the game, though, he knew, not really following orders. She was only doing exactly what *she* wanted. She was sexy and empathetic; she'd *chosen* to go along with him.

'I'm in my room. Alone. I've turned the key.'

'Good girl. Now . . . what *are* you wearing?'

He'd imagined that little silky turquoise robe of hers – and nothing underneath. There was a longish pause, and he guessed that she was deciding whether to lie and fabricate, or just tell it like it was.

'White jeans, tee shirt, bare feet.'

'Delectable, but I'm more interested in what's underneath that.'

'White bra and knickers, both cotton with a little bit of lace trim.'

'Gorgeous, and very virginal.'

'Not any more . . . thanks to you.' Her voice was delicious, provocative.

Did she regret it though, he wondered. Giving that great gift to a man who wasn't the Mr Right she'd waited for so long. Better not go there, and get heavy. He'd had enough of heavy thoughts. He needed the lightness and pleasure of sexual jousting with a woman who could instinctively give as good as she got.

'It was my pleasure to relieve you of that burden, Ms Lockhart. You should be grateful.'

Across the miles and the ether, he could feel her momentary and instinctive feminist indignation. It seemed to crest, then he imagined her wry smile, a shake of her head, making her silky hair flutter. Men were idiots, but smart women like Jess Lockhart were prepared to indulge their ridiculous ways.

'I am, Mr McKenna. I am. I'm very mindful of the fact that you're a super-stud and I'm very privileged to have had the benefit of your massive . . . sexual expertise.'

'Careful, madam.'

'Sorry.'

'I don't think you are, but you could at least try to show it by taking some of those far too many clothes off for me.'

'Okay.'

'Does your phone have a decent speaker?'

'Yes.'

'Well then, put it on speaker and set it close by while you strip off . . . and tell me what you're doing while you do it.'

A moment passed, and when she spoke again, the quality of her voice was different, more echoing, telling him that she'd obeyed him. 'The phone's on the bedside table, and now I'm taking my tee shirt off.' He heard a tantalising rustling sound, soft fabric brushing against soft skin, and perhaps the faintest slight whoosh of her hair again as it settled back to her shoulders. He wasn't sure he could really hear all that, but it was good to imagine it.

'Are the curtains drawn? Perhaps there's some pervert in a bedroom across the back from you, watching you take your clothes off?' As his memory served, there wasn't actually any way anybody could overlook her, even with the curtains wide open, but the pervert was right here in this car anyway.

'There's nobody looking in.'

'Imagine there was. How would you feel? Would it turn you on to know a stranger was admiring your body?'

'I'm not sure . . . it might.' Was she touching herself already? There was a breathy quality to her voice. 'Yes, actually, it does. It did when you kidnapped me at work and whisked me upstairs.'

Yes, I knew that, beautiful girl. I knew that.

'Excellent. Now then, there's a stranger sitting in a bedroom across the way from you. He's sitting in his window seat, admiring you . . . and touching himself.'

'What does he look like?'

Oh, you minx!

'This is supposed to be my game, not yours, madam. But seeing as it's you, he's got dark hair, a bit of a beard thing going on, and he's in his thirties. He's got a fabulous body and an enormous cock.'

'Sounds like he's got an enormously high opinion of himself too.'

'He probably has, but enough about him. What are you doing now? Any progress on that white bra with fine lace trim?'

'I'm taking it off now.'

Ellis closed his eyes, shutting out the night and the motorway and the cars speeding along in other lanes. All he could see was Jess, gracefully revealing herself to him. She still had a sublime modesty about her, being so recently untouched, but her innate sensuality reached out like her slender hand to stroke him.

'I'm touching myself now . . . I'm playing with my nipples and stroking them and squeezing them . . . the way you do.'

Oh dear God . . . I can't take this any more . . . I've got to . . .

To hell with tacky. To hell with out of control.

Ellis jabbed the control for security, locking the windows, the doors and the privacy screen.

With a groan he knew she'd hear, he unfastened his belt, then his trousers . . . and reached inside.

Jess panted. She'd been holding her breath. What was he doing? Was he actually masturbating while he was in the back of his limousine?

How sleazy was that?

How incredibly, incredibly hot!

He's doing this for me? Because he desires me . . . so much? Jesus Christ . . .

Slumping back against the pillows, Jess reached down and cupped her crotch through her jeans. Her aching clit leapt, and she squirmed. She wouldn't tell Ellis about that. Well, not yet. She was jumping ahead of his instructions in the game.

'What are you doing now? Is that filthy pervert with the beard thing still watching you?'

Jess grinned to herself, hitching herself about on the bed. Two could play at this game.

'I'm pinching my nipples. It hurts a bit, but I like it.' All true. 'The pervert's got his cock out and he's rubbing himself, the filthy sod.' Also true, she suspected. She could see that marvellous shaft, clasped in his strong elegant hand, the ruddy crown taut and shiny, a little wet with his pre-come.

'He sounds like a disgusting sex maniac to me.'

'He is!'

'You should report him to the police,' said Ellis, and she could tell he was either fighting not to laugh . . . or fighting the wayward behaviour of one particular part of his anatomy.

'Oh, I don't know about that. He's rather cute,

actually, and with that huge cock and all, he's a real turn-on.'

'Speaking of turn-ons, madam, how about taking the rest of your clothes off now? For me and the pervert.'

One and the same, Mr McKenna.

'Okay, I'm stripping now.' After a last squeeze of her pubic mound, Jess set about her jeans, fumbling with button and zip in her haste and excitement. She was alone in her room, and yet burning in the spotlight of Ellis's avid gaze. He was as good as there with her as she wriggled out of her denim chrysalis like a butterfly of sex, her senses unfurling. She flung the garment away, then sent her panties flying after it.

'I'm naked,' she said, wondering if he'd heard her. She almost didn't have enough breath for a volume sufficient that the phone's microphone would pick it up.

'Good. Now play with yourself, gorgeous one. Stroke your nipples and your clit. I want to hear some gasping and moaning. Put on a show.'

Shedding all inhibition, it was easy to do. Whether she could have done the same if he was actually here was a moot point, but the touch of her own fingertips, the proxy of his, stirred her more intensely than she'd expected. Just one light press of her middle finger against her clit made her gasp out loud, shocked and pleasured.

'That good, eh?' he purred from the speaker. In her mind's eye Jess saw the dark flare of lust in *his* eyes.

'Yes, very good. It's the pervert. Having him watch

me is exciting. It gets me going.' She squirmed against the mattress, circling her fingertip, rolling the silky bead of her clitoris in a complex, instinctive pattern. It was the way Ellis touched her, as if the fine muscles and tendons of her hand had learnt the action via the reaction it induced.

'You're killing me, woman,' groaned Ellis, 'you and your ruddy pervert. If I was there now there'd be no performing and watching . . . well, maybe later . . . but right now, I'd be in you, fucking you like fury, hammering you into the mattress, making you come until you can't see straight and you pass out.'

Jess tossed her head against the pillow, wanting, wanting, wanting that ferocious onslaught, Ellis powering away between her thighs, their bodies angled so that with each thrust his pelvic bone knocked her clitoris. With her hand jammed between her legs and her finger right at her centre, she rolled over, face down on the bed and rocked and rocked, using her own weight to massage herself too. Her nipples rubbed against the bedding as she rode her own fingers, making the sensations whip and whirl like a high, sweet wind.

'Oh God, yes! Yes! Yes!' she shouted like every cliché of an orgasming woman as the crisis battered through her and her vagina contracted and contracted, reaching for the divine cock of the man miles and miles away from her. Fifty, a hundred, who knew? She just wanted him to be with her and in her, or just with her and touching her, making her come with every part of him . . . maybe even just his voice.

'Are you coming, Jess? Are you coming for me?'

He might still be able to speak, but Jess was beyond it. She gasped for air. She sobbed. Damn, she even whimpered. The orgasm seemed to have turned her inside out, and now she just wanted to be held.

And Ellis wasn't there. She buried her face in the pillows for a moment, stifling the cries of her loneliness.

'Jess? Jess? Are you okay?'

'Yes, I'm fine,' she said, rolling back over then sitting up, shaping up, pulling herself together. 'Just a bit shagged out . . . remotely, that is.' She tried to laugh, but it came out a bit weird.

'Are you sure?' demanded Ellis, on it in a flash. 'I haven't upset you, have I, love? I know you're not used to all this, sex games and everything.'

Still naked, Jess reached for the water carafe and glass she kept at her bedside and poured herself a drink. The fluid was a bit warm and flat-tasting, but still the act of sipping it settled her. She found herself smiling. What a ninny. Getting in a state of post-coital melancholy without actually having shagged anybody, fool. Setting aside her glass, she dragged her throw from the bottom of the bed and snuggled it around her. That was better.

'Don't worry, Ellis. I'm good. I liked it. My first ever phone sex.'

'But not the last, I hope. It's going to be a long week. I might need to call you up again before Friday for a top up.' She could sense him smiling now. They'd had a weird moment there, but she felt herself lightening again, feeling more relaxed, feeling the benefit of the climax now. The familiar glow.

Shuffling further up in the bed, she clutched the throw more closely about her, as if enfolding herself in the sensation. Ellis was far away, physically, but he'd been with her in spirit. He'd been the source of her excitement. A real man, not Dream Lover. A real man she could enjoy and share pleasure with, even if it was only for a finite amount of time. He was hers, now. She shared him with his memories, but any woman would have had to.

The glow. Hang on to the glow. The enjoyment . . . and the naughtiness.

And a naughty thought occurred to Jess now too. Had he? Had he really?

'Ellis? Are *you* okay?' She grinned, even though he couldn't see her. Maybe they should Skype next time? 'Did you . . . um . . . did you do anything?'

'I did, you provocative, seductive minx!' He laughed, and she loved the rich, happy sound of it. 'I told myself I wasn't going to . . . but I did. You drove me to it, you irresistible trollop, you. It's a damn good job there's a healthy supply of paper tissues in this jalopy, or things would have been incredibly messy.'

An enormous sense of power made Jess giddy for a moment. She'd done that. She'd made this glamorous, sophisticated man into a helpless schoolboy who couldn't contain his urges and had been compelled to pleasure himself in the back of his own limousine, whilst thinking of her, pleasuring herself.

'You're a very naughty man, Mr McKenna. Fancy, tossing yourself off while you're being driven down the M1. What on earth would people think? All these minions of yours, who look up to you with respect as their boss. All your business associate type people, who think you're like this . . . financial machine, all analytical and cool as ice and all that.'

'I don't care what they think, gorgeous. I'm only interested in you at the moment, and thinking about what you're doing, back there in your bedroom. Where I wish I was right now. All I want is to leap into your bed right now and throw myself on top of you in the most delicious and primitive way. And I'm going to do that as soon as you arrive in London.'

'I thought I was going to be allowed to visit some galleries and do some sightseeing?' she pointed out pertly.

Ellis laughed again. 'I think there'll be time for both, sweetheart. And I want you to do what *you* want to do.'

'Well, tempting as culture is, being ravished by a handsome man with a big cock certainly sounds like something I want just as much as seeing a bunch of pictures.'

'Maybe I could buy a Manet and have it fixed to my bedroom ceiling? Kill two birds with one stone?'

'You're a very silly man as well as a very horny one.'

'I know . . . I know . . .'

A thought occurred. Something she almost always forgot, because Ellis was so easy to get on with, so . . . so normal in many ways.

'You *could* buy a Manet, couldn't you?' Another thought . . . 'I bet you've already got one, and you're laughing at me.'

'I would never, ever do that, Jess.' He sounded

suddenly serious. 'And no, I don't have a Manet. As I said, the family does own some good art, but I don't possess any old or modern masters.' He paused, and she could feel him lightening up, across the miles. 'Personally, I'm thinking of starting to collect Jessica Lockhart. I've seen some examples of her nudes and they're spectacular.'

'Get away with you.'

'I'm serious. I hope you're going to finish that self-portrait for me. And do that other one . . . that one from memory, from the mirror.'

Oh God, that. She'd done a few rough outlines, just shapes and lines. Another thing she'd kept secure from Cathy's eyes.

'Yes, I'm going to try. The subject matter is a bit distracting, though, especially the mirror one. But I'm not one to shy away from a challenge . . . as you well know.' And yet once she would have done. How knowing him had changed her and brought out her confidence! They barely knew each other, but he'd prompted so much in her.

Pausing, she grinned to herself. 'The members of my art class usually bring work they've done away from the classroom for group critique . . . Do you think I should take in those particular pieces?'

Ellis's bark of laughter rang from the speaker. 'I dare you to!'

Wicked foolhardiness swelled like a wave. But no, she wouldn't do it. Those were moments and images for her and Ellis alone.

'No, I'm not showing them. Not even for you, Mr Sex,' she said firmly. 'But I will work on them, and maybe bring the results to London to show you. Or failing that, take pics of them with my phone and email them to you.'

'I want them to keep.' He sounded quite masterful.

'We'll see.' She hoped she sounded just as assertive.

'I'm in your hands.'

I wish you were . . . and not just in a sex way.

'There's no answer to that,' she said lightly, and he laughed again.

'If it wasn't getting late, and I wasn't almost at my destination, I'd suggest a replay of our festivities just now,' he said softly, 'but you've not exactly had the most restful of weekends, satisfying my enormous lust for you every two minutes, so I think that for your sake, we should hang up now, and take a rain check for more phone sex later in the week.'

She suddenly didn't want him to 'go'. Talking to him was so right. So natural. Even the erotic games. Once again, she got that odd feeling that somehow she'd known him forever, perhaps in a former life, who knew.

But he was right. It was late. And she was tired. She needed sleep, even if the solitary bed that had always been so accommodating and so appropriate to her now seemed half empty, without his lean and powerful form in it beside her.

'Consider the check taken, Mr Sex.'

'Good. Now at the risk of starting the "you hang up, no you hang up" dance, I'm going to ring off now, and let you get your sleep. I would say beauty sleep, but you don't need that, as you're beautiful already.'

'Sweet talker.'

'Truth talker,' he said emphatically, 'Get some rest. I will text you your travel arrangements later in the week, and we'll speak again before Friday. Goodnight, Jess.'

'Goodnight, Ellis.'

But the line had already gone dead, and she doubted that he'd heard her.

Ellis called again several times during the week, but the conversations were mostly of a strangely non-sexual nature, more the gossipy touching base of a friend rather than the provocative erotic challenges of a lover.

Jess laughed aloud when his opening gambit was 'How was your day?' quickly followed by 'What's so funny?'

'Nothing. Nothing at all . . . actually it's really nice to know that somebody other than Cathy and my sister cares about my mundane life.'

'Never mundane, Jess . . . but seriously, how *was* your day?'

So they both chatted on, sharing funny stories from their vastly different working lives, confirming her travel plans, and swapping opinions – often wildly different – on news and current issues.

Things became a little more risqué when the talk turned to art, later in the week, and Ellis enquired about her progress with the self-portrait and the image of them on the ottoman, fucking.

'I wish I was back there now . . . back inside you . . .' he said huskily, and one thing led to another, and she never did get to report on the status of the drawings.

Ellis also sent Jess presents throughout the week, the naughty man, showering her with thoughtfulness. The hoard included a selection of gorgeous deluxe art books – some of them titles that he must have seen in her bedroom, on loan from the local library – and new supplies of her favourite pencils and drawing pads. She'd never even *noticed* him noticing these things when he was with her, but he clearly had, memorising the brands in order to gift her with them later.

He also sent her subscriptions to a number of journals she could never have afforded for herself, and he made her a 'Friend' of just about every major art gallery and museum in London, including the National Gallery, the National Portrait Gallery, the Tate, and, most appealing of all to her, the Courtauld.

'I'm afraid I'll be busy with meetings on Friday and part of Saturday, so hopefully, you can fill in the time exploring art to your heart's content. I'm sorry I can't explore with you, but if I can get away, I will do, and we'll do some culture together.' He paused, and she could easily picture the wicked twinkle in his eyes. 'Well, a little bit. There are other things I'd much rather be exploring while you're here, as you can well imagine.'

Jess *could* well imagine, and she knew she'd happily forgo even the lure of the Courtauld, in order to explore the fabulous work of living art that was Ellis McKenna.

One thing Jess didn't discuss in too great a detail with Ellis was her life class. She felt irrationally guilty, even though there was nothing to be guilty about.

The model this week had been a young woman with a very slight, almost emaciated physique. She'd seemed healthy and relaxed enough, but her body-shape was tough to draw without making her appear skeletal and, of course, there was no way Jess could draw Ellis instead this time. Something that Josh Redding, the guy who seemed interested in her had remarked upon, teasing her good-naturedly in the college canteen during the class break.

'No fantasy man this week?'

'No, he was just a passing fad,' she'd lied, 'He's some rich supermodel guy I saw in a celebrity mag and fancied. I'm over him now.' She grinned, but inside it was as if she'd betrayed Ellis in the most profound way.

'Glad to hear that. These film star looking hunks make the rest of us ordinary guys feel inferior.'

Oh dear. He likes me. I should like him. I would have . . . before . . .

'You're not an ordinary guy, Josh. You're a very talented artist to say the least.' At least that wasn't a lie. He *was* good.

'Thanks. I think.' He grinned back at her, but didn't press the matter.

After that, they'd fallen into conversation about the difficulties with the latest model. Josh was fun to talk to, and he knew his art. He wasn't bad looking either, in a quiet, buttoned-up sort of way.

If I hadn't met Ellis, I think there really might have been just a bit of a flicker there. I might just have taken a chance, this time.

But as they'd been about to go their separate ways

at the end of the class – Jess lived within walking distance of the adult education centre, and Josh came by car from the other side of town – Josh had asked, tentatively, if she'd like to take in a film at the weekend, at the local art house cinema.

'The *Exhibition on Film* of *Munch 150*. I was going to buy the DVD, but I think it'll be much better on a big screen. How about it? We could go for pizza afterwards, if you like?'

More guilt. It had been such a relief to have a 'prior engagement'.

'I'm afraid I'm away for the weekend. Staying with a friend . . . I'm sorry.'

She was. She wasn't. God, she didn't know what she felt. Josh was nice, but Ellis was . . . Ellis.

'No worries. I think it's on for a few weeks. Maybe another time, eh?'

'Yeah . . . sure. Rain check?'

'Rain check.'

They'd parted then, a little awkwardly, leaving Jess feeling very strange indeed.

Thrown into deep shadow by the brilliance of Dream Lover made flesh, a perfectly nice man like Josh Redding seemed merely a sketch compared to a dazzling, accomplished masterpiece. But would she be able to see him with more clarity . . . afterwards?

Because 'afterwards' would soon come, sooner than she wanted. Ellis had left her under absolutely no illusions about that, and much as she knew she loved him, she also knew that she just couldn't crawl back into her burrow of celibacy and half-life when he was gone. She'd be letting herself down, and letting Ellis down, wasting the gifts of sensuality that he'd given her.

She would miss him terribly, but she wouldn't pine and close herself off again. Ellis had chosen to turn his back on the life of the emotions forever . . . but she couldn't do that. She owed it to herself to forge a new way, after him, and perhaps giving Josh Redding a chance would be a way to try and achieve that.

You're just shadow-boxing with yourself, kid. It'll be hard. It'll be well-nigh impossible. Ellis McKenna will be a tough act to follow, if only because you love him to distraction.

21

But there had been no internal debates about Josh Redding once Jess began her London adventure. Her lover's giant presence in her mind didn't leave room for anything else, and even just thinking about her art class friend felt like being unfaithful.

Especially when she reached her destination . . .

Ellis's London apartment was much more like the billionaire pad she'd initially expected him to have. Like a wonderland, a glossy photo spread made real. The colour scheme surprised her though, and made her laugh the instant her brain made certain connections. When he'd told her the location, she'd checked out properties in this same giant building, on Zoopla and Rightmove, and when the housekeeper had shown her in, she'd expected the classic sea of white and chrome, as in the illustrations.

Instead, to her delight, she found a warmer, much more welcoming palette. Tones of rich dark brown, near black polished wood, all lightened with sand and cream and fawn, and high-lit with zingy little accents of blue and green, in jewel tones. The more she looked at it, when the housekeeper had left, the more an impression formed. And then it clicked.

It's got the same colour scheme as you have, Mr McKenna.

The blacks and browns for his hair, creamy tan for his skin, blue-green for his fabulous eyes. She wouldn't see him until later, but somehow, his presence was all around her as she settled in and explored, strengthened by his colour aura.

The concierge/housekeeper had offered a dazzling array of in-house services, but Jess had wanted to be alone in Ellis's space.

'Of course,' the quietly efficient woman had said, 'you'll find the kitchen is stocked with all the staples you'll need, and just press 0 on the house phone if there's anything else you require.'

And now Jess was taking five, sitting in a vast living room area that overlooked the Thames, sipping a reviving cup of tea.

And here comes the rain again. *Why is it always raining? We met in the rain and it seems to follow us wherever we go.*

The London weather was indeed disappointingly wet and grey, but somehow even that had an impressionist charm, imparting a misty blue-grey aura to the busy City view, that almost might have come from the brush of Monet. Or Whistler.

I can't believe I'm here. It's like stepping into a dream. Even more so than Windermere Hall.

Her tea finished, Jess decided on a quick snoop around the apartment before she ventured out onto the rainy streets of London.

Ellis had been right when he'd said he didn't have a great many pictures and works of art in his London pad. But the ones he did have were much more to Jess's taste than the few rather dull country scenes he had on the walls at Windermere, which she suspected had been in the house when he'd first arrived there.

Here though there were three rather nice, impressionistic London views that were vibrant and accomplished. Not by artists she knew though, and she cursed the limitations of her artistic education. She knew mainly those 'greatest hits' that she cherished, and the pre-eminent art movements and their exponents, but beyond that was a very great world of painting, still unexplored.

There was nothing on the bedroom walls, as yet, which surprised her. She'd half expected some gems of tasteful eroticism, art to set the mood when Ellis brought his temporary conquests here for seduction.

Conquests like you, kiddo. You're just the latest.

Jess had blushed when the female concierge had shown her into this football-field sized room rather than a guest room, on her little introductory tour. But then she'd thought, what the hell, why worry?

She's probably perfectly used to different women sharing his bed. It isn't as if I'm the first. He's never deceived me about that!

Back in the room shortly after, on her own, Jess couldn't resist the siren call of Ellis's wardrobes, curious about his clothes.

The sliding door glided on its track, revealing hanger after hanger. Suits. Shirts. Razor-sharp business attire such as the billionaires of film and fiction might wear. She tried to imagine him clad that way, so different from the casual, unstructured beach bum look in which he'd made such a stunning first impact on her. She loved that style. It just seemed so right for him. She'd always remember him that way . . . either that, or stark naked.

Checking the label on a shirt, she grinned.

I might have known.

Paul Smith. She checked another and another. It almost seemed as if Ellis had every flowered or patterned shirt the man had ever designed. She pulled out one adorned with tiny washed out cornflowers and held it against her face. The cotton was very soft, and it smelt of Ellis's fresh yet spicy cologne. The lovely odour made her heart twist, and she was tempted to stash the shirt in her bag, as a keepsake, and hope he wouldn't notice it was missing.

It was time to head out on her gallery pilgrimage now. Hanging around here, her thoughts were arrowing inexorably in familiar, dangerous directions that she knew they shouldn't.

The pursuit of great art would distract her from the recurring and inconvenient truth that she'd fallen for a man she couldn't have.

Getting around London isn't nearly as time-consuming when you have a luxury hire car to take you wherever you want to go.

Great galleries were still great galleries, though, and each had to be lavished with all the attention its precious collection deserved. With hours outside Ellis's bedroom strictly limited, Jess asked the driver to take her straight to the venue right at the top of her list.

The Courtauld.

The limo drivers of London clearly had the same knowledge that the world famous black cab drivers possessed, and knew all the same clever rat runs that lesser mortals simply weren't privy to. Staring out at the rain and the scurrying crowds with their mackintoshes and umbrellas, Jess was shocked at how quickly the car drew up at the Strand entrance to Somerset House.

'Would you like me to see you to the door with an umbrella, miss?' the driver asked.

'No, but thanks very much. I'll be fine.'

'If you're sure, miss. Just give us a call on the number on the card when you want to move on. It won't necessarily be me, but whoever it is will get you exactly where you want to go.'

As the long black car sped away, weaving neatly into traffic, Jess headed for the arches that led into the Somerset House courtyard. She popped out to take a quick look at the fountains, but just as she was doubling back, her phone rang, so she darted beneath cover again, just in front of the gallery entrance, to take the call.

'Jess, it's me. Where are you?' Ellis's voice. Her heart trembled every time she heard it. He'd only texted so far today, presumably in his meetings.

'Just about to go into the Courtauld Gallery. I'm very excited. I can't wait to see the Impressionists.'

I wish you were here to see them with me.

'Good! You enjoy, sweetheart. Take your time

looking around. I'm almost finished here, so I'm hoping I can get to you there, and we can maybe enjoy some of those pictures together.'

Jess's spirits leapt. Sharing this experience with Ellis would be just as wonderful, in its own way, as making love.

'That's great! I'd love that. I'll mooch around. There's masses for me to see before you get here. Shall I wait for you in a particular room or something?'

He probably thinks I'm crazy. I sound like a giddy kid . . . but I don't care!

'I'll find you, Jess. It's a relatively small gallery. I shouldn't be too long, but if I haven't tracked you down in an hour and a half, keep doubling back to the Impressionists and I'll look for you there. Does that sound like a plan?'

'It does indeed. I don't need any excuse to loiter around in front of *La Loge* or *A Bar at the Folies-Bergère*.' She could hardly believe she was going to soon see those sublime artworks . . . with her sublime, albeit temporary lover.

'Okay, Jess. Got to go again now. Enjoy the pictures. *Ciao!*'

The connection went dead, and Jess realised she was shaking. Was it the art? Or was it Ellis? Probably both.

I could spend days in here. It's a house of treasures . . .

The Courtauld is a small gallery, but to Jess's mind, it was perfect. The rooms are relatively small, and the atmosphere intimate, almost like viewing art in someone's beautiful home rather than in a sterile, formalised environment. She moved from room to room, not ashamed to be open mouthed in wonder at the superb collection of works, doubling back on herself to look at particular pieces again, following no set pattern of viewing, entranced by the genius displayed.

Rubens. Botticelli. Gainsborough. Goya. Turner. Every one a jewel.

She was conscious though, of saving the best until last, so she could share her thoughts with Ellis. But finally, she had to give in and enter the rooms where the Impressionist paintings were hanging.

Manet. Monet. Degas. Cézanne. Renoir. Magical names.

It hardly seemed possible that she was seeing them for real. They were the stuff of her dreams, almost in the way Ellis was. They reminded her how barely formed her own artistic aspirations were, and yet at the same time they fired her with ambition. She'd never be famous, but she could try new things, push her skills, and learn and grow in the journey.

Ellis was the start of a journey too.

He'd prompted her to find her inner heart as a sexual woman. She knew he would not be with her much longer on the path, but she had no qualms about giving herself and her virginity to him. She was happy, in a bittersweet way, to have known him and loved him at all.

She stared hard into the face of the barmaid in *A Bar at the Folies-Bergère*. The face was enigmatic, weary, the eyes sad, resigned. Had she known a special lover? Had she lost him? There was regret there, Jess was sure of it, and she resolved not to ever, ever feel that way when looking back on her time with Ellis McKenna.

It was difficult to tear herself away from the great Manet masterpiece, but she felt tugged towards her other particular favourite. Renoir's *La Loge*.

A happier painting, yes, and prettier in a more obvious way, but although the central figure – the cocotte? – seemed to be confident, and to gaze out boldly, Jess still wondered . . . what was her background? Did she too hide some doubt about her status? And who was her male companion ogling at, in another theatre box?

Don't you care? Or does he always do that? And it's nothing . . .

As she stared at the details of the pretty girl's hair, her face, and her striking black and white gown, Jess had the oddest feeling.

No . . . Nobody has sixth sense like that. You can't just know he's here.

And yet her body shuddered finely. Her heart began to race. She wanted to turn around, but somehow she couldn't.

Knowing she'd see a sight more dear to her than any French Impressionist masterpiece!

She's the masterpiece. Art pundits would throw up their hands in horror at me saying that. But she's the sight I most want to see here, the most beautiful.

Ellis paused in the doorway, as entranced by the image of Jess standing before *La Loge*, as she was by that famous work. Her face was aglow with wonder, illuminated almost. He felt in awe of her and the pure communion between her and the great painting.

Seeing Jess like that made him glad to be in the gallery. He'd experienced a gut-wrenching shudder on entering, irresistibly drawn back to family plans that had once been made. Julie had been so keen to visit this gallery, and he was sure that even though Lily and Annie had been only little girls, they too would've been able to appreciate the experience. They'd certainly have loved the pretty opera box girl, with her black and white dress and her flowers. Lily had loved to dress up, and would probably have requested a dress like that for her next birthday.

The pang of pain struck him again, but ebbed a little when he focused on the woman who waited for him in the here and now, so slim, yet shapely, elegant in her simple summer outfit, cornflower blue cotton trousers and a short, toning jacket. He loved the way her dark hair hung shiny to her shoulders, and her face was so fresh with barely the lightest touch of makeup.

You know I'm here, don't you?

Something subtle about her stance had changed, as if she'd sensed him in the way he was sure he'd have sensed her with their positions reversed. But she wasn't giving in to the urge to turn around, the minx. She was making him come to her, like the goddess she'd become, and perhaps always had been, unknowingly.

Smiling, he lingered a moment longer, enjoying the invisible push-pull between them. It made him want her furiously, stirring the hunger that had gnawed him since Sunday last. The primal beast part of him wanted to hustle her imperiously from this wonderful gallery, bundle her into a limousine and speed back to the apartment to fuck her hard, then slow, then kinky, then gently vanilla. Maybe even start the process in the back of the car.

But most of him, perhaps even a greater part, just wanted to be with her, and to share experiences. This gallery. London. Simply being together.

He wanted to say, *Look, all you people, I can actually be happy. I can stop being an emotional cripple, at least for a little while, and take pleasure in the company of this wonderful, enviable woman.*

Oh, what the fuck was he waiting for?

Ellis strode across the room, weaving through fellow Impressionists devotees. He walked softly across, and snuck up behind Jess, following her eye-line to the painting.

'What do you think he's looking at? If it were you and I in that box, my eyes would be only for you, never mind the audience, or even the opera.'

'I knew you were there,' she said, turning to him, her face provocative, smiling. 'I was just wondering how long it'd take you to come across to me.'

'Whoa, super powers now, as well as your many other talents.' He reached for her hand, and drew it to his lips. The gesture felt perfectly natural; she was a queen, and he was her courtier.

'I suppose so,' she answered, then took his breath away, by leaning in towards him as he straightened up, and pressing a quick kiss to his lips.

Oh God. He stiffened in his underwear, suddenly

glad of a loose, longish jacket. He'd have to focus on art appreciation or he was going to embarrass the both of them.

'I'm glad you're here, Jess. I've missed you. It's been a very long week.'

She frowned a little, as if she didn't quite believe him, but then smiled again, her face openly happy. 'Yeah, I've missed you too, Ellis.' She paused and winked. 'Although all the presents have helped to ease the pain. You're a very extravagant, but very, very kind man. Thank you so much.' She reached up and touched his face, making his erection jerk again. 'I'm not going to embarrass you, by saying I can't accept your gifts. I think I know you enough to know that you don't . . . um . . . mean anything by them. You're not trying buy me or make me obliged to you. You're a better man than that, and the books, and the pencils and everything . . . well, they make me feel happy.'

Emotion stole away Ellis's voice. She was a wonder. So honest. So fresh. She played no mind games. For a moment that spear of pain pierced him again. Jess's frankness and lack of guile reminded him of Julie, even though in most ways they were very different women.

'I'm glad,' he said at last. 'Very glad. Now, shall we admire the art?'

'Yes, isn't this amazing?' She turned back to *La Loge*. 'I love it, but it's a bit of an enigma, just like the best things always are.' She turned back quickly to him, with a wag of her eyebrows. 'Is she a lady? Or is she a prostitute? That's what you always wonder . . . what they were trying to say, as a comment about their times. She looks contented enough, doesn't she? Not like the girl in the *Folies-Bergère* . . .' She nodded towards that other painting, not too far away. 'She looks sad to me.'

Ellis stepped back a way, trying to think critically about the paintings when all he wanted to do was take Jess in his arms and hug her and kiss her. 'I don't know . . . I think she's just a young woman out for the night with her boyfriend, really. And he's being a bit of a git, as we mostly are.'

Jess turned from the picture and gave him an appraising look. Was she wondering about the word 'boyfriend'? *Was* he her boyfriend? He'd never been anyone's boyfriend since Julie. His relationships, or whatever they'd been until now, had not really merited that term.

'Let's look at this gal then,' he said, resisting self-analysis and taking her by the arm and leading her towards the Manet.

'So, what do you think?' As they stood in front of the famous bar scene, he experienced an insane urge to hold her hand, or put his arm around her. But he resisted that too. Too possessive. Too mine, mine, mine. Too confusing for them both.

'It's hard to know what she's thinking. Or what Manet wants us to believe she's thinking. The whole thing is a bit unsettling. The reflection is all skew-whiff but he must have meant it to be that way.' Jess pursed her lips, staring hard at the image. 'It's wonderful, truly, but it makes me uneasy. And even more so, seeing it for real.'

Wonderful but uneasy. That's how I feel.

Suddenly Ellis wanted to get out of here, absurd as that seemed. He'd wanted to share this experience with her, but the provocative art was dredging up thoughts he didn't want to face.

You bloody coward, man.

He glanced at his watch, and saw the perfect out.

'When did you last eat, Jess? I hate to raise mundane matters in the presence of high art, but it's way past lunchtime.'

Her frown wasn't puzzled, but knowing. As if she saw right through him. Her perspicacity was far more unsettling than any Impressionist masterpiece. 'I had some biscuits on the train.'

'Biscuits? You can't live on biscuits, woman.' He did reach for her hand now. He needed the touch of her flesh to centre him, and return him to territory he felt secure on. 'You need to build yourself up. You need fuel . . .' He leaned in and whispered in her ear. 'For later. For stamina.'

Jess turned her face towards him, still with that smart, all-seeing expression, and Ellis could have sworn she gave him the very faintest of nods, as if affirming their return to safer ground.

'How about a late lunch?' he continued, not nodding himself, except psychically. 'I'm certain we can get a nice table somewhere . . . Maybe the Savoy Grill? Or somewhere quieter, if you prefer? I know plenty of restaurants.'

Jess regarded him steadily. 'Would you think me ungrateful if I said I'm not very hungry? It's been such an exciting day. My stomach feels too jittery for a proper meal.'

Me too. But I'm not sure it's about food. And the only hunger I have is for you, Jess Lockhart, only for you.

'But don't you want to see more of the gallery?' Jess enquired as they made their way out of Room 6, and then down the stairs.

'I had a quick look around while I was looking for you,' he lied. 'Maybe we can come back tomorrow, eh? Although I'm sort of jealous of you spending so much time and attention on all these dead guys . . . when we could be doing other things.'

He was being crass, and he knew it. Despite his ground rules coming into this thing with Jess, it was more than just sex and bed, which was the problem. Getting back to the focus on the carnal was what they needed to do.

For both their sakes.

When Ellis had summoned a car, and like magic it had arrived in a couple of minutes, they piled inside, still not having settled on where to eat.

'How about tea at The Ritz then?' he said suddenly, sounding like an indulgent relative, offering a niece a delicious treat, but the way his thumb stroked the centre of her palm seemed to suggest something far more earthy. She was torn. She'd always wanted to take tea in a high class London hotel, but the sweetness of wild sex with Ellis was just as tempting.

'I thought you had to book months in advance for afternoon tea in these big posh places?'

Ellis laughed, and waggled his dark eyebrows at her. 'As you've pointed out before, I don't tend to live like a billionaire. But I can, if I want to. They'll find a table for me, don't you worry.'

Such arrogance. But somehow it got to her, turning her on. She wanted to throw herself at him there and then, and test the veracity of his claim that the window-glass was completely one way. Yet, at the same time, she wanted to test his other claims too.

'I'd love tea at The Ritz then,' she said, lifting her chin, challenging.

'Right-ho.' Pulling his slim phone out of his inner pocket again, Ellis spoke to someone for a few moments, pausing every now and again whilst this person, presumably some PA or other, spoke to a third party on another line. Ellis beamed at Jess throughout, as if he completely understood that she was testing his billionaire credentials.

'Great! Fantastic! Thanks so much . . . Tell them we'll be arriving in about ten minutes.' When he rang off, he slipped the phone in his inner pocket, and began fishing around in the outer pockets of his suit jacket.

'What are you doing?' It was Jess's turn to laugh as Ellis drew a pair of fine-knit silk socks from one pocket, and a dark blue tie from the other.

'I might be lord of all I survey, but I've got standards. And so has The Ritz.' He kicked off his leather slip-on shoes and began pulling on his socks. 'There's a dress code in the Palm Court, and I'd hate to embarrass you by not adhering to it.' Sartorially socked, he attacked his shirt collar and slid the tie into place, knotting it expertly without the help of a mirror. 'How do I look?' The knot was perfect, and the blue tie toned perfectly with the small flowers on his shirt.

'Absolutely divine,' said Jess facetiously, although it was true. 'But what about me?'

'Also divine. You look perfect.'

Dubiously, Jess looked down at her summer jacket and cotton trousers, and her fairly sensible lace-up shoes, which she'd chosen for walking. No fashion plate, but tidy enough she supposed. Somehow it'd been important not to look like a total scruff in the presence of sublime art. And the sublime man who was passing through her life.

Within a few minutes, they reached The Ritz, and the sense of being in a dream, the way she often felt with Ellis, intensified. They were greeted by the hotel manager himself and escorted personally to a prime spot in the Palm Court. Jess tried not to rubber neck, either at the sumptuous surroundings, the gilded mouldings and furniture, or the enormous floral display in the centre of the room, but it was impossible not to. She looked for celebrities too, but couldn't spot anybody she recognised. It was mainly a lot of people just like her, tourists visiting the city. Well, perhaps not quite like her; all the other tea-takers had probably booked six months in advance for their table. Whereas she, in the presence of a genuine celebrity, her billionaire prince of glamour, had just swanned in on spec, like the Queen of Sheba.

'Hungry?' enquired Ellis, surveying the bill of fare.

'Very!' She *was* hungry. And the cakes and sandwiches and scones being served at an adjacent table looked breathtaking. But she would have gone hungry and left this beautiful fairy-tale ambience without a second thought . . . if Ellis had suddenly announced that he was hungry for her rather than lemon cake, fluffy scones and crust-less ham sandwiches.

So lost was she in her fantasy scenario of hopeless desire that it was quite a shock when the waiter arrived and Ellis began to order.

But the tea they shared could only be described as scrumptious. And Ellis's almost schoolboy pleasure in the delicious confectionery kept a smile on Jess's face, and expunged any hint of her own guilt at over-indulging.

'Another scone?' he said with a wink.

'Oh, I can't. I'll just burst.'

'Don't worry . . .' He leant in close, his mongrel voice low and thrilling. 'I intend that you shall work off all the calories later . . .' He winked outrageously. 'In fact you'd probably better have at least three more, plus cream . . . because you're going to need plenty of energy.'

Jess compromised with another tiny but divine petit four.

'So, how has work come along on the self-portrait? And the other thing?' Ellis enquired, fussing with the teapot. 'Do you have any progress to show me?' His eyes glittered provocatively.

'Well, not here, and that's a fact,' Jess told him pertly. 'But yes, I think I've more or less finished both of them.' She'd brought that sketchbook and another with her, in her largest bag. The drawings had both turned out scarily well, although they still made her blush, because they were so raw, so graphic. It was one thing to do life drawing, of some figure, somebody who wasn't a part of your life. But when you were the subject yourself, intimately portrayed . . . it was another matter.

'I look forward to seeing them. Especially the self-portrait . . .' He dropped his voice. 'And the model, for comparison.'

And I want to draw you again . . . and see your body.

'I'm guessing you didn't show those works to your friends at the life class?' Ellis grinned as he topped up both their teacups.

'Hell no!' Jess looked around in alarm, hoping nobody nearby had heard her exclamation. Luckily everybody was busy, munching and chattering about their own concerns. 'There's life drawing and there's life drawing . . . and that part of my life I'd rather nobody knows about. Well, not the details . . .'

Ellis lounged back in his chair. 'But they must suspect there's a man . . . Didn't you say they'd noticed you weren't drawing the models a lot of the time?'

'Yes, it was remarked on.' Jess paused, feeling a twinge of guilt over Josh Redding. Which was ridiculous, because she hadn't done anything or agreed to anything with him. Had she even flirted? She didn't think so . . . although new, sexually empowered Jess might even do that instinctively, without even realising it. 'One of the guys from the class asked me out on a date, to the movies,' she blurted out, feeling as if the Palm Court had suddenly turned into a confessional.

Searching Ellis's face, she saw barely a reaction. His smile remained playful, equable. Or did it? Was there just a slight flick of something in his eyes? But why would it bother him? He'd impressed the score on her from the start, and the fact that he was 'educating' her about sex, for the benefit of future boyfriends.

'His name's Josh. He's really good at drawing, and he knows his art,' she went on, wondering why she had to justify herself, but knowing in her gut that she had to.

'I hope you said "yes",' Ellis said, then paused to sip his tea, 'as long as you think he's good enough for you.' His eyes narrowed just a bit.

'Of course he's "good" enough! He's a very decent person. Really nice. And quite good looking too.' She sipped her own tea, flustered. 'Obviously not as fabulous as you, but cute in his own way.'

'But did you accept his invitation?'

'Well, no, I couldn't. It was for this weekend.'

'Rain check?'

Jess took another petit four, and nibbled it, even though she'd told herself she'd already eaten far too much. 'Sort of . . . It's an art film I really want to see. It's on at the local cinema for a few weeks.'

'Good. You should go.' Ellis took another scone. Was he a nervous eater too? Why would he be though . . .? 'You never know, he might be Mr Right. You should give him a chance.'

'I'll see . . . But I'm not going out with him while . . . while I'm still seeing you. I know our thing is just . . .' She leaned in, then went on in the lowest voice she could. 'I know our thing is just sex, but even so, I don't two-time.'

'You're a very honest woman, Jess, but it wouldn't matter, really.'

Damn the man, wasn't he in the least bit jealous?

'Well, it would to me.'

'And that's why I admire you so. You've got scruples and a noble heart. As well as – ' now it was Ellis's turn to lean in ' – the most fabulous body and the most breathtaking instinctual knowledge of how to use it. And believe you me, gorgeous woman, I appreciate being the man who has exclusive access to it, even for only a few weeks.' His eyes glittered, filled with desire now, and no shadows.

How could I possibly want anybody else when you're around, Ellis McKenna? You make men like Josh seem insignificant, even though they're perfectly nice and attractive. I'm sure that if you asked me, I'd lie down amongst the scones for you, gladly!

But later, when they were out in Piccadilly and Ellis was about to summon their 'carriage', Jess touched his arm.

'Look . . . it's not that I don't want to plunge into bed with you this very moment, but I think if I do, I'll just bounce off you again, I'm so stuffed with cake and scones . . .' She glanced up the famous street, wondering why she was suddenly prevaricating. Some shyness did still linger. Would she ever be rid of it? And the talk about Josh, and 'afterwards' had unnerved her. 'Could we just have a little bit of a stroll, to walk some of this carb excess off before we head back? There are tons of small galleries in this area and maybe we could window shop a bit?'

Ellis smiled, and reached for her hand. 'Good

idea, gorgeous. It'll be all the more fun for a bit of
anticipation, eh? Not that I haven't been anticipating
since Sunday . . .' He squeezed her fingers and they
set off. He clearly wanted to get to bed, but he
seemed happy enough to humour her whims. 'And
never mind window shopping. I'm in the mood for
buying! I need some more art for both the London
pad and for Windermere. You've piqued the connoisseur in me, Ms Lockhart, and I fancy a splurge.'

'Not for a Manet or a Renoir . . . surely stuff like
that only comes up at auction once in a blue moon?'

'Oh no . . . something slightly more modest. An
investment. Something that might be sought after one
day.' He turned to her and gave her a very arch glance.
'Although I'm saving some wall space for a few
Lockharts too. I want to see the stuff you've got in
storage as well as your latest work.'

'Don't be silly.'

Ellis just blew her a kiss and upped his pace,
drawing her along. The earlier rain had all gone now,
and blue skies hung above the famous street.

Thinking about her pictures and belongings in
storage, Jess realised she'd have to open the unit sooner
rather than later. She and Ellis wouldn't be together
all that long. Oh, that ticking clock was driving her
crazy. She *mustn't* think about it!

After a brief stroll, seeing nothing much in windows
that took their fancy, they found themselves standing
outside a small, discreet gallery called 'LaPierre and
Hornby'. A receptionist sat at her desk in the window
space, and on a low window shelf in front of her, mounted
pages from the shop's catalogue were spread out.

'That looks more like it,' said Ellis, pointing to something that had already caught Jess's eye.

A dazzlingly vivid, impressionistic oil of a gorgeous bunch of flowers. Roses, she thought, but the vivid, energetic dabs of pink and peach and mauve were open to interpretation. Two pieces of fruit on a lightly sketched in plate gave Jess a clue.

'I think that might be a Leslie Hunter . . . possibly. I can't be sure. It's just that I saw a documentary about the Scottish Colourists, and that's a bit like the work of that school.'

Ellis grinned at her. 'Now this is why it's useful to have an art expert with me. I pick out something I like, and you tell me what it is. You're a woman of very many qualities, Ms Lockhart . . .' He leaned in close again. 'Both out of the bedroom and in. Now –' he drew her on by the hand, ' – I think I'm going to buy this "Hunter" and any more Hunters or similar that they've got on offer.'

LaPierre and Hornby specialised in British art of the twentieth century, and there was indeed another Hunter on sale, even though that artist's work, and other output by the same group, was now much sought after. Ellis ended up with the pink roses still life and a scene from Provence, almost pulsating with yellow light, by Hunter, and a gorgeous interior by another colourist, F.C.B. Cadell.

Jess's jaw dropped at the prices, but Ellis smiled. 'Don't worry . . . I can afford it.'

Damn, she always kept forgetting he was who and what he was. He'd flexed his billionaire magic at The Ritz, but most of the time, he kept his profile low and behaved, well . . . like a normal person. He liked nice things but he made no fetish of his wealth, or designer brands. She imagined that if he saw a patterned shirt that he liked at a local market, he'd happily hang it in his wardrobe with his Paul Smiths.

'Right, anything you fancy?' he asked cheerfully, once the purchase details of his booty had been finalised.

Jess almost said yes and drew him to a Peploe still life, but then checked herself. He could buy it for her out of his pocket change, but it would also have seemed too much like a parting gift, a pay-off.

Instead she just smiled, and said, 'Thanks, but I'm good. It's kind of you though.'

Ellis raised his eyebrows, as if he'd read her little rationalisation, but as she shrugged and turned away, something intriguing caught her eye, across the gallery.

Salon Privé.

'What's in there?' Ellis demanded of the assistant who'd been attending to him.

'Ah, that's our collection of erotic art for sale . . . Some people are a little shy of it, so we have a private area for the most explicit works.'

'Fancy a look in there, then?'

The expression on Jess's face was priceless. Adorable. Even though she went to life drawing classes, even though she'd worked on that stunning, blood-thundering self-portrait, and dozens of sketches of his own naked body, she was still blushing at the thought of entering this private gallery.

But that was one of the things that was so exciting about her, her quintessential blend of innocence and sensuality. Ellis would have put even money on the fact that she'd never lose that lovely, tantalising modesty, even long after she was married and had been having sex with her husband for years and years.

Not that you'll ever see that. Some lucky sod with no tortuous history and no hang-ups will be with her then. A man who's worthy of her. A man without emotional baggage.

Turning away from the gloomy thoughts, Ellis smiled at Jess, giving her his most saturnine pantomime seducer leer, loving the little pink flags on her cheekbones. 'What's the matter? After all the naughty drawings you've done of me, surely you don't think it'll be too daring for you?'

'No way!' Her chin came up, and her eyes flashed. 'I'm just worried it might be too risqué for *you*. Come on, let's take a look.' She grabbed his hand and darted forward, pushing open the frosted glass door into the *Salon Privé*.

The first thing that met their eye was a sizeable bronze on a white plinth. A couple had been frozen for all time in what looked like the moment of orgasm, savage expressions contorting both the faces of the man and the woman, and their bodies, unusually elongated, were almost arched away from each other, looking more pained than ecstatic.

'Blimey, they don't really look as if they're enjoying it very much,' observed Jess, leaning in for a closer look at the detailing, 'although I must admit, it's a very fine piece of art.' She turned to him, pinker than

ever. 'I hope I don't look as ugly as that when I . . .
um . . . when I'm in the throes.'

'You look beautiful, Jess. Transcendent.'

It was true. Her face might twist a bit, and she had
a habit of scrunching up her eyes, but nothing could
take away the loveliness and honesty of her features,
in the throes or otherwise.

'Liar.'

'How can you say that? Didn't you even look at
yourself in the mirror when we were making love on
the ottoman back at Windermere? Haven't you looked
when you're having your fantasy sessions with Dream
Lover?' The rosy, impressionistic dabs on her cheeks
brightened, suggesting she might have done, and that
she'd had mirror sex with herself before she'd done
it with him. 'I think we need to do it in front of a
looking glass again at the earliest possible opportunity
so you can see how gorgeous you really look.'

Her mouth quirked. She bit her lip. Then grinned
broadly.

Bingo! As usual, she was up for it, and he couldn't
wait. He wanted to bundle her into a limousine straight
away and rush her to his apartment. Then fuck her
furiously in front of the sliding mirrored doors in his
dressing room. Or maybe when the image of the room
reflected back from the windows, at night. Perhaps,
for a tease, they could perform without him telling
her they were one way glass and nobody could look
in on them.

*Are you an exhibitionist, Jess? Lord knows you've got
plenty to be proud of.*

'Yikes, the prices!' she exclaimed, clearly avoiding

the issue for the moment. 'I thought the colourist works were expensive, but at least they're by noted artists. This is ridiculous . . . I've never even heard of this sculptor.'

Ellis took a look at the ticket. Not desperately expensive by his standards, but he didn't like it enough to consider buying. 'Let's look at some of the drawings,' he said, leading her away. A display of coloured drawings along one wall had caught his eye. They were relatively small, but something about the arrangement of the bodies in the nearest one spoke to him much more excitingly than the contorted looking bronze.

The suite of drawings had one major theme. BDSM. Ellis leant in close, to see the detail. The style was almost naive, nowhere near as accomplished and vibrant as Jess's work. But the artistic spanking enthusiast's enjoyment of his or her subject was obvious and joyous. Whoever they were, they very clearly had an intimate experience of the games they portrayed.

Buxom babes with rounded bottoms lay across the laps of stern looking gentlemen, mostly dressed in black. Pink splodges to match those adorning Jess's elegant cheekbones were in evidence on these shapely backsides, and when they twisted around, to look at the target zone, the expressions on the spanked women's faces were wide-eyed, full of feigned horror and undisguised excitement.

Some of the drawings were heavier in content, whips and chains and leather collars abounding, but they all had an unabashed aura of strangely wholesome enjoyment.

The spankers were loving it.

The spanked were loving it.

The artist was loving it.

I'm loving it myself, thought Ellis, with an inner smile. His fingers flexed, recalling the divine firmness of Jess's bottom when he'd caressed it. She was a goddess of slim but curvy perfection in that department.

Would she like to try all that? He cast a sly sideways glance at her. He didn't want to pressure her into anything she didn't want to do. There was no pleasure for either of them in that. But she was curious, and she'd expressed an interest in 'experimentation', so who was he to deny her any experience? He was supposed to be tutoring her, after all.

Jesus, it was difficult to view images like these with such a beautiful and desirable woman as Jess beside him. A woman he'd be bedding sooner rather than later. Surreptitiously, he adjusted the fall of his jacket, in an attempt to disguise the sudden, fierce erection he was sporting. Hiding his hard-ons in pubic was an occupational hazard with Jess around.

The expression on her face was intent, almost avid, although not awestruck in the presence of greatness as she'd been in the Courtauld Gallery. Was it the artist's style she was scrutinising so closely? Or the subject matter? The latter, he suspected. He nearly moaned out loud when the pink tip of her tongue dabbed at her lower lip. Was she trying to goad him into embarrassing himself, the gorgeous minx? It almost seemed that way.

'So, what do you think?' he said at last, to break his own inner tension. 'I don't think the artist is anywhere near as talented as you. If you chose to draw this kind of subject matter, you could clean up here at these prices.'

The sketches were indeed priced with a great deal of chutzpah, based more on their sprightly content than on the skill involved.

Jess frowned, and yet Ellis could see her turning thoughts over.

My God, woman, you're amazing! You're almost considering it, aren't you?

But was it the idea of selling erotic art . . . or playing the games the drawings depicted?

Both, he hoped, as she turned to him with a grin. 'If I were to draw it, I'd have to understand it, wouldn't I?' Her eyes twinkled.

Ellis's cock lurched. Desire, and a pounding excitement thrilled through him. She wanted to play. She was a goddess; inexperienced yet seductive and sensual to her artistic fingertips.

'You would indeed.'

'Know anybody who could give me a bit of instruction?' She glanced at the nearest sketch, a pretty dark-haired girl with sleek, reddened buttocks, across the lap of a man with a saturnine, rakish look. If Jess herself had drawn it, it would have been the two of them.

'You know I do.'

'I thought so.'

There was nobody else in the *Salon Privé*, so he kissed her, his lips brushing hers lightly, when really he wanted to ravish her mouth, and grind his body against hers.

'Shall we get out of here?'

'Yes please.'

He took her by the hand, and led her away from the provocative art. 'Can you wait a few more minutes though?'

'Yes . . . yes, of course.' She looked puzzled.

'Good girl. I want to buy a couple of these naughty spanking drawings.' He winked at her. 'They're nowhere near as good as your work, but I want to reward the artist for giving us interesting ideas.'

Jess laughed. 'Ever the philanthropist. Where are you going to hang them?' she asked as they passed into the main gallery.

'I've no idea . . .' He hadn't either, but he'd think of something. 'Maybe I'll establish myself a secret sex room for kinky activities, like the billionaires in the bestsellers do.'

'I wouldn't put it past you,' said Jess, returning his grin as they approached the eager-looking gallery assistant, who clearly already thought of Ellis as the handsome Santa Claus of her commission.

'Could you summon a car please, Jess, while I settle up?' Ellis asked, turning to her. 'It'll save a bit of time . . .'

Oh, he loved the heat in Jess's eyes. The eagerness. The sensuality. She was growing in sexual assurance with every moment that passed. Yet she didn't flaunt it. Everywhere they'd been today, he'd seen men eyeing her up. Sometimes he was sure she'd noticed, other times not so much. But she didn't preen or flutter, simply accepting admiration as her right.

When they were out on the pavement, it was the

same. The appreciative glances came her way. It made Ellis smile, so used was he to catching attention himself. Now he was in the shade.

You can look, but not touch, he said to the massed ranks of Jess's new admirers, touching her back as a long dark car eased out of traffic to slow in front of them.

For the moment, she's mine. Because she permits it. But soon, I'll have to give her up, because I'm not worthy of her and I can't give her what she needs.

She'll take her pick of you then. Choose a prince from amongst her helpless slaves.

Watch out, you guys, she'll eat you alive!

22

'You're looking at me very strangely, Mr McKenna.'

It was true. Ever since they'd got into the car, an unusually quiet Ellis had been looking at her in a way that was both measured, and what she could only describe as impressed. There was desire there too, in his darkened eyes, and yes, in the bulge in his trousers that she'd noticed as his jacket slid aside . . . but for some reason, he didn't immediately act on it. Or lunge at her.

But then, Ellis had far too much class to lunge at a woman. He didn't need to. Presumably they always fell at his feet with ease, just as she'd done herself, pretty much.

'I'm just thinking about the way men everywhere look at you, Jess.' He reached out and ran a fingertip along her cotton-clad thigh. 'Are you aware of the fact that almost every heterosexual male who crosses your path would give his eye teeth to get what I'm getting? Because you're a goddess.'

'And you're a nutcase. And you're imagining things.'

But was he? She was aware of the looks she got from men now. She'd noticed a change after that first night with Ellis, but had they *always* looked, and she'd been too blinkered to see it?

'No, I'm dead on the money. You're gorgeous. The admiration and worship of us poor males is your birthright.'

Jess laughed. Whether he was bullshitting her or not, it was good to hear. She wasn't afraid to admit she enjoyed the flattery.

But still . . .

She narrowed her eyes at him. 'Okay, so I'm a gorgeous goddess and men are unworthy, but doesn't that rather fly in the face of what we were just discussing in the *Salon Privé*?' Her heart started to thud, and the engine of need turned over, deep in her belly. 'I'm assuming, if we're going to play, that you'll be in charge . . . the master . . . the one with the upper hand? Like in the drawings . . .' His hand was still moving on her thigh, and she had the sudden flash fantasy of it pulling back sharply, then landing in a slap. 'Now, it almost sounds as if you want *me* to be dominant instead.'

He gave her a long look. Contemplative. Almost sly. 'Now there's an interesting thought.' His fingers curved, caressing the inner slope of her thigh now. 'But yes, I've always been the dominant. It's what comes naturally to me . . .' He shrugged. 'But I'm not saying I wouldn't ever switch. I just haven't got around to it yet.'

And you probably never will. With me. We won't have the time.

Jess pushed the sobering thought away. Their time *was* limited. And the moment was too electric to waste.

'I like the idea of you being dominant,' she said, meaning it, 'on a temporary basis, of course. I . . . I feel safe with you.'

'Thank you.' Ellis's voice was solemn. Her trust wasn't displaced, she'd never been surer. Then he smiled again. 'And yes. Just a temporary basis. You're too strong a woman, Jess Lockhart, for anything other than that.'

I think I am, Mr McKenna. I think I'm getting there. And I'm going to need all my strength soon. When we part . . .

When they entered the apartment, Ellis caught her by the hand. His grip was firm. Not cruel. Not rough. But attention-catching.

'So, how about it? Are you ready to play? To go a bit further, be more daring?' He drew her to him, right into his personal space . . . or perhaps he was in hers, already playing?

He was calling her bluff.

'Do you have to ask?' She looked him right in the eye, not wavering.

Ellis beamed. 'So, do we play now? Or later?'

Jess's heart pounded. Now, definitely now.

'Now.'

Heat flared in his eyes, and she imagined him monitoring her eagerness through the way the blood pounded in her wrist.

'You've got the heart of a lion, Ms Lockhart.' Moving closer, he whispered in her ear, his voice dark and husky. 'Shall we try little spanking then? Nothing too elaborate . . . just enough to put a little heat in that fabulous bottom of yours.'

Should she even speak at all now? Were they already in the zone?

'Yes . . . I think I'd like to try that.'

'Very well then.' Ellis released her, the move brisk, and decisive. He *was* in the zone. 'I'd like you to prepare yourself. I'd like you to wear a skirt, and no knickers. You can keep that blouse on if you like. It's pretty.'

The words almost made Jess sway, dizzy with excitement, and rocked by the stern little edge in Ellis's smile. His dominant act would be just that, an act, but ever the showman he would play it to the hilt.

'Is there anything else I should do?' She needed to ask. She didn't want to disappoint him.

'Just be ready. Do anything you need to. Now, you may go . . . but don't take too long.'

The way Ellis looked at her suggested that it wouldn't be a good idea to say anything else, so instead, Jess gave a quick little nod, and sped away to the bedroom.

Not sure what making herself ready for anything entailed, she hurried through the most logical preparations. The soft blue blouse, she kept, but put a prettier bra beneath, with a front clasp. Luckily, she'd brought a blue cotton skirt that looked good with the blouse, and her flashiest shoes, a pair of navy high heels she'd once bought for a party, long ago. They were steeper than her usual choice, but perfect for the moment. She supposed she should've had stockings and suspenders for a gig like this, but they were too much of a palaver, and her legs looked perfectly fine with fake tan. Better than fine.

A bit more makeup seemed a good idea too. A bolder look to show she'd made a proper effort, and that she was still Jess, his goddess, and only temporarily playing a submissive role because she wanted to.

Just about as ready as she'd ever be to play at spanking, Jess surveyed herself in the mirror.

Face serene. Clothes cute and flattering. Hair shiny. Legs spectacular! She half imagined going out there, and turning the tables. Telling Ellis that she'd take charge. He wouldn't complain, even if it wasn't what he was expecting.

But you have no idea what to actually do, you silly mare!

Maybe another time. If there was one. Don't think of that now . . .

Holding her head high, she walked smartly out of the bedroom, heading for the spacious sitting room area.

There, she suppressed a little gasp. Ellis must have entered his dressing room by the other door, because he too had made his preparations. Gone were the soft linen suit and flowered Paul Smith shirt, and in their place were dark denims and a midnight blue shirt that was unmistakably silk. The effect was pure drama, and a perfect foil for his supermodel looks. He'd done something to his hair too, dampened it and combed it back a little.

From gilded beach bum to dark shadow-god in the wink of an eye.

'You—'

'Shush,' he said softly. It was just one word in a low voice but it rang with power. 'There's no need to speak. Not until I tell you. Do you understand?'

Jess nodded. She knew she should affect a respectful attitude, looking down submissively, but she couldn't take her eyes off him. He made her knees wobble, and desire roll heavy in her belly. Who would have believed that Ellis McKenna could be any more of a lust object than he normally was? But apparently it was possible.

'I won't do anything heavy, Jess. I'm not a brute or a sadist, or even all that much of a master . . . but I need to know that what we do is good for you. That you have a way out, do you understand?'

She nodded again.

'I guess you've heard the expression "safe word", if you've read all those naughty books?'

She gave another nod.

'I thought so. Now tell me what your safe word is. You may speak.'

Jess nearly cracked a smile. Ellis himself was trying not to grin. It was there in the fine muscles of his face, and that made her feel safer than any word.

A vision of the Courtauld flashed before her eyes, and the pretty cocotte in her black and white dress. 'Renoir.'

'Good choice. Renoir it is then.' He allowed himself the ghost of a smile. 'Now, come here.'

She walked towards him like a goddess, her head held high, her eyes clear and confident. If he'd been a real 'master', he'd have reprimanded her, but he was just a man playing an erotic game, for diversion, with a beautiful and exceptional woman.

'Stand very still,' he instructed her when she reached him. He could smell a faint whiff of her light and delectable floral toilette water, and it almost made him sway with desire. Almost made him grab her and hug her and kiss her and sweep her up in his arms, to carry her to bed and simply and delightfully fuck her.

But, he'd offered her an experience. Something to add to her repertoire, so he'd better deliver on the act that he'd promised her.

He looked down into her eyes and, for a moment, she looked back, unfazed. But then, like the good submissive of fiction, she lowered her gaze. Respectfully? Well, a fair approximation of it. She was a damn good actress when she wanted to be. But he'd seen the sweet quirk of her lips just before she'd looked down.

'You're a very wayward submissive, Ms Lockhart. You don't seem to have any respect for authority at all. I was going to allow you a glass of champagne before we started, to calm your nerves, but I'm not sure now that you deserve it.'

Goddamn, the bubbly wasn't for her, it was for *him*!

She didn't respond, or even move a muscle, standing there, a poem in blue. But he knew somehow that she would love a glass of champagne. In the brief time they'd been together, she'd taken quite a liking to it, and in a cool, melancholy moment, he resolved that when they parted, he would send her a case of whatever marque she preferred, on a regular basis.

Enough of that. The moment is now. There's no future . . . and no past. Just us. Playing.

'However, as I'm feeling magnanimous, I think we will have a little champagne, first, before I start touching you.'

At the word 'touching', she licked her lips, the she-devil, and Ellis fought for self-control. His cock was already like iron, pressing against the unforgiving fabric of his jeans. 'Stay right where you are,' he added, striding to the long, polished sideboard, where he'd placed the wine in a glass ice bucket, along with a couple of other items that he'd seen her glance at, noting them.

He filled a single flute with the pale golden fizz. It was the house champagne of the building, and though he'd always liked it, he wondered now if he'd short-changed Jess. Perhaps he should have ordered up a more luxurious brand for her? Something world famous and sought after? But she wasn't like that. Celebrity labels meant nothing to her. She had higher values; true quality and worth were what interested her.

So why is she with me? She doesn't give a toss about my money, and she knows I'm damaged goods . . .

Dismissing the thought, he brought the brimming flute back to where she stood, so slim and elegant. He took one sip himself, and then held it to her lips, cradling the back of her head as he did so. Letting her hands hang graceful and inert at her sides, she took a drink from the glass, a real one with obvious enjoyment, and cracked that tricky little imp of a smile again.

'Good, eh?' She nodded. 'More?' She nodded again.

He proffered the glass again, and she took another swallow. The game was supposed to be him watching her, him scrutinising her and controlling her, but she looked back at him levelly over the brim of the glass, eyes full of irrepressible challenge.

Taking back the glass, he drained it then returned it to the sideboard, his back almost burning from her subtle scrutiny. He was supposed to be in charge, but her hold over him was total. Running his hand along the edge of the polished wood, he breathed in deep, then selected an item from the surface.

His tie. The blue one he'd worn to the Palm Court. When he returned to her, with it stretched taut between his two hands, her eyes widened.

'So, Miss Lockhart, are you ready to play?'

For a moment, she didn't speak. Was she shaking? He certainly was. And fully erect too. For a moment her glance skittered to his groin, then she met his eyes again, her expression bold.

'I'm yours to command . . . master. Whatever you wish is my wish.'

Good answer!

'Let's start with this then, shall we?' He stepped behind her, and drew her hands together at the small of her back, securing them loosely with the tie. His cock leapt. She was bound. Her body available to him. She couldn't stop him making free with her in any way he chose.

Plunging his hand into her silky hair, he held her

face to his and kissed her hard, pushing in deep and rough with his tongue, tasting the wine on her tongue as she no doubt tasted it on his. He kept kissing, wildness rising as he plundered her mouth, gripping the back of her shapely scalp. A moan rose in his throat, and he almost thought he'd uttered it, until he realised that it was Jess who was moaning not he. She was shifting her hips too, as if so turned on that she couldn't contain the energy.

'So randy,' he growled against her mouth, and with his free hand, he reached down and gripped her crotch, massaging her through her pretty blue skirt.

Jess gasped sharply. Ellis imagined the flutter of her aroused flesh, stirred by his hold. He squeezed hard and she struggled, rocking herself on his hand, moaning again.

He could almost imagine she was already coming. Maybe she was?

Being bound made Jess dizzy with desire. She couldn't explain why. It didn't make sense. Normally she would have kicked against being in any man's power. Even when she'd been a virgin, she'd valued her own sense of agency, and being subject to someone else's will, man or woman, had never sat right with her.

But this was Ellis, and everything was different with him. And exciting in a way she could barely quantify. The urge to touch herself raged through her, amplified by the inability to do it. Her sex ached, and weird yearnings to do strange things wracked her body.

Crazy things like falling to her knees to kiss his

feet. Kiss the scars of his long ago operation, as if to assuage the pain he'd once experienced. He was bare-foot, as he so often went indoors, but no less dominant for that. Ellis McKenna didn't need boots and leather to be her master. His mere presence ruled her world in this game. With his mouth so close, she pressed forward and stole another kiss.

'Naughty, naughty, naughty,' he whispered against her lips, and she could almost taste the laughter in his voice. This was piquant fun between the two of them. There would never be anything really heavy or cruel. He wasn't like that. He wasn't selfish.

'I'm sorry, master,' she replied, trying to keep her own voice straight and respectful.

Still close, he shook his head, as if despairing. 'You mustn't speak until I give you permission, *slave*,' he pointed out, placing special emphasis on the noun, round and fruity. 'Now, what do you want me to do with you? And this time, you *may* speak.' Still gripping her aching crotch, his strong hand tightened, pressing her skirt against her.

Everything. I want you to do everything.

'If it pleases you . . . I'd like you to touch me, and spank me, and fuck me, master. But only if it pleases you.'

'But I'm already touching you . . .' Squeeze, squeeze, squeeze . . . 'Do you want more? Do you want me to touch your skin? Your sex . . . your naked sex?'

She couldn't answer. It would have come out as a long moan of pleasure. The zone he'd named seemed to tingle, and leap . . . she was almost coming. Jess nodded her answer, unable to stop herself bearing

down on his containing hand. The tie around her
wrists seemed to amplify the sensations. She was
fizzing and bubbling inside, like the champagne.

'Very well, then,' he said, 'You shall have everything
you want. But first . . . a final touch, I think. Stay right
here.'

Jess kept still, even though her body was screaming
for release. If her hands had been free, she might even
have played with herself, and to hell with the consequences. Those consequences were what she wanted,
after all.

Heart pounding, she watched her lover stroll to
the sideboard and pick up the other item that had
been lying there. With eyes only for Ellis, Jess hadn't
really fixed on it, but it'd been in the back of her mind
all the same; a patterned silk scarf, decorated with
some of Monet's water lilies, unless she wasn't
mistaken.

*Don't be dumb, Jess . . . He's going to use it as a blind-
fold, you ninny!*

Ellis twirled the length of silk around his fingers,
tensioning it as he had the tie, making Jess shudder
harder. What would it feel like to be in the dark, not
knowing what was coming next, what he was going
to do to her? Waiting for the next touch. The next
kiss. The first spank . . .

'Will you mind being blindfolded?' His voice was
arch now, more English, his accent purer. Within the
parameters of the game, she hadn't much choice but
to accede to him, and for a moment apprehension
gripped her.

It was all new. The blindfold, the potential pain of

the spanking, the reddened bottom. All new to her. Intriguing but alarming.

But then she relaxed. 'No, I shan't mind at all, master,' she whispered, still not sure whether she was supposed to speak at this juncture.

She was safe with Ellis. She had no doubt about that. He might be closed off from romantic love by his loss, but his kindness and his humanity were unimpaired. His heart wasn't arrogant, selfish, or controlling, and he would always put the well-being of a partner before his own needs, his own pleasure.

Even in their brief acquaintance, he'd proved that to her time and time again.

In a deft, quick move, he covered her eyes with the soft scarf. The silk was heavy gauge, and surprisingly dense, creating a velvet darkness. Disorientated for a moment, she swayed, and Ellis instantly supported her, letting her part her feet so she could stand more squarely.

'Good girl,' he said, right next to the side of her face, ruffling her hair, beneath the containing silk, with his breath. 'Can you see anything?'

She shook her head.

'Excellent . . .' He paused. 'But all of London, beyond the window, can see you. They can see how beautiful you are . . . how vulnerable . . . And they'll see your gorgeous body, too, when I show it to them.'

Jess suppressed a 'yeah, right'. On the balcony earlier in the day, she'd wondered whether people – across the river, or in another building, and in possession of strong binoculars or a telescope – could see into the apartment when it was lit. But on checking, she'd discovered the windows were privacy glass showing only a mirrored surface. There was no possibility of a voyeur observing their game.

But imagining a voyeur was fun. They'd done it before when playing at phone sex, and look how well that had turned out. She pictured a thousand watching eyes, avid for the show. The sight of herself and Ellis in performance. Her body exposed and played with. Deliciously tormented. Spanked and compelled to orgasm; most likely soundly fucked too.

Beneath her skirt, her sex rippled again, and the silky fluid of arousal welled from her cleft and trickled down her thigh.

'Now, stay very quiet and still, while I prepare you.' Jess licked her lips.

'Wicked girl. You'll pay for that.' His thumb pressed down on her lower lip, then thrust inside her mouth. Instinctively she sucked on it. 'And you'll do that, too, I think, sooner or later.'

The vision of Ellis's beautiful cock filled her mind. She saw herself on her knees, still bound, sucking furiously on it. Her mouth watered at the thought and she swallowed, almost as if gulping down his come.

Oh yeah!

And then his hands were gone, and she was left in the dark, aching and anticipating. The imaginary metropolitan audience watched hungrily, anticipating Ellis's next move. Jess sensed steps . . . Oh, he was wily. Because he was barefoot, there was no way to hear him stomping about the room, and she wished for spider senses so she could tell where he was and what he was doing.

For a full minute, nothing happened, then just when she was about to crack and demand, where the hell are you, he touched her. Quick and deft, he unbuttoned her blouse, then pushed the fabric off her shoulders, to expose her bra.

'Sublime.' His voice was low as his flat hand settled on her chest above the lace and satin. His little finger slid beneath the edge of the fabric. 'Your skin is very hot, slave. Are you burning for me?'

She nodded.

'Good.' Reaching around, he squeezed her buttock with his free hand, kneading the flesh. Still working her, he kissed her again, thrusting with his tongue.

Kiss. Squeeze. Breathe. The slither of narrow fingertips inside the cup of her bra, searching and finding her nipple.

'Do you like that?'

'Yes . . .' she whispered, barely recognising her own voice.

'Good,' he repeated crisply, then released her. 'Let's find some more things you like.'

With no further ado, he snapped open the front clasp of her bra, baring her. Pausing only to play his fingers across her nipples, he reached down, grasped the hem of her slim skirt, and eased it up her thighs and up over her belly, tucking the cotton cloth at her waist.

'What a beautiful sight. I'm sure the men in our "audience" are loving this. Gorgeous tits, lush pussy, perfect thighs . . . what more could they ask for?'

Jess moaned when he gripped her crotch again, this time with no barrier. Desire surged as he slipped a finger into her cleft and rocked it against her clit, still playing with her nipples with his free hand. Counterpoint . . .

'Would you like an orgasm now?'

She nodded her head furiously. All resolve to hold out had evaporated.

'I'll spank you harder.'

'I don't care.'

Soft laughter was his only answer. That, and imperious attention to her clit. His touch was hard, wild, nowhere near as millimetre perfect as his usual subtlety, but Jess came almost immediately, shouting out, 'Oh God,' as her hips jerked and rocked, uncouthly thrusting. Still working her, Ellis flung his free arm around her waist, keeping her steady.

The orgasm was blinding, intense, going off like a rocket, too much yet too little, far too soon. Even though she'd climaxed, it wasn't enough. She needed more. But when she tried to coax him into it, pushing against his hand, he whispered, 'No, no, no, greedy girl. You have to wait now. You have to take your punishment first.'

In her mind's eye, she saw him clearly. Her handsome, dazzling god, a prince of drama in his dark clothing. Merciless, he pinched and rolled her left nipple, tweaking and toying. Jess pursed her lips hard, fighting the groans, not sure whether they were of pleasure or pain, but wanting more, more, more . . . her voice escaped as Ellis's fingers tightened on her, flattening her nipple and sending streaks of sensation along secret pathways to her clit.

Her eyes watered behind her blindfold. It wasn't

tears, just an overflowing of sensation. An echo of her arousal welling again in her pussy, the fluid flowing down her bare thigh like a river of sex.

The whole of her loins seemed to be on fire as Ellis repeated the procedure with the other nipple.

God damn it, he was infernal. He'd noted her susceptibilities, right from the beginning, what seemed like a lifetime ago. Now he was using it to lay down another sweet layer of erotic torment, alternating pressure with exquisitely delicate flicking and feather-light stroking.

You devil!

One of the drawings she'd seen in the *Salon Privé* came to her mind. A submissive posed very much as she was, but with heavy clamps hanging from her nipples. Jess imagined that weight, wondering if she could have taken it, and still been able to stand proud, with a defiant smile, like that model.

As if he'd read her mind, Ellis tweaked her nipple again. It hurt. She was dying to come again . . . yet loving the denial. How kinky was that?

Like the girl in the drawing, she lifted her head, echoing that bold expression beneath the silky blindfold.

Bring it on, Mr Sex! Bring it on!

'If only you could see yourself . . . you look divine,' said Ellis, swapping pressure for pleasure again, and making her dance in her high heels.

Well, I could see myself if you'd take the blindfold off.

She didn't say it. She wasn't supposed to speak without permission, and seeing herself in the window glass might shatter the magic.

In her darkened world, Ellis's hands settled on her bottom and, as he reached around to cup the cheeks of her arse, the wall of his body pressed against her beleaguered breasts. His cock was hard against her belly, pushing at her through the denim of his jeans, as he squeezed and fondled her, testing the resilience of her flesh and the tone of her muscles.

'You have a gorgeous arse, slave,' he purred, giving her bottom a little pinch, 'sweet and curvy, yet perfectly firm. Ideally designed for a bit of a spanking. I can't wait . . .'

Me neither. Get on with it!

Why so keen to be punished? Something else that didn't make sense . . . even though it did!

Time seemed to warp and waver as he handled her body. Breasts, buttocks, thighs . . . sex. His touch was vigorous, moving abruptly from zone to zone, surprising her, exciting her more and more. She adored it, yet wanted to cry out to him to move on to the next phase. Fear and apprehension were doing a tango in her belly. The urge to fight her bonds, to touch and caress Ellis just as he touched and caressed her, was bordering the unbearable.

But just when she was about to shout out to him, he took her by the elbow and guided her across the room to one of the deep leather sofas. His hold on her was solicitous, as if she were infinitely precious to him. Fugitive thoughts flitted across her mind, and she nearly stumbled. But Ellis caught her in a flash, supporting her with both hands, holding her safe.

'Are you all right?' His voice was soft and caring,

completely out of his role. The real Ellis concerned
for her, and her well-being.

'Fine. Thanks.'

'Good girl.'

Something in the quality of his hold on her changed
again, and they were back in the drama.

Game on . . .

23

If only he could express how gorgeously desirable she looked. How supreme. How goddess-like despite her exposed and vulnerable state. Her hands might be tied, but she had him in the palm of one of them. Trying to play the 'master' was like climbing a mountain in the face of her magnificence.

'Very well then, how shall we do this?' he posed the question, laughing inside at his attempts to be magisterial.

Jess didn't speak, but stood before him proud and perfect, her exposed body and her elegant demeanour turning him into her slave far more than she was his. When she lifted her chin, and breathed in, making her breasts rise too, his poor aching cock almost erupted in his jeans.

'Do you wish to kneel on the settee to be spanked, or will you take your punishment across my lap?'

Lap! Lap! Lap! his erection howled, longing for the contact. It'd put him in even greater danger of embarrassing himself, but he didn't care.

'Across your lap, if you wish it, master,' she answered. She was so composed, and yet as excited as he was, he could tell.

'Excellent choice.'

Happy, he leant close and kissed her on the lips. His face brushed against the silk scarf, and he recalled purchasing it, on impulse, when it'd caught his eye in the window of one of the boutiques in the building's atrium. The motif of the water lilies had made him smile, refreshing the thoughts of Jess that had been floating in his consciousness, like the aquatic blooms. It hadn't occurred to him until afterwards that the scarf might be used in a sex game. He'd just wanted it because it was pretty . . . and so was Jess.

Taking his seat on the tawny leather sofa, he breathed in deep, loving the fresh scent of her light, flowery toilette water, and the deeper, more visceral tang of her aroused sex, so close to his face as she stood before him. The glint of her silky moisture gleamed on her pubic hair and on the inside of her thighs. Damn, he wanted to be there now, and to hell with spanking. But he'd promised her a game, an experiment, a bit of erotic fun . . . and he was committed to deliver. Reaching up, he took her by the waist and guided her across his knee. Despite her bonds, she descended with grace, and seemed to settle in exactly the right spot.

Parting his thighs, he made a steadier platform for her body, almost gasping aloud as she jostled his hard and throbbing cock.

'Sorry,' she said quickly, then wriggled again, the minx, giving him another rub with her flank.

He wanted to say 'no worries' as his Australian friends and family might have done but instead he replied with a mock-stern, 'I should think so too.'

But it wasn't just the feel of her that had him on a hair trigger. The sight of her crumpled his self-control. Her bottom was the loveliest, the lushest shape. Just the right degree of roundness, yet neat and tight and toned. Even the most diffident of spankers would be tempted to lay a hearty slap across it, and then want to do it again and again as the firm flesh bounced and the skin went rosy.

Despite the impish sense of disobedience he sensed in her, Jess lay still, steadying the target for him. Still as a living statue, she made it impossible for him to miss or fluff the blow.

Settling his left hand at the small of her back, by her bound hands, he was astonished that the sight of his wedding ring didn't stab him with guilt. In this cool, clear moment he felt detached from the life it represented, although he knew that was only a temporary phenomenon, only a fleeting escape.

With his other hand spread, he lay it across her beautiful curves, the rounds of her bottom. Her skin was velvety and warm. Not hot yet, but delightful to the touch. He rubbed her and stroked her for a few moments, exploring the inner slopes, and her thighs, and even dipping round into her sticky cleft. She maintained her poise, but he could feel it was a strain; her body was electric.

'Are you ready?' he asked, fingertips just resting against her sex lips, where the honey was pooled. 'You don't want to go "Renoir" on me, do you? It's all right, if you do . . . I understand.'

Again, he knew he wasn't acting the classic master, but it didn't seem to matter. This was their own game, not governed by rules and conventions and 'scenes'.

'I'm ready,' she replied.

There was nervousness in her voice, but a smile there too.

Ready as I'll ever be.

Jess tried not to tense. Even within the limits of her knowledge, she knew that it would hurt less if she let herself go loose and not tense up.

'Okay then . . .'

But almost before he'd spoken, the first slap landed, square on the crown of her left buttock.

'Jesus Christ!'

It *did* hurt. It hurt like crazy, even though she'd relaxed, or so she'd thought . . . Her bottom blazed at the point of impact, as if he'd struck her with a piece of well-seasoned hardwood rather than his hand.

'No . . . just me,' he said, spanking her again on the other cheek, balancing the fire.

'Ow! Ow! Ow!' Her body was in shock, everything disconnected, not reacting right.

Or maybe it was? Her desire surged, burning like her bottom, making her crazy. Wriggling like the proverbial eel, she almost fell off Ellis's knee, not able to tell where pain ended and raging lust began.

Another spank fell, and she squealed, really squealed, her voice high and squeaky.

'It hurts! It hurts!'

'Of course it does.' Ellis fell still. 'It's a spanking. That's the whole point.' His hand settled more gently across her rear, even the feather-light contact stirring things up and increasing her squiggling and squirming. 'Do you want me to stop? If you don't like it . . .'

'No! Don't stop. I don't know if I like it or not, but it's turning me on. Give me more!'

It was the truth. The actual truth. The heat in her bottom pulsed out into her pussy too, transubstantiated into gorgeous, gouging need. The spanking pain was insubstantial beside it.

'Are you sure?' For a moment he sounded doubtful.

'Of course I'm sure . . . why are you even asking me?' Half laughing, she ground herself against him. 'You're the master. Just do what masters do!'

Ellis broke out into laughter too, wickedly squeezing her punished bottom cheek, and making her yelp again. 'Yes, indeed, I am the master, aren't I?' He squeezed the other cheek. 'From the way you've started ordering me around, I was beginning to wonder there . . .'

'I'm sorry.'

'I should think so. I'm going to spank you even harder for that, you minx.'

Thank God for that! She didn't say it. She was too busy grunting and gritting her teeth, as new spanks landed.

The pain was fierce. Red. Fast-spreading, even though Ellis stayed on target like a marksman. Lust bloomed in Jess's belly, and she flung herself about, working her crotch against him. Yet still he managed to find her bottom every time, stoking the fire with a sweet, unerring accuracy.

Panting, fighting for control, Jess saw a picture of the two of them, on the dark canvas of her mind. Ellis stern yet smiling, his hand descending again and again. Herself bound and blindfolded, clothes half on, half off, her buttocks naked and raggedly crimson.

Hissing at a particularly crafty blow, she was able to smile too.

Against her hip a mighty erection swelled, rock, rock hard.

Sod this!

'Enough already! Let me up! Let me loose!'

'Renoir?'

'Whatever! Renoir! Manet! Monet! Toulouse-Lautrec! I want to see you . . . You're beautiful! I want you to fuck me!'

Ellis laughed out loud, but he was already working the knot that bound her hands. The instant Jess was free, she shuffled off his lap and onto her knees beside him on the sofa, cursing through her teeth as she wrenched off the silky scarf too. Awkwardly, she twisted round to look at her bottom. 'Golly! Talk about flaming crimson . . .' She poked her buttock gingerly, and swore again.

'I thought you wanted to look at me, not your arse,' pointed out Ellis. When she turned back towards him, he was grinning delightedly.

'Just checking.' She lunged at him, almost forgetting her tender bottom, throwing her arms around him and then kissing him hard and messily. She'd never felt more voracious, more filled with lust . . .

Ellis responded in kind, fighting her in the kiss, tongue pushing back. 'You devil!' she growled against his mouth when he cupped the flaming cheeks of her bottom, holding tight.

'And you, madam, are the bossiest submissive in the world. I don't think I was ever really in charge there, Ms Lockhart. Not for an instant.'

Perhaps he was . . . perhaps he wasn't. Did it matter? He'd spanked her. It'd hurt. But she'd loved it!

And now she wanted him to fuck her. Fuck her hard.

She drew back a little, eating him up with her eyes. He *was* beautiful. His dark hair was wild, and his expression was too. His face was flushed, the pink across his cheekbones an echo of the cherry glow across her bottom.

'You *are* beautiful, Ellis . . .' She touched his face, her twinges forgotten.

'I'm not,' he said, still smirking.

'Liar! You know you are!'

'Okay then, I am, but nowhere near as beautiful as you are . . .' He settled his hands on her shoulders. 'Just look at you. Face of an angel. Breasts of a goddess. Rosy pink bottom of a courageous, stoic heroine. Perfection . . .'

She knew she wasn't. Not for him. But now was not the time to visit those issues. Now was the time to snatch pleasure with this wonderful man while she still had access to him.

'Fuck me, Ellis. You've stirred up fires . . . now do something put them out. Use that great big hose of yours!'

'So domineering . . .' Laughing, Ellis moved in close again, his breath riffling her hair. 'We shall have to play this game the other way sometime soon . . .' He pressed his lips to the side of her face. 'Like I said before, I'm not much of a submissive . . . but for you, I'd certainly be prepared to try it.'

Ah, the future again. The land that could not be visited.

'I'll look forward to that,' she said lightly, 'now, can we please make love?'

Taking the initiative, she slithered off the sofa and onto the rug. It was soft, with a deep, lush pile, but even so, the floor beneath was hard on her tender bottom. She didn't care though. The aching glow, the twinges as she moved, they only seemed to pour fuel on the conflagration of her need.

'Isn't this a bit painful for your bum?' Ellis slid down beside her; much more gracefully, she noted with wry chagrin. He spread his fingers and slid them down the side of her thigh, skirting the red zone. 'Would you like to be on top?'

Jess reached for him, pulling him down for another kiss. 'No, not really . . . and I don't care about the pain. What pain? I just want you in me, Mr Sex. Now jump to it!'

Looming over her, Ellis's face was full of wonder, illuminated, and the expression a thrill in itself. Yes, she had power. Sexual power. A strength that astonished her. How far she'd come in this game, in such short a time. Whatever happened with Ellis, in their very brief future together, she would adore him forever for showing her how to be herself . . .

As well as being the man she'd always love.

'I live to serve,' he answered puckishly, ripping at the buttons of his shirt, then tugging the garment off and flinging it aside. He prised a condom from the pocket of his jeans, then shimmied out of them too, delighting Jess with the fact he was rampantly commando.

'No knickers, Mr Sex. What a dirty boy you are!'

'Why waste time with pants when there's pussy to be had,' he shot back, with the condom already out of its package. Within a flash, he had it rolled on, armed and ready for action. 'Are you sure you don't want to ride me?'

'Sure . . . for now. Maybe later.' Grabbing at his flank, she urged him over her as she parted her legs, squirming her sizzling bottom against the rug.

Moving between her thighs, Ellis reached down to touch her. 'Ooh, like silk . . . Obviously your subconscious likes spanking, even if your conscious isn't quite sure yet.' With delicate accuracy, he rolled her clit like a pearl.

'Ellis! Please!' cried Jess, feeling orgasm gather, and desperate that he should be inside her when it arrived.

Pressing a kiss to her forehead, he complied, using his fingers to position his glans at her entrance, then swinging with his hips to push inside her.

Oh yes, oh yes, would she ever tire of this? The wonder of his possession was as fresh as first time, and the push was still a discovery of her boundaries. Her body was still tight, not virgin but barely explored.

He thrust in deep, pressing her bottom against the rug, making her grunt. Ignoring the new aches, she wrapped her arms and legs around him, arching to press hard into the contact between their bodies.

Growling, Ellis responded in kind, powering into her, in primal shoves, just what she wanted.

It was a wild chaotic ride, pleasure and pain, but mostly pleasure, pleasure, pleasure. A hair away from orgasm to start with, Jess came again and again, soaring and shouting under Ellis's relentless fucking. With the last scrap of her wits, she knew he was holding back, and determined that he should pinnacle with her, she geed him on, stroking his back and arse and thighs.

'You devil woman,' he hissed, 'you delicious sexy piece of ass, you blow my mind.'

'Ditto, devil man,' said Jess on a gasp, then grabbed at Ellis harder, another climax blanking her mind.

As she clung to him on instinct, he spent inside her, shouting her name.

Afterwards they lay in a shattered heap on the rug: Ellis gasping on his back, Jess rolled over onto her front, beside him. Somehow in the melee she'd found the Monet scarf, and had clutched it between her fingers like a talisman.

'This is beautiful,' she said, running her thumb over the fine silk, comparing it to the texture of Ellis's thick, dark hair. 'How did you come to have it? Did you buy it especially for BDSM games?'

Ellis opened his eyes and glanced at the scarf. 'No . . . actually, I noticed it in the window of one of the boutiques down in the atrium, and the water lilies made me think of you, and how you like the Impressionists.' He reached out and touched the silk, brushing her fingers. 'I loved the colours, and I thought it'd look great for fastening back your hair . . . or something. I just thought you'd like it.'

'I do. It's lovely. Thank you.'

Emotion choked her. He was such a kind man. It was the simplest of gifts, and yet chosen with genuine thoughtfulness.

They lapsed into silence. Peaceful, but also troubled for Jess.

Oh Ellis, how will I ever let you go?

24

Mm, more champagne.

Obviously Ellis lived slightly more of a billionaire life when in London because there was a new bottle of bubbly chilling in the ice bucket when Jess emerged from the bathroom. One flute stood beside it, and some wine was gone from the bottle.

Where was Ellis?

The spanking game had been a trip but intense. Jess had needed a bit of time out to herself afterwards and, as ever, Ellis had respected her space.

As a dominant, he'd been a revelation, and clearly knew exactly what he was doing. When Jess examined her body, she'd expected to see a mess of ragged redness and bruises covering her bottom, but her rear was surprisingly unscathed. It was still pink, yes, and a bit tender, but nowhere near as sore as she'd anticipated. Especially after a lavish application of another of Ellis's white label toiletries, an after-exercise rub that Jess suspected contained arnica and other beneficial herbs.

But now that she'd showered and tended to herself, she wanted to tell him she was okay. So where was the man? Somewhere in the apartment drinking champers, obviously. Pouring herself some, Jess took a welcome sip, and looked around the room.

Aw, he'd folded her clothes and laid them across a chair, bless him. He was such a creature of contrasts. An ultra-wealthy man who commanded the destiny of thousands of employees . . . yet endearingly domesticated. He cooked. He folded clothes. He was a treasure in so many more ways than just fabulous in bed.

On top of the pile was the beautiful silk scarf, and she ran her fingers over it, loving the vibrancy of the colours: multiple blues, lavender and purple. It was exquisite. Ellis could probably quite easily buy a real Monet if one came on the market, but this meant more to her because of the thoughtful way he'd chosen it.

Smoothing the delicate surface she'd ruffled, she set out to find her lover, glass in hand.

Almost immediately, she heard his voice. He was speaking. On the phone? No, there was his mobile on the coffee table in the living area. Had someone arrived while she was showering? She didn't think so.

Perhaps he was video conferencing? On his laptop. It sounded as if he was out on the patio and, being rather curious, she began moving that way . . . then hesitated.

None of my business. Probably high finance. Commerce never sleeps and all that. I should just watch the television or get my sketch pad out.

Yet she did neither, and, feeling vaguely guilty at
being so nosy, she continued towards the patio. The
long glass doors were open, and in the sheltered area
the tiles and the furniture were all dry, and the evening
air was fresh and perfect after the rain earlier in the
day. Remaining out of view behind the blinds, Jess
could see Ellis out there, relaxing in one of the lounging
chairs with his laptop on his knee. Yes, as she'd
suspected, he was conversing with someone on Skype.

Don't do it, Jess. Don't do it.

'I've always hoped you and Christobel might get
together . . . eventually . . . once you're over Julie.'

It was a woman's voice, coming from the speaker.
Quite strong, but a bit quivery. Perhaps someone
older? A relation?

'No, that won't happen. I'll never get over Julie.'

Oh, that cold, bleak tone. It cut to the quick. Jess
was familiar with his grief, but she'd never heard it
so plangently expressed, so bitter. Whoever he was
speaking to knew him well, and was privy to his sad
history. It must be a family member, or a very long-
standing friend. Jess knew in her gut it wasn't another
woman, at least not someone like her.

There was another question, but distracted, Jess
didn't quite catch it. Only Ellis's reply.

'Yes, I am with someone right now, Augusta. And
no, it's nothing like that. It's nice, but very, very
temporary.'

Jess gripped her glass in both hands. She wanted
to back away now, but her feet seemed glued to the
carpet. Ellis was talking to his Aunt Augusta, the one
with the island, and discussing someone temporary.

Me.

Why did it hit her in the gut to hear it? Ellis had been perfectly frank with her about what he could offer. Why think things would be otherwise? Ellis couldn't let himself get over the guilt, and he couldn't get over the loss of his beloved wife. There was no way she could get inside his head and know which pained him the most, the guilt or the loss, but they were both unequivocal. And now, to her horror, it dawned on Jess that despite what she thought was her logical and pragmatic handling of the situation, she'd subconsciously started to harbour certain hopes. Stupid hopes. Idiot hopes. Probably fostered by the tender way he'd nurtured her, and encouraged her to bloom.

Now she saw those hopes like smoke in the rain, without substance. Ellis would never allow himself to move on. It was sad and unhealthy, and she wished that for his sake as well as her own that things could be different. But she knew that no matter how much she tried to help him, there was probably no point.

His aunt made a small sharp sound of impatience that carried clearly from the speaker. 'But could you not try a bit harder to make something of your relationship with her? At least give this person a chance, Ellis. You won't give *anyone* a chance.'

Despite everything, Jess almost smiled. A matchmaking well-wisher, urging him to give love a chance . . . where had she heard all *that* before? The reasons were different, but both she and Ellis had closed themselves off from possibilities. What was different though was that Jess was finally ready to open the door and grow.

There was a long pause. Jess held her breath.

'We're just friends, Augusta, that's all. Jess and I enjoy each other's company. But like I said, it's strictly temporary. We both agreed that from the start. I offered to help her . . . help her out with something. And out of the goodness of her heart, she's keeping me company for a while. She's a lovely woman, and I am fond of her, but that's it. Nothing more. So don't get any big ideas, eh?'

Oh, that hurt. Even though she knew the score. Because of her own idiotic if barely formed ideas.

But no more. No more big ideas. Ellis was the most wonderful man she'd ever met, and the most human and humane, despite his voracious sexuality. But he would never be hers, and it would be better and less painful for both of them if they parted their ways as soon as possible.

When I get home from London, that's it. Back to reality . . . in every sense. No more Ellis. No more Dream Lover stuff. It's time to make a brand new start in the real world. Get the paints and the easel and everything out of storage. Accept Josh Redding's invitation.

Ha, all very fine. Easy to make resolutions; harder to follow them. But she'd do it. She had to. There were no other options.

Leaving her hiding place, she headed silently away, back towards the bedroom. The urge to draw was overpowering, a therapy for her hands. She couldn't turn off her heart, but at least she could do something that made her feel less powerless in the face of emotion she couldn't control.

No, she wasn't going to give up on having a life.

Ellis might impose on himself a strict set of emotional parameters, but she wasn't going to. It would hurt like hell not to be with the man she loved, but she couldn't take ten steps back now that she'd made so many forward.

But it was a horrid irony. Ellis McKenna was the man who'd helped her move forward after marking time for so many, many years.

But he couldn't do the same thing for himself.

A couple of glasses of champagne didn't seem to have interfered with Jess's ability to draw. Quite the reverse. She worked and worked, tearing through several fast sketches of Ellis in a raw and angular style. The pencil strokes were jagged, in a break from her usual preference for realism, but the results were good.

No wonder the great artists loved their booze and bad living and their torrid, tricky relationships. It obviously all helps with the creativity!

She sketched on and on, tossing sheets of paper aside, knowing exactly when each drawing was done, even if it looked half finished.

What was Ellis doing out there? Working on his computer? Still talking to his aunt?

Brooding?

Thinking about his temporary 'thing' and how to end it kindly?

Jess was pretty sure that Ellis was as aware as she was that they'd become too close for comfort. Getting up at last, she crossed the room to top up her champagne glass, never more sober in her life, despite the alcohol.

As she turned from the sideboard, Ellis entered the room, clutching the lapels of his robe together with one hand, and with the second champagne flute dangling from the fingers of his other. He looked chilled, as if the temperature outside had plunged.

Or maybe it was an inner coolness. Without speaking, he crossed to the bed, and his eyebrows shot up as he glanced at the drawings. Not sure how to find words, Jess brought the bottle across, took his glass from him and topped it up.

'Thanks . . .' He took a deep drink, then set the glass on the bedside table and resumed his perusal of her work. Jess joined him on the bed, at the other side, abandoning her own wine. Suddenly, it didn't taste quite so good.

Ellis set down the drawings and stared at her, frowning. She could see in his eyes that her wild new drawing style had told him all he needed to know.

'These are very, very good,' he said, touching the surface of the paper. 'Some of them look a bit turbulent though . . .' He frowned. Jess could read his face, and the struggle. He didn't want to hurt her, but it was coming . . . 'You're not in pain, are you? I didn't hit you too hard? I tried not to . . .'

Shadowboxing with a different kind of pain?

'No, you barely hurt me at all. I can't feel a thing now . . . You're very clever.' She smiled. Or tried to.

But there was no fooling Ellis. 'You heard what I said out there, didn't you? Me talking to Augusta on the computer.' His glorious face looked stricken again. 'I . . . I'm sorry, Jess. I really am. But . . . well . . . I am what I am. I wish things could be different.'

Ellis was usually so lithe, so loose, but now his body screamed tension in every nerve. Jess could feel it herself, singing in the air.

'Yes, I did hear,' she said quietly. Her fingers itched to reach out for his, and maybe a couple of hours ago, she might have done it, but now there seemed to be too great a gulf. 'But it's okay, Ellis. Really it is. I know the score. I always have. You've never deceived me . . .' She did reach out then. She couldn't help herself. His fingers were very cold, but at least he didn't flinch away. 'You're a good man, and we've had a wonderful time together. I wouldn't change a thing . . . but I know you're not mine.'

Ellis heaved a sigh, yet he smiled at her, his eyes filled with respect. He might not love her, but what he did feel for her was real and had a value.

'And you're a good woman, Jess. More than good. Miraculous.' He lifted her fingers to his lips and kissed them. 'And you deserve a marvellous man who can give you all the love that's owing to you. Not an emotional cripple like me . . .' Small muscles in his face twitched and moved as if he was fighting for control. Was he sad? Was he angry with himself? It was hard to tell.

'I wish I could turn back time,' Jess found herself saying. The words came from somewhere un-thought out, but she couldn't stop herself. 'I wish I could turn back time and change things for you, so Julie was still alive, and your daughters too, so you could be really happy again. I really do.' A lump in her throat balked her, and she wasn't sure who it was for . . . 'I know it means you and I would never have met, but it's maybe better that way. I'd never have missed what I hadn't had . . . and I know my life would have sorted itself out eventually.'

'Oh Jess . . .' He kissed her fingers again. Because he dare not kiss her lips? Because he didn't want to taunt her with a closeness that couldn't go anywhere?

When he looked back up again, his eyes were agonised. He wore the face of a man fighting to change, but locked in place. She wanted to throw her arms around him and comfort him and love him, but that would only hurt him more. And hurt her too.

Still holding her hand, he said, 'You *do* want more, don't you?' His voice was low and steady.

Time for truth.

'Yes. I do. I want what I know I can't have. Not with you. But I accepted the terms of the original deal, and now I must abide by them. It's me that's gone back on the agreement, not you. My bad.'

'You're not bad. You're wonderful. Any other man would be grabbing you with both hands, to hold you and keep you.'

'Maybe . . . maybe not.' She drew in a deep breath, fighting herself as much as the situation. 'But I . . . I think I need to set out and see if I can find that "grab, hold, keep" man. I can't stay in a holding pattern all my life.' She looked at him very intently, hoping he could understand things that she wasn't expressing well. 'You've done me a very great service, Ellis. It would probably have taken me a long, long time to break out without you.'

He didn't speak, but his face was a mask again, hiding a turmoil beneath.

'I think I need to get out and kiss a few frogs, to find a prince. Well, another prince . . . know what I mean?'

'I'm not a prince.' That brought a wry smile.

'Oh you are . . . Have you looked at yourself in a mirror lately?' She straightened up, steeling her spine. 'And meeting you has helped me find my inner princess.'

'You were a princess already, Jess. A queen. A goddess.'

'But not *your* goddess. Not your princess.'

For a moment his mouth worked. He was fighting not to break down. 'No . . . I lost mine. But you'll be somebody else's princess . . . some lucky, unscrewed-up guy. And the sooner you find him, the better.'

He was right. She'd fallen for him and she loved him. But, there was no future with Ellis, and the longer she moped for what she couldn't have, the more likely she was to slip back into her half-life. It would be hard. Perhaps the greatest fight of her life, but she had to ride forth and into battle as soon as she could.

'I think you're right. Better to pull the sticking plaster off now . . .'

'So the wound can heal.'

They both laughed, suddenly, at the piled-on melo-drama. The pain was still there, but they were both adults, and they could both hack it.

With a last squeeze of Ellis's hand, she slipped off the bed, and went to the sideboard, retrieving the champagne bottle. She brought it back with her, and topped up both their glasses.

'Here's to a night of outrageously muddled metaphors . . . and to moving forward.'

They clinked their glasses and finished the wine.

'I think I ought to go,' she said, feeling a strange layer of calm settle over the ferment inside her. 'I know there won't be a train at this hour, but maybe I could get a hotel room and then the first train north in the morning.'

Ellis shook his head. 'Don't be absurd.'

Jess could feel herself wavering. Wanting to stretch things out longer. Have more closeness. More sex. More Ellis. But that wasn't the answer, because there wasn't an answer where she and he were concerned. Hanging around, dragging out a one-sided love, was good for nobody.

'I don't mind . . . and I know you could get me a room. Pull some strings. Maybe get me a suite at The Ritz?'

With a wry shrug, Ellis returned her smile, and took her hand again. 'I could do that. And I totally respect and understand that you'd like to leave as soon as possible.' He pulled in a great breath. 'But if you leave now, there'll be no schlepping around to hotels and catching trains. I'll arrange for a company jet from the City airport . . . and you'll probably be home in not much more than a couple of hours.'

'But . . .'

'No buts. If you'll feel better leaving now, that's how you're leaving. Understand?' He was so decisive, suddenly Ellis the mover and shaker, who could make anything happen.

She nodded. Yes, why prolong the pointlessness?

A clean, sharp, almost instant break now was best. This way she could put half the country between herself and temptation in a matter of hours.

'I'll make the arrangements for you now.' He squeezed her fingers, then kissed them again. 'Do you need any help with packing your things? Anything else I can do? Maybe arrange for some food before you go? You haven't eaten anything since the Palm Court. You must be starving.'

Still so thoughtful. He *was* a prince. An unavailable prince, but kind and courtly all the same.

'I'm okay, thanks Ellis. I've nothing much to pack, and I'm not really hungry . . .' This was hard, so hard, but it had to be done. 'Think I might just finish off that last inch or two of bubbly though . . . Seems a shame to waste it.'

Ellis gave her a strange little smile, then filled her glass. 'Cheers, Jess,' he said softly, clinking his empty glass to hers. 'Right, I'll get things sorted. Be back in a few minutes.'

Then he rose from the bed and left the room, not looking back.

Jess clenched her fingers, digging nails into her palm.

Now was not the time to fall to pieces.

25

'What the hell are you doing back here? I thought you weren't coming back until Monday . . . what happened to the luxurious sex weekend with your billionaire?'

Jess switched on the kettle, and then reached for a mug for Cathy. Small, mundane tasks kept her focused. Made everything normal. Kept a lid on things.

'He's not *my* billionaire and it wasn't a fixed thing, staying until Monday,' she said, forcing her voice to sound normal, with a lid on that too.

Cathy strode across the room, and put her hand on Jess's arm, forcing her to turn. 'If he's dumped you, I'll bloody well hunt him down and kill him, millions notwithstanding. The shit! The absolute shit!'

Jess let out a tight little laugh. It was funny, really. She'd been the one to finish it herself, not Ellis. His style would probably have been to complete the weekend and make it as lavish and hedonistic for her as possible. A parting gift laden with gorgeous food, more champagne and orgasm after orgasm after orgasm. He would have taken her wherever she wanted to go by day, and held her in his arms at night. Which would only have made it harder to part. A clean break was far better for both of them.

Keep telling yourself that . . .

'No! He hasn't dumped me. Not in the slightest. He's been perfect and wonderful and kind . . . and the ideal lover . . .' She gave Cathy a very firm look. 'But that's just the problem. He's *too* fabulous. So I'm going cold turkey now, rather than carry on enjoying all the fabulousness and then find that I've gone and got addicted to him.'

Cathy pursed her lips and shrugged. 'If you say so. I guess that makes good sense, really. It's just that I was hoping this was Cinderella and you and he would stay together. Like a movie, you know?'

The kettle whistled and Jess brewed the tea before speaking.

'Nope, not a movie. Just a wonderful, magical interlude type thing. A lot of people don't even get that.' She fussed with the milk bottle and sugar bowl. 'He can't get over his wife, and in a way, I sort of admire that, even though he'd be a much happier person if he could move on.' She turned and rested her hip against the counter top. 'And it's much better for me to just have these three . . . um . . . encounters with him . . . so I *can* move on.'

'But who to?'

'I don't know. But I've got to try . . .' Jess looked at the sugar bowl, and somehow couldn't help but smile. 'I've had a taste of sweetness now, and I'm not going to give it up again, even if the finest and rarest honey to end all honey is unavailable.'

'Bloody good for you!' Cathy said, taking charge of the teapot, giving it a stir, then pouring the tea.

'But don't worry, I'm not going to turn into some kind of slag, sleeping with every man who crosses my path. I'll be very selective. Only ones that have clear potential to be something more.'

Cathy nodded. 'Very wise . . . and I think you should probably start with Josh Redding. He sounds as if he has potential. He's an artist like you, and he sounds really nice from what you've said about him.'

'He's a prospect, certainly.' Jess took her mug of tea.

'Well, if you really do want to move on, you should go out with him. Didn't you say he'd asked you to go and see some arty movie with him?'

Was it too soon? Was all her bravado about sugar and moving on a façade? 'I'm thinking about it, Cathy. Really thinking . . . But what I do really need to do now is get some sleep. I think I'll take this up. Sorry to have disturbed you . . . and don't worry about me, will you?' Cathy's forehead crimped in a frown. 'I don't have any regrets, Cath, really I don't. Ellis McKenna is something I wouldn't have missed for all the world, even if he wasn't Mr Right, you know?'

'If you say so.'

'I do. Now, let's get some sleep, eh? I think I might have a day out tomorrow. Go to the City Art Gallery, and have a snoop round the shops. Get some Starbucks . . . Are you available?'

Yes, much better to get out, get fresh and act normal.

Anything other than mooching about home, letting yourself get maudlin, and pining for the perfect love that could never be.

The week that followed passed in an odd sort of cotton wool state. Jess got on with life during the day, living in the moment, not allowing herself to think too much about anything.

It was only at night, lying in bed alone, that she allowed herself to think about Ellis, and replay all the precious memories of being with him. Not just the sex. In fact, memorable as it had been, she didn't revisit it all that much. It was the other things that were so drilled in that she just couldn't quit them.

Talking. Laughing. Swimming in his pool. Sharing views on art. Eating that enormous and fabulous tea at The Ritz. The Courtauld. Little moments of pure, perfect gold.

It's going to take a long time is this getting over him, she told herself in the darkness. *So, I'm really going to have to try hard, and try soon.*

Ellis had asked her if she'd mind if he called her, or whether she'd prefer him not to. Jess had said that not was probably best, at least until they'd put some distance between each other.

'But if you need anything. Anything at all. Contact me immediately. Promise me that,' he'd said as she was about to board the jet. He'd also asked if she wanted him to accompany her back home, but she'd declined, and he'd acceded to her wishes.

The only thing I really want from you is what I can't have.

So it was best to get on with life.

At life class, she was glad that Josh came to chat at break-time and didn't ask any probing questions about her weekend. She almost wondered if he sensed something, especially when he repeated his invitation to the Munch film.

'Yes, I'd love to,' she'd answered, feeling vaguely mean when his face lit up.

I hope I don't turn into his 'Ellis'.

But still she knew she had to give him a chance.

This is crazy. I need to get a grip. I can't go on like this.

Again and again in the week after Jess's London visit, Ellis found his spirits lifting, and experienced an almost boyish sense of anticipation that made him smile.

But then he'd remember . . .

He and Jess had parted. He would not be seeing her at the weekend. There was nothing to look forward to.

What was wrong with him? He'd never felt like this before. With his previous girlfriends and lovers, he'd always enjoyed the sex, and also the temporary companionship. But no matter how much he'd liked them, he'd never *missed* them when he'd not been with them.

The only person he'd ever missed was Julie. And his daughters.

Now it was Saturday night, and he was at Windermere Hall. Alone and missing . . . someone.

Julie? Yes, insomuch as he would always remember her. Always love her. But she was gone, and somehow now, that simple fact didn't produce the sharp lance of pain that it always had done. He could accept it now. Live with it.

What's the matter with me? Julie, what's the matter with me?

He prowled the house. In the sitting room, he paused in front of each of his new Hunter pictures, pleased with the way they looked, but unsettled. In the bedroom, he admired the vibrant Cadell. In the pool room, he trailed his fingers in the water, wondering whether to swim, but too restless.

Julie had never been here, nor had the girls, but he was still looking for someone, missing someone who *had* been here. Someone who'd talked and laughed and swum with him, who'd helped him choose the pictures. Someone who'd given her beautiful body to him, shared pleasure and experimentation, always smiling. Someone who'd created amazing art here, especially the two drawings she'd left in his London flat as a gift, to stir not only his libido but other deeper, finer emotions that left him shaking.

Jess, oh Jess!

She was the one he was missing. The one he ached for now. He wanted her, but he wanted more. Oh hell, he wanted what she'd admitted, in her honesty, that she wanted herself. It was what *he* wanted and needed too. And now he'd let her go. Almost sent her away. Encouraged her towards a new life, with some notional new man she'd probably marry. Possibly even this Josh character she'd talked about and whom he'd as good as pushed her towards.

God damn it to hell, what if this Josh is Mr Right?

No! No! No!

I'm your Mr Right, Jess Lockhart. I'm the one who loves you.

And yet . . . still . . . he had to make his peace with Julie first. Purposeful now, he strode to the small library he used as an office, pulling open a drawer in the sideboard that he rarely opened, because of the pain it contained.

Drawing out the album from within, he took it to the desk and sat down in his leather wing chair. Julie had been an aficionado of what she'd staunchly declared to be 'real' photography: vintage cameras, film, prints lovingly developed and preserved. He was glad of it now, as he turned the pages, not saying goodbye, but allowing them to leave him peacefully, and let spirits both lost and still alive grow tranquil.

His wife had been beautiful, and their children adorable. But now there was no guilt in longing for a different beauty . . . and musing perhaps . . . examining the possibility that one day there might be other children to adore.

He studied the smiles in the prints, still wondering . . . Had they thought of him in those last moments? Had there even been time? Onlookers had reported that all the gunman's victims had dropped like stones, gone in the blink of an eye. So Ellis could only go on what he felt, on what he believed without knowing how.

He wasn't a superstitious man, and his faith was nebulous at best, but looking at the smiling images of his wife and daughters . . . his *late* wife and daughters . . . he knew. He just knew.

He understood what he'd not allowed himself to truly accept until now, not completely. Which was that generous, huge-hearted Julie would never want him to lead a sterile, loveless life if she wasn't there, and that his sweet daughters would always want their daddy to be happy, whatever happened.

And the only way for me to be happy is with you, Jess.

He smiled, echoing the expressions of his lost family, knowing he had their permission to be happy again too. And permission to release the guilt he'd felt over their deaths . . . and the new guilt over falling in love again.

I haven't known you long, Jess, but I know I can be happy with you. Because I do love you. I'm a love at first sight guy. I was with Julie and I am with you too.

Pressing a last kiss against each cherished face in the album, he closed it and slid it onto the sideboard. No need to hide it any more.

There was just one last thing to do. A big step, but he could do it now. Touching the gold of his wedding ring, he slid it off his finger, kissed it, and then placed it in the ring box that had been tucked away in the drawer along with the album.

His heart suddenly pounding, he reached for his phone and started dialling.

What do you think you are, you fool? Some kind of spook or private detective? Sitting here in the dark, watching her front door. You're pathetic!

Why was he lurking here, slumped down behind the wheel of his Mercedes SUV, across the road from Jess's place, waiting for her to come home?

Ellis had tried to ring Jess repeatedly, but her phone was turned off. He'd tried to compose texts, but the limitations of the medium had caused him to end up swearing and nearly stomping his mobile into tiny pieces before abandoning the effort. Business messages he could compose with consummate ease, but this, God, this was so much more important.

Finally, he'd rung the house, and spoken to Cathy.

'She's out. She's gone to the pictures with a bloke from the art class. She's probably turned her phone off so they don't disturb people in the cinema. The last time we went, there was some inconsiderate git who was calling and texting his mates all the way through the movie.'

Logical, but Ellis still wondered. What if she'd turned the damn thing off so she didn't have to speak to *him*? Because she didn't want there to be a possibility of him interrupting her while she was trying to forge a bond with a new male friend, this nice Josh she'd spoken of, who was suitable and who could be Mr Right.

Jess's house-mate had been going out herself, but she had asked if she could pass on a message. Ellis had said, *Yes, yes please, just tell her that I called*.

But now he was here, sitting in the darkness, because he was a lovelorn idiot and he had to make Jess his, and prevent her forging that bond with another man.

Tapping his fingers on the wheel of his Mercedes, he was almost glad the Citroën was in the garage, undergoing an expensive refurbishment. If she came back now, she wouldn't recognise this chunky SUV, and he could watch, surreptitiously, weaving his strategy, if she should happen to bring her art-loving friend home with her.

But what if it was already too late? What if courageous Jess had decided that a man still married to his own dead wife was a hopeless cause, and she'd plunged forward, impulsive and passionate, into her future?

After all, she plunged in with you, didn't she? Like a lioness . . . It was one of the greatest, bravest leaps a woman can make.

Ellis was bemused by his own thoughts. This was the antithesis of his usual modus operandi. He was decisive, determined, almost ruthless sometimes. He had to be. And sometimes he was arrogant and overpowering with women too.

But he couldn't be that way with Jess. He respected all women, but he respected her more. He respected her as much as he had done Julie, the first woman he'd respected and loved.

Driving here, he'd compared the two loves, finally able to do so. He loved Jess just as much as Julie. Not more, but differently, and it felt just as wonderful. He wasn't a conventionally religious man, but again he felt that somewhere, somehow, Julie had watched his deliberations over the photographs and said, *Go for it, you silly bugger! Go on! Be happy!*

A taxi hove into view, interrupting his metaphysical musings. His heart went thud, thud, thud, like that of a callow youth sighting his first date. Was it her? Was she back? Was the goddamned nice Josh from life class with her?

Atavistic possessiveness surged in Ellis's gut like

acid. No woman could belong to one man, but try telling his caveman brain that.

In every rational way, he's probably a better man for you than I am . . . but he can't have you!

But her expression as she paid off the taxi – yes, it was his gorgeous Jess – stopped him in his tracks, and kept him slouched low in his seat in the dark SUV that she wouldn't recognise.

Jess was smiling to herself. She was glowing. She looked almost triumphant.

Fuck! Hell! Damn!

It *had* worked out. She'd had a successful date. She really liked nice Josh and, disaster of disasters, she was going to see him again . . . and more.

Ellis realised he was now clutching at the steering wheel so tightly that his fingers were hurting. He relaxed them, but he couldn't relax his whirling mind. He almost moaned when his beautiful, smiling Jess disappeared into the house.

What was going on? If the date had been so fabulous and made her so happy, where was Nice Man? Thank God, at least it seemed as if they weren't going to sleep together this first time. Was there still a chance for Mr Wrong? For Mr Sex, the man so deeply in love that he hadn't even realised it until it was almost too late?

Ellis still couldn't understand his own hesitancy. He *had* to move now. Speak to her. Declare himself. And yet he remembered how, sometimes, with Julie, he had been more cautious and measured, holding back to think through what was best for her, rather than charging like the proverbial bull at a gate and ruining everything by grabbing for what he wanted rather than what she needed.

For ten minutes, Ellis sat there, working out how best to lay his heart before Jess and reveal his feelings to her. How most effectively to state the case for himself rather than that other man. Most of those ten minutes involved more cursing and blinding at himself for being a hesitating fool.

Just bloody well go and knock on the door, you clown!

But just as he was reaching for the handle, another taxi drew up outside Jess's house, with a toot of its horn.

No! She's going to him!

And yes, here came Jess from the door, still looking bright-faced and happy and determined. She had her overnight bag with her too.

No! No! No!

It seemed a slightly odd way to go about things, but she was going to wherever her new man was, and they were going to sleep together. And it would be the start of 'something wonderful' for them, and a new lifetime of loss and agony for Ellis McKenna.

She would be happy. He had to face that. It was what he wanted for her. Her happiness was a priority that over-rode every single one of his own feelings, and maybe someday, he'd find a kind of peace in knowing she was leading a happy life with another man.

Someday . . .

No! Fuck it! Bloody hell!

Ellis hurled himself out of the SUV, almost stumbling, but not caring if he fell or twisted his ankle or worse. Like a sprinter, he hurtled towards the taxi. Jess was already inside, and the brake lights went off. Summoning a turn of speed he hadn't achieved since he was a teenaged runner, trying to prove to himself that his damaged foot would never hold him back, Ellis raced along the pavement, then jumped out into the road, in front of the black cab, waving his arms, knowing he looked like a raving lunatic, but still not caring at all what anyone thought except Jess, and she already knew he was a crazy man anyway.

The cabbie looked shocked, but pulled up just inches from Ellis's shins. He looked angry then, instead, and rolled down the window.

'What the hell are you doing, you stupid bastard?'

Ellis ignored him, and ran to the rear passenger window, banging on it. 'Jess! Jess! Please wait . . . don't go!' Her face looked pale inside the cab, but thank God, she was still smiling. She had her phone in her hand, as if about to turn it on.

'Shall I drive on, miss?' the cabbie asked.

'No, it's okay,' Jess said, and Ellis saw her stuff the mobile in her bag and rummage about, presumably for money. Digging in his own pocket, he pulled out his wallet, almost tore a wad of notes in half getting them out, and thrust them at the driver.

'Are you sure you'll be all right, miss?' Ellis couldn't fault the cabbie's concern for his passenger, even in the face of being massively overpaid, but he just wished the man would shut up, and let Jess get out.

'Everything's fine . . . now.'

When the passenger door was released, Ellis half climbed in and almost hauled Jess and her bag out bodily, his arms encircling her as if that were their default position. Holding her . . .

With a last nod in Jess's direction, the cabbie put his vehicle in gear, and then sped away. Ellis held on to Jess for dear life, tightening his embrace, breathing in her scent and feeling the sweet strength of her seep into him and restore his sanity.

'I'm sorry about that,' he said, kissing her hair and rubbing his face against hers, 'I just couldn't let you go to him. I know he's probably a much better man for you. He's everything you need . . . and he'll make you happy.' A lump formed in his throat, and he found himself blinking, his eyes tearing up. 'But give me a chance, Jess, and I'll do everything in my power to make you just as happy. I'll really try . . . I'll do anything you want!'

Her body shook in his hold. Damn, was it shock? Had he frightened her with his deranged antics? He held her closer, running his hands over her hair, her back.

But it wasn't a reaction. And, realising that, Ellis found himself smiling, then laughing . . . because Jess was laughing too.

'Fuck, yes, I know I'm a raving lunatic. But it's *you* that makes me crazy, Jess. The thought of losing you, that's what's made me behave like this.'

She looked up at him, her lovely eyes glowing, warm with . . . with beautiful emotion. A positive emotion. The emotion she'd expressed with such dignity before, back in London.

'You *are* a lunatic, Ellis McKenna, you really are.' She leant in and pressed her lips to his. The kiss was the sweetest they'd ever shared, and possibly the most chaste. 'Where on earth do you think I was going just now, you crazy man?'

'To your artist guy, to Josh's house, to spend the night together.'

'Oh, you are a plonker, Ellis, really!' She shook her head, her shiny hair rippling. 'I was on my way to Windermere Hall, to you, you fool!'

'But I saw you come in about fifteen minutes ago, and you were smiling. You looked really happy.' Despite his words, he was beginning to believe in miracles, and his heart was pounding faster than ever. If it hadn't meant letting go of Jess, he would have leapt up in the air and punched the sky in triumph.

'I was happy. I am happy,' said Jess gently, her face glowing more than ever if that were possible. 'I had a very pleasant evening with Josh, but it made me realise something crucially important.' She paused to kiss him again. 'It made me realise who I really had to be with. The man I really want and love. I was looking happy because I'd made a decision and I'd found the strength to follow up on it. I was coming to *you*, Ellis, to tell you that I love you. I rang Windermere Hall, and I got transferred to one of your PA people, who said you were in residence there, but out at the moment.' She gave a little shrug. 'I was just about to phone your mobile from the cab, but then I thought, to hell with it, I'd be better off telling you how I feel in person. Face to face. I might have chickened out otherwise . . .' She hesitated again, as if reaching a tipping point. 'I know you had a perfect marriage with Julie, but I think you and I can be happy together too. If we give it a chance. So, that's why I'd rung for a taxi . . . to take me to Windermere Hall, so I could wait for you there, and then state my case.'

For once in his life, Ellis was lost for words. He just muttered, 'Oh my God, oh my God,' and tightened his arms around Jess, lifting her up off her feet and whirling her around in his hold, for pure joy. His heart nearly burst with happiness when she grabbed onto him, just as tight.

'Are you all right, Ellis?' she enquired when he set her down, reaching to stroke his face. 'You look totally thunderstruck.'

'I am,' he said, laughing again. 'I'm thunderstruck by the things that have dawned on me tonight, and I'm just about as all right as it's possible to be.'

Jess stared into his eyes. He knew she saw all, saw his nonsense, understood it, and accepted it. 'So, do you want to go inside, or do you want to whisk me away in what seems to be an alternative chariot, to your local sex lair?' She nodded to the black SUV. 'Where is the Blue Whale, by the way?'

'In the garage, for a bit of an overhaul . . .' Cars seemed so unimportant at the moment, other than a means of getting him and the woman he loved to privacy and a bed. 'Let's go to Windermere, eh? It's not that far and the drive will give me a chance to get my head together.' He released her, and picked up the small overnight bag she'd dropped in all the kerfuffle. 'And I'll bet you haven't got any champagne in the fridge in there, have you?'

'No, I haven't, although I was thinking about getting some . . .' Her smile became creamy, knowing

. . . supremely female, but at the same time with a jittery, excited quality. 'Why do we need champagne, Ellis?'

'To celebrate the fact that I've fallen in love with you, and that I love you, and I don't think I can go on living without you!' With his free hand, he grabbed hers, and led her towards the SUV. 'Now, are you coming, or do I have to pick you up and carry you?'

Her answer was a grin as she broke into a run, leading him.

Another bed. Another glass of champagne. But how different were the circumstances this time.

Jess hitched herself up, to sit up straight against the pillows for the toast. Ellis's beautiful eyes sparkled like the famous wine in the glasses that they clinked.

'To you, Jess.' He paused, and his naked chest lifted as he took a deep breath. 'Thank you for saving me. Thank you for giving me a chance and loving me.'

Now it was Jess's turn to feel breathless. It was real. All real. Not one of her pre-Ellis daydreams. This was actually happening.

'To you . . . Mr Right. After all.'

The champagne was the best stuff this time, but even flat lemonade would have tasted like nectar to Jess under these circumstances. Fresh from tender, passionate lovemaking and with Ellis's many heartfelt iterations of *I love you* still singing in her ears.

He'd loved another woman deeply, and probably still did and always would, but now Jess knew it was possible for Ellis to love again, to love her, the one love not taking anything away from the other. Okay, she was human and there might be times when she was jealous, and when she wished she'd been the first, but loving Julie had made Ellis the man he was today . . . the man *she* loved.

'I hope so,' he said with a wry smile. 'I'm sure I won't be an easy ride, but you're a smart woman. If anybody can cope with me, you're the one.'

'I know . . . it's going to be such a trial for me, isn't it? Living with a breathtakingly handsome billionaire who's amazing in bed? How will I survive?' She clinked her glass to his again.

'Seriously though . . . I'll do whatever I can to give you the life *you* want.' Their glasses were empty now, so he set them aside on the bedside cabinet. 'Your terms, Jess. If you want to live together, we live together. If you want us to just see each other to start with, that's our pace.' He paused and, for a moment, he snagged his lower lip. 'If you want marriage, that's what I want. As soon as you want, or after whatever "getting to know you" period you feel comfortable with.'

'Crikey . . .'

'I know that in real terms, we've not been together long. Barely a few weeks.' He took her hands in his, and smothered them in kisses. 'But *I'm* sure. This is how it is for me. I know myself again, the way I once did . . . and that's all down to you.'

Jess found herself shaking and, an instant later, she was wrapped in Ellis's arms. She *was* sure. This was her first relationship, but still she knew herself, and she was sure.

'Marriage, yes,' she said, snuggling in close, loving

the warmth of Ellis's body. Sex with him was amazing, but simple proximity had its own sweet charm. 'Maybe not quite next week or anything . . . Let's give it a month or two, to give your family and my sister and my friends a chance to get used to the idea. But in the meantime, well, maybe I could start to move in here?'

Ellis's arms tightened. 'Good! I know it'll be a big adjustment for both of us . . . I spend the week in London. I travel a lot. But I can travel less. It's not impossible to run large business empires nowadays barely travelling at all. Unless you want to travel, to see the world with me?'

'I'm not sure yet. It's all a bit crazy. I think I should sort of ease into things.'

Ellis laughed softly, and she had a feeling he was thinking something naughty, but at the same time, trying to remain rational. 'One thing . . . please tell me you don't want to continue working at Windsor Insurance. Now that would be just too weird.'

It was Jess's turn to laugh. 'Oh, I think I can quite safely say that working as a drone in one of your lesser companies is far from my life's ambition.' She paused, trying to make sense of her happy overload. 'But I will have to have something in my life . . . something of my own. I've been thinking about what you said, about making a career of my art. And I've decided I want it . . . just as I want you. I've been given a talent, and I shouldn't waste it. I should celebrate it.'

She pulled away, and looked closely at his face. He was smiling. 'I most heartily concur. I want you to fulfil your potential and make the most of your gifts.'

Then he looked more serious. 'You *should* pursue an art career. Pursue it seriously. I'll help in any way I can, and support any path you choose. Study. A degree. Whatever you want, you can have it now.'

With Ellis at her side, Jess felt as if she could achieve anything. She'd always had a quiet self-belief, but now it was as if any goal she chose to reach for was attainable.

'Not entirely sure about a full-on art degree, but there are short courses and lectures and summer schools at the Courtauld I'd like to attend, definitely. The London sex lair would make a great base for all that.' She gave him a wink. 'And we could do *all* the galleries and *all* the exhibitions . . . that is, in between shagging each other senseless and you jazzing about making your billions.'

'You make the most rational and appealing plans, Ms Lockhart.' He hesitated, taking the moment to kiss her. 'That makes perfect sense . . . but right now, do you think we might make a start on the senseless shagging. Lying in bed next to you always seems to have a rather marked effect on me.'

Jess followed his eye-line to the very marked bump beneath the sheet in his general groin area. And that had a marked effect upon her too.

I'll wake up soon, she thought. *This is just a delicious figment of my imagination. A Dream Lover scenario gone wild.*

But as she subsided onto her back and pulled him towards her, she was far too horny and too happy to even consider that possibility.

'Come on, Mr Right, show me what you're made

of . . .' She grinned up at him, letting her thighs open wide, inviting him to pleasure her. 'I need some more of your billion dollar lovemaking!'

'I'll have you know that the McKennas are *sterling* billionaires, Ms Lockhart,' Ellis shot back, laughing as he paused to roll on a condom.

'Even better. Now service me!' she commanded, drawing his lips down onto hers as he pushed his cock inside her.

The next morning Jess woke up, rolled onto her side, and there was Ellis McKenna, the most beautiful man she had ever seen, sleeping peacefully with a serene, contented smile on his glorious face.

Dream Lover.

Mr Right.

The man who loved her just as much as she loved him.

Epilogue

'It looks a bit . . . um . . . cubist somehow,' said the artist's model, considering the half done drawing.

The artist frowned. 'You're right. Your thighs aren't in the least bit chunky like this . . .' The eraser hovered over the chunks in question, but then the artist tossed it aside, and shrugged at the work. 'I think I'd better stick to my sex skills, don't you? And making money. I'm pretty good at those, so I'll leave the art to you.'

'Oh, I don't know,' said Jess, picking up the sketch pad Ellis had been working diligently on for the last half hour. 'You've got something there, Ellis. Believe you me, I used to see a lot worse at life class. A helluva lot worse. And mostly by people who thought they were Leonardo da Vinci.'

Ellis pursed his lips. He was such an achiever. But then he grinned. 'I'll have another bash at it later . . . Let's do something different now. What do you fancy, Mrs McKenna? Another cocktail? A fruit plate? Sex?'

'Decisions, decisions.' Jess smiled at her new husband. She'd been about to adjust her sarong, because it'd slipped down and was barely covering any of her, much less the thighs Ellis had been sketching, but she decided to let it slide even further.

They were on their honeymoon, at Ellis's 'shack', Blue Breezes, and he was relaxed there now that the ghosts of his past no longer hurt him.

'Oh I do wish I could really draw,' he said earnestly, lunging forward, 'because this is the greatest work of art I've ever seen.' His warm hand slid over her breast and her belly, and then her decidedly non-cubist thigh. Jess had been pampering her skin with deluxe body lotion and buffing and toning and beautifying ready for the honeymoon, so she'd look her best in skimpy bikinis . . . and, more often, out of them.

And she was mostly out of her bikini, because the staff had instructions only to come at certain hours, and to sing loudly when they were approaching, to warn the honeymooners. Jess wasn't actually a sun worshipper, but a little of it at the least hot times, and plenty of pleasant shade from broad rustic umbrellas, or on the veranda, suited her to a tee. They were almost naked in the shade right now, wearing only their colourful sheets of printed cotton fabric, and their matching narrow wedding bands in simple white gold.

Ellis's own sarong had fallen open at his lunge, and offered a treat that Jess found far more appetising than any fruit plate. He was huge and hard, as he'd seemed to be almost all the time since they'd got here . . . apart from the times when they visited Aunt Augusta to dine. Then, he was the perfect dutiful nephew and caring, tactful spouse, bringing Jess together with the first of her many new relations in a relaxed and friendly setting. Jess was already becoming quite fond of the irascible old lady, finding much in her wisdom and sharp humour that reminded her of her own gran.

Their wedding had been a very quiet, but happy affair at the local registry office, with just a few of Jess's friends to support them, and her closest uncle on her late father's side to give her away. They'd decided not to announce their marriage to Ellis's extended family yet, because neither of them wanted any fuss or hoopla. The time would come when they had to let the secret out, but despite her natural nervousness, Jess knew that with Ellis beside her, she was perfectly capable of facing up to in-laws, no matter how rich and exalted they were. Basking in his love bolstered her self-belief with each new day. They could meet any challenge that lay ahead of them, stronger together.

And now, Jess reached for her husband confidently, taking him in hand. Ellis was thrillingly masterful in bed, but she too was learning to be dominant from time to time. Something he loved from her as a piquant change of pace.

'This is the work of art,' she pronounced, rubbing him slowly and carefully. Ellis's staying power was phenomenal, but she didn't like to take chances. 'What do you think the patrons of LaPierre and Hornby would think if I sent them one of these for the *Salon Privé*?'

'I'd like to think they'd sell like hotcakes . . .' Ellis gasped when she fondled him with her thumb, just beneath the crown of his cock.

Jess had been selling a few works to LaPierre and Hornby for a while now, for their risqué collection. Drawings by 'J. Lockhart' were much in demand, especially by female art lovers. The sketches Jess sold were always carefully posed, and didn't show the man's face, just his magnificent body.

'Yes, just think, Mr Sex, you're probably a Dream Lover for all sorts of lovelorn spinsters now . . . They'll be looking at your gorgeous bod, and weaving their fantasies around you, just the way I wove fantasies around some imaginary man.'

Ellis just moaned softly and fell back against the cushions. It was Jess's turn to press forward now, looming over him.

She found it difficult to remember what her own sexual fantasies had been like before Ellis. She'd pictured a body, sometimes a vague face, but that shadow-play had been totally eclipsed by reality now.

The reality of his heart and mind; the reality of his cock, his strong sleek thighs, his smooth powerful chest . . . and his handsome face.

'I hope I'm your only fantasy now, Jess McKenna.' He caught his breath as she climbed astride his thighs and positioned him at her entrance.

'Oh, you are . . . you are . . . you're more than enough for any woman,' she purred, beginning to sink down, down, down and fill herself with his heat and hardness. Even now it was still a wonder every time, that something so big and stiff and beautiful could fit inside her. Shuffling into a better position, she flexed her inner muscles mercilessly, making Ellis shout out loud and grab her hips.

'And you're more than enough for me, devil woman.' He bucked up from the blanket, thrusting. 'The wicked, sexy virgin who seduced me . . .'

'It was you who seduced me!' Jess cried happily, reaching down to touch herself, though she scarcely needed it. With the push and pull and the tug and tension she was barely a whisper from orgasm after only moments. Posing half naked while Ellis had drawn her had been more than ample foreplay.

'Okay, I'll give you that one. We seduced each other.' His eyes meeting hers, he grunted and gasped as she worked him again.

'Sounds about right,' replied Jess, grinning in triumph. The pleasure was winding and circling inside her, growing like a shimmering vortex, ready to pop.

When she stroked her clit, she lost control, coming hard and fast.

'I love you.'

'I love you.'

Together they laughed and cried and climaxed, forever in love.

Ready for more?

Read on for a sneak peek at

The Accidental Call Girl

The first steamy book in the Accidental series

Also by

PORTIA DA COSTA

BLACK
LACE

1

Meeting Mr Smith

He looked like a god, the man sitting at the end of the bar did. Really. The glow from the down-lighter just above him made his blond hair look like a halo, and it was the most breath-taking effect. Lizzie just couldn't stop staring.

Oops, oh no, he suddenly looked her way. Unable to face his sharp eyes, she focused on her glass. It contained tonic, a bit dull really, but safe. She'd done some mad things in her time, both under the influence and sober, and she was alone now, and squarely in the 'mad things' zone. She'd felt like a fish out of water at the birthday party she was supposed to be at in the Waverley Grange Hotel's function room with her house-mates Brent and Shelley and a few other friends. It was for a vaguely posh girl who she didn't really know that well; someone in her year at uni, who she couldn't actually remember being all that pally with at the time. Surrounded by women who seemed to be looking at her and wondering why she was there, and men giving her the eye with a view to chatting her up, Lizzie had snuck out of the party and wandered into the bar, drawn by its strangely unsettling yet latent with 'something' atmosphere.

To look again or not to look again, that was the question. She wanted to. The man was so very hot, although not her usual type. Whatever *that* was. Slowly, slowly, she turned her head a few centimetres, straining her eyes in order to see the god, or angel guy, out of their corners.

Fuck! Damn! He wasn't looking now. He was chatting to the barman, favouring him with a killer smile, almost as if he fancied *him*, not any of the women at the bar. Was he gay? It didn't really matter, though, did it? She was only supposed to be enjoying the view, after all, and he really was a sight for sore eyes.

With his attention momentarily distracted, she grabbed a feast of him.

Not young, definitely. Possibly forty, maybe a bit more? Dark gold-blond, curling hair, thick and a bit longer than one would have expected for his age, but not straggling. Gorgeous face, even though his features, in analysis, could almost have been called average. Put together, however, there was something extra, something indefinable about him that induced a 'wow'. Perhaps it was his eyes? They were very bright, and very piercing. Yes, it *was* the eyes, probably. Even from a distance, Lizzie could tell they were a clear, beautiful, almost jewel-like blue.

Or maybe it was his mouth too? His lips were mobile, and they had a plush, almost sumptuous look to them that could have looked ambiguous on a man, but somehow not on him. The smile he gave the lucky barman was almost sunny, and when he suddenly snagged his lower lip between his teeth, something went 'Oof!' in Lizzie's mid-section. And lower down too.

What's his body like?

Hard to tell, with the curve of the bar, and other people

sitting between them, but if his general demeanour and the elegant shape of his hand as he lifted his glass to his lips were anything to go by, he was lean and fit. But, that could be wishful thinking, she admitted. He might actually be some podgy middle-aged guy who just happened to have a fallen angel's face and a very well-cut suit.

Just enjoy the bits you can see, you fool. That's all you'll ever get to look at. You're not here on the pull.

With that, as if he'd heard her thoughts, Fallen Angel snapped his head around and looked directly at her. No pretence, no hesitation, he stared her down, his eyes frank and intent, his velvet lips curved in a tricky, subtle quirk of a smile. As if showcasing himself, he shifted slightly on his stool, and she was able to see a little more of him.

She'd been exactly right. He *was* lean and fit, and the sleek way his clothes hung on him clearly suggested how he might look when those clothes were flung haphazardly on the floor.

The temptation to look away was like a living force, as if she were staring at the sun and its brilliance was a fatal peril. But Lizzie resisted the craven urge, and held his gaze. She didn't yield a smile. She just tried to eyeball him as challengingly as he was doing her, and her reward was more of that sun on the lips and in the eyes, and a little nod of acknowledgement.

'For you, miss.'

The voice from just inches away nearly made her fall off her stool. She actually teetered a bit, cursing inside as she dragged her attention from the blue-eyed devil-angel at the end of the bar to the rather toothsome young barman standing right in front of her.

'Er . . . yes, thanks. But I didn't order anything.'

There was no need to ask who'd sent the drink that had

been placed before her, in a plain low glass, set on a white napkin. It was about an inch and a half of clear fluid, no ice, no lemon, no nothing. Just what she realised *he* was drinking.

She stared at it as the barman retreated, smiling to himself. He must go through this dance about a million times every evening in a busy, softly lit bar like this. With its faintly recherché ambience it was the ideal venue for advances and retreats, games of 'Do you dare?' over glasses of fluids various.

What the hell was that stuff? Lighter fluid? Drain cleaner? A poisoned chalice?

She put it to her lips and took a hit, catching her breath. It was neat gin, not the vodka she'd half expected. It seemed a weird drink for a man, but perhaps he was a weird man? Taking a very cautious sip this time, she placed the glass back carefully and turned towards him.

Of course, he was watching, and he did a thing with his sandy eyebrows that seemed to ask if she liked his gift. Lizzie wasn't sure that she did, but she nodded at him, took up the glass again and toasted him.

The dazzling grin gained yet more wattage, and he matched the toast. Then, with another elegant piece of body language, a tilt of the head, and a lift of the shoulders, he indicated she should join him. More blatantly, he patted an empty stool beside him.

Here, Rover! Just like an alpha dog, he was summoning a bitch to his side.

Up yours!

Before she could stop herself, or even really think what she was doing, Lizzie mirrored his little pantomime.

Here, Fido! Come!

There was an infinitesimal pause. The man's exceptional eyes widened, and she saw surprise and admiration. Then he slid gracefully off his stool, caught up his drink and headed her way.

Oh God, now what have I done?

She'd come in here, away from the party, primarily to avoid getting hit on, and now what had she done? Invited a man she'd never set eyes on before to hit on her. What should her strategy be? Yes or no? Run or stay? Encourage or play it cool? The choices whirled in her head for what seemed like far longer than it took for a man with a long, smooth, confident stride to reach her.

In the end, she smiled. What woman wouldn't? Up close, he was what she could only inadequately describe as a stunner. All the things that had got her hot from a distance were turned up by a degree of about a thousand in proximity.

'Hello . . . I'll join you then, shall I?' He hitched himself easily onto the stool at her side, his long legs making the action easy, effortless and elegant.

'Hi,' she answered, trying to breathe deeply without appearing to.

Don't let him see that he's already made you into a crazy woman. Just play it cool, Lizzie, for God's sake.

She waited for some gambit or other, but he just smiled at her, his eyes steady, yet also full of amusement, in fact downright merriment. He was having a whale of a time already, and she realised she was too, dangerous as he seemed. This wasn't the kind of man she could handle in the way she usually handled men.

'Thank you for the drink,' she blurted out, unable to take the pressure of his smile and his gently mocking eyes. 'It wasn't what I expected, to be honest.' She glanced at his identical glass. 'It doesn't seem like a man's drink . . . neat gin. Not really.'

Still not speaking, he reached for his glass, and nodded that she take up hers. They clinked them together, and he took a long swallow from his. Lizzie watched the slow undulation of his throat. He was wearing a three-piece suit, a very good one in an expensive shade of washed-out grey-blue. His shirt was light blue and open at the neck.

The little triangle of exposed flesh at his throat seemed to invite the tongue. What would his skin taste like? Not as sharp as gin, no doubt, but just as much of a challenge and ten times as heady.

'Well, I am a man, as you can see.' He set down his glass again, and turned more to face her, doing that showcasing, 'look at the goods' thing again. 'But I'm happy to give you more proof, if you like?'

Lizzie took a quick sip of her own drink, to steady herself. The silvery, balsamic taste braced her up.

'That won't be necessary.' She paused, feeling the gin sizzle in her blood. 'Not right here at least.'

He shook his head and laughed softly, the light from above dancing on his curls, turning soft ash-blond into molten gold. 'That's what I like. Straight to the point. Now we're talking.' Reaching into his jacket pocket, he drew out a black leather wallet and peeled out a banknote, a fifty by the look of it, and dropped it beside his glass as he slipped off the stool again. Reaching for her arm, he said, 'Let's go up to my room. I hate wasting time.'

Oh bloody hell! Oh, bloody, bloody hell! He's either as direct as a very direct thing and he's dead set on a quickie . . . or . . .

Good grief, does he think I'm an escort?

The thought plummeted into the space between them like a great Acme anvil. It was possible. Definitely possible. And it would explain the 'eyes across a bar, nodding and buying drinks' dance. Lizzie had already twigged that the Lawns bar was a place likely to be rife with that sort of thing, and it wasn't as if she didn't *know* anything about escorting. One of her dearest friends had been one, if only part time and not lately, and Brent would most certainly be alarmed that she'd fallen so naively into this pickle of all pickles. She imagined telling him about this afterwards, perhaps making a big comical thing out of her near escape, and hopefully raising some of the old, wickedly droll humour that fate and loss had knocked out of her beloved house-mate.

Trying to think as fast as she could, Lizzie balked, staying put on the stool. Escort or casual pick-up, she still needed a moment to catch her breath and stall long enough to decide whether or not to do something completely mental. 'I think I'd rather like to finish my drink. Seems a shame to waste good gin.'

If her companion was vexed, or impatient, he didn't show it. In a beautiful roll of the shoulders, he shrugged and slipped back onto his stool. 'Quite right. It *is* good gin. Cheers!' He toasted her again.

What am I going to do? What the hell am I going to do? This is dangerous.

It was. It was very dangerous. But in a flash of dazzling honesty, she knew that the gin wasn't the only thing that was too good to waste. The only question was, if he *did* think she was a call girl, did she tell him the truth now, or play along for a bit? She'd never done anything like this before, but, suddenly, she wanted to. She really wanted to. Perhaps because the only man she knew from the wretched party she'd left, other than Brent and some other friends from the pub, was a guy she'd dated once and who'd called her uptight and frigid when she'd rebuffed a grope that'd come too soon.

No use looking like a pin-up and behaving like a dried-up nun, he'd said nastily when she'd told him to clear off.

But this man, well, there wasn't an atom in her body that wanted to rebuff *him*!

What would it be like to dance on the edge? Play a game? Have an adventure that was about as far from her daily humdrum routine of office temping as it was possible to get?

What would it be like to have this jaw-droppingly stunning man, who was so unlike her usual type? She usually went for guys her own age, and Fallen Angel here certainly wasn't that. She was twenty-four and, up close, she could see her estimate of mid-forties was probably accurate. A perfectly seasoned, well-kept, prime specimen of mid-forties man, but still with at least twenty more years of life under his belt than she had.

And if she explained his mistake, he might well just smile that glorious smile at her, shake her hand, and walk away. Goodnight, Vienna.

'Cheers!' she answered.

He didn't speak but his eyes gleamed a response.

I bet you know what to do with a woman, you devil, paid for or otherwise.

Yes, she'd put any amount of money, earned on one's back or by any other means, that when Fallen Angel was with an escort, it was no hardship to be that working girl.

And she couldn't keep calling him Fallen Angel!

On the spur of the moment, she made a decision. This was a game, and she needed a handle. A name, an avatar that she could hide behind and discard when she needed to.

Looking her companion directly in the eye, and trying

not to melt, she set down her glass, held out her hand and said, 'I'm Bettie. Bettie with an "ie". What's your name, Gin-Drinking Man?'

Apparently ignoring the offered handshake, he just laughed, a free, happy, hugely amused, proper laugh. 'Yes, obviously, you *are* Bettie.' Looking her up and down, his laser-blue eyes seemed to catalogue her every asset; her black hair with its full fringe, her pale skin, her lips tinted with vivid bombshell red, her pretty decent but unfashionable figure in a fitted dress with an angora cardigan over it. When she went out, especially to a party, she liked to riff on her superficial resemblance to Bettie Page, the notorious glamour model of the 1950s. And being an Elizabeth, Bettie was a natural alternate name too.

Having subjected her to his inspection, he did reach for her hand then, grip it, and give it a firm shake with both of his clasped around it. 'Delighted to meet you, Bettie. I'm John Smith.'

It was Lizzie's turn to laugh out loud, and 'John' grinned at her. 'Of course you are, John. How could you possibly be anyone else?' The classic punter's name. Even she knew that.

He rocked on the stool, giving his blond head another little shake, still holding on to her. 'But it's my name, Bettie. Cross my heart . . . Honestly.'

The way he held her hand was firm and no nonsense, yet there was a tricky quality to the way his fingertip lay across her wrist, touching the pulse point. She could almost imagine he was monitoring her somehow, but the moment she thought that, he released her.

'OK, I believe you, Mr John Smith. Now may I finish my drink?'

'Of course.' He gave her the glittering smile again, laced

with a sultry edge. 'Forgive me, I'm being a graceless boor. No woman should be rushed . . .' There was a pause, which might have included the rider, *even a prostitute*. 'But once I know I'm going to get a treat, I'm like a kid, Bettie. When I want something, I tend to want it now.'

So do I.

Lizzie tossed back the remainder of her gin, amazed that her throat didn't rebel at its silvery ferociousness. But she didn't cough, and she set the glass down with a purposeful 'clop' on the counter, and slid off her stool.

'There, all finished. Shall we go?'

John simply beamed, settled lightly on his feet and took her elbow, steering her from the crowded bar and into the foyer quite quickly, but not fast enough to make anyone think they were hurrying.

The lift cab was small, and felt smaller, filled by her new friend's presence. Standing, he was medium tall, but not towering or hulking, and his body was every bit as good as her preliminary inspection in the bar had promised. As was his suit. It looked breathtakingly high end, making her wonder why, if he was looking for an escort, he didn't just put in a call to an exclusive agency for a breath-takingly high-end woman to go with it? Rather than pick up an unknown quantity, on spec, in a hotel bar. Leaning against the lift's wall, though, he eyed her up too as the doors slid closed, looking satisfied enough with his random choice. Was he trying to estimate her price?

'So, do we do the "elevator" scene?' he suggested, making no move towards her, except with his bright blue eyes.

Oh yeah, in all those scenes in films and sexy stories, it always happened. The hot couple slammed together in the lift like ravenous dogs and kissed the hell out of each other.

'I don't know. You're in charge.'

'I most certainly am,' he said roundly, 'but let's pretend and savour the anticipation, shall we? The uncertainty. Even though I do know that you're the surest of sure things.'

Bingo! He does *think I'm an escort.*

Confirming her suspicions like that, his words should have sounded crass and crude, but instead they were provocative, exciting her. Especially the bit about him being 'in charge'. Brent had always said it was the whore who was really in charge during a booking, because he or she could just dump the money, say 'No way!' and walk out. But somehow Lizzie didn't think it'd be that way with Mr John Smith, regardless of whether or not he believed she was a call girl.

This is so dangerous.

But she could no sooner have turned back now than ceased to breathe.

'And anyway, here we are.' As he doors sprang open again, he ushered her out, his fingertips just touching her back. It was a light contact, but seemed powerful out of all proportion, and Lizzie found herself almost trotting as they hurried along the short corridor to John's room.

As he let her in, she smiled. She'd not really taken much note of their surroundings as they'd walked, but the room itself was notable. Spacious, but strangely old-fashioned in some ways, almost kitsch. The linens were in chintz, with warm red notes, and the carpet was the colour of vin rouge. It was a bizarre look, compared to the spare lines and neutrals of most modern hotels, but, then, the Waverley Grange Hotel *was* a strange place, both exclusive and with a frisky, whispered reputation. Lizzie had been to functions here before, but had never seen the accommodation, although she'd heard about the legendary chintz-clad love-nests of the Waverley from Brent's taller tales.

'Quite something, isn't it?' John grinned, indicating the deliciously blowsy décor with an open hand.

'Well, *I* like it.' Perhaps it was best to let him think she'd been in rooms like this before; seen clients and fucked them under or on top of the fluffy chintz duvets.

'So do I . . . it's refreshingly retro. I like old-fashioned things.' His blue eyes flicked to her 'Bettie' hair, her pencil skirt and her angora.

Lizzie realised she was hanging back, barely through the doorway. Now *that* wasn't confidence; she'd better shape up. She sashayed forward to the bed, and sat down on it, trying to project sangfroid. 'That's good to know.' Her own voice sounded odd to her, and she could hardly hear it over the pounding of her heart and the rush of blood in her veins.

John paused by the wardrobe, slipping off his jacket and putting it on a hanger. So normal, so everyday. 'Aren't you going to phone your agency? That's what girls usually do about now. They always slip off to the bathroom and I hear them muttering.'

Oops, she was giving herself away. He'd suss her out any moment, if he hadn't already. 'I'm . . . I'm an independent.' She flashed through her brain, trying to remember things Brent had told her, and stuff from *Secret Diary of a Call Girl* on the telly. 'But I think I will call someone, if you don't mind.' Springing up again, she headed for the other door in the room. It had to lead to the bathroom.

'Of course . . . but aren't you forgetting something?'

Oh God, yes, the money!

'Three hundred.' It was a wild guess; it sounded right.

Sandy eyebrows quirked. 'Very reasonable. I was happy to pay five, at least.'

'That's my basic,' she said, still thinking, thinking. 'If you find you want something fancier, we can renegotiate.'

Why the hell had she said that? Why? Why? Why? What if he wanted something kinky? Something nasty? He didn't look that way, but who knew?

'Fancy, eh? I'll give it some thought. But in the meantime, let's start with the basic.' Reaching into his jacket pocket, he slipped out the black wallet again, and peeled off fifties. 'There,' he said, placing the notes on the top of the sideboard.

Lizzie scooped them up as she passed, heading for the bathroom, but John stayed her with a hand on her arm, light but implacable.

'Do you kiss? I know some girls don't.'

She looked at his mouth, especially his beautiful lower lip, so velvety yet determined.

'Yes, I kiss.'

'Well, then, I'll kiss you when you come back. Now make your call.'

2

Something Fancy

Well, well, then, 'Bettie Page', what on earth did I do to receive a gift like you? A beautiful, feisty, retro girl who's suddenly appeared to me like an angel from 1950s heaven?

John Smith considered having another drink from the mini bar, but, after a moment, he decided he didn't need one. He was intoxicated enough already, after the barely more than a mouthful of gin he'd drunk downstairs. Far more excited than he'd been by a woman in a long time, and certainly more turned on than he'd ever been with an escort before. Not that he'd been with a professional woman in a while. Not that he'd been with a lot of them anyway.

It was interesting, though, to pretend to Bettie that he had.

Sinking into one of the big chintz armchairs, he took a breath and centred himself, marshalling his feelings. Yes, this was a crazy situation, but he was having fun, so why deny it? And she was too, this unusual young woman with her vintage style and her emotions all over her face. That challenging smile was unmistakeable.

'Bettie, eh?'

Not her real name, he was sure, but perhaps near to it.

She looked the part for Bettie Page, though. She had the same combination of innocence, yet overflowing sensuality. Naughtiness. Yes, that was perfect for her. But *how* naughty? As an escort she probably took most things, everything, in her stride. Surely she wouldn't balk at his favoured activities? And yet, despite her profession, there was that strangely untouched quality to her, just like the legendary Bettie. A sweet freshness. A wholesomeness, idiotic as that sounded.

How long had she been in the game, he wondered. What if she was new to this? She was certainly far younger than his usual preference. His choice was normally for sleek, groomed, experienced women in their thirties, courtesans rather than call girls, ladies of the world. There might be a good deal of pleasure, though, in giving something to *her* in return for her services, something more than simply the money. Satisfaction, something new . . . a little adventure, more than just the job.

Now there was the real trick, the deeper game. And with any luck, a working girl who styled herself as 'Bettie' and who was prepared to take a client on the fly, after barely five minutes' chat, was bold enough to play it.

Suddenly he wasn't as bored with life and business as he'd been half an hour ago. Suddenly, his gathering unease about the paths he'd chosen, the insidious phantoms of loss and guilt, and the horrid, circling feeling that his life was ultimately empty, all slipped away from him. Suddenly he felt as if he were a young man again, full of dreams. A player; excited, hopeful, potent.

When he touched his cock it was as hard as stone, risen and eager.

'Come on, Bettie,' he whispered to himself, smiling as his

heart rose too, with anticipation. 'Hurry up, because if you don't, I'll come in there and get you.'

When Lizzie emerged from the bathroom the first thing she saw was another small pile of banknotes on the dresser.

'Just in case I have a hankering for "fancy",' said John amiably. He was lounging on the bed, still fully dressed, although his shoes were lying on their sides on the carpet where he'd obviously kicked them off.

'Oh, right . . . OK.'

Fancy? What did fancy mean? A bit of bondage? Spanking? Nothing too weird, she hoped. But it might mean they needed 'accessories' and she had none. You don't take plastic spanking paddles and fluffy handcuffs to the posher kind of birthday party, which was what she was supposed to be at.

'I don't have any toys with me. Just these.' The words came out on a breath she hadn't realised she was holding, and louder than she'd meant to. She opened her palm to reveal the couple of condoms she'd had stashed in the bottom of her bag. 'I wasn't originally planning to work tonight, but the event I was at was a bit tedious, so I thought I'd take a chance in the bar . . . you know, waste not, want not.'

What the hell am I babbling about?

John grinned from his position of comfort and relaxation. A tricky grin, as sunny as before, but with an edge. He was in charge, and he knew it. Maybe that was the 'fancy'?

Something slow and snaky and honeyed rolled in her belly. A delicious sensation, scary but making her blood tingle. His blue eyes narrowed as if he were monitoring her physical responses remotely, and the surge of desire swelled again, and grew.

She'd played jokey little dominance and submission games with a couple of her boyfriends. Just a bit of fun, something to spice things up. But it had never quite lived up to her expectations. Never delivered. Mainly because they'd always wanted her to play the dominatrix for them, wear some cheap black vinyl tat and call them 'naughty boys'. It'd been a laugh, she supposed, but it hadn't done much for her, and when one had hinted at turning the tables, she'd said goodnight and goodbye to the relationship. He'd been a nice enough guy, but somehow, in a way she couldn't define, not 'good' enough to be her master and make her bow down.

But golden John Smith, a gin-drinking man of forty-something, with laughter lines and a look of beautiful world-weariness . . . well, he *was* 'good' enough. Her belly trembled and silky fluid pooled in her sex, shocking and quick.

Now was the moment to stop being a fake, if she could. Maybe explain, and then perhaps even go on with a new game? And yet she could barely speak. He wasn't speaking either, just looking at her with those eyes that seemed to see all. With a little tilt of his head, he told her not to explain or question or break the spell.

But just when she thought she might break down and scream from the tension, he did speak.

'Toys aren't always necessary, Bettie. You of all people should know that.'

Had she blown it? Maybe . . . maybe not. Schooling herself not to falter, she shrugged and moved towards him. When she reached the bed, she dropped her rather inadequate stash of condoms on the side table and said, 'Of course . . . you're so right. And I love to improvise, don't you?'

Slowly, he sat up, and swivelled around, letting his legs swing down and his feet settle on the floor. 'Good girl . . .

good girl . . .' He reached out and laid a hand on her hip, fingers curving, just touching the slope of her bottom cheek. The touch became a squeeze, the tips of his four fingers digging into her flesh, not cruelly but with assertion, owning her.

With his other hand, he drew her nearer, right in between his spread thighs. She was looking down at him but it was as if he were looking down at her, from a great and dominant height. Her heart tripped again, knowing he could give her what she wanted.

But what was *his* price? Could she afford to pay?

He squeezed her bottom harder, as if assessing the resilience of her flesh, his fingertips closer to her pussy now, pushing the cloth of her skirt into the edge of her cleft. With a will of its own, her body started moving, rocking, pushing against his hold. Her sex was heavy, agitated, in need of some attention, and yet they'd barely done anything thus far. She lifted her hands to put them on his shoulders and draw the two of them closer.

'Uh oh.' The slightest tilt of the head, and a narrowing of his eyes was all the command she needed. She let her hands drop . . . while his free hand rose to her breast, fingers grazing her nipple. Her bra was underwired, but not padded so there was little to dull his touch. With finger and thumb, he took hold of her nipple and pinched it lightly through her clothing, smiling when she let out a gasp, sensation shooting from the contact to her swollen folds, and her clit.

Squeeze. Pinch. Squeeze. Pinch. Nothing like the sex she was used to, but wonderful. Odd. Infinitely arousing. The wetness between her labia welled again, slippery and almost alarming, saturating the thin strip of cloth between her legs.

'I'm going to make you come,' said John in a strangely normal voice, 'and I mean a real one, no faking. I think you can do it for me. You seem like an honest girl, and I think you like the way I'm touching you . . . even if it *is* business.'

Lizzie swallowed. For a moment there she'd forgotten she was supposed to be a professional. She'd just been a lucky girl with a really hot man who probably wouldn't have to do all that much to get her off.

'Will you be honest for me?' His blue eyes were like the whole world, and unable to get away from. 'Will you give me what I want? What I've paid for?'

'Yes, I think I can do that. Shouldn't be too difficult.'

Finger and thumb closed hard on her nipple. It really hurt and she let out a moan from the pain and from other sensations. 'Honesty, remember?' His tongue, soft and pink slid along his lower lip and she had to hold in a moan at the sight of that too.

She nodded, unable to speak, the pressure on the tip of her breast consuming her. How could this be happening? It hurt but it was next to nothing really.

Then he released her. 'Take off your cardigan and your dress, nothing else.'

Shaking, but hoping he couldn't detect the fine tremors, Lizzie shucked off her cardigan and dropped it on the floor beside her, then she reached behind her, for her zip.

'Let me.' John turned her like a big doll, whizzed the zip down, and then turned her back again, leaving her to slip the dress off. He put out a hand, though, to steady her, as she stepped out of it.

She hadn't really been planning to seduce anyone tonight, so she hadn't put on her fanciest underwear, just a nice but fairly unfussy set, a plain white bra and panties with a little edge of rosy pink lace.

'Nice. Prim. I like it,' said John with a pleased smile. Lizzie almost fainted when he hitched himself a little sideways on the bed, reached down and casually adjusted himself in his trousers. As his hand slid away, she could see he was huge, madly erect.

Oh, yummy.

He laughed out loud. He'd seen her checking him out. 'Not too bad, eh?' He shrugged, still with that golden but vaguely unnerving grin. 'I guess you see all shapes and sizes.'

'True,' she replied, wanting to reach out and touch the not too bad item, but knowing instinctively it was forbidden to do so for the moment. 'And most of them are rather small . . . but you seem to be OK, though, from where I'm standing.'

'Cheeky minx. I should punish you for that.' He laid a hand on her thigh, just above the top of her hold-up stocking. He didn't slap her, though perversely she'd hoped he might, just so she could see what one felt like from him. 'Maybe I will in a bit.' He stroked her skin, just at the edge of her panties, then drew back.

'You're very beautiful, you know,' he went on, leaning back on his elbows for a moment. 'I expect you're very popular. Are you? Do you do well?'

'Not too badly.' It seemed a bland enough answer, not an exact lie. She had the occasional boyfriend, nothing special. She wasn't promiscuous, but she had sex now and again.

John nodded. She wasn't sure what he meant by it, but she didn't stop to worry. The way he was lying showed off that gorgeous erection. 'Do you actually, really like your job, then?' He glanced down to where she was looking, unashamed.

'Yes, I do. And I often come too. The things you see on the telly. Documentaries and stuff . . . They all try to tell people that we don't enjoy it. But some of us do.' It seemed safer to cover herself. If she didn't have a real orgasm soon, she might go mad. He'd barely touched her but her clit was aching, aching, aching.

'Show me, then. Pull down the top of your bra. Show me your tits. They look very nice but I'd like to see a bit more of them.'

Peeling down her straps, Lizzie pushed the cups of her bra down too, easing each breast out and letting it settle on the bunched fabric of the cup. It looked rude and naughty, as if she were presenting two juicy fruits to him on a tray, and it made her just nicely sized breasts look bigger, more opulent.

'Lovely. Now play with your nipples. Make them really come up for me.'

Tentatively, Lizzie cupped herself, first one breast, then the other. 'I thought you were going to make me come? I'm doing all the work here.' A shudder ran down her spine; her nipples were already acutely sensitive, dark and perky.

'Shush. You talk too much. Just do as you're told.' The words were soft, almost friendly, but she listened for an undertone, even if there wasn't one there.

Closing her eyes, she went about her task, wondering what he was thinking. Touching her breasts made her want to touch herself elsewhere too. It always did. It was putting electricity into a system and getting an overload in a different location. Her clit felt enormous, charged, desperate. As she ran her thumbs across her nipples, tantalising herself, she wanted to pant with excitement.

And all because this strange man was looking at her. She could feel the weight of his blue stare, even if she couldn't see him. Were his lips parted just as hers were? Was he hungering just as she did? Did he want a taste of her?

Swaying her hips, she slid a hand down from her breast to her belly, skirting the edge of her knickers, ready to dive inside.

'No, not there. I'll deal with that.'

Lizzie's eyes snapped open. John was watching her closely, as she'd expected, his gaze hooded. Gosh, his eyelashes were long. She suddenly noticed them, so surprisingly dark compared to his wheat-gold hair.

In a swift, shocking move, he sat up again and grasped the errant hand, then its mate, pushing them behind her, and then hooking both of them together behind her back. Her wrists were narrow and easily contained by his bigger hand. He was right up against her now, his breath hot on her breasts.

Bondage. Was this one of his fancy things? Her heart thrilled. Her pussy quivered. Yes. Yes. Yes. He held her firmly, his arm around her, securing her. She tried not to tremble but it was difficult to avoid it. Difficult to stop herself pressing her body as close to his as she could and trying to get off by rubbing her crotch against whatever part of him she could reach.

'Keep still. Keep very still. No movement unless I say so.' Inclining forward, he put out his tongue and licked her nipple, long, slowly and lasciviously, once, twice, three times.

'Oh God . . . oh God . . .'

His mouth was hot and his tongue nimble, flexible. He furled it to a point and dabbed at the very point of her, then lashed hard, flicking the bud. Lizzie imagined she was floating, buoyed up by the simple, focused pleasure, yet tethered by the weight of lust between her thighs.

'Hush . . . be quiet.' The words flowed over the skin of her breast. 'Try not to make any noises. Contain everything inside you.'

It was hard, so hard . . . and impossible when he took her nipple between his teeth and tugged on it hard. The pressure was oh so measured, but threatening, and his tongue still worked, right on the very tip.

Forbidden noises came out of her mouth. Her pelvis wafted in a dance proscribed. A tear formed at the corner of her eye. He dabbed and dabbed at her imprisoned nipple with his tongue, and when she looked down on him, she could see a demon looking back up at her, laughter dark and merry in his eyes.

He thinks he's getting the better of me. He thinks he's getting to a woman who's supposedly anaesthetised to pleasure, and making her excited.

Hard suction pulled at her nipple and her hips undulated in reply.

I don't know who the hell this woman is, but the bastard's making me crazy!

Lizzie had never believed that a woman could get off just from having her breasts played with. And maybe that still was so . . . But with her tit in John Smith's mouth she was only a hair's breadth from it. Maybe if she jerked her hips hard enough, it'd happen. Maybe she'd climax from sheer momentum.

'Stop that,' he ordered quietly, then with his free palm, he reached around and slapped her hard on the buttock, right next to her immobilised hands. It was like a thunderclap through the cotton of her panties.

'Ow!'

The pain was fierce and sudden, with strange powers. Her

skin burnt, but in her cleft, her clit pulsed and leapt. Had she come? She couldn't even tell, the signals were so mixed.

'What's the matter, little escort girl? Are you getting off?' He mouthed her nipple again, licking, sucking. Her clit jerked again, tightening.

'Could be,' she gasped, surprised she could still be so bold when her senses were whirling, 'I'm not sure.'

'Well, let's make certain then, eh?' Manhandling her, he turned her a little between his thighs. 'Arms around my shoulders. Hold on tight.'

'But . . .'

'This is what I've paid you for, Bettie' His blue eyes flashed. 'My pleasure is your compliance. That's the name of the game.'

She put her hands on him, obeying. The muscles of his neck and shoulders felt strong, unyielding, through the fine cotton of his shirt and the silk of his waistcoat lining, and this close, a wave of his cologne rose up, filling her head like an exotic potion, lime and spices, underscored by just a whiff of a foxier scent, fresh sweat. He was as excited as she, for all his apparent tranquillity, and that made her dizzier than ever. This was all mad, like no sex she'd ever really had before, although right here, right now, she was hard pressed to remember anything she'd done with other men.

'Oh Bettie, Bettie, you're really rather delightful,' he crooned, pushing a hand into her knickers from the front, making her pitch over, pressing her face against the side of his. His hair smelt good too, but fainter and with a greener note. He was a pot-pourri of delicious male odours.

'Oh, oh, God.' Burrowing in with determined fingers, he'd found her clit, and he took possession of it in a hard little rub. Her sex gathered itself, heat massing in her belly she was so ready from all the forays and tantalising gambits he'd put her through.

'If you have an orgasm before I give you permission, I'll slap your bottom, Bettie.' His voice was low, barely more than a breath. 'And if you come again . . . I'll slap you again.'

'But why punish me? If you want me to come?' She could barely speak, but something compelled her to. Maybe just the act of forming words gave her some control. Over herself at least.

'Because it's my will to do it, Bettie. Because I want you to come, and spanking your bottom makes me hard.' He twisted his neck, and pressed a kiss against her throat, a long, indecent licking kiss, messy and animal. 'Surely you understand how we men sometimes are?'

'Yes . . . yes, of course I do . . . Men are perverts,' she panted, bearing down on his relentless fingertip that was rocking now. 'At least the fun ones mostly are, in my experience.'

'Oh brava! Bravissima! That's my girl . . .' Latching his mouth on to her earlobe in a wicked nip, he circled his finger, working her clit like a bearing, rolling and pushing.

As his teeth closed tighter, just for an instant, he overcame her. She shouted, something incoherent, orgasming hard in sharp, intense waves, her flesh rippling.

The waves were still rolling when he slapped again, with his fully open hand, right across her bottom cheek.

'Ow! Oh God!'

John nuzzled her neck, still making magic with his finger, and torment with his hand, more and more slaps. Her body was a maelstrom, her nerves not sure what was happening, pain and pleasure whipping together in a froth. She gripped him hard, holding on, dimly aware that she might be hurting him too with her vice-like hold.

'Oh please . . . time out,' she begged after what could have been moments, or much longer.

The slaps stopped, and he curved his whole hand around her crotch, the gesture vaguely protective . . . or perhaps possessive?

'Not used to coming when you're "on duty"?' His voice was silky and provocative, but good-humoured. 'It's nice to know I managed to make you lose it. Seems that I've not lost my touch.' He pressed a kiss to her neck, snaking his arm around her back, supporting her.

Lizzie blinked, feeling odd, unsorted. She hadn't expected to feel quite this much with him. It had all started as a lark, a bit of fun, testing herself to see if she could get away with her pretence. She still didn't know if she'd achieved that, and she wasn't sure John Smith would give her a straight answer if she found a way to ask him.

Either way, he'd touched her more than just physically. He'd put heat in her bottom, and confusion in her soul.

For a few moments, she just let herself be held, trying not to think. She was half draped across the body of a man she barely knew, with several hundred pounds of his money in her bag and on the dresser. His hand was still tucked inside her panties, cradling her pussy, wet with her silk.

'You're very wet down there, sweetheart,' he said, as if he'd read her thoughts again. He sounded pleased with himself, which, she supposed he should be if he really believed she was an escort and he'd got her as dripping wet as this. 'And real, too . . . not out of a tube.' He dabbled in her pond.

'It's not unknown, John. I told you that . . . Some of us enjoy our profession very much. We make the most of our more attractive clients.'

'Flatterer,' he said, but she detected a pleased note in his voice. He was a man and only human. They all liked to be praised for their prowess. His hand closed a little tighter on her sex, finger flexing. 'Do you think you could oblige this attractive client with a fuck now? Nothing fancy this time. Just a bit of doggy style, if you don't mind.'

In spite of everything, Lizzie laughed out loud. He was a sexy, possibly very devious character, but she also sensed he was a bit of a caution too, a man with whom one could have good fun without sex ever being involved.

'I'd be glad to,' she replied, impetuously kissing him on the cheek, wondering if that was right for her role. Straightening up, she moved onto the bed, feeling his hand slide out of her underwear. 'Like this?' She went up on her knees on the mattress, close to the edge, reaching around to tug at her knickers and make way for him.

'Delightful . . . Hold that thought. I'll be right with you.'

Over her shoulder, Lizzie watched him boldly, eager to see if his cock was as good as it had felt through his clothes.

Swiftly, John unbuttoned his washed-slate-blue waistcoat, and then his trousers, but he didn't remove them. Instead, he fished amongst his shirt-tails and his linen, pushing them aside and freeing his cock without undressing.

He was a good size, hard and high, ruddy with defined, vigorous veining. He frisked himself two or three times, as if he doubted his erection, but Lizzie had no such doubts. He looked as solid as if he'd been carved from tropical wood.

'OK for you?' Jiggling himself again, he challenged her with a lift of his dark blond eyebrows.

'Very fair. Very fair indeed.' She wiggled her bottom enticingly. 'Much better than I usually get.'

'Glad to hear it.' He reached for a condom, and in a few quick, deft movements enrobed himself. A latex coating didn't diminish the temptation.

Taking hold of her hips, he moved her closer to the edge of the bed in a brisk, businesslike fashion, then peeled off her panties, tugging them off over her shoes and tossing them away.

'Very fair. Very fair indeed,' he teased, running his hands greedily over her buttocks and making the slight tingle from where he'd spanked her flare and surge. 'I'd like to spank you again, but not tonight.' Reaching between her legs, he played with her labia and her clit, reawakening sensations there too. 'I just want to be in you for the moment, but another time, well, I'd like to get fancier then, if you're amenable.'

'I . . . I think that could be arranged,' she answered, panting. He was touching her just the way she loved. How could he do that? If he kept on, she'd be agreeing to madness. Wanting to say more, she could only let out a moan and rock her body to entice him.

'Good, very good.' With some kind of magician-like twist of the wrist, he thrust a finger inside her, as if testing her condition. 'I'll pay extra, of course. I don't like to mark women, but you never know. I'll recompense you for any income lost, don't worry.'

What was he talking about? She could barely think. He was pumping her now. Not touching her clit, just thrusting his finger in and out of her in a smooth, relentless rhythm. And when her sensitive flesh seemed about to flutter into glorious orgasm, he pushed in a second finger too, beside the first. As she wriggled and rode them, she felt his cock brushing her thigh.

'Are you ready for me?' The redundant question was like a breeze sighing in her ear, so soft as he leant over her, clothing and rubber-clad erection pressed against her.

'What do you think?' she said on a hard gasp, almost coming, her entire body sizzling with sensation.

'Ready, willing and able, it seems.' He buried his face in her hair, and nuzzled her almost fondly. 'You're a remarkable woman, Bettie.'

And then she was empty, trembling, waiting . . . but not for long. Blunt and hot, his penis found her entrance, nudging, pushing, entering as he clasped her hip hard for purchase and seemed to fling himself at her in a ruthless shove.

'Oof!' His momentum knocked the breath out of her, sending her pitching forward, the side of her face hitting the mattress, her heart thrilling to the sheer primitive power of him. She felt him brace himself with a hand set beside her, while the fingers of his other hand tightened on her body like a vice, securing his grip. His thrusts were so powerful she had to hold on herself, grabbing hunks of the bedding to stop herself sliding.

'Hell. Yes!' His voice was fierce, ferocious, not like him. Where were his playful amused tones now? He sounded like a wild beast, voracious and alpha. He fucked like one too, pounding away at her. 'God, you're so tight . . . so *tight*!' There was surprise in the wildness too.

Squirming against the mattress, riding it as John rode her, Lizzie realised something. Of course, he had no idea he was taking a road with her that not too many men had travelled. She'd had sex, yes, and boyfriends. And enjoyed them immensely. But not all that many of them, throughout her years as a woman. Fewer than many of her friends, and hundreds fewer than an experienced escort.

But such thoughts dissolved. Who could think, being possessed like this? How could a man of nice but normal dimensions feel like a gigantic force of nature inside her, knocking against nerve-endings she couldn't remember ever being knocked before, stroking against exquisitely sensitive spots and making her gasp and howl, yes, howl!

Pleasure bloomed, red, white heat inside her, bathing her sex, her belly, making her clit sing. Her mouth was open against the duvet; good God, she was drooling too. Her hips jerked, as if trying to hammer back against John Smith as hard as he was hammering into her.

'Yes . . . that's good . . . oh . . .' His voice degraded again, foul, mindless blasphemy pouring from those beautiful lips as he ploughed her. Blue, filthy words that soared like a holy litany. 'Yes, oh God . . . now touch yourself, you gorgeous slut . . . rub your clit while I fuck you. I want you to be coming when I do. I want to feel it around me, your cunt, grabbing my dick.'

She barely needed the stimulus; the words alone set up the reality. The ripple of her flesh against his became hard, deep, grabbing clenches, the waves of pleasure so high and keen she could see white splodges in front of her eyes, as if she were swooning under him, even as she rubbed her clit with her fingers.

As she went limp, almost losing consciousness, a weird cry almost split the room. It was high, odd, broken, almost a sob as John's hips jerked like some ancient pneumatic device of both flesh and iron, pumping his seed into the thin rubber membrane lodged inside her.

He collapsed on her. She was collapsed already. It seemed as if the high wind that had swept the room had suddenly died. Her lover, both John and *a* John lay upon her, substantial, but not a heavy man really. His weight, though, seemed real, in a state of dreams.

After a minute, or perhaps two or three, he levered himself off her, standing. She felt the brush of his fingers sliding down her flank in a soft caress, then came his voice.

'Sorry about calling you a "slut" . . . and the other stuff. I expect you've heard a lot worse in this line of work, but still . . . You know us men, we talk a lot of bloody filthy nonsense when we're getting our ends away. You don't mind, do you?'

'No . . . not at all. I rather like it, actually.' Rolling onto her side, then her back, she discovered him knotting the condom, then tossing it into the nearby waste bin. His cock was deflating, naturally, but still had a certain majesty about it, even as he tucked it away and sorted out his shirt-tails and his zip.

'God, you look gorgeous like that.' His blue eyes blazed, as if his spirit might be willing again even if his flesh was currently shagged out. 'I'd love to have you again, but I think I've been a bit of pig and I'll be *hors de combat* for a little while now.'

You do say some quaint things, John Smith . . . But I like it.
I like you.

'Perhaps we could go again? When you've had a rest?' She glanced across at the second pile of notes on the dresser. It looked quite a lot. 'I'm not sure you've had full value for your money.'

John's eyes narrowed, amused, and he gave her an odd, boyish little grin.

'Oh, I think I've had plenty. You . . . you've been very good, beautiful Bettie. Just what I needed.' He sat down beside her, having swooped to pick up her panties, then pressed the little cotton bundle into her hands. 'I haven't been sleeping too well lately, love. But I think I'll sleep tonight now. Thank you.'

A lump came to Lizzie's throat. This wasn't sexual game playing, just honest words, honest thanks. He seemed younger suddenly, perhaps a little vulnerable. She wanted to stay, not for sex, but to just hug him, and hold him.

'Are you OK?'

'Yes, I'm fine,' he said, touching her cheek. 'But it's time for you to go. I've had what I've paid for, and more, sweet girl. I'd think I'd like to sleep now, and you should be home to your bed too. You don't have any more appointments tonight, do you?'

'No . . . nothing else.' Something very strange twisted in her mid-section. Yes, she should go now. Before she did or said something very silly. 'I'm done for the night.' She got up, wriggled into her knickers as gracefully as she could, then accepted her other things from John's hands. He'd picked them up for her. 'I'll just need a moment in your bathroom, then I'll leave you to your sleep.'

She skittered away, sensing him reaching for her. Not sure she could cope with his touch again, at least not in gentleness.

John stared at the door to the bathroom, smiling to himself, but perplexed.

You haven't been working very long, have you, beautiful Bettie?

How new was she to the game, he wondered. She didn't have that gloss, that slightly authoritative edge that he could always detect in an experienced escort. She was a sensual, lovely woman, and she seemed unafraid, but her responses were raw, unfiltered, as if she'd not yet learned to wear a mask and keep a bit of herself back. The working girls he'd been with had always been flatteringly responsive, accomplished, a massage to his ego. But there'd always been a tiny trickle of an edge that told him he was really just a job to them, even if they did genuinely seem to enjoy themselves.

But Bettie seemed completely unfettered by all that. She was full throttle. There was no way she could have fabricated her enjoyment of the sex; there was no way she could have faked the unprocessed excitement she'd exhibited, the response when he'd spanked her luscious bottom.

She loved it, and maybe that was the explanation. Most whores encountered clients who wanted to take the punishment, not dish it out. Maybe she wasn't all that experienced in being on the receiving end of BDSM? But she was a natural, and he needed a natural right now. Someone fresh, and vigorous, and enthusiastic. Unschooled, but with a deep, innate understanding of the mysteries.

He *had* to see her again. And see her soon.